She heard the familiar voice before she saw him. Inexplicably, even after all this time, the low resonance was capable of causing her pulse to flutter. Its measured tones were explaining to unseen listeners, "We've still sun above the beach. Let's finish with the festival scene before we pack it in tonight."

And then Molly saw him cresting the rise of the path from the beach, surrounded by people hurrying to keep up with his brisk stride. The saffron rays of the late afternoon sun caught in his pale hair like gilded mesh, and as his lean, broad-shouldered form emerged fully over the ridge of the slope, shirtless, barefoot, clad only in worn jeans riding low on his slim hips. Molly decided that he was altogether too handsome and always had been.

Molly already had one foot inside the car when she heard his deep voice cry, "Molly? Molly Darian?" The words held a question. And before she'd returned her foot to the ground, he was running toward her, shouting her name.

Also by Susan Johnson

SUSAN JOHNSON

HOT STREAK

Previously published under the
pseudonym Jill Barkin

BANTAM BOOKS

HOT STREAK
A Bantam Book

PUBLISHING HISTORY
Previously published under the pseudonym Jill Barkin by Berkley Books /
March 1990
Bantam mass market edition / September 2004

Published by
Bantam Dell
A Division of Random House, Inc.
New York, New York

This is a work of fiction. Names, characters, places, and incidents either are
the product of the author's imagination or are used fictitiously. Any
resemblance to actual persons, living or dead, events, or locales is
entirely coincidental.

ISBN 0-553-56115-4

Manufactured in the United States of America
Published simultaneously in Canada

OPM 10 9 8 7 6 5 4

HOT
STREAK

CHAPTER 1

SPRING, 1983

All spring days should be so verdant, all April suns so warm, all assassins so reliable.

They looked like ordinary tourists. Dressed in cotton slacks and knit shirts, the four dark-haired men entered Rome's Leonardo da Vinci terminal through different doors and quietly took their places. They were waiting for the arrival of one of the passengers for the four-fifteen flight to Athens. The Uzis packed in their carry-on bags were loaded and capable of firing 650 r.p.m.

Jacobsen would be traveling alone, under a Belgian passport, they'd been told, and could be expected to check in by 3:40 at the latest. So stationed within machine-gun range of the check-in counter, they waited, relying on Jacobsen's weakness for order—a dangerous vice for a courier. The plan had been walked through so many times it was etched on their memories like a perfectly choreographed ballet: From 3:30 to 4:00, get in, assassinate Jacobsen, and get out. At 4:07 their driver would leave, with or without them.

With an apparent casualness that disguised the adrenaline pumping through their senses, each watched the clock behind the counter. The minutes ticked by. Three-forty came and went . . . By 3:45 a restless unease set in. Where was he? Were the planners wrong? The men waiting were zealots, not accountants: They followed orders. And if the orders were faulty . . . Two of the men were visibly sweating, although the air conditioning was on in the modern glass-fronted terminal.

Three-fifty. The crowd was increasing. Children were everywhere. Was it a holiday? One of the Italian saints' days? A toddler's ball rolled too close to one of the waiting men and he roughly kicked it away. Three fifty-two. One of the assassins extracted a cigarette from his shirt pocket, lit it, and inhaled deeply on the dark Turkish blend.

Three fifty-four. A carabiniere walked directly toward the gunman stationed near the phone boxes. The man with the cigarette signaled briefly with a half-lifted hand, palm down. Do nothing. The policeman walked to within a foot of the phones, reached out and picked up the receiver, resting it on one shoulder while he slipped in a coin and began dialing. All four men began breathing again.

Three fifty-five. The youngest, his moustache only a fuzzy suggestion, nervously checked the zipper on his nylon bag, then glanced at the clock. Time was running out.

But at 3:56 and ten seconds, Jacobsen swung through the glass doors and strode toward them, looking fit, sporting a new tan. And also sporting a beautiful traveling companion. She was young, dazzling, long-legged in a mini-skirted pink sundress, looking thoroughly western from the top of her raggedy cut golden hair to the tips of her painted toes. The planners had been wrong on two counts: He was late and was not traveling alone, although Jacobsen's reputed libido no doubt accounted for the adjusted priorities. It was common knowledge the man favored a libertine's lifestyle although his excesses didn't evidence themselves in his healthy physique. But perhaps the edge was off. One could but hope.

In the next two seconds zippers on nylon bags were ripped open. Safeties flipped off a second later, and, with the precision of practice, four Uzis opened up with a barrage of deadly fire.

Three machine guns simultaneously swept over Jacobsen, the woman, and the crush of people around him; the fourth detoured briefly to swing toward the carabiniere on the phone. One side of the policeman's head disappeared. The gunmen made a last pass of the area of tile floor where Jacobsen lay in a tumble of bodies, a tidy, methodical act to see that no one moved. Professional thoroughness. Then, satisfied he was dead, they sprinted for the glass doors.

The screaming crowd scattered before the running men like frightened birds. A policeman blocked their way for a few foolish seconds before eighty rounds of spraying death spattered bits of his shredded flesh on the shrieking throng scrambling out of the way. His body hit the shiny black floor in a widening pool of blood.

Outside, just past the line of legal cabs, a car idled with its parking lights on. The lights flashed once before the sedan wheeled over to the running men and slowed enough to let them jump in.

It was 4:02 when the black Mercedes with West German plates smoothly accelerated and sped away from Leonardo da Vinci airport.

CHAPTER 2

Egon had had several leisurely grappas while waiting for his flight to Paris. His throat still felt warm from the liquor as he left the coffee bar and turned the corner into the main hall, but it closed up in terror when the guns opened fire. He froze, gasping for air, clutching the wall, his instincts screaming, Back! Go back! But he was paralyzed with fright, incapable of movement. How did they know I was *here*? he hysterically thought. He'd only decided himself on the spur of the moment to accept Jean-Claude's invitation for the weekend. No one should have known. He hadn't told a soul. Not his valet, not his housekeeper. Not even Jean-Claude.

It took a full ten seconds while he anticipated bullets ripping into him before he realized the gunmen's target was at the counter across the floor from him. And then another five seconds more before he found the strength to slide back around the corner, out of sight. He clung to the wall, shaking, drenched in sweat while visions of falling bodies, blood, unearthly screams with almost a corporeal quality assaulted his mind.

He wasn't the target; someone else was, he concluded for a short moment before an irrational fear overwhelmed the logic. Egon had been living on the brink of collapse since the dramatic warning last month when his favorite sports car had been wired and blown up in his own courtyard. The car had been parked only ten feet from his front door. In broad daylight. Every window on the palazzo facade had been shattered, the entrance door blown off its hinges. The damaged building had resembled jaws of hell, explicit in its threat. Not that he'd needed the additional persuasion.

Egon von Mansfeld knew what Shakin Rifat and his cadre were capable of. He'd been a fool to indulge him beyond the polite amenities of the society they both occasionally frequented. Shakin Rifat was no ordinary arms broker. As head of a family once influential in Turkish government, Rifat had connections in Europe. Supporters and sympathizers. He was always in the market for arms. And Egon von Mansfeld was one of the heirs to West Germany's second largest munitions works. Even high, Egon knew why Rifat had approached him. But the euphoria was too strong that night at the party after the races. He hadn't politely declined and walked away. He'd listened to Rifat's proposition. And bragged too much. The next day, after he'd come down, he'd backed out of the preliminary negotiations for the submachine gun prototypes the Von Mansfeld Works were developing.

Shakin Rifat hadn't been pleased. He'd been coveting the weapon ever since word of its revolutionary features had first leaked out. It was a caseless submachine gun radically different from any weapon design of the last fifty years. In experimental trials it had fired up to 2000 r.p.m., a virtual impossibility with conventional firearms. The single smooth outer casing had no protuberances or holes, and the pistol grip was at the point of balance. It had an unusual fifty-round throwaway magazine of plastic with small windows in the casing to allow the firer to see how many rounds were left. But its most novel features were its rotating cylinder mechanism and moving magazine, a design entirely different from anything that had been seen before in small arms, or in any other weapon for that matter.

And Egon, under the influence of drugs, had promised Rifat two hundred.

He'd sent two of his attorneys to repudiate his indiscretion the following afternoon. Rifat sat straight-backed behind an enormous desk topped with a single slab of exquisite malachite. He was late middle-aged, lean, with dark skin that proclaimed his origins. His body was still hard. At first impression he looked like a businessman; at second impression a soldier; at third impression an officer.

The attorneys tactfully explained that Mr. von Mansfeld had gone beyond his authority. They made all the usual excuses for Egon. And they returned the cash down payment in a Hermès satchel.

Shakin Rifat had listened. He understood. He knew what Egon was—a weak, spoiled wastrel. But he also knew that Egon von Mansfeld on his name alone could deliver the small number of experimental weapons if he wished. Anger flared in Rifat's dark eyes—a cold, dispassionate hatred—and in that moment, alarmed at such chill malevolence, the two von Mansfeld attorneys earned their generous retainers for the month. His face set, the fury concealed, Rifat dismissed the high-priced messengers and turned to some papers on his desk.

But Egon remained as a possible future source, filed away against some eventuality when all portions of the equation balanced: drugs—fear—threats—need. The car bombing had served a dual purpose. It was a warning for silence, but it was also a reminder that Shakin Rifat was angry, and their business was unfinished.

When the screaming stopped . . .

When the carabinieri and the ambulances had come and gone . . .

And the morticians . . .

Trembling and white, Egon skirted the blood on the floor,

stepped over a child's blood-soaked teddy bear, and shakily walked outside. The fading sun had the look of blood, too, crimson and intense. Squinting against its apocalyptic glare, he searched for a taxi in the disordered clutter of police vehicles still crowded around the airport entrance. Noting a yellow car halfway down the drive, its driver surreptitiously motioning and mouthing "Tassi," Egon made his way slowly through the tangle of cars and vans to the cab. A sudden dizziness assailed him, and when he came within three feet of the Fiat 750, he plunged through the open back door and collapsed on the seat. He had to get out of town, far away, he thought, shivering in the warm air. His eyes followed the short, bulky driver as he slammed the door shut, walked around the back of the cab, and slid into the driver's seat. "I want to go to Nice," Egon blurted. Sylvie was there. She'd take care of him. She'd see that Carey came.

"You crazy?" the driver asked brusquely, jerking his head around to look at the slender blond man, white as his linen shirt.

"Not yet," Egon said, his voice strangely raspy, as if there wasn't enough air in his lungs to force out the words.

"You know how far that is?" the cabbie asked, stretching his hirsute arm along the back of the seat and looking Egon over with critical appraisal. The tobacco-colored suit was expensive, as were the shoes, the two rings, the Bulgari watch. Maybe he did know how far it was.

Egon nodded wearily. He'd recognized the Neapolitan accent, confirmed with a brief glance—no meter—that he was in an illegal cab. A Neapolitan's disregard for the system was as natural as their ingrained privateering mentality. Egon relaxed fractionally. For money, this man would do anything. Sliding further into the corner of the seat, he stretched his legs out and said, "Seven-hundred kilometers, at least."

"You got money?" It was more a statement now than a question.

Egon nodded again. The rough, low-class dialect brought

back long-forgotten memories. Raising his heavy-lidded eyes, he replied quietly, "Enough."

"Show me." It was an eleven-hour drive and, surface appearances aside, Gennaro was a businessman.

Pulling crumpled currency from his jacket pockets, Egon tossed them into the front seat.

Gennaro's dark eyes widened. Mostly American. Large bills. He could exchange them on the black market for a good profit. Nice—next stop.

"Get your ass in gear. I'm in a hurry," Egon ordered in a brutish Neapolitan slang he'd picked up when he was very young. He'd not only mastered the broad inflection of the Naples dialect that summer long ago, but Gianni had introduced him to spaghetti alle vongole at Zì Teresa and sex tableaux in waterfront taverns. Spaghetti alle vongole was still his favorite food, although it was best with the pungent smell of the bay invading your nostrils. For the rest . . . sex tableaux had long since failed to pique his jaded appetites, and beautiful young Gianni had died at twenty in a drug war.

Casting a swift glance back in the rearview mirror, Gennaro decided the rich man wasn't from Naples. Not with that pale, sculpted face, although the accent was pure Camora. Shooting the gears home, he stepped on the accelerator and snaked his way around the parked cars. When he reached the open road, he asked without turning, "Who taught you that?"

"Some friends," Egon said, the inflection so perfectly Naples, Gennaro was startled anew.

"Are they still alive?" The answer would satisfy several more unasked questions.

"No."

Drug smuggling, Gennaro understood with clarity. "Do you want to go on the coast road or on A-1," he asked, a faint deference in his tone now. One never offended the Camora and lived long.

Egon felt for the kit in his breast pocket. He had four

points left. Enough till Nice, and then some. "Whatever's fastest, and turn the radio down." He was feeling better already, beginning to tune out, and the music was distracting. Reaching over, he rolled down the window. Warm evening air rushed against his face, fanning his silky hair back in ruffled waves. He could feel the tenseness leave his neck and shoulders, the heroin come to the fore again. Glancing out at the landscape, he took in Siumiciano's peaceful expanse. Flat and featureless, it fit his current mood. His mind began to withdraw to its own internal landscape, and he stared unfocusing for several minutes. But just as he began to forget, the music was interrupted by a sharp news report. The airport attack had already been attributed to Shakin Rifat. Egon stiffened. Had they been after him? Were they still after him? He began shaking again, the fresh surge of fear more powerful than the opiates.

CHAPTER 3

It was eight in the morning in Minneapolis. Margaret Rose Darian, known as Molly to everyone but the remotest stranger, flipped on the TV before she set her daughter's breakfast on the table. "Hurry, Carrie, your eggs are getting cold." Hearing a muffled response from the direction of the bedroom, she poured the milk and slid the jam jar closer to the plate.

"Morning, Mom, and don't say anything until I explain," her daughter said in a rush of words.

That snapped Molly's head around from the morning newscast. "Good God! When did you do that?"

"Last evening."

"That's why you had a scarf on when you came in from Lucy's." Her young daughter stood before her with pinkened earlobes and small pearl studs in her previously unblemished ears . . . looking too grown up. "You're too young."

"I'm eight, almost nine," Carrie replied matter-of-factly, dropping into her chair. "Amy's had pierced ears since she was four. And Tammy's had them since—"

"I know the list, honey, by heart. You couldn't wait—"

"I waited five years for you, Mom. Look at it that way," she said, her huge, dark eyes watchful.

Molly laughed, an abrupt, spontaneous helplessness at her daughter's curious logic.

Feeling a little braver, Carrie added, "I promise not to wear really long, dangly earrings until I'm older."

"The way your peer group's going, that'll be next week," Molly said with a heartfelt sigh, not in the mood for discipline. Her blue eyes took on a sudden maternal directness. "But I want your word of honor, on one thing."

"Sure, Mom." Carrie was magnanimous in her victory.

"I don't want to see three earrings on each ear. Never. Understand, Munchkin?"

"Promise." A radiant smile shone back at her.

Molly sighed one more time, a reflex action to their somewhat disparate notions of childhood. Did every eight-year-old girl in America have holes in her ears, a closet full of designer clothes, and the knowledge that rockabilly didn't mean what rockabilly used to mean? One glance at the clock reminded her that the riddles of the universe would have to wait. In the tone that all mothers acquire after watching children dawdle through three thousand and nineteen mealtimes, Molly admonished, "Now eat. You're going to be—" Her sentence was interrupted by a news bulletin flashing across the TV in stark black letters.

TERRORIST ATTACK! it proclaimed, and then the announcer's face replaced the clamoring headline. "Terrorist attack at the Rome airport!" The newsman's voice was excited. "Only minutes ago, four gunmen opened fire on passengers at the air terminal. We don't have all the details, but twelve people are known dead, two of them children. The death toll could—"

Molly switched the set off. "Lord, it's happening all the time. No one's safe." Regret and resentment blended oddly in her voice.

"We are in Minneapolis," Carrie replied with the calm

innocence of insulated youth. "No terrorists have ever killed anyone in Minneapolis. Do I have time for hot chocolate?" And with that, terrorist attacks were dismissed from Carrie's mind.

" 'Fraid not, dear. Are you sure your ears aren't infected? They look pinkish."

"They're fine. Relax, Mom. Lucy says if they begin to throb, to take a Tylenol."

"A professional opinion is always appreciated," Molly said dryly, "but if they're not paler by this evening, I'm taking you to the clinic for a second opinion. Lucy's not my idea of trustworthy expertise."

"Okay, okay," Carrie mumbled with a mouthful of muffin and jam. "You're the boss."

"I don't want to be the boss," Molly replied on a quiet exhalation. "I just want us to get along. And I don't want problems . . . like your ears falling off," she went on, slipping her arms into an Irish tweed jacket in an unusual lavender tone. "I don't want you looking like an eighteen-year-old starlet when you're eight either. And why the hell do terrorists keep killing innocent people?"

"I think they don't have land or food or something."

"It was a rhetorical question," Molly murmured half to herself as she searched through her purse for her car keys which were misplaced *again*. "Have you seen the car keys?"

"On the counter in the bathroom."

"In the *bathroom*?"

"Face it, Mom, you're not organized."

"Don't get smart, kid, at eight o'clock in the morning or I'll—"

"What, Mom?" Carrie teased.

"Just eat now," she muttered. Intimidating threats were not part of her repertoire with her daughter. She loved her too much. "I'm leaving in five minutes, and if you're not ready you'll have to take the bus to school."

"Mommmmm!" It was a long, drawn-out wail. "Don't be *cruel*."

Molly paused in the doorway, remembering the unwritten code apropos bus riding. No one *ever* rode the bus unless every other possible option for transportation to school had been wrung dry and discarded. Inadvertently, she'd struck a raw nerve of childhood protocol. "Don't panic, I'll wait. I'm the owner, right? I can come in when I want. But hurry," she reminded her daughter. Owner or not, if she didn't put in long hours every day her fledgling business, which seemed to be creeping into the black after two precarious years, could just as easily go under. That would make her ex-husband Bart happy as hell. And she'd resist *that* happening with the last breath in her body.

Her high heels clicked on the parquet floor as she walked down the hall to the bathroom to get her car keys. There shouldn't be people like Bart, she thought, her long-legged stride causing her blond shoulder-length hair to sway gently from side to side. There shouldn't be hunters and victims. There shouldn't be terrorists killing innocent children. It was so damned Machiavellian. So barbaric. Hadn't civilization progressed at all? Oh, damn, she silently swore, glancing out the terrace door next to her bedroom, the rain still hadn't let up. Her hair would frizz up like crazy again.

CHAPTER 4

It was an appalling day to be out. His father had warned him in his customary quiet way. His stable master had been less polite. "Day for a damned fool to kill himself," he'd said.

"Shorten the leathers a shade then, Leon. That'll keep me alive."

"Shit. Take more than that today," Leon muttered, but he'd seen the restrained fire in his employer's eyes, and had done as he was told. When Charles Fersten's mouth clamped shut in that thin straight line, everyone did his bidding or stayed out of sight.

For the fifth day in succession, cold, driving rain swept the northern Minnesota countryside. There were pools of water on the practice track near the stables, and the first curve of the private steeplechase course visible from the paddock resembled a snipe bog.

"Positive you want Tarrytown?" Leon tried one last time to dissuade his employer.

"He's surefooted in heavy going," was the curt reply.

Also had a bad mouth, which combined with his phenomenal strength, made him a difficult horse to hold, Leon thought. But maybe that was a masochistic fire in those black eyes and the count was out to match his temper against Tarrytown's gigantic strength.

Leon wasn't so far off the truth, although Charles Bernadotte Carrville Fersten, a count if he chose to acknowledge his father's lineage, normally didn't scrutinize his motives too closely. He just *needed* to ride.

His father had seen the morning news, too. As they watched, the death toll had mounted from the terrorist attack in Rome. Sixteen dead last count. The attack, reporters said, had Shakin Rifat's mark.

Whenever Shakin Rifat struck, Egon fell apart.

And then the phone would ring, and Sylvie would make demands.

Charles swore and swung himself up into the saddle.

Tarrytown jumped the first two timber fences beautifully, even under the adverse conditions. He was a massive horse of remarkable power, and a smile flashed briefly across Charles's mouth in appreciation. A half mile into the three-mile course, both horse and rider were thoroughly soaked and splashed with mud. Tarrytown took the first water turn without breathing hard and cleared the third and fourth hurdles like a leaper. Then, his head stretched out like a racer on the straight, his hooves scarcely touching the dark ground, Tarrytown flew down the treelined course. The pines were dark against the gray northern sky, in contrast to the silvery birches wet with rain, their tiny buds still tightly curled, waiting for a warm spring sun. Charles's spirits soared with Tarrytown's burst of speed and, despite the cold driving rain, he felt a warm surge of pleasure, a familiar elation synonymous with reckless wild rides.

But at the next water jump thoughts of Sylvie intruded like unwelcome messengers of doom, and he inadvertently tightened his grip on the reins. Tarrytown had already launched himself before the unexpected tug at his mouth. He cleared the water, but not with his usual rise, having faltered midair with the cut of the bit. The huge bay slipped on landing, slithering for several yards. It was touch and go for several breathless seconds before he recovered his legs. But his formidable strength pulled him through, and he managed to struggle upright, leaving both horse's and rider's hearts pumping furiously. A rider had to give his horse its head going over a jump; a rule Charles knew instinctively. Bending over, he apologized softly to Tarrytown, stroking him gently beneath his ear. "Sorry," he murmured, "my fault . . ." and added a few pithy comments concerning his ex-wife.

Dismounting, Charles walked Tarrytown back to the stables, talking aloud to his old companion . . . about Sylvie and her stupidity, about Sylvie and her arrogance, about Sylvie and her weak-willed brother. During the mucky walk back the rush of adrenaline slowly subsided and, like a cleansing tonic, it washed away much of his tension. Or maybe it was the wild ride that eased the tension. Since boyhood, a horse and speed had been comfort, therapy, intoxication—all things to Count Charles Fersten.

"Didn't go the whole," Leon laconically remarked when they returned.

"You were right, Leon," Charles replied with his familiar smile, the fire gone from his eyes. "Damn near got killed out there." He even felt restored enough after the exhilarating ride to ask, "Any phone calls?"

"Nope."

She hadn't called yet. Maybe this time she wouldn't, Charles thought, his normal cheerfulness renewed.

Bitch must not be able to get a call through, Leon uncharitably thought. And a cable wouldn't do her much good. If you're going to threaten and plead, it loses impact somehow on paper.

"See you tomorrow," Charles said, turning to go, the light from the open door silhouetting his powerful frame and the spiky outline of wet windswept hair.

"If the rain lets up." Leon was busy wiping Tarrytown down.

Charles's dark brows quirked like the grin lifting one corner of his mouth. "Can't take care of me forever."

"Someone has to. Besides all the eager women, that is."

"I don't know, Leon. You might lose against that kind of competition."

And he had on numerous occasions. But not for long. "Any woman last more than a week?" his stable master bluntly asked. "Besides the bitch, I mean. And from the looks of it, you might never shake her loose."

"Now, Leon, a little respect for my ex-wife." But the grin accompanying the words was wickedly boyish.

"I'd like to give her a whole lot more, but she never gets close enough to put my boot where it'll do her the most good."

"Speaking of boots. Did my boots come back for the Maryland Hunt Cup?"

"This morning."

"Good. I'll try them tomorrow. Think Tarrytown can take those terrifying timbers two years in a row?"

"If he can't, there's not a hunter that can. The Ferstens are the best breed of jumpers in the world."

"Thanks to you."

"And to your pa."

The phone line from the house trilled tinnily in the stable and they both stiffened, their expressions instantly altering. Charles's heavy brows creased into a frown.

"I'd say it's the bitch," Leon growled.

"Wouldn't bet against you on that one," Charles quietly replied. "If it's Sylvie, I'll take it in the house."

When Leon picked up the receiver, he nodded darkly and said, "Sit tight, Countess, he's on his way to an inside phone."

And Charles reluctantly started across the muddy paddock.

CHAPTER 5

Sylvie von Mansfeld was a countess in her own right, rich, beautiful, spoiled, and young. She'd met Charles one summer when she'd turned to acting in an attempt to escape boredom. She was captivated by Carey Fersten, the brilliant young director from America who had roots on the continent. She was delighted that his aristocratic family north of the Baltic held a knight's title a thousand years older than her family's mercantile nineteenth-century coat of arms. She was bewitched by his compulsive decisions. When they first met during filming in Yugoslavia, the young genius director was operating on instinct alone. Carey was drinking too much then, using recreational drugs in an excessive way that appealed to her excessive nature. It wasn't until the second week of sharing his bed that he'd stopped in mid "Darling" and asked her name. It still sent tingles down her spine recalling those days, old memories freshly rekindled by the sound of his deep, husky "Hello."

"I need you," Sylvie purred into the phone.

"The feeling is not mutual, Sylvie. What do you want, as if I didn't know," Charles said bluntly, settling into a worn leather chair in the library.

His cool tone brought Sylvie back to her present problem. "You have to come and talk to him. Egon called. He was at the airport during the shooting, and now he's worse than ever. God knows his fear is reasonable. Especially after what Rifat did to the car. He was barely coherent when he called. You *have* to come and talk to him, Carey!"

"Jesus, Sylvie." Charles kept his voice steady, despite his feelings on the subject. "I was just there a month ago. Put him in a sanitorium. Find him a confessor. Find him a woman, for Christ's sake. I can't come and hold his hand every time he OD's on terrorism."

"Those madmen are using him, Carey, you know that. Capitalizing on his nerves and drug habit. He's terrified. No one else can calm him when he's in this state."

"I can't this time, Sylvie. I'm sorry. I'm scheduled to ride in a meet in Maryland next week, and my next film starts two days after that."

"I need you. Egon needs you. You *owe* me!"

Carey sighed. "I can't keep paying for that mistake forever. Everyone was doing drugs out there."

"But you started him."

"I didn't, but I'll never win that argument with you. Oh, Christ, it could have been anyone. He was out looking for it."

"You made him what he is," she snapped.

"Lord, grow up. He is what he is, with or without me."

"If you don't come, he's going to die. I could barely understand him on the phone."

There was a silence on the overseas connection while Charles damned the day Sylvie von Mansfeld first slipped into his bed. "Okay, all right," he said at last, his feelings for Egon overcoming his aversion to Sylvie, "I'll be there, but I *have* to be back Wednesday next."

"We're at the villa in Nice."

"This is the last time, Sylvie, I swear." Hanging up, his expression grim, Charles angrily punched the phone number for the stable. "Tell Jess to have the jet fueled. We leave in an hour. And bring my saddle, will you Leon? Maybe I can get in a few hours of riding before the Hunt Cup." In a brisk cadence he finished his instructions to Leon. Then he dropped the phone receiver in its cradle and turned to his father. "Damn and bloody hell," he softly swore. "When will it end?"

His father had been seated at the marquetry desk near the window during the phone conversation, his eyes half-closed. Opening his eyes fully now, he glanced at his only child with tolerant affection and quietly said, "The sins of your youth, eh?"

"With Sylvie and Egon, I'm never going to be allowed to forget them."

"Surely there must be some treatment center with an effective program for"—his father paused delicately—"his variety of problems."

Bernadotte had never understood Egon's bisexual idiosyncrasies. Firmly heterosexual, he viewed them as an aberration. "He's tried most of the drug treatment centers," Carey replied, ignoring the other insinuations, "but so far none of them have turned him around. And Sylvie's right, he does respond to me. It makes it harder though since Egon's witless flirtation in the arms business last year. With Rifat leaning on him, he needs the heroin more to blot out the insecurities and fear, just at a time when he'd be better off facing them clean."

"I understand your attachment for the young man, my concern is your mother," Bernadotte said, dismissing Egon with a casual wave of his hand. "She's going to be disappointed if you're not back for the Maryland Hunt Cup. The house was opened last week and she has a full guest list waiting to visit with her 'darling' boy."

"I know." Sliding down on his spine, Charles stretched out his long, mud-spattered legs and contemplated the soiled toes of his handmade boots. Then, stretching to relieve the tightness in his shoulders Sylvie's calls always induced, he said, "Tell Mother I'll be back in time."

His father smiled his rare smile. "She'll be pleased."

"And *don't* tell her I went to see Egon," Charles said, rising from the depths of the comfortable chair. "She'll worry needlessly."

"I'll make some excuse."

"I'll call when I'm heading back." Charles stood in the library doorway and flashed a quick smile, both brows rising speculatively. "I did tell Sylvie this was the last time, didn't I?"

"Distinctly," his father agreed.

"Then I'm on my last mission of mercy," Charles replied. "Ciao." And with a wave he walked from the room.

"Godspeed," his father murmured in the quiet library as he began concocting a story that would satisfy Juliana.

Although Bernadotte and Juliana had chosen to live apart since Charles was three, they maintained a friendly parenting relationship and a true friendship apart from their duties as parents. Charles was really more like Juliana in many ways, Bernadotte thought. He was a Carrville in size; the Ferstens had always been larger than most but without the extreme height of the Carrvilles. And his love of horses was mysterious, with a gravity like Juliana's that bordered on the pagan. Like his mother, he socialized with ease; there was very little of the hermit like Bernadotte in Charles. But in other ways he was his father's son: reckless and instinctive, inquisitive until he found satisfactory answers. He was, above all, the joy of his father's life, and Bernadotte never regretted meeting Juliana.

Juliana Carrville had been seventeen the spring Count Bernadotte Fersten came to Baltimore to ride in the Hunt Cup. His reputation had preceded him, and every lady invited to the Hunt Ball that night had vied for his attention. He'd just turned forty, was rumored to have spent the previous month with his latest lover, the Maharani of Narayan at her estate outside Delhi while awaiting the beginning of the spring steeplechase circuit. It was a dangerous liaison—especially with her jealous husband in residence—but evidently the count had survived, as he had all his other scandals of the postwar years.

When his estates bordering the Baltic in Eastern Finland were in danger of being overrun by the Russians in the closing days of World War II, Bernadotte had taken leave from the Finnish army and managed to rescue his retainers and his stable of Fersten hunters just hours ahead of the Russians. But his wife Kirsti, whom he'd adored, had been killed in the flight, a victim of exploding shrapnel from artillery pressing the Russian front westward. Her loss, it was said, hurt Bernadotte more deeply than all his ancestral estates left behind.

Heartbroken, he'd pensioned off all the servants, except those needed for his small stud farm near Helsinki, and left for the continent, not caring whether he lived or died. During the next five years he rode in every steeplechase of consequence. Heedless of death, he won most of them. He drank champagne till dawn, slept with whomever clutched his arm that night, and entertained beautiful women from Oslo to Rome with wit, charm, and intoxicating, moody sensuality.

But his icon of Kirsti was always the first object he looked at on waking each day, and his standing order dictated that her grave would always be covered with fresh violets, the flower she'd adored. Bernadotte hadn't been able to forget the only love of his life. Her loss so haunted him that he avoided being alone, and was desperately afraid of solitude. Riding, hunting, gambling, sailing, boudoir games, and a reckless pursuit of pleasure obsessed him. And with his capacity to acquit himself well at all these games, he was in great demand.

When he walked into the drawing room that night in Baltimore before the Hunt Ball, he thought for a blinding moment that Kirsti was waiting for him. But when the tall, blond woman, dressed in violet chiffon turned around, his disappointment must have shone on his face.

"I feel I should apologize for some reason," Juliana Carrville said, her large hazel eyes attentive.

Count Fersten recovered instantly. "Of course not. I'm afraid I mistook you for someone I once knew. She liked violet, too."

Thanking her lucky stars she'd picked this dress for the ball, Juliana put out her slim hand and introduced herself.

Bernadotte recognized the last name. "Your father's on the National Hunt Committee."

"No, my brother. You're the odds-on favorite to win tomorrow, you know," she said, her smile warm.

"I hope you're right. The course is formidable." It was a modest reply by a man who'd outclassed everyone in the field, and had ridden the course the previous year in record time.

"Did your horses get in yet?"

"Came down yesterday from Louisville."

"Where you won the Oxmoor."

"A bit of luck, actually."

Juliana had heard otherwise. On a treacherous course where only four of the original twenty riders finished, the count had ridden so aggressively in mud left over from two days of rain that bets had been taken on which hurdle would account for his broken neck. "I hear you may decide to settle in America," Juliana went on hurriedly, for Bernadotte's glance was beginning to stray.

"I may," he said absently, his attention drawn to a spectacular redhead in cream lace and diamonds who was bearing down on him.

"There's an estate for sale next to ours. If you'd like, I'll show it to you Wednesday."

"Thank you. I'll let you know," he politely replied and turned to greet his old friend Mrs. Percy-Wilson.

The day after the Hunt Cup race, Bernadotte's manservant woke him after the all-night celebration of his win and informed him that Miss Carrville was waiting in the parlor downstairs. She'd come to show him a nearby house on the market.

"Give her my excuses, Anders . . . politely."

"Miss Carrville already advised me she isn't leaving until she sees you." Anders coughed discreetly, but didn't so much as glance at the lady sleeping next to his master. "She's prepared to join you up here, sir." Anders had considerable experience forestalling women and was paid handsomely for this important skill. He was very good in a standoff, but Miss Carrville was better. It had taken all his persuasion to keep her from following him upstairs. "I think you'll have to speak to her personally, sir."

Bernadotte groaned softly, cast a swift look at the drowsy Mrs. Percy-Wilson lying beside him, and decided she was not sufficiently awake to require an explanation. Quickly throwing on some clothes, he went downstairs to give his excuses to Miss Carrville *personally*.

CHAPTER 6

Juliana had decided to give her virginity to Count Fersten that day. The romantic notion was the first sexual goal for a girl normally consumed with her passion for riding. Perhaps this unusual stirring of emotion was related to the fact that Count Fersten was considered the finest amateur horseman in the world—a godlike figure, as far as Juliana was concerned.

A less polite man may have succeeded in putting Miss Carrville out of his parlor, but Bernadotte had a natural courtesy that contributed in large part to his enduring charm. And, after all, Miss Carrville was divinely motivated.

So while Mrs. Percy-Wilson slept off the fatigue of her champagne intoxication and sexual enthusiasms alone, Count Fersten accompanied Miss Carrville on a tour of Spring Green Manor. Everything had been arranged with a wealthy young woman's eye to sybaritic detail. Juliana wore yellow and white piqué, fresh and youthful against the golden glow of her Palm Beach tan. The sleeveless dress accentuated her slender arms, its neckline titillating yet still in good taste. She wore no underclothes, sure that they would only get in the way.

Servants had been sent ahead to the empty country home. Juliana preferred using her own staff, although the present owners, who had moved to a larger estate to accommodate their expanding stable yard and nursery, had generously offered theirs.

Juliana had gone to great lengths to discover the count's favorite country food and wines. He was astonished and said so when they rested on the south terrace after a tour of the house and grounds. Seated at a small, glass-topped table shielded from the slight breeze, they enjoyed an alfresco breakfast. After a night of drinking, the food piqued his appetite, and Bernadotte ate seriously until each taste was satisfied.

"How did you know?" he asked when he finished, his tanned hand sweeping over the table. "Everything's perfect."

"Mental telepathy?" Juliana smiled, and her face took on an appealing softness.

The count raised his brows skeptically and said, "A charming asset. Does it extend to my brand of cigarettes?" After a night of overindulgence, his urge for nicotine was reaching withdrawal proportions. Having hurriedly dressed to forestall Miss Carrville coming upstairs and meeting Mrs. Percy-Wilson without her makeup, he'd forgotten his cigarette case.

"Northern Turkey, handled by Dunhill in London and Jasper in New York," Juliana said with a studied carelessness.

His brows rose again, this time in appreciation. "And you have some."

"Of course." She reached over to a square Meissen box set next to the small vase of yellow roses and lifted the cover.

"Have you forgotten *anything*?" he asked, reaching for a cigarette. His mouth curved into a smile. It was all very flattering, and she was pretty in a fresh, healthy schoolgirl way.

"Champagne's chilling upstairs."

"Are you always so forward?" Although he was familiar

with aggressive females, she somehow eluded the stereotype. They rarely came this young.

"Never." She pointed out the lighter.

Never, he thought and immediately asked the obvious question. "How old are you?" He lit the cigarette, inhaling deeply.

"Seventeen."

He exhaled the smoke slowly before he said, "I'm forty."

"I know."

"Seventeen's too young."

"Too young for what?" Juliana retorted.

"Too young for chilled champagne upstairs."

"What if I was nineteen?"

Bernadotte paused for a moment, considering.

"See, you wouldn't say 'no' right off if I was nineteen."

"I still would."

"No you wouldn't."

"I should." His brows came together above his fine bridged nose. "That's damn young."

"Pretend I'm twenty."

"Where the hell are your parents?"

"Dead."

"Guardian, then."

"My brother's sleeping off his hangover with someone else's wife. Don't ask me who. His social secretary has trouble keeping up."

"So you're on your own, keeping your own social secretary busy with musical beds."

"I've never slept with a man."

"Good Lord," he said softly, but an ungovernable sensuality stirred at her admission. "Why me?" he asked, aware that he shouldn't be asking any more questions. He should be saying a polite good-bye.

"You're beautiful," Juliana said, staring at him.

"No I'm not, but thank you." Bernadotte was realistic about his looks. They were unconventional, severe in their modeling, slightly oriental across his cheekbones and eyes, sensual at times, but never beautiful.

"And your body's perfection," Juliana added, secure in her own assessment of Bernadotte despite his demur. Bernadotte had the physical presence of a natural athlete: broad-shouldered and muscular, with a leanness through his torso and hips, a classical symmetry personified. "You're one of the few men who can tower over me. Your size is unusual for an amateur rider."

"My family's bred the Fersten hunters for generations to accommodate the Fersten males," he modestly replied. The Turkish leaf was soothing, like an old addiction, and Bernadotte relaxed against the wrought-iron chairback.

"What does your horse carry?" she asked.

"Ninety-three kilos."

"The course was wicked yesterday. You didn't make one mistake."

He smiled at her breathless flattery. "I've been riding competitively since I was eight."

"I ride at least four hours a day," she responded, proud of her interest.

"You hunt, then?"

"All season."

"With the Grendale Valley?"

"No, the Worthington. You're astonishing over the jumps," Juliana went on in a breathy voice. "Your balance is superb."

"My father's trainer taught me to walk a high wire. It makes balance in the saddle second-nature," Bernadotte replied, more comfortable now that the conversation had returned to horses.

"Would you go riding with me, someday?" The question was naked, her voice pleading, her eyes asking for more.

The mood had altered suddenly. "I don't know how long I'll be staying," he answered evasively, putting out his cigarette, thinking it was time to go.

In her enthusiasm Juliana leaned forward, and her full breasts rose slightly above the shallow scooped neckline of her dress. "*If* you stay?" she persisted.

"I'd like to, then," he quietly replied, his dark eyes drawn to the soft, ivory curve of her breasts.

"I could show you the river and Alder's Bluff and Crane's Nest and—" While she swiftly recited the points of interest in the Worthington Valley, Bernadotte's libido, at variance with his mind's commands, envisioned Miss Carrville's large breasts unclothed. "It would be fun to ride together," Juliana blithely declared.

Indeed, his carnal urges agreed. She was tall for a woman . . . and slender, except for those enormous breasts. Indeed, it would be a pleasure to ride her.

"Say you will," she urged a moment later.

"I'd like that," he said, and was startled out of his musing when she instantly stood, put out her hand to him, and invited, "Come, then." Momentarily bewildered, he decided he must have missed something, but he took her small hand in his and asked, "Where?"

"Upstairs."

He inhaled slowly, feeling the heat of her hand in his, feeling the silky smoothness of her skin against his calloused palm. "No," he replied on a soft exhalation of breath, and let her hand drop. In the aftermath of a long night's drinking, every nerve, all sensation seemed acute and close to the surface. He could practically feel the damp heat of her body closing around him.

"I don't have any underclothes on," she said, coming over to stand beside him. He felt his erection rising. "See." She lifted the yellow and white pique skirt, and suddenly he was inches away from smooth, tanned thighs and pale, satiny hair growing in a faint iridescence pathway up the sleek curve of her stomach.

He should have said, "Put your skirt down," but instead he murmured, "The servants—"

"Sent home."

His hand delicately brushed against the pale silky hair. If she wasn't seventeen he wouldn't have asked again, "We're alone?" His dark eyes lifted to hers, and she nodded.

His flaxen head bent to kiss the glossy golden thighs and silvery hair, and she moaned, a low, luxurious sound. Of their own accord his hands came up, and he grasped her gently by the hips.

His palms felt rough on her skin; she'd noticed he'd ridden without gloves. Bare hands on the reins suited his style— no pretense. His touch was light, though, the barest pressure on her slim hips. But heated. She could feel his warmth. And she pressed into that warmth, wanted to be engulfed by the fire of this man whose reputation was torridly wild, whose daring skill as a rider balanced precariously between commanding his fate and plunging into the fires of hell. There were fires burning inside this man, and she wanted to dance in the flames.

Feeling her move into his caress, his tongue slid deeper into her ready wetness. For an untried virgin, she was anything but timid. He tasted her sweetness, tightened his grip on the soft flare of her hips, and felt an unfamiliar impatience. He usually played at love with a jaded man's composure. Maybe it was the fresh air today or the fresh young girl; maybe it was the last of the champagne bubbles colliding in his bloodstream. Maybe she smelled like long lost innocence and artless desire. It didn't matter. The playboy of the leisured society of western Europe wanted this sweet, lush, horse-mad young woman, and he'd denied himself nothing in the last five years.

His head lifted abruptly, leaving a coolness between her thighs. "Does this come off?" he asked, his lean fingers flicking lightly over the millefiori buttons gleaming on her bodice. It wasn't a question, but an order, and she let her skirt fall while she reached to undo the buttons.

He didn't move to help but passively watched, sprawled

back against the ornate, wrought-iron chair. Well, perhaps not altogether passively. Juliana glanced once at the elegant line where his casually splayed legs converged, and the enormous rise in the soft, dove gray flannels heightened the desire pulsing through her senses.

The dress slipped off from her shoulders first, and Bernadotte felt himself quicken when her jutting breasts were exposed. Her nipples were erect, as though sculpted in pink marble. "Hurry," he said. And she pushed the fabric over her hips, obedient to his urgent tone. Her obedience was a loving pleasure though, for she'd wanted him far longer than he'd felt the need for her. Count Bernadotte Fersten had been her hero for as long as she could remember.

As her dress fell in jonquil folds about her feet, she stepped out of her sandals.

Rising from the chair, Bernadotte took her hand, leading her the few scant feet to where the flagstone terrace met the lush, green lawn. Drawing her into his arms, he kissed her on the mouth for the first time.

While the warm sun bathed her nude body and the count's powerful embrace held her tightly, she felt a delicious dizziness. Juliana had to lift her face to meet his mouth, arching her graceful throat. With shameless eagerness she opened her mouth to his demands, laced her arms tightly around his neck, and brushed her hips against his rigid arousal.

She only did that once before she found herself beneath him on the lawn, her legs nudged wide while Bernadotte swiftly opened his trousers. With a craving that matched his own, she wanted him deeply inside her. It was all she'd thought of for years. His erection free, he entered her immediately, lacking his normal finesse, only murmuring "I'm sorry," into the softness of her hair. Then, in the next instant, he buried himself with a low moan into her tight virgin passage.

What a strange thing to say, she thought, smiling her

welcome, luring and surrounding him with a natural instinct, capturing, at last, the lover of her adolescent dreams.

He was moving inside her slowly, his eyes closed, his strong arms holding his weight lightly above her, his white silk shirt gathering grass stains at the elbows, his light-colored flannels ruined with green knees. The second strong thrust of his hips forced him so deeply inside her, she felt her toes tingle with pleasure. His rhythm was slow and instrusive, as though he had all day, as though the lady beneath him expected her pleasure to be prolonged. He'd learned of dalliance young, in both discreet and flamboyant boudoirs; to him, making love was like superb riding—a natural bent.

Moving up, he pressed exactly where Juliana most felt the ripples of ecstasy. As her breathing changed, when the exhilaration of her senses forced her breath into small, quiet gasps and the first orgasmic quivers began, she breathlessly whispered, "I want your child."

He almost stopped midthrust, but his own pulsing tide was already racing toward a shattering climax and the threat of hell itself couldn't have stopped it. Buried deep inside her, he poured himself into her trembling warmth, and while she sighed in abandoned pleasure, he whispered, "No."

Juliana was infinitely more persuasive than a novice courtesan had any right to be and, before long, Bernadotte found himself upstairs in bed, sipping chilled champagne. She had a natural proclivity for pleasure, and since it was too late to retract the first offering of his lust, he decided you can only hang once.

They spent the afternoon in bed, the evening as well, and he said, "Enough," before she did. "I'm not seventeen, puss, and that's all I can do for you today."

Her warm tongue and soft lips put the lie to that pronouncement, several times more . . . but it was the phone that put an end to the hours of lovemaking. Her brother, it seemed, needed her to negotiate with one of his overwrought mistresses. When a crashing noise and a few heated comments vibrated across the wires, she agreed to come home and soothe the distraught woman.

Her driver was asleep in the car, but he came awake amiably. She had Bernadotte driven home first. "Call me," she said when they arrived at his lodgings. She kissed him lightly on his lean, tanned cheek.

"If I stay," he replied, brushing his fingertip gently across her bruised mouth.

"I'm going to have your baby, so you really should call."

There was no suitable answer to her startlingly cheerful statement, so he simply said, "Thank you for a lovely day, Juliana." Then he opened the door and walked away.

He didn't call, of course. He very sensibly left Baltimore the following day.

CHAPTER 7

That summer, Bernadotte found a place like home. A landscape so similar to his ancestral country that he bought five thousand acres outright. He took Kirsti's picture with him the day after the purchase was completed, lifted it to the pine and birch forests and the rocky granite hills, and said, "We're home, sweetheart. At last."

His workmen had finished the masonry of the small country house and were beginning the interior plastering when Juliana called in August.

"Your child is due in January." Her voice was sunny, just as he remembered it.

After a grimace of astonishment there was a short silence while he weighed his wishes against his obligations. "Where would you like the wedding?" he asked.

"Baltimore," she said. "Do you mind if it's large?"

There was an infinitesimal pause this time, and then he answered, "No, of course not. Whatever suits you."

"Do you have a guest list?" she inquired.

"No," he said.

"Is Friday next all right?"

He briefly looked at the calendar on his desk near the

phone, glanced around the unfinished room, thought something like this couldn't possibly be happening to him when he'd found peace at last, and quietly answered, "Friday next is fine."

They were married on a sultry August day before every friend and relative Juliana's family had ever known. Everyone at the reception agreed that:

Juliana looked radiant—considering . . .

Count Fersten was remarkably charming—considering . . .

And if the marriage lasted a year, it would be four months longer than anyone expected.

Extra workmen were hired to speed the completion of the house and stables in order to accommodate Bernadotte's growing family. Juliana adored her husband with a young girl's worship which, while flattering, was unnerving. They were, however, extremely compatible in bed.

When Charles was born, Bernadotte was pleased to find that his wife's smothering affection was easily transferred to her son. And it was with great relief that he found he'd taken on the less demanding role of "father" in Juliana's life now that her loving attention was focused on her baby.

They outlasted the speculators in Baltimore who'd predicted a swift demise of their marriage. Juliana stayed at his country estate for three years, although she traveled often with Charles to her homes in Baltimore and Palm Beach. Despite Bernadotte's preference for his hermitage near the Canadian border, he found his new family warm and loving.

When Charles was three, Juliana decided that she and her son were better off on their own. The separation was amiable, and Bernadotte extended an open invitation to return for visits. Charles spent his summers with his father, while Bernadotte traveled to Palm Beach for Christmas each year.

Their son grew into a sturdy youngster, assured of his parents' love and support. However, he had inherited the taint of wildness bred through generations of Ferstens. In the middle of his senior year Charles was expelled from the sixth in a line of prep schools when it became clear that his boyish pranks were motivated by a dangerous compulsion for lawlessness.

After Charles's latest escapade, Juliana called Bernadotte. "He needs a man's touch now, dear," she said. "I can't control him. Would you mind?"

He didn't mind, of course. He doted on his only child, by now a rangy, big-boned youth whose whipcord body hadn't quite caught up to his growth. So when Charles returned to his father in disgrace yet again, Bernadotte said that first evening after dinner, "I won't say you shouldn't have done all those things at school, Charles, and I understand nonconformity. But the escapades have worried your mother. I'd appreciate," he gently admonished, "if you could put these rebellious high jinks into some kind of proportion."

"There's too many rules, Father. I can't stand it," said Charles, a maverick by deepest instinct.

"Living here will eliminate most of the rules," his father assured him. "If you remember to act like a gentleman and have respect for other people's feelings, I won't expect much more."

And with responsibility on his own youthful shoulders, Carey, as his mother called him—a family diminutive for Carrville males—developed a grudging maturity. As his parents' son, he was a naturally skilled rider. Under his father's guidance he began taking an active interest in the Fersten stables. A tutor was brought in to finish out the last few months of school, and then Carey entered his first European steeplechase event. It was too much for a young boy. He won and won and won, and at eighteen the adulation overwhelmed him. In December his father brought him home to recuperate; he'd been living on nerves and liquor for the last month.

Although barely eighteen, he'd seen much of the world and indulged his senses past prudence for a long time, more so lately with the hedonistic partying accompanying the race circuit. Women were interested in a winner—and a rich, handsome winner increased the offerings to dizzying proportions. He was worn out, worn down in body and spirit. Pleasure had somehow lost its fine edge.

It can happen at any age, the questioning . . . What is happiness? What sustains it? How is it measured? Or would satisfaction be a plainer word for a plainer world?

His spirits at low ebb, Carey came back to the States at a time when newscasts were pressing home the need to save a small Asian country struggling toward democracy. The first U.S. war fought on television showed young children dying before the viewer's eyes, depicted old, helpless people displaced from their lifelong homes, pitilessly presented footage of entire villages disappearing under napalm attacks. The politicians were talking then about "the light at the end of the tunnel," and Carey felt a surge of the spirit that had called his father and his father's father and countless Ferstens from the days of medieval baronies to fight other peoples' wars. Instead of resting, Carey impetuously joined the marines, a spontaneous decision based on a fugitive combination of melancholy, youthful idealism, and remembered stories of Fersten ancestors who had fought through a thousand years of Europe's history.

He may not have taken so drastic a step had his life been less off course. But the decision didn't seem drastic at the time; it seemed as if he'd been handed an opportunity to do something more significant than proving one's skill as an athlete on and off the course. He told himself it was wise to at least make his own choice by enlisting at a time when the draft was hot on the heels of eighteen-year-olds without deferments. But he realized the flaw in that rationalization: Generals' sons weren't fighting this war, nor were senators' sons or rich men's sons. He wouldn't have had to go. But, brooding and moody, with an elusive desire to test himself and somehow help in the tragedy five thousand miles away,

Carey Fersten joined up. At the time he thought of himself as another Fersten male going off to war, another generation. There was pride in that.

When he came back from Vietnam two years later, the boyishness was gone and his bright idealism had faded. He stayed in his room for two weeks, not even coming downstairs for meals. His father had been aware of the drugs, but he'd only watched and waited, careful not to intrude upon the painful readjustment.

During his third week home, Carey received a visit from the widow of his best buddy in the corps, a man who'd died in his arms. Dhani MacIntosh had taken the bus from Chicago—a day and a half trip with transfers and layovers—and had walked the last three miles from the highway. She brought the pictures Mac had sent back to her, all the ones in which he and Carey had been standing arm-in-arm or clowning around with the usual rude gestures and uplifted beer bottles. And she wanted to talk about Mac, wanted to know everything that the brief letters hadn't been able to say, wanted to be with someone Mac had loved like a brother.

It was the first time Carey had cried since he'd come back. They both cried, held each other and cried.

"The first time I saw Mac, he was nineteen," Carey began. "He had just flunked out of college and decided the marines might pay the bills for you and Mac Junior. He walked into our temporary camp after carrying a basketball through five miles of jungle. Best damn sight I'd seen in four long months of hell. He called me 'Shorty' . . . it was the first time in years I'd looked up at anyone . . . and asked me if I played basketball. We set up a makeshift hoop and played horse or twenty-one or one-on-one. Sometimes when we went back to the main camp for a few days, we'd put together a real game. Mac and I, Luger and Ant, along with a pickup guard or sometimes without one. We whipped everyone's ass."

"He said you were the first cool honkey he'd ever met," Dhani said with a smile.

"I had fewer hang-ups than a lot of folks out there, and Mac and I liked to party. No women," Carey quickly interposed. "There weren't any out where we spent most of our time. Mac and I and some of the crew would just party up and talk about what we were going to do when we got out. He wanted to start up a community center in your old neighborhood, he said, and help a few kids out of the ghetto. Mac always felt if he'd paid more attention in school, he wouldn't have flunked out. The basketball scholarship got him to college but couldn't keep him there."

"He never learned how to read real well," Dhani said softly.

"I know. He knew. But he wanted to make it better for some other kids. It's the only fast track out of the ghetto, he'd say, sports and school."

"I'm in a job training program now. I think I might be able to start college next year."

Carey's eyes filled with tears, and he brushed a quick hand over the wetness. "Do you know how happy Mac would be to know that? Hey, Mac, you hear that?" he said, looking up. "You hear how smart a wife you've got?" He smiled a rueful smile at Dhani. "I talk to him all the time. Christ, people'll call me nuts, I suppose, but I do."

"Me, too. He was the kind you just know would always listen."

Carey looked out at the late fall landscape and swore under his breath. Turning back abruptly, he said, "You know what pisses me off something fierce? There's plenty of assholes living . . . and Mac's dead. It's not fair!"

"Did he suffer?" Dhani asked after they'd talked about the futility and the injustice, after they'd discussed the good memories and the good times. She had avoided the question until the last because she wanted to know, but was afraid of the answer.

"No," Carey replied. Sitting on the porch railing in the late afternoon sun, he looked down at the even rows of planking below his feet before he looked back at her. "No, he didn't suffer," he lied.

Dhani exhaled a great breath of relief. "I was afraid . . . he'd . . . the end was . . . awful."

"It was fast," Carey said. "Really. How's Mac Junior?" he asked. And while Dhani talked about her son, Carey tried to press back the terrible memories of Mac's death.

They had just been dropped into the clearing they'd already taken twice in the last six months. He was at point and Mac was slack man, five yards behind him when Mac stepped on the mine. The explosion knocked Carey flat. When he turned back to the anguished screams, he saw what was left of Mac thrown on a heavy jungle bush. Mac's arms and legs were gone. If he lived a million years, he'd never forget the sight of Mac crying for him. As he scrambled back, Carey screamed for a corpsman. "It's all right, Mac, I'm here. I'm here." Very gently he lifted the man who had been six foot six into his arms, carefully eased himself onto the ground, and held him. Staring out of the dense green growth of underbrush that for a suspended moment in time seemed to isolate them as the last two men on earth, Carey roared, "If there's not a corpsman here in two minutes, I'm going to kill somebody!"

Mac's eyes were open wide. "I don't want to die," he whispered.

"You won't," Carey said fiercely. "I won't let you. Corpsman!" he screamed. "Dammit, we need a fucking corpsman over here!"

"I can't feel anything, Shorty. Am I going to make it?"

"It's shock, Mac. The feeling will come back. Your body's in shock." But with each beat of his heart, Mac's arteries were pumping away his life. "We'll have you fixed up in no time," Carey reassured him.

Just then a VC artillery unit began a dropping pattern along the tree line sheltering the company. No one could move. No medic came. As soon as the mortars started exploding, the Hueys that had dropped them in the clearing lifted like big, lumbering birds and flew away. Carey swore at them as they disappeared over the treetops.

He told Mac the copters would be there in a minute for him, that he'd be taken out to the nearest field hospital, that he'd earned a good, long R and R. He lied and lied and lied while his best friend died in his arms.

When Mac was dead, Carey made a soft bed for him in the undergrowth. Oblivious to the VC mortars systematically sweeping across the tree line while the firebase on the hill got their bearings on target, he raced toward the drop point where he knew the corpsmen would be. He manhandled a protesting corporal through the exploding shells to where Mac lay and said to him in a cold, level voice, "I want his arms and legs sewn back on."

The horrified man stared at him. When the medic opened his mouth to object, Carey lifted his M-16, pointed it directly at the man's head, and said, "Mac was my best friend."

The gruesome task, performed hastily but done, was accomplished only moments after the VC bombardment stopped as suddenly as it had started. And now we'll take this clearing for the third time, Carey thought cynically. Mac was dead. For what? The Cong would own this piece of land again an hour after they left.

"Thanks," Carey said softly into the eerie silence after a steady hour of ear-shattering explosions. He lowered his weapon. "Thanks. He needs them to play basketball." The corpsman nervously eased himself away from the tall blond man whose glazed eyes stared at the gruesome body on the ground. "Is that better now, Mac?" he heard him say before he turned and ran out of range of the crazy soldier's M-16.

Carey stayed with Mac until his body was lifted aboard a chopper. And then he cried.

―――――

Dhani stayed overnight, and that evening at dinner Bernadotte saw a glimpse of the Carey of former days as his son entertained Dhani with humorous anecdotes of Vietnam. It was the first visible break in the brittle, self-contained man who'd come back from Vietnam, the man who'd stayed in his room watching TV, not sleeping, hardly eating, trying to deal with some inner nightmare that wouldn't loosen its hold.

They sat afterward over Drambuie and made plans for the center Carey wanted to fund as a memorial to Mac. For the first time in weeks, he was animated, making suggestions as fast as Dhani could write them down, giving orders as he'd always had the tendency to do, then apologizing to her with a quick, flashing smile. Bernadotte had to excuse himself briefly when he saw that first smile. It brought back images of a chubby two-year-old toddler riding his first pony, and a young boy coaxing his father to let him have a motorcycle years too early. It was the smile Carey warmed rooms of cold-eyed cynics with. His son had returned to him, and Bernadotte needed a moment alone for his tears to subside.

The following day, after Bernadotte's chauffeur had driven Dhani away, Carey turned to his father and said, "I think I'll go for a ride."

Controlling the impulse to dance a jig for the first time in his life, Bernadotte calmly replied, "It's a pleasant afternoon for a ride. I'll have Leon saddle Tarrytown."

The riding helped Carey's recuperation; day by day the familiarity of the stark countryside so different from Vietnam slowly blurred his most horrifying memories. In a month the taut edginess had diminished, and in another month Carey came home one day with a movie camera, and announced he'd signed up for a film course at the nearby college.

What started as something to allay the recurring nightmares, a diversion to fill in time until the next steeplechase season began, became an obsession. He had found his métier in an artistic discipline that struck a rudimentary chord in every nerve and pulsing beat of his restless soul. He had the eye and the rhythm and the inherent genius to cut right to the core of human feeling, and he made the supremely difficult art of moviemaking look effortless.

It was as if a door had opened into the promised land. All the wealth in his life had never given him the joy and excitement that film-making did. With an artistic, creative mentor who recognized his talent, Carey spent the next two years learning his craft. And then after a summer spent fluctuating between high highs and low lows, when he kept a picture on his dresser of himself and a lovely blond girl sitting on a dock, he decided to finish school at USC. "It's the place to go for film," he said, "and there're lots of blonds in California." Grown men didn't die of love. Grown men said, "Get a grip on yourself. Life goes on." But he'd never before been without something he wanted. And he was badly out of sorts.

So once he was settled at USC, he proceeded with a demolishing vengeance to test the theory that "blonds have more fun." His master's thesis won a Cannes Film Award, and he was launched. Phrases like astonishing, phenomenal, a unique talent, an inner eye like Leonardo, Michelangelo, and Van Gogh combined, potent sensitivity that stirs the soul— flamboyant praise in the hot glare of the world's most prestigious gathering of talent described the newest wunderkind of the celluloid world. He was a sensation.

His mother was pleased he'd found some direction in his life, though she never understood his films and still found horses less demanding. His father watched his progress as a film-maker with keen interest and regarded his son's personal life with a lenient indulgence.

CHAPTER 8

In Nice, Rutledge greeted Carey at the open door. The surveillance cameras had followed the car from the front gate. "Good evening, Monsieur le Count." Rutledge was always punctilious in his address, though Carey preferred less formality.

"Evening Rutledge. Good to see you. Is Sylvie here?"

"Yes, sir, in the library."

Carey's brows rose questioningly. Sylvie was not known for her bookish habits.

"She's having a Cognac, sir," Rutledge said in answer to the silent question. "This way, please."

Carey followed him down a corridor of trompe l'oeil landscapes and open-door vistas he'd always considered the villa's best feature. They were very early nineteenth-century work, the villa having been built as a country retreat before the Edwardian influx of aristocracy crowded every square inch of precious sea view with an ornate pile of derivative architecture. Sylvie's villa was pure palladian, its airy rooms open to the Mediterranean sun.

Carey patiently stood back while Rutledge opened the door to the library after one knock and announced in his deep basso, "Count Charles Fersten."

Sylvie jumped up and ran toward Carey, her silver hair shining in the lamp-lit room, the fuschia silk jumpsuit she wore an incongruous color amid the muted brown tones of old leather-bound books and cherrywood paneling. With dainty sandaled feet flying over the kilim carpet, she crossed the broad expanse of floor, her arms held wide. Carey braced himself for one of her impetuous hugs.

Rutledge discreetly shut the door at her first purring words. "I missed you, dear husband."

"Ex-husband, Sylvie," Carey murmured, gently extricating himself from her scented embrace, suspiciously wondering if he'd been lured here on false pretenses. "Where's Egon?"

"You look wonderful, darling," Sylvie breathed in dulcet tones, her beautifully made-up eyes taking in the full impact of one of the handsomest men on six continents. "I like your new haircut."

"It's not new."

"It looks new," she replied with a wifely intonation.

"Cut it out, Sylvie. I've been hacking my own hair for years and you know it." Carey's streaked blond hair was spiky and unkempt, as usual.

"Well, I haven't seen you for so long," she cooed, exuding seduction with practiced skill. "It looks different. Do you like my new Messilina outfit?" she went on, stepping back and holding out her arms so the svelte beauty of her silk-sheathed body was fully visible. "He did it exclusively for me."

"Sylvie," Carey said with more patience than he was feeling after an eight-hour flight, "I didn't fly all day to come here and exchange pleasantries. The Messilina's wonderful; he's got a helluva touch. You look marvelous, as always, but Egon better be here, or I'm going to want your throat. Right on the spot." His hands were jammed into his jacket pockets, and his look bordered on glowering.

"What a suspicious man." A small, studied moue accompanied the delicate affront.

"Living with you for two years develops the faculty, or one doesn't survive."

"Not nice, love, but then you always were hard to handle with your evil temper," she reproached with the tiniest smile.

"Hard to handle . . . because I won't take your orders twenty-four hours a day? True, Sylvie, I'm harder than hell to handle."

"Pooh . . . you're no fun anymore. Can't you take a little teasing?" She looked up at him from under tinted lashes and softly said, "If I remember, you adored teasing in Yugoslavia and in Florence the first six months we were married."

Carey looked back at her with a dark glance. "If *you* recall, Yugoslavia and Florence were only blurs; neither of us had a single straight day until we woke up in Rome at Easter. So if I seem serious in contrast to that, it's called living in the real world. Which I'd like to try and help Egon do, if you'd kindly show me which room he's strung out in."

"No memories, Carey?" Her voice was soft, her violet eyes ardent. Although he was all business, she had other plans for his five-day stay.

He gazed at her and thought, as he had a thousand times over the past three years, how much Sylvie reminded him of Molly. Molly, the woman who loved him, but not enough. Molly, who married her fiancé because she was too frightened to tell her parents two weeks before the wedding—planned down to the last crabmeat canapé for over a year—that she was in love with someone else. It was probably the only reason he'd married Sylvie—that resemblance. Not exactly the memories she had in mind. "We had some good times, Sylvie," Carey said kindly. "Now what you should do," he went on with a pleasant smile, "is marry one of those young men hanging around on your yacht. You'd make some banker papa ecstatic."

"They're boring, love. Everyone's boring, except you."

"I'm boring now, too. Just work and ride, ride and work. Boring as hell."

"Boring?" She ran a practiced glance over his body. Her hand, provocatively slow, touched him lightly on the fine wool of his jacket sleeve. "*That* will be the day."

He moved back just out of reach in a casual way. "Swear to God, Sylvie. Even my mother is complaining of how dreary I've become. She compared me to my father the other day, and that's the ultimate in disparaging remarks about hermit types." And yet, it was true. Since his days with Sylvie, Carey's life had altered drastically. He was working hard and doing some of the best filming of his career. He was riding better than ever, with total concentration, and it showed. He and Tarrytown had picked up firsts at Autueil and Liverpool and if the Hunt Cup race next week went well, he had a good chance at the triple crown in steeplechase. It had never been done before. Dickson-Smith had taken the Hunt Cup and Grand National in 1975, but came in second at Autueil. Which reminded him just how little time he had here with Egon before the race. "Now if you'll let me get my hands on Egon, I'll try to talk some sense into his beautiful addled head."

CHAPTER 9

Egon was lying on his bed, his eyes half shut, looking at nothing. Three TV screens opposite the bed were tuned to different stations. Carey walked over to the elaborate communications system, pressed some switches, and the screens went dead.

"Goddammit, turn those on. I'm watching *Dallas*." Egon's eyes remained unfocused for a moment, and then closed.

Carey approached the bed and said, "I'll turn it on in a minute. Hi, Egon. You're on the nod again, Sylvie says. Need some help?"

Egon's head turned in slow motion and his eyes filled with tears. "I'm scared, Carey. They bombed my car. You know that. They bombed my car. Sylvie won't give me anything. I'm out and she won't get me any more. I need a hit, Carey, *now*." His skin was cold, moist, bluish; the hand he held out to Carey trembled.

Carey squatted down near the bed so that their eyes were level. Egon's pupils were contracted to pinpoints. "Egon, now listen to me. You've had too much already. You look like hell, like some damn ascetic monk. Have you eaten this week?"

"I haven't been hungry." Egon's eyes closed.

Carey shook him hard, and his eyes slowly opened. "Listen to me, Egon. I've got five days before I have to fly back. Now I'm willing to hold your hand and talk to you and feed you spaghetti alle vongole—"

"With fresh raspberries for dessert," Egon whispered.

"With fresh raspberries, you brat," Carey said, grinning. "But you've got to take hold. You hear? I've only five days."

Egon's eyes twitched slightly in his effort to smile. "I love you, Carey."

"I love you, too, but don't get any ideas," he bantered. "Now, do you think you can stand if I lift you up?"

"Sure, Carey." But he was dead weight, although he pathetically tried to steady himself, sweat dripping from his tortured body. His slender form shuddered. "I need a hit. I can't make it," he whispered, hanging in Carey's arms.

Carey felt his heart contract at the infinitely fragile ownership Egon had on his own life. His muscles taut with the effort, Carey lifted Egon into his arms and carried him over to a chair by the window. He lowered him into it, setting Egon's hands carefully on the chair arms for support. "I've got some chemicals," he quietly remarked, bending close so Egon could see his face. "Just to take off the edge, but you have to promise to eat."

Egon's voice was a thready whisper. "I'll eat, Carey. I promise."

"Sit up, don't fall," Carey cautioned, his smile kind and accepting. "I'll get a glass of water for these pills."

After a touching attempt to swallow a few mouthfuls of food to please Carey, the drugs began to ease Egon out of his stupor. It reminded Carey of Vietnam, carrying a grown man, but the bed was large and white and clean when he brought Egon back from the chair, and there was a servant there to help him dress Egon in dry clothes. No mud, no blood, no stench of death. Ten minutes later Egon was sleeping, this time peacefully.

Resting in a sprawl on the sofa, Carey ate a sandwich and

sipped on a beer the cook had sent up. He knew it wouldn't be long before Egon was wide awake and agitated. And that stage would peak anywhere from thirty-six to seventy-two hours. So he relaxed while he could. The city below twinkled with lights. The sea, awash with pleasure craft marked by their running lights, stretched darkly to the horizon where a thin outline of mauve defined its limits. The night air lifted the sheer curtains in a lazy pattern, bringing currents of warm, scented air into the room. Nice was a paradise for the senses. But Carey's thoughts were melancholy; it was such a waste. He wondered how long it would be before Egon grew up—or worse, didn't grow up but died from the heroin.

Egon also reminded him of Molly, and he didn't know why. With Sylvie it was obvious—the same height, the same slender shape, the same blond hair. But with Egon it was more elusive; maybe it was Egon's vulnerability, his uncertainty. Molly had spent the whole summer they were together traumatized over whether she could get out of the marriage that had been so long in the planning. It could have worked out. She could have canceled the wedding; they could have left town and moved anywhere.

But, he reminded himself, taking a long draft of the fine German beer, what good did it do playing "what if?" ten years later? Those kind of opium dreams didn't happen in real life. Never. And the sigh he exhaled was for his youthful impotence against respectable plans by respectable people more than ten years ago. He never had been able to understand why someone couldn't just cancel a wedding. But Molly had been afraid of causing a breach between her parents and Bart's. "They'd be crushed," she'd said.

"It's your life, not theirs. Don't be some damn sacrifice," he'd retorted.

"I've known Bart since grade school."

"Jesus Christ," he'd said in disgust.

"Our dads play golf together."

"Are we talking marriage here, or a golf foursome?"

"Everyone in town's been invited."

"I don't care if everyone in the universe has been invited. All I want to know is do you love him?"

She opened her mouth to answer, then shut it again.

"That's what I thought. Why don't you cancel the wedding?"

"Why should I?" Molly retorted in a sudden rush of anger, annoyed that Carey could harangue her but offer no commitment himself.

"Because you don't love him," he said. In hindsight he recognized he was a fool for not tossing his heart at her feet, but at twenty-two he hadn't realized what a mistake he was making. He supposed it was his fault he'd let her slip out of his life. But in the next heartbeat he changed his mind. Hell no, he thought. It was her fault. *She* married someone else. He didn't go out to California until after she married. Damned if the reminders of Molly didn't surface at the oddest times, and he couldn't ignore the intangible sense of loss that always accompanied them. What was she doing this warm April night, he wondered . . .

But then Egon whimpered in his sleep, and Carey's mind came back to Nice.

CHAPTER 10

"S o are you going?"

"Of course I'm going. Would I miss the gossip session of the decade?"

"*Ten years.* I can't *believe* it. *Everyone's* going. I called Liz yesterday and she said acceptances are almost ninety percent."

"We had a *great* party class," Molly said, her smile reminiscent of glorious high school memories.

"No kidding. Remember Bucky and Tess at the beach the day after graduation? They were quite entertaining . . ."

"Or Rod . . . or Billy? Lordy, what a fun day, but I'm getting too old to drink forty-eight hours straight anymore."

"We're only twenty-eight, Molly. *Don't* say old. Just in our prime. Just *absolutely* in our prime." Georgia was a best friend who'd stayed a best friend through marriages, divorces, children, and grouchy moods.

"Speak for yourself. I have my moments when my energy levels are zip."

"You're working too hard." Georgia's concern was evident as she gazed across the luncheon table. Molly was almost too thin at times, her eyes large in her fine-boned face. In a way, Georgia had always envied the classic bones and willowy body, especially considering her own predisposition to put on weight just looking at a piece of chocolate cake.

"Gotta make a living," Molly replied with a quiet ferocity, her dark blue eyes flashing.

"Especially after Bart stole your last business," Georgia retorted, censure heavy in her tone.

"*Especially* after that," Molly agreed, brushing a wave of her heavy, honey-colored hair from her forehead. "Ours was *not* an amiable divorce. Or an amiable marriage. It was a damned enormous mistake, to be perfectly frank."

"Aren't they all?" Georgia casually remarked, a cynic about the joys of matrimony. "How *is* the utterly charming ass?" she asked. "Still using that fraudulent white smile so effectively?"

"I don't see much of him, but presumably that smile is still making secretaries' hearts flutter."

"Every man's dream," Georgia commented, "the office harem."

"That didn't bother me so much as the selfishness, the pure arrogance that his behavior was acceptable because he was a man. It came as a great shock and irritation to Bart when *I* asked for the divorce. He said, 'Why would you want a divorce? You can't support yourself. You need me.' He really felt he was doing me a favor, and I should be satisfied regardless of his lifestyle." It was strange, Molly thought, because she'd always secretly felt she'd been the one doing the favor marrying him. She'd never told him that, of course, and he had his own conception of their marriage.

"Chauvinism is alive and well as we march into the twenty-first century," Georgia remarked dryly. "Give it another thousand years or so, and maybe we can dilute it with careful breeding. And then again," she sardonically added, "maybe we can't. In the meantime, save me, dear God, from ambitious men. They always feel they can tell you what to do."

"Amen to that. Bart always felt his career success somehow offset all his liabilities, like never coming home, putting work first, second, and third above his family, which somehow ranked just below his weekly haircut. For Bart a wife was only supposed to be pretty and agreeable, children quiet and agreeable, the house clean, meals miraculously on time regardless of his arrival . . . Don't ask me why I put up with it. You know as well as I because Larry wasn't a scrap better."

"*Au contraire*, sweetie, I do not know the answer. Self-analysis is not my forte. I do know, however, that life is infinitely more fun since I replaced thirty-eight-year-old Larry with two nineteen-year-olds."

"Lecher," Molly said with a grin.

"Come in, the water's fine," Georgia drawled.

"Carrie's too nosy for me to bring two nineteen-year-olds home." It wasn't the real reason Molly wouldn't bring them home, but she could be blasé, too.

"How is Carrie?" Georgia probed in a kindly way. "Still stable as Mount Olympus? Any sudden missing Dad?"

"You know Bart's idea of fatherhood—Christmas, birthdays, and ask me later, I'm busy right now. He actually prided himself on never having changed a diaper. And he couldn't even remember Carrie's age, for God's sake. What's to miss? Actually, I think she's adjusted better than I. I'm struggling with a fledgling business and edgy as hell at times."

"She's a darling."

"I know."

"Modest mother."

Molly smiled. "She's smart, too, and as of yesterday has pierced ears. I could kill her."

"Get with it, modern woman."

"I'm trying, but she's only eight."

"And so," Georgia teased, "what are your views on makeup for eight-year-olds?"

"Don't get me on the subject." Molly stabbed at a chunk of her chicken salad.

"Kids grow up faster today."

"So I'm told. Call me old-fashioned." She chewed

thoughtfully, wondering if she was the last mother in America who disapproved of eye liner for eight-year-olds.

"Speaking of old-fashioned. Been getting anything lately?"

Molly choked a little, not because she was prudish, but because Georgia's blunt delivery still threw her. She should have been familiar with it by now. Georgia had been eight when she asked Molly one warm summer day as they sat in her tent under the maple tree in the backyard, "Do you know what fucking is?" Twenty years later, Georgia was still capable of asking startling questions between "Pass the butter" and "Do you think the Democratic Party has lost its credibility as a working man's party?" Molly swallowed before she answered, "Don't start, Georgia." She smiled in a winsome way that made her look much younger than twenty-eight. "Not after my fiasco with Grant last weekend."

"Did you chicken out?"

"Didn't have to. I was saved by the bell."

"Why the hell would anyone want to be saved from Grant Duncan?"

"Don't ask me. I haven't the money for analysis. I had actually gone out on his boat Saturday with the thought that a handsome, solicitous charming date was what I needed to blow the cobwebs out of my psyche."

"And? I adore gory details . . ."

"We sat in the sun while we cruised on the St. Croix, and then early in the evening we pulled into his slip. Thought we'd have another drink or so . . . maybe go out for dinner, maybe eat there . . ."

"Maybe eat each other," Georgia blandly proposed with a lift of her dark brows.

"The thought," Molly mildly replied, "had occurred to me. Anyway, he brought out a bottle of wine he'd gotten at auction last month because he knew it would enchant me, and the wine was absolutely heaven in a bottle. I was planning on staying the night, Carrie was set at Mom and Dad's.

Everything was perfectly orchestrated as a be-good-to-Molly weekend, because frankly, I was beginning to fear for the soundness of my mind apropos men turning me on. Now anyone should be thrilled to go to bed with Grant, right?"

"He's definitely a thrill," Georgia bluntly agreed.

"And you should know," Molly teased. "When will you be moving into the ranks of the Guinness Book of Records?"

"I'm thinking," Georgia replied with a lazy insouciance, "of writing a book called *A Woman's Trip Through Paradise*. Volume One—America, sequels to follow. The way *you've* been going lately, you could do one on celibacy as an alternate lifestyle. So you didn't get it on with Grant even with the wine and the river and the seclusion of his cruiser—all the props."

"Call me stupid, but I don't want the props. I want this feeling to hit me . . . Wham! And if it's an oatmeal feeling, I don't want it."

Georgia groaned theatrically. "Oh, Lord, don't tell me you said that to him."

"No, his daughter called just when I was telling myself it was silly for a grown woman to feel she had to have the earth move in order to go to bed with a man."

"You should have thought of your marriage and known better."

"Or yours."

"Or any marriage more than two-and-a-half months old. But Grant hardly fits into that boring category," Georgia pleasantly noted. "That man is hung."

"*Now* you tell me," Molly smartly replied.

"If I'd known you were going down to the river with him, I would have sent you a registered letter, saying, 'This man is hung. Get a baby-sitter.' And after his daughter called?" Georgia prompted, pouring some more wine in her glass.

"He apologized when he got off the phone. She wanted a good-night kiss from New York."

"Long distance parenting. We're raising a new breed of

children. Four or six parents; eight or twelve grandparents; aunts, uncles, and cousins by the score. At least they'll know how to mingle. On with the story . . . Now, you wanted to tell him your heart didn't pit-a-pat and a handshake would be your preferred way to end the evening."

"How did you know?"

"We've been friends since kindergarten. What do you mean, how did I know?"

"Okay, so that's what I wanted to say, but I didn't. I was feeling guilty because I didn't want to hop in bed with him. How do I get myself into these pickles?"

"You're too damned selective. You want the right chemistry up front. My philosophy has always been, make your own bloody chemistry."

"No one looks good anymore," Molly bemoaned, then her eyes sparkled with a buoyant levity, "and I wish someone did, dammit. Am I crazy? Why doesn't anyone look good anymore?"

"Look, Scott has a friend who's gorgeous and available," Georgia ventured. "Want me to talk to him?"

"God, no," Molly quickly retorted. "I know you adore young flesh, and I'm not knocking it, but it's just not for me." She smiled. "I'd feel like his mother—or aunt, at least."

"Scott's nineteen, he's of age," Georgia replied with a negligent shrug. "And he's wonderful. Face it, they're not so damned opinionated at that age."

"Only you would find your newest boyfriend defending him in traffic court," Molly bantered. Although her style differed, she'd always marveled at Georgia's carefree attitude.

"Scott's mature for his age," Georgia said with a Cheshire-cat smile, giving the wine in her glass a soft twirl.

"His body is definitely mature, I'll give you that," Molly answered with a smile. She had seen him at Georgia's a few weeks ago dressed in a tank T-shirt and surfer shorts, and he was as near perfection as nature could devise.

"He's sweet, too, and he pampers me. He runs errands for

me and insists on cooking, which is wonderful because no one else knows how to when Magda's off on weekends. He's really quite charming to have around."

"Plus great in bed. Don't forget that," Molly pleasantly reminded her.

"Never, sweetie. *That* comes first." Her expression one of complacent well-being, her eyes half-lidded with luxurious memory, Georgia looked across the linen-covered table and, in a low, throaty voice, demanded, "Haven't you ever been *hot* . . . I mean really *hot* for a man?"

Even now it hurt to think about him, Molly reflected, even after all those years. Yes, she'd been flame-hot for Carey Fersten. Devouringly. Ceaselessly. So hot, she'd tremble for half a day before she'd see him. So hot that when he smiled, she shivered. But not since then. Never since then. Including her married life with Bart. "I'm not the hot type, Georgia," she dissembled. "You're hot over anything that flexes good pectorals. I should learn the technique."

"It makes for some really great recreation," Georgia assured her, lifting one arched brow and tossing a silky fall of long black hair over her shoulder.

"Maybe if I get this last bank note paid off and I'm finally operating the business in the black, I'll get into your style of recreation. Right now my mind's on surviving financially the next few months."

"If you need some money, hon, just ask."

Georgia was doing well in her law practice, in addition to taking in a princely sum in child support from her ex-husband. But the kind of money Molly had needed to begin anew when Bart had taken her (*his*, he'd said during the divorce proceedings, and the papers were all in his name) small design studio was not something Georgia could write a check for. Now after two hard years, her mini-merchandise mart developed from an abandoned eight-story factory was open, completely renovated and beginning to get critical reviews as the smartest, trendiest, most complete, centralized array of wholesale manufacturers in the midwest. "Thanks, Georgia, I appreciate the offer, but I'm keeping my head above water."

"Well, don't forget to take a break from your all-consuming obsession with work and save the weekend of the class reunion for fun."

"You can count on it. Would I miss seeing Liz and Adele claw at each other?"

CHAPTER 11

Carey spent the next five days with a cranky, agitated ex-brother-in-law who drank coffee nonstop and yawned a lot. He brought a sweater when Egon shivered, and took it off when he began sweating. They sat on the terrace outside the bedroom, watched the yachts and launches cruising on the Mediterranean, made an attempt to eat at mealtimes, and talked about anything but the reason Egon had bolted Rome and come running to Nice. Finally, though, on the evening before he had to leave, Carey felt Egon was stable enough to come to terms with the fear. The stars seemed alive in the sky, brilliant against a blue-black canopy of night. The air was like velvet on one's skin. It was warm even late in the evening, and the scent of bougainvillaea invaded the senses with sweet reminders of spring. Carey was nursing his second Campari and ice; Egon had three empty espresso cups on the table beside his chaise. "If Rifat still wants those prototypes from you, remember they need you alive. He won't get them if you're dead." Carey's voice was temperate, his eyes watching for Egon's reaction.

"They could kidnap me," Egon nervously retorted, his long fingers clasping and unclasping restlessly. "I can't stand pain, Carey, you know that. I don't want my ear or my finger cut off. And with the current mood of the board of directors, even with a message like that, I'm not sure they'd exchange any prototypes for me."

"You own the company, you and Sylvie. You own their jobs, don't forget. And even though they may not approve of your lifestyle, they'd be sensible about their obligations. Also," Carey said with a flash of a smile, reluctantly admitting to himself that one had to admire her nerve, "don't think Sylvie wouldn't raise holy hell."

Egon sat up straighter, rubbed his sweaty palms on the knees of his linen trousers, and smiled back. "You're right." When Sylvie put her mind to something, she usually got it. "That makes me feel slightly more courageous. Keep in mind though," he said, dropping back against the cushioned lounge chair, dolor replacing the brief elation, "everyone doesn't have what it takes to get two silver stars and a purple heart in Vietnam. That sort of bravery is genetically lacking in my DNA."

Emptying his glass, Carey chewed on the last bit of crushed ice before answering. How could he explain to Egon that no one consciously prepares to be brave? "Everyone who went over there was afraid," he said, his voice soft, "wondering how they were going to respond, whether they could actually shoot another human, if they'd let down their buddies someday, or die in a Saigon café innocently drinking a beer when a damn bomb went off. You're not lacking some shining virtue, Egon. There was more luck involved than anything when it came to survival in 'Nam. No one was doing much thinking over there—including the brass. Damn terrifying thought, so you just kept moving fast to cut down the risks or dug in and kept your head down. When someone's shooting at you there's no time to think, anyway; and when there was time, why waste it? Everyone got high. So it wasn't courage that kept me alive, but luck, and . . ." Carey softly added, putting the heavy tumbler on the flagstone beneath his chair, "a helluva lot of anger. It was a pretty stupid thing to do, enlisting like that, but at that age you don't readily admit to major blunders. So I figured I'd better learn how to use those weapons they gave me better than the guy who was trying to kill me. In a way," he mused, his eyes on the stars, "I was fascinated by the ways man has devised to kill his neighbors on this planet. Do you know you can kill a man by jamming his nose into his brain? Really simple," Carey said so quietly Egon had to sit forward to hear. His mouth twitched into a chill facsimile of a smile Egon had never seen before. "Hell, I wasn't brave, Egon." Carey shook away the damning memories. "Just madder than blazes I'd ended up in a dripping jungle in delta mud up to my ass in the middle of nowhere for no good reason. We weren't stopping the VC, we weren't making progress that I could see in winning the hearts and minds as the general liked to say. There must be a better way, I thought, seeing the hundredth village burned to the ground to make the world safe for democracy. So I was damned determined not to die on that sweltering piece of real estate." Shaking his head in an abrupt gesture of dismissal, Carey glanced up at Egon. "Don't let Shakin Rifat scare you into living on heroin. Don't," he emphasized with a rough severity, "let anyone scare you into giving up your life. You just have to say fuck you!"

"I'll try, but I don't know . . . For me to say fuck you to Rifat would probably take the world's current supply of crank," Egon replied with a simple honesty.

"Look," Carey said, reaching over to splash another few inches of the red liquor into his glass, "why don't you get away for a while! You're a first-class rider. Come back, stay with me, do part of the circuit this year."

Egon grimaced. "It's too much work."

"It'd be good for you," Carey encouraged. "Breathe fresh air at dawn, eat well . . . tone up."

"I can do all that on the party circuit," Egon teased, "although the exercise is different."

"You can't do the party scene and stay off drugs. It's killing you faster than Rifat ever could. I can't help after tomorrow with the race and filming and Sylvie can't do it alone. Would you consider a treatment center?" He knew he was on shaky ground after Egon's last experience where they'd put him in solitary confinement for a day and he'd freaked.

"Don't ask." Egon's voice was soft but decisive. "I'm over the worst now anyway; Sylvie and I'll manage. Speaking of whom," he continued, determined to change the subject, "you've been side-stepping my sister these past few days."

"With extreme difficulty," Carey admitted with a rueful smile. Since the first night he'd arrived, he'd been politely evading Sylvie's sexual advances with various excuses. He'd slept on the couch in Egon's room not only to discourage Sylvie's presence, but because he slept when Egon did and woke when he did and in general served as nursemaid. He'd worn a two-day stubble of beard out of laziness until Sylvie had brushed her fingers across his jaw one afternoon when she'd come to visit Egon and said in her throaty contralto, "Ummmm . . . sexy . . ." Immediately after she'd left he'd gone into the bathroom and shaved.

"You must be the exception to the rule: What Sylvie wants, Sylvie gets," Egon observed.

"*Now* I'm the exception," Carey reminded him. "*Now*. But I paid for the privilege of that hard-earned experience. I married her."

"She *can* be a trial," Egon agreed with the frankness of a younger brother.

"The understatement of the millennium."

"Whatever came over you?" Egon asked. "I mean, to marry her."

"Lord, I don't know . . . wish I did." He shrugged, and the silk shirt he wore unbuttoned shimmered with the small movement. "I woke up one morning and said, 'What the hell?' That was that rainy day in Belio, when we couldn't do any filming, remember? It rained buckets all during the ceremony. I should have recognized the ominous portents."

"It was a swell party after, though." Egon had his own fond memories of Carey that summer. Carey had been the first person since his parents died who listened to him and took him seriously, who didn't treat him like an obtrusive child.

"Yeah, it was." They'd invited everyone in the small village to the reception, closed down the shops, and danced and drank till dawn. "At least one good thing came out of the marriage," Carey said, his expression mildly amused as he recalled the festivities at Belio.

"Two things," Egon softly rejoined. "I've you for a friend, and I don't have friends. Not real friends. I'll pay you back someday, Carey. For all you've done for me."

Carey saw Egon's eyes fill and felt his heart go out to the young man who'd lost his parents too young and had been forced to rely on Sylvie for stability. And stable she wasn't. "Hey, what are ex-brothers-in-law for," Carey responded quietly, putting out a hand to touch Egon's shoulder. He'd spent long enough growing up himself to recognize the problem. "Why don't you come back to the States with me?" he offered. "You can cheer me on at the Maryland Hunt Cup. There'll be parties there, too. It won't be completely tame." He went on talking about the race because Egon was perilously close to tears and needed time to recover. The drugs did that, made every problem more intense, every emotion shaky, hairtrigger, turbulent.

"Maybe later," Egon replied short moments later after he'd swallowed hard, "but Sylvie's dragooning me into going up to Paris with her for a shopping spree. She needs my company, she says. Actually, she wants an excuse so Bernhardt won't barge in. And I'm the excuse. I know how to be obnoxious. He's too old, she says, and dreary."

"She's right there, poor devil; he's boring as hell. Well, come later if you can. You've an open invitation. But try to stay straight. Shakin Rifat isn't near as frightening when you're off the stuff."

"I'm going to try. Really. I'm not as shaky today, am I?" He was pale under his tan and still very thin, but the tremor in his hands was almost gone.

"You look great," Carey lied. "Absolutely."

CHAPTER **12**

The men on surveillance that morning reported in their log that Charles Fersten left Villa Mariabelle at eight-ten with his groom, pilot, and chauffeur, then the logbook marked "Charles Fersten/Nice" was closed and sent by courier back to Shakin Rifat in Rome.

Egon was being watched by Rifat's staff, who noted that Egon von Mansfeld was once again cutting back on his excessive drug habit, and Charles Fersten was a prominent part of that rehabilitation. Shakin Rifat knew Fersten was someone of importance to Egon. He just didn't know yet exactly how he could make use of that association. In the meantime, the surveillance would continue.

CHAPTER 13

W hen Carey walked into his mother's house in the late afternoon, she greeted him warmly with a hug and said, "I didn't believe your father for a minute. Now sit down and tell me where you've been."

"Baby-sitting Egon," Carey answered, settling into a large overstuffed chair.

"The poor boy. Will he survive?"

"This time he will."

"It doesn't sound too hopeful," Juliana replied, perching on the arm of a love seat that had graced the empress's drawing room at Malmaison. Her hazel-eyed glance scrutinized her son.

Carey shrugged. "It's hard to tell. Someone or something gets him hooked again and who knows . . . But enough of that mess. You look wonderful, Mother. When are you going to start looking old? *I'm* starting to look old."

Juliana was slender, tanned, and toned. Her blond hair was short and fluffy this season, making her look girlish although she was fifty now. "Just good clean living, darling. Something you aren't too familiar with." And she grinned.

Carey smiled back. His open, winning smile came easily

in his mother's company. "I've reformed, Mother. Only caffeine and an occasional Twinkie now. I'm disgustingly healthy."

She looked at him with a mother's searching gaze for a moment and, discounting the fatigue of his session with Egon, she decided he looked well. "Have you found some nice woman to take care of you?"

"No, Mother." She always asked and he always gave the same answer. "I'm trap shy after Sylvie."

"She was most unusual, I'll agree." Juliana was tolerant beyond the normal. "But not a very good rider." On that criteria, she had exacting standards.

"She didn't ride at all."

"Perhaps, dear, that was the problem."

"The problem, Mother, was she screamed very early in the morning, often during the day and always at night after several drinks. I was beginning to get hearing loss."

"Perhaps some therapy would help."

"When I suggested it once, she broke most of the glassware on the table."

"I see . . . well, it's lovely to have you here and after a good night's sleep and a restful day tomorrow, you'll be ready for the race." Her interest in Sylvie, exhausted, she moved on to topics which concerned her.

"No houseguests yet?" Carey asked. He'd expected full battalion strength.

"I put them off, love. I knew you'd be tired when you arrived. They'll be here in plenty of time."

"How did you know I'd be tired?"

She snorted softly, then smiled. "Your father was always charming but he's never learned to lie. The story he gave me was reproachfully poor. I knew straightaway you were mixed up in something unsavory and would show up exhausted. Now tell me what you want for dinner."

The day of the race the house was filled to overflowing. Breakfast was served to 200 guests and neighbors, all family or friends of Juliana and cheerful well-wishers of luck to her only child. The mimosas served with a hearty country breakfast buffet induced an early morning good humor, and Carey responded to his share of jovial back-slapping and animated advice. But his mother could see he was becoming impatient, and she excused him so that he and Leon could drive out to the course early enough to see to Tarrytown's preparation.

Tarrytown had been flown in four days before, and was rested and placid—unlike his rider.

Purses had been going up the last few years; steeplechase was becoming a growth sport in the States, and crowds of 30,000 people were no longer a rarity. Money had much to do with the boom. The $700,000 purses were a viable way to earn a living for trainers and riders, and steeplechase had actually become more than just a tax write-off for owners.

However, money hadn't changed the Maryland Hunt Cup. Forty years ago when timber racing was struggling to return from the World War II doldrums, an editorial bemoaned the lack of entries for the postwar renewal. Someone had suggested a $50,000 purse might encourage more owners and trainers to run their horses. The editorial argued against a large purse, suggesting entries would be swelled by horses unsuitable to the course.

The Hunt Cup didn't offer a purse until 1972, and it was only $15,000 now. The few horses and riders here today, Carey thought, were up for the unique challenge of this race. The purse was only a minor bonus.

He'd entered for several reasons, some less tangible than others. First, the Hunt Cup was by reputation the most terrifying, most formidable course in the world with timber jumps lethal to both man and beast. Carey thrived on that danger—the cutting edge excitement of survival. Secondly, this hunt country had been home to his mother's family for generations; a Carrville always risked his life in the Hunt

Cup. Faithful to its original intent as a race for gentlemen sportsmen through home fields, the Hunt Cup was still the only steeplechase in the world charging no admission. So he rode for the sense of adventure and family. And, last but not least, the thought of winning the triple crown in world steeplechase brought a rush to his senses. He'd had eight wins in fourteen mounts in *this* race but the perfect combination of victories at all three—Aintree, Autueil, and here at home, had always eluded him. If he won today, he would have achieved something no American rider had ever done before.

He wished he were less tired.

He wished he'd had another day to rest after the sleepless nights in Nice.

Maybe the field would fall away, he speculated with casual hope and considered expectation. It was known to happen here and at Aintree. There had been times at both races when the last horse standing had won, and this year only a field of twelve had been entered. The famed third fence usually took out a few riders, and the sixteenth and seventeenth of the twenty-two fences often claimed their victims. Perhaps simply staying on would be enough to win.

But his cynical sigh brought Tarrytown's ears forward as though he, too, understood more than luck was involved. Reaching out, Carey stroked the velvet softness of Tarrytown's coat as they waited to move up to the starting post. "You've got a nice long rein today," he said, his fingers trailing down the gleaming chestnut's powerful, deep neck, "so carry me through and I'll just stay on one way or another."

Tarrytown twisted back and nuzzled Carey's leg as if to reassure him. And Carey grinned, oddly relieved, knowing his horse understood his weariness. In the years they'd been riding together, they'd developed a communication distinctly their own with a telepathy peculiar to their special natures.

"It's a slop course," Carey added. "Pray we lose a few competitors to that." Early morning thunderstorms had softened the ground so the turf was going to be muck to anyone not in the lead. They had to get out front and hold it from the start.

Tarrytown apparently had decided on the same strategy—a favorite of his—because he broke away at the starting post with power and speed that was both remarkably elegant and economical. Coming into the first fence, Tarrytown lowered his head to see what he was up against, and Carey allowed him to make his own arrangements. He knew from experience Tarrytown was bold but careful. This horse didn't take any chances. Although he had the courage to face any steeplechase fence and the weight to hit them without necessarily falling, he preferred a clean jump. All Carey had to do was keep himself under control and watch.

Tarrytown shortened his stride and jumped, tucking his front legs under in his own peculiar style to avoid the top rail. As they soared over the fence with extravagant inches to spare, Carey's weariness lightened.

Eleven riders followed them over the first two fences but predictably the third fence took its toll, and four horses either fell or were brought down in a terrible struggling mass. The field was precipitously cut to eight, and further dwindled to six when two horses failed to get over the ninth fence, hitting the top rail simultaneously and splitting it as they went down. Another rider fell at the twelfth fence when his mount balked at a loose horse.

By the fifteenth fence, Carey could feel Tarrytown's mood as if he were saying, "I'm going." They were in balance, in complete harmony, physically flowing as a single component of motion. It was the bareback training from age three and the high wire, his father always said, that made a rider one with his mount. Similar to dance, one had to feel and hear and sense the movement with intrinsic emotion, not logic. That purist training made Carey the supple, effortless jumper he was today, lifting his weight completely off his horse while it was in the air, yet touching down smoothly, exhibiting unparalleled poise from lift-off to finish. With good reason,

Carey Fersten was heralded as the most stylish rider in the sport.

At the nineteenth fence, Tarrytown was still strong and jumped the next two timber obstacles with a gutsy speed and power that was part conceit and part elation. He was the kind of horse who liked to take the lead and hold it against the competition, and the diminishing field was far behind. Moving into the inside position by habit, they turned toward the finish and both felt the irrepressible stirrings of triumph. Victory beckoned, the cheering crowd was faintly distinguishable above the beating of their hearts, the straight green stretch of turf was all that was left between them and the first triple crown in steeplechase history. Carey tried not to think of the melodramatic stories of horses falling or stumbling just short of the finish line, or the instances when some physical hazard abruptly ended a seemingly triumphant victory. "Let's take her home," Carey murmured, his voice deliberately calm. But the electric energy pulsing through his body was more potent than the tranquillity of his tone. ·

And Tarrytown dug in, cruising down the stretch with ease and enjoyment, as though he were finishing a country meeting flat race instead of four miles of the most treacherous racing in the world.

"Show off," Carey whispered, exhilaration in his voice, Tarrytown's boundless stamina and gallant heart never ceasing to amaze him.

The handsome bay turned on an additional burst of speed in response, as if the stopwatch mattered and he had his own private goals.

Their winning time was the second fastest on record.

An American had won the triple crown for the first time.

An amateur rider, rare in the ranks of professional jockeys, had attained the remarkable prize.

The most brilliant contemporary rider had finally brought it home.

CHAPTER 14

I t was getting late. He'd talked to old friends, danced, drunk, enjoyed the congratulations, and pleased his mother by being solicitous to all her favorite people. The victory was sweet. He'd done it—the triple crown. Actually, Tarrytown had done it and he'd been along for the ride. His spirits were high, and he was accepting some cordial parting compliments from the Benchley master of the hounds when he felt a tap on his shoulder. Turning slightly, Carey recognized the tall brunette, smiled at her, swiftly concluded his conversation with Elliot McLeod, and, turning back to her said, "Good evening, Mrs. Garrett. How did I miss you earlier?"

"I only recently arrived. Family things to do."

"Ah, that explains it. How are all the little Garretts?"

"Fine, healthy. Asleep."

"And Mr. Garrett?" He glanced around briefly.

"In Europe."

"How nice," Carey said pleasantly, his eyes sliding down to her toes and up again. "For him, I mean," he added in a tone which belied his words; his dark eyes were provocative with inquiry.

"Yes," Sarah answered.

"Would you care for a nightcap somewhere?" Carey asked, looking over the busy ballroom still full of guests.

"I'd love one." Her voice was decisive, not coy. It was the Sarah he knew.

"Your place or mine is the customary response," he said with a teasing grin.

"My children are more curious than these people here," she responded, her gaze sweeping the room.

"My place, then," he said smoothly. "How convenient. Shall we walk over?" He put out his hand.

Her long silk gown trailed along the damp grass as they walked hand-in-hand across the moonlit pasture. Tilting her head to look up, she asked, "Do you remember the first time we went riding?"

His smile flashed white. "Do you?"

"Pickney's pond was high."

"And you were the cutest girl in the county."

"Why did you divorce?" she asked in the same girlish voice that always reminded him of summer sun and swimming in cool, shady places.

"Are we changing the subject?" His heavy brows quirked in a tentative inquiry but his smile was wide.

"Yes, and don't try to be evasive. Remember I knew you when you didn't even have fuzz on your upper lip. No practiced charm, Carey, darling, just an answer." Her angelic expression contrasted the bulldog directive.

"You always were a persistent brat," he acknowledged with amused tolerance. "Why did I get married would be a better question. But marriage didn't seem to suit me, to answer your question about my divorce. Are you happy with Edward?" It was a sincere inquiry, like a young child asking how high the sky is.

"We get along."

His grin was boyish, dégagé. "What more can one expect?" He swung her hand lightly back and forth. "How do you feel about a swim with an old friend? I can't promise

Pickney's pond with wild strawberries and flitting dragon-flies, but Mother's pool is at least secluded."

"I don't have a suit," she said with a mischievous smile.

"I was counting on that," he replied. "Lord, you look good, Sarah." And stopping, he pulled her close. Her arms lifted high around his neck, sliding over the silk collar of his tuxedo, their eyes meeting under the spring moon. "You feel wonderful," he murmured, pressing her warm body intimately near. The silk beneath his hands was smooth and heated.

"You feel . . . interesting," she whispered, her face lifted to his.

"I hope you don't have to be home early." He was moving her slowly back and forth in languid arousal.

"The servants will manage." Her eyes were half closed, her voice low.

"Till next year?" Carey lightly kissed the top of her winged brow.

"Not without a raise," Sarah breathed, her mouth brushing slowly over the cushion of his lower lip.

"I'll talk to my business manager," he murmured, enticing her lips with gentle, tugging nibbles.

It didn't matter that Sarah spent most of her life chauffeuring her children to dance lessons, riding lessons, music lessons, Little League games; chairing the Junior League, volunteering at the museum two afternoons a week—in short, taking motherhood seriously. It didn't matter that Carey knew he was leaving tomorrow. Tonight was joyful friendship and pleasure and sweet lust. They stood under a bright yellow moon after a day of victory, absorbing each other's happiness. Their kiss was long and luxurious, the taste of each other triggering lush memories of lazy summer days.

"Why is it always so delicious with you, Carey? Like a dear treasure that never loses its luster."

"I think it has something to do with being fifteen at the time, Sarah. And agreeing then that we never had to go home.

Some blood pacts last for centuries with undiminished gilding. Trust me." His fingers glided gently over her bare shoulders, his dark eyes alive with passion. "You were enchanting at fifteen. Beautiful," he whispered, his finger tracing a slow path downward until it reached the heavy curve of her breast. "Always will be . . ."

"Are the daffodils in bloom at your mother's?" Sarah's hands drifted slowly down Carey's back until they rested just below the base of his spine, then splayed over the taut muscles of his lower back while her hips moved in a slow, undulating rhythm.

He groaned very low, like a contented lion, and nodded twice in time to her intimate dance. "You feel like you need a daffodil shower," he murmured, his voice husky with desire. And then a smile of remembrance creased his lean face.

Sarah laughed softly. It was a private joke, a private keepsake shared by only two people in the world. "Do you ever wish you were fifteen again?" she asked, her fingers moving upward.

Carey thought for a minute. "Yes, for the summer with you. No, for the lack of control over my life."

Sarah tilted her head in a small, graceful inclination. "Are you in control now?"

"As much as a horse-mad, iconoclastic dreamer can be. We're talking *simulated* control." And he kissed the tops of her fingers that had crept over his shoulder and drifted across his cheek.

"My therapist says I should be less passive, more aggressive, take charge of my life more often," Sarah softly declared, tapping a fingertip on Carey's lower lip for emphasis of each word.

Carey knew how unstable Sarah's childhood had been, how her father had remarried four times. Her extended family was a byzantine snarl of half-brothers and sisters, stepmothers and shared vacations. Hardly a lesson on how to take charge of your life. "Therapists usually have a few ex-wives or ex-husbands in the woodwork. Don't take everything they say to heart. If they were so great in dealing with relationships and the world, they'd be celebrating silver wedding anniversaries instead of raising their third family. If you're satisfied, who cares? Do you like your kids?" He was not so tactless as to ask the same about her husband.

"Love them."

"Lucky for them," he replied with solemn gravity.

"You don't have any children, do you?" Sarah said, reading the traces of regret in his tone.

Carey shook his head.

"Why not?"

His hands dropped away from her shoulders, and, slipping his fingers through hers, he resumed their journey toward his mother's house. They walked several steps before he responded to her blunt inquiry. "After Vietnam and all the Agent Orange problems," he said very quietly, "I didn't think it was wise. We were drenched in that stuff up in the jungle. They were spraying round the clock. No one mentioned side effects, but several of my buddies had children with severe problems. You want to cry when you see those babies struggling to do simple things every child takes for granted. I couldn't deal with that."

"How terrible!" Sarah exclaimed. Regardless of her ambivalent feelings toward Edward, her children were her greatest joy. "Oh, Carey," she said, sympathy reaching out in her voice, "I'm sorry. How awful for you."

"Hey." He pulled her to a stop. "It's not that big a tragedy. The world will get along just fine without any more Ferstens. Now," he went on, tugging on her hand like an insistent child, "if this conversation doesn't lighten up, I'm taking back my offer of a daffodil shower."

"I won't let you!" Sarah cried. "A promise is a promise, Carey Fersten! You have to!"

"Make me," he teased.

"With pleasure," she cheerfully replied.

And it was.

Juliana's driver took Sarah home the next morning after a late breakfast poolside. Carey took a second breakfast with his mother before leaving for Minnesota. She only mentioned the daffodils once in passing, a casual remark about how "boys will be boys." Carey apologized. "It must have been the spring moon. I'm sorry, Mother."

"Sarah's a sweet girl," was all she said. "Will we be seeing you again soon?" she asked with a motherly inquisitiveness.

"*You* will be seeing me again when I've finished shooting. Probably in two months. Maybe three if the weather doesn't cooperate. Come up though, if you're interested in a starring role. We'll write you in," he said with a grin.

"As if I'm inclined to be a movie star at my age. I can't even remember a telephone number, let alone pages of dialogue."

"Just so you don't forget mine. Call me."

After saying his good-byes, Carey boarded his plane at a small local airstrip and slept the few hours it took to reach his father's.

The next day, production began on the film Carey had been wanting to make for eleven years. It was a personal indulgence he hadn't been able to afford until now. But his last two films had grossed so much money, his accountants were scouring the tax laws for hidden loopholes.

He'd always wanted to do an immigrant story.

He'd always wanted to explore the beginnings of the union movement in the iron mines.

He'd always wanted to bring the diverse ethnic mixture of the Iron Range to the screen.

It was an ambitious project. Some of his advisors had warned him that it was *too* ambitious, *too* self-indulgent.

"Not commercial enough," they'd said, now that he was considered "commercial."

"Not my first priority," he'd replied. "Nor my forty-ninth, either," he'd added.

"Too esoteric," they'd cautioned.

"Bull," he'd retorted. "Give the audience some credit, guys."

"Immigrant sagas don't sell," they'd protested.

"Good stories do, though," he'd pleasantly responded.

"Carey, fella, you're going to lose a bundle on this concept."

"But it's my money, isn't it? We start May first. Everyone be ready."

"There's not even a decent restaurant in that outland," one assistant director in a foul mood and a stylish leather jacket had muttered.

Carey gave a thin smile. "I just want to remind everyone this is not a corporate decision. And to those uncertain of the structure of Golden Bear Productions, Allen will fill you in. *Bon appétit.*"

CHAPTER 15

The decibel level had been rising steadily since the cocktail hour at the class reunion began. Molly was smiling at one of Marge's facetious remarks about girls' field hockey. Years ago they had all agreed that field hockey was the pits, and their opinions were unaltered by time.

It was comfortable, genial, like old home week, back with the group that had shared every bit of whispered high school gossip. The five friends had kept in touch with the usual Christmas cards, birthday cards, and birth announcements, but this was the first time in ten years they'd all been together again.

In the course of the last two hours, all the pertinent information had been exchanged: who was married, divorced, remarried, moved, working, happy, unhappy, bored, ecstatic. Husbands and ex-husbands had been thoroughly dissected. With a relaxed sigh, Molly leaned back in an antiquated leather chair in the Moose Club's old-fashioned, blatantly masculine interior. Immune to the decorating fads of the last sixty years, the board had resisted change with a stalwart stubbornness that was somehow comforting, Molly decided, gazing at a room untroubled by the passage of time.

"Molly, do I have a piece of gossip for you," Linda, whose tennis body had remained unchanged, said with a knowing lift of her brows.

"Don't keep me in suspense, then. You know how I adore gossip," Molly said, resting her head against the timeworn leather that had seen three generations come and go.

"Carey Fersten came into town yesterday with his film crew."

For a stark moment the noise, the people, the reunion, and her sense of reality were all suspended. Molly was in a vacuum of arrested motion, and she saw him as she had the last time almost ten years ago, two weeks before her wedding to Bart.

Carey was leaning against the carved column of Mrs. Larsen's front porch, the night was hot like tonight, Sweet William and phlox were in bloom, their fragrance as beautiful as his dark, accusing eyes. His pale hair, rough like a dog's coat, shimmered in the moonlight, and his tall, broad-shouldered form in an old polo shirt and worn riding pants was silhouetted against the moon's glow. He'd been detached, withdrawn, his face careful to show no emotion. When she'd asked him why he still had his riding boots on, had he been riding at night, he'd enigmatically said, "Riding clears my head. It's a distraction. And," he'd added, "Tarrytown's wild at night. I love it." Tarrytown had been a partially trained two-year-old then, untamed and unbridled like his master.

She remembered touching him on the shoulder, feeling his sweat-damp shirt and wondering how reckless the ride had been; but a moment later he'd pulled away and stood upright, no longer casually leaning against the pillar. "What are you going to do now?" she asked, wanting to say something so their time together wouldn't end, wanting to reach the cool, remote man who stood only a foot away from her but seemed to be a world away.

"Do?" he said in a mildly astonished way, as though she'd asked him to explain the theory of relativity.

"I mean . . . for the rest of the summer."

"Oh." He shrugged. "Ride, I guess. Finish my film, and—" He stopped abruptly, his black eyes burning through her like a flame.

She felt the scorching heat as she always did with Carey, but he seemed so far away. This was their last night together and, other than his heated glance, he was as distant as the moon shining down on them.

"And . . ." she prompted, not wanting him to stop talking because then it might be over.

"And," he said so softly the words were almost lost in the tinseled night air, "I thought I'd give you what you came for." Putting his hand out, he touched the creamy whiteness of her cheek, his thumb sliding slowly between her quivering lips. He gently massaged the lush softness of her mouth, then the pad of his thumb probed deeper, exerting a slight pressure on her teeth, slipping past them to the wet interior of her mouth.

She licked his thumb, and he drew in a sharp breath.

With a startling abruptness he withdrew his thumb and, taking her by the wrist, started across the porch to the stairway, not caring this time whether Mrs. Larsen saw him or not. Pulling her up the stairs in a rapid ascent, he pushed her in when they reached his room, slammed the door shut behind him, and locked it.

He left her standing in the center of the room and, without a word, methodically pulled off his riding boots and stripped off his shirt. With his hand on the zipper of his pants, he looked at her and said, "I don't plan on forgetting this night."

A moment later he undressed her with swift efficiency and took her the first time standing right there in the middle of the room. Afterward, he carried her to his familiar bed and followed her down, his hard body impatient, as if he hadn't climaxed just moments earlier. For the first time since Vietnam he made love without reserve, because when the world was being blown away, nothing mattered.

They made love like two young animals—he, aggressively with a pent-up frustration, she, with her own devouring need. It was feverish: kisses and touching and plunging madness that left their mouths and bodies burning in the desperate wildness of their passion. It was bittersweet, hours long, and a lifetime too short.

And neither ever forgot it.

Much later, lying in his arms, she'd felt the quiet words against her hair. "I'll take you away."

Twisting in his embrace, she looked up at him, her heartbeat suddenly rapid. "Where?" she asked, hearing at last the words, however vague, she'd been waiting all summer to hear. He'd said that he loved her, adored her, needed her, but never more. "Could we get married?" she asked, her eyes dark in the moonlit room. It was a woman's question to a man she loved beyond bearing.

"Married?" he blurted out, and she saw his startled look before he quickly recovered. "Sure," he responded hastily in the next moment, "we'll get married." He nodded once, a swift dip of his chin, swallowed, and said, "Sure. Good idea."

And Molly's heart sank. He didn't want to. He hadn't meant *that* when he'd said, "I'll take you away." Her mother's words came back to her, the ones she'd overheard long ago when Hazel Brewer was over for tea and they were talking about the old count and his son. "Boys like that marry their own kind," her mother had pronounced. "And don't even stay married most of the time," she'd added. "Look at the old count. He hasn't lived with his wife in years."

Hazel had informed in a breathy voice of disclosure, "Ethel knows everything that goes on up there because her cleaning lady knows the count's stableboy—and she says that young boy is always getting letters and calls from princesses. Can you imagine? *Princesses!*"

"He'll marry one of them when he's done sowing his wild

oats," her mother had replied. "They never marry young. Why should they?"

Oh, God, why hadn't he responded differently? Molly sadly thought. "It's not a good idea," she said suddenly, sitting up and moving away. Her heart ached when Carey didn't reach for her or disagree.

"If you want it, it's a fine idea," he said quietly.

"You don't really want to, though."

There was a short silence before Carey replied, "I've never thought of it before, that's all." He shrugged. "I'm not opposed."

The shrug was too casual, the words too negligent, like saying Cheez Whiz and Hi Hos are fine when you're used to caviar. Her temper flared at her humiliation and at all the differences in their lives, suddenly magnified. "Fuck you," she snapped.

"Hey," he said, sitting up. "What was that for?"

"For your damn undying declaration of devotion. For your information, Carey Fersten, I don't *want* to marry you!"

"Only fuck me, is that it?" The hot anger in her voice sparked his own quick temper and distress. "In between visits from your wonderful fiancé. Someone has to keep your hot little body satisfied when he can't."

"And it might as well be you, right?"

"Why not? I've got time on my hands," he drawled, then swore under his breath and said, "Oh, hell, come here. I don't want to fight."

She shook her head and moved off the bed, afraid that she would lose control, throw herself into his arms, and make him marry her even if he didn't want to. She had some pride. And he had his rich man's world—a world in which she didn't belong. "I'd better go," she whispered.

"Look, we'll get married. It's okay, really."

"It wouldn't work, Carey."

"Why not?"

"I don't really know you. You don't know me. Not like we should."

"Bull."

"We don't have anything in common . . ."

"Jesus God, you can talk something to death."

"That's what I mean. You don't understand me at all."

"And Bart does?"

"We grew up together."

"Sounds boring."

"It's a good basis for a marriage."

"If you're trying to convince me, you're wasting your time."

"Anyway, it's too late. I don't have the nerve to stop it even if I wanted to."

"You mean you don't want to," he replied sullenly.

"I don't know . . ." And she didn't. She was confused, too young to single-handedly resist the full weight of parental opposition, bear the burden of Bart's disappointment, and defy the overwhelming momentum of a small-town wedding only two weeks away. "You don't really *want* to get married, anyway," she declared flatly.

"It's not that." Carey dropped back on the pillows. "It's just kind of sudden," he explained. "Give me a day or two to get used to the idea."

"Or a year or two."

"Look, don't get your temper up. I'm just telling you how I feel."

"Fear."

"Not exactly."

"Thanks a lot." Damn, everything was wrong. She wanted ardent vows of love, and he stopped cold when the word "marriage" was mentioned. "It was nice this summer," she said, moving to pick up her clothes. "Let's leave it at that."

"I don't want to."

She held her blouse in her hands, and it shown white against her shadowed body. "What *do* you want?"

"I want *you*."

She knew that. There'd never been any question of his *wanting* her. The only question was how much, and, weighed against her marriage plans, it appeared he didn't want her enough. "I really have to go," she said with a small sigh, slipping her arms into her blouse sleeves.

"Are you going to marry him?"

"I don't know."

"What do you mean you don't know."

"I mean," she said with soft resignation, "I have to. I can't back out now."

"I'm going to throw up." His brows were drawn together in a scowl.

"Your life is different."

"Damn right."

Why didn't he say he couldn't live without her? He hadn't even said he loved her tonight. Maybe her mother was right; Carey's kind played around, but didn't marry.

Why did she persist in this martyrdom? he wondered. If you didn't look out for yourself, who did? He'd never known of a stable marriage, so the notion of a prescription for successful matrimony, all her talk of mutual background as the basis for stability in a marriage, seemed utterly alien. There weren't any stable marriages.

"It's under the chair," he said to her, pointing out the shoe she couldn't see. Molly had one sandal in her hand and looked lost. Her blouse was unbuttoned, her long legs bare, the partial curve of her bottom visible beneath the hem of her shirttails. When she twisted toward him, the delicate swell of one breast was exposed, as was the supple slope of her hip where it gently flared out from her narrow waist. A waist he could almost circle his fingers around. They had shared so much pleasure and sweetness this summer. "You're going through with it?" His voice was gruff.

She nodded, and his jaw stiffened. He lay motionless and silent in the rumpled bed while she dressed, watching her with dark inscrutable eyes, the room heavy with the odor of warm bodies and sperm. He was distant, so unlike the wildly passionate man who had made love to her so recently. He made her feel like a stranger.

And when she'd started to stumble over a clumsy adieu, her bottom lip trembling with sadness, he'd broken in and said, "Lots of luck," half-meaning it because he loved her, half-sarcastic with anger.

All she heard was the anger.

"You'll have to unlock the door to get out," he added in a lazy drawl, as if he were finally through with her now and she could leave.

The next morning Molly tried to talk to her mother after breakfast. She hadn't slept much, torn with doubts, aching with her loss, and she only abstractly listened to her mother's discussion of their scheduled dinner with the Coopers that evening. "Bart will be in town now until the wedding. Won't that be nice, dear? I know it's been hard on you with him gone at school all summer, but if he graduates early and steps into that wonderful internship . . . Well, what could be better?"

"Mom," Molly hesitantly began, the words rehearsed a hundred different ways during the sleepless night hours, "did you ever wonder if you were doing the right thing marrying Dad?"

Her mother looked up from the latest change to her seating arrangements for the dinner reception after the wedding, a seating chart she'd been juggling since May. "Would you believe Aunt Mae refuses to be within fifty feet of Gloria Dahlstrom? And George doesn't speak to Harold Mitchel since he ran against him for mayor. Well . . . they talk if you count a few short phrases and air so thick you could cut it with a knife." She sighed distractedly and set a small square of cardboard three spaces down the diagram in front of her. Looking up, as if noticing Molly for the first time, she said,

"Aren't you gone yet?" She glanced at the clock. "It's almost eleven. You're usually on your way to the beach by now."

Molly and Carey had spent most of the summer at his private lake, but since Molly couldn't tell her mother that, she'd ostensibly been off to the municipal beach every day. "Not today, Mom. I think it might rain." Like it's raining on my life, she thought miserably.

"Those days at the beach have given you a beautiful tan, perfect with your wedding dress."

The tan she'd gotten with Carey. Her mother would die if she knew that.

"Now what were you saying, dear? I heard something about marrying Dad?"

She'd lost her nerve. "Nothing, Mom. Forget it."

"Honey, if there's something you want to talk about, tell me," her mother gently insisted, taking note of her unnaturally subdued daughter. "You and I have always been able to discuss things." They had, but it was trivial stuff, like tears over fights with friends or what to wear to a dance or how Mrs. Hansen was a bear over piano technique. This wasn't the same. This was earth-shakingly different.

Working up her courage again, Molly began, "Did you ever wonder if Daddy was the right man for you?"

"Cold feet, sweetheart?"

Molly nodded. "Sort of."

"Everyone has that feeling at one time or another, dear," her mother reassured her. "It's perfectly normal with all this wedding commotion. Sometimes I wonder if it wouldn't have been easier to have you two kids run off to Hawaii or somewhere." She smiled and reached over to pat Molly's hand. "You'll get over it, honey. Have you seen the silver service Aunt Edith sent yesterday? It's terribly florid but solid and useful I suppose, and, after all, we all know her—"

"I really mean it, Mom," Molly interrupted. "I don't know if I want—"

The motherly words of comfort broke in. "A case of the

butterflies is typical. Marriage can seem so final when you're young. Now that Bart's back, you two will have your usual fun times together and, mark my words, the butterflies will disappear. He's just been gone so much this summer, the whole wedding doesn't seem real to you."

"It's not only that. I don't know if I care about him enough." There, she'd said it, or at least part of it; the part where she didn't have to mention Carey Fersten.

"Nonsense. You two have been chums since grade school. Bart's like a son to us and very handsome, too, I might add."

Her mother was saying all the things that didn't matter to Molly, talking about Bart as if marriage were based on a list of positive assets. Taking a deep breath, her heart tripping inside her chest, Molly said, "What would you say if I told you I didn't want to get married?"

She watched the blood drain from her mother's face, saw the nervous flutter of her hands spread the seating charts in disarray. "I don't know what to say," her mother answered after what seemed a very long time. "What do you want me to say?" she asked, bewildered and pale.

"Say it would be all right," Molly said in a small, frightened whisper.

She always recalled with affection her mother's endearing attempt at understanding. Her face frightfully white, she replied, "Of course, dear, it would be—" she swallowed, and the last word came out more faintly than normal "—fine."

But Molly could see it wouldn't be fine at all, and the whole crushing weight pressed on her shoulders.

"Tell me what's wrong, sweetheart," her mother urged. "If it's any consolation, these last-minute jitters happen to everyone."

Could she tell her mother she was thinking about throwing over Bart, who really was fun to be with and—yes, handsome and a chum, too—because she'd met a young man who made her tingle just thinking of him? Because this young man had hands that could slide over her body like silk and take her over the edge with a practiced skill that was pure heaven? Of course she couldn't. There'd be talk about lust versus love, and how similar backgrounds were the real basis of enduring marriages. There'd be the questions: "Why haven't we met him, dear? If he was serious, why hasn't he come to the house to meet your family?" And then, when they heard who it was, there'd be alarm because Carey Fersten was too wild, too strange, too rich to fit into this small, northern community.

The doorbell rang and for a moment Mrs. Darian looked distracted, her mind filled with disastrous visions of complete chaos. What to do with a thousand-dollar wedding dress. How to return the hundreds of presents. What would the caterers want for reneging on the contract on this short notice? And the band and hall rented for the dance. And the minister! Good God! And the Ladies' Auxiliary who'd been making yards and yards of satin streamers and bows to decorate the flower-decked sanctuary, altar, and pews. And the flowers ordered specially from Oregon where the weather was still cool enough this time of year to allow splendid roses. The doorbell pealed loudly, and this time she heard it. "I'll get it," she said, and wearily rose from her chair.

Returning a moment later, she carried in a large bouquet of yellow daisies. "They're from Bart." Her mother's voice was tentative, her expression uncertain. Placing them on the table, Molly saw the card pinned to the bouquet: To my sunshine girl. Love and kisses, Bart.

Molly felt terrible.

"What should I do, Mom?"

Her mother slowly shook her head and she suddenly looked older than she had ten minutes ago. "Whatever you think is right. No—" she quickly interposed "—I don't mean that. Just do what makes you happy. Daddy and I only want you to be happy. Don't worry about the rest."

Molly looked at the yellow daisies and the hastily scrawled note. There was an energy and cheerfulness about Bart that was captivating and potent. If you stood in his wake, he'd carry you along. She may not love him the way she loved Carey, but what guarantee did she have that their intense passion would last? She'd known Bart all her life. Carey had entered her world like a blazing meteor, as exotic as a far-off star—and just as unpredictable.

"I'll take you away," he'd said. And that was all he really meant.

"It would be a terrible bother to send back all the presents," Molly said with a small smile. "Right? And if Liz can't sing at my wedding, she'll throw a fit. Besides, neither you nor I would have the courage to tell Pastor Helms it's off when his daughter is a flower girl. It's gypsy fate, Mom, and the butterflies are better already."

A faint blush of color reentered her mother's face. "Bart is sweet," she said hesitantly.

"And handsome," Molly added with a smile. "What should I wear to the Coopers' tonight?"

Her mother let out a breath. "Are you sure, dear?" she ventured.

But Molly had seen the expression of relief. "I'm sure, Mom," she lied with a pleasant smile, while a poignant sadness inundated her soul.

The feeling of sadness and things left unsaid had stayed with her over the years. Not that it mattered. She'd married Bart two weeks later, and Carey had gone out to school at USC the next month. Except for occasional newspaper and magazine articles with photos depicting America's finest young director, Carey Fersten had disappeared from Molly's life.

The snippets of information available from newsprint revealed very little of the man, although the bare bones of his life in the ensuing years were known to her and millions of other people. He won the Cannes Film Festival Prize at age twenty-five with his first major work. She read of his sudden defection from Hollywood a year later to make more esoteric films; his numerous liaisons with well-known beauties all over the world, his marriage to a young German countess-cum-actress, his divorce two years later. And now. Here on the Range. Here in this town, making the immigrant movie he'd talked about years ago.

How could his name still stun her after all this time? So many years had passed, so much had happened: her marriage; the birth of her daughter; the business; the divorce; so many edges had blurred, memories tarnished.

But not his.

That image in the moonlight was as fresh and pure as a rose under lucite. And as disturbing as it had been that night in August.

With heroic effort, Molly shook away the shattering remembrance, forcing her face into a polite social smile. Share as she had with these friends of her youth, she had never completely shared Carey with them. He'd been too special, too different, and perhaps she'd known her feelings were too intense to share. "So the world-renowned director is back in this little burgh," she said in a neutral tone. "He's going to find it dull as dishwater after his travels."

"Want to see him again, Molly? Hmmm?" Marge teased. "There was something between you two that spring and summer, even though you wouldn't admit it. Now that you're divorced, why not look him up?"

"No thanks," she said in a deliberately cool voice. "Too much competition from all those glamorous beauties." She shrugged, but was annoyed to feel her face flushing. "Every paparazzo photo shows at least one groupy clinging to his arm, and usually there's more. He's probably never heard a woman say 'no.'" Every one of those pictures she'd seen over the years was cinema verité, sharp in her mind: the one taken when he and some duke's wife were slipping out of the back door of an exclusive hotel in London early one morning; the full array of shots taken with telephoto lenses on the Greek island where everyone was bathing au naturel; those in St. Moritz with a deposed monarch's youngest daughter smiling up at him; and the nightclub scenes with starlets entertaining one of the handsomest men in the world. "At my age, with an eight-year-old daughter in tow," Molly reminded them, her face set now to disclose no emotion, "I don't stand a chance against all that fair pulchritude surrounding him. I'll settle for the memories and leave the flash-and-dazzle Carey Fersten for the jet set."

"His films aren't like that at all," Nancy, who'd flown in from California, interposed. "Quiet, intimate mood pieces. No flash and dazzle anywhere."

"His life apparently doesn't follow his art, then, because lean, suntanned, sexy Carey Fersten is almost always 'where the action is,'" Molly rebutted.

"How do you know?" Linda remarked, and for a moment Molly had the distinct impression her friends were defending him.

"Because I read—"

"Those articles aren't always true," Georgia cut in, her voice moderate, her eyes on the slight flush reappearing on Molly's cheeks.

"None of the publications have been sued for libel," Molly replied.

"Well, those kind of pictures and headlines sell; they could be innocent friends," Linda acknowledged.

"Like hell," Molly said. "And don't forget Sylvie von-what's-her-name, the young wife and actress of slightly blue reputation. That was real."

"But not long-lasting," Georgia reminded her.

"Do me a favor, will you?" Molly retorted in a small huff of exasperation. "Stop gushing over him. He could be a saint in monk's clothing, misunderstood by the world at large, but I'm not interested. It all happened ten years ago, for God's sake."

"So you don't want to see him," Marge declared.

"No. You can't dredge up the past. People change, times change, circumstances change. It's impossible." But even as she emphatically pronounced the trite maxims, a tiny voice deep in a forgotten, locked-away corner of her mind cajoled, *I wonder what he looks like in real life, stepping out of the photographs? Does his hair still glisten in the moonlight? Are his hands still as gentle?* With sheer willpower, Molly wrenched her mind from the disturbing thoughts and, upending her rum, finished it in one great gulp. "Another drink, anyone?"

CHAPTER 16

After the banquet and the speeches, the dancing and drinking, after the Moose finally closed down, the party moved to the motel where most everyone was staying. Situated on the freeway south of town, the Holiday Inn was the largest, the best the small town of Amberg had to offer.

Hours later, temporarily escaping the smoke and noise of the transferred party, Molly was leaning on the balcony railing overlooking the indoor pool. She was in the midst of a struggle, trying to subdue a curious sense of longing and indelible images of Carey when the subject of her musing strode into the atrium.

Her mouth went dry.

A stunning redhead was hanging onto Carey's arm, and they were laughing. My Lord—her pulse leaped treacherously—his smile hadn't changed. Warm, open, intensely vital. And nothing else had changed, either—except the burnished tan. He hadn't had a tan like that then, the permanent kind, testifying to life in southern latitudes. His tall, rangy body, the body of Creswell's leading basketball scorer that year, was still lean and elegant. And those powerful muscles, shoulders, arms, and thighs, clearly visible under the white knit shirt he wore tucked into tight-fitting jeans, were taut and youthful. He was wearing sandals—almost barefoot, as he preferred. He'd had a phobia against shoes, not a sensible eccentricity when living in Minnesota's climate, so he'd always compromised with the lightest possible footwear the weather allowed.

His light hair was rough-cut, perhaps a shade longer than before. She remembered he had a habit of raking it back with his fingers when it got in the way. And even from this distance, across the illuminated pool, his dark eyes and heavy brows, the sensual, predatory eyes that had earned him her intimate name "Tiger" were potent as fevered memory. The opulent redhead was gazing adoringly into those eyes at the moment, and that heated adoration drove Molly away from the balcony railing, just as those intense, dark eyes looked up as if answering a sixth sense.

Molly was gone by that time—only a flash of honey-colored hair and a gleam of azure silk registered in the dusky eyes.

Raucous good cheer greeted Molly when she returned to the large motel room crowded with ex-classmates seated on chairs, on the floor, on the beds, and dressers.

"What you need, Molly baby, is another drink. You're falling behind. Don't want to let down the reputation of our entire class, do you?"

She smiled at Pucky Kochevar and blew him a kiss. "Have I ever let you down, Pucky?" And before the sentence was finished a drink had materialized in her hand.

Needless to say, no one rose early the next day. In fact, it was close to two when Molly opened her eyes and gingerly flexed each muscle and appendage, all of which responded normally if somewhat slowly. She'd survived her first class reunion.

Georgia and Marge were at her door first and within the half-hour had rounded up Linda and Nancy for a late lunch. Sitting beside the pool, eating with the ravenous appetites peculiar to the morning after a long night of drinking, the old friends relived the previous night. So-and-so hadn't changed, so-and-so had changed immeasurably. Professional job choices were analyzed, new husbands or wives scrutinized, who had danced with whom and who hadn't were noted. The conversation was fluid, rapid, neurotically funny as it can be with old friends who share the same sense of humor.

"Should we go and knock on Carey's door? He's here, you know," Marge teased, her audacity as prime as it had been at fourteen.

"I don't think his bed-partner would appreciate it." With a grin, Molly pulled Marge back into her chair.

"You saw him?" Linda breathed, wide-eyed and awestruck, her naiveté undiminished by the years.

"Briefly," Molly said. "He and a model-type redhead walked in around three. I was out on the balcony getting away from the smoke."

"Did you talk to him?" Marge asked, and every eye at the table swiveled to Molly. They could all display a certain blasé facade—all except Linda—but Carey Fersten was as close to a star as any of them had ever known.

"No, so put your tongues back in. Jeez, he's only another guy—not some superhero," Molly replied, a sudden image of Carey and the adoring woman last night provoking her nettled tone.

"Just another guy?" Marge repeated in accents heavy with disbelief. "Are you blind, deaf, and dumb? He's the sexiest guy I've ever seen, and if I could be certain Bill who's snoring three doors down wouldn't wake any time soon, I'd be tempted to knock on his door. I could introduce myself as Molly Darian's best friend. I'm sure he'd remember you."

"Don't be so sure. I expect several dozen women have come and gone since my little fling with him."

"He was a hunk," Nancy reminisced with a small sigh. "Do you remember how he looked on court? Nobody had muscles like Carey Fersten."

"An ex-marine back from Vietnam," Marge added. "Experienced, older, the women were panting after him even then. You met him in that film appreciation class, didn't you? The one on Saturday mornings at Creswell."

Molly nodded, but she wasn't about to reminisce about that. It was one of the most enduring memories in her life, and hers alone—not available for public consumption. It was the spring quarter of her senior year, and honor students were allowed to take college courses across campus at Creswell. Carey was doing T.A. work for the professor, and did most of the grading for the course. She'd gone in one afternoon to pick up her test score, and he'd asked her out to a movie.

She said, "I'm engaged."

He'd looked down at her from under those half-raised, heavy brows and said, "So?"

She'd heard all the stories concerning the old count's wayward son; the one who'd been expelled from every good prep school in the country. The rich kid–bad boy image had evolved somewhat with maturity, Vietnam, and his enthusiasm for film, but a touch of the renegade lingered in the improved persona. And that nervy insolence was manifest in the softly spoken, "So?"

But he was experienced enough to recognize the modest uncertainty in the young woman who'd attracted his attention since the first day of class, so he damped the predatory fire in his eyes and suggested coffee at the student union. Molly could say yes to that, and before twenty minutes had passed she'd said yes to the movie as well. It was the beginning of her introduction to passion Carey Fersten-style; it was also the spring prelude to a glorious, passionate summer that served forever after as a merciless measure of perfection.

"They're filming out at Ely Lake Park, I hear," Linda said, "using the pavilion for some midsummer kind of festival. Judd's folks have been working as extras."

"What's the story about?" Georgia asked.

"I don't know exactly . . . something about the early emigrant labor movement."

"Sounds socially significant."

"None of his movies have been pure fluff."

"You mean those good looks and that sexy charm and he's got brains, too?" Marge jestingly commented. "Do you suppose women love him for his mind?"

"And money, and title—all of the above previously mentioned," Linda answered.

"So is he really some kind of intellectual, Molly?" Marge persisted, intrigued by the celebrity in their midst, alive with lurid curiosity.

"He was on the dean's list, if that means anything. I don't know much about his intellectual aspirations. We didn't discuss literature and philosophy much," she replied with a touch of mockery.

"I'll bet you didn't. If I had Carey Fersten within arm's reach, I'd use my mouth for better things," Marge smartly retorted.

"Vulgar as ever, Marge," Linda remonstrated, casting her eyes skyward.

"I meant I'd kiss him."

"Sure, sure, we know you. Kiss him where, darling?" Nancy said pointedly. "You didn't mention *where*."

"Talk to Molly about kissing Carey Fersten," Marge said, her smile broad. "Is he really as good as all the jet-set gossip implies?"

Molly went quiet for a moment, then said, "He's nice."

"Nice?" Marge exclaimed. "*Nice?* What the hell does that mean? You mean he goes to church twice on Sunday and doesn't step on ants?" Leaning across her plate, she looked directly at Molly and, with a playful leer, softly asked, "How nice?"

Molly sighed in friendly resignation, her pink flamingo earrings swaying gently with the movement of her breathy sigh. "If you must know, you lecherous ladies," and Molly couldn't help but smile at the expectancy on each face, "nice means he's very good at pleasing you."

"Oh, Lord," Nancy breathed, "I'm going to *die* right here. I'm always sexy as hell after I drink. What do you think he'd say if I knocked on his door?"

" 'Good morning' and 'I didn't ring for the maid'?"

Nancy shot Marge a black look. "Screw you."

"Hey, I'm only teasing. You look great. I love your California tan." And Marge smiled her warm, sincere smile that endeared her to her Sunday school students, her karate instructor, her husband Bill, and the world at large.

The waitress interrupted with fresh coffee, and by the time everyone had been served, the conversation centered on whether Jane Wilcox had said "I own a Mercedes," thirty or forty times the night before.

CHAPTER 17

Two hours later farewells were exchanged, promises to see each other more often solemnly pledged, and each woman went her separate way.

Molly slid behind the wheel of her four-year-old sedan, the only remnant of her marriage not expropriated by a vengeful husband at divorce time. And Bart would have tried to take that too, she thought, starting the car, if the title hadn't been in her name.

Bart Cooper had been extremely uncooperative when their marriage broke up. It had to do with the fact she'd asked for the divorce. It had to do with his ego and anger and statements like: "You want out of this marriage? I'm not the husband you married? You're growing away from this?" He'd swept his arm out, taking in the antique furniture, the enormous living room, the lake view beyond the bow windows. "Fine!" he'd shouted. "That's *just fine!* But you're not taking me to the cleaners, and you're not taking this all with you because I worked for this and paid for this. And if this style of living isn't *good* enough for you, find out what it's like on your own. And I mean *on your own!* I'm not supporting you and your new boyfriend."

"There isn't any boyfriend."

"I'm sure there will be. For the record, he'll have to make his own living."

And even though his vice presidency of the area's largest advertising agency carried with it a substantial salary, out of retribution he'd pirated Molly's design business into his hands, as well. It hadn't been too difficult to accomplish; all the papers were in his name. Naive female that she'd been, when she first set up her own Design Center after finishing college, it hadn't seemed unusual to have the business management side of the center in Bart's name. Bankers were notoriously slow to lend liberal sums to a woman starting a business, and it had seemed sensible at the time. The loans had been paid off swiftly as the Design Center flourished. Unfortunately, it had become so successful, when they divorced, Bart decided to appropriate it for himself.

At first she'd tried to fight it, but their accountant was a friend of Bart's, their banker was a friend of Bart's, and the agency he worked for conveniently arranged for most of his salary to be masked as commissions and bonuses. Unsubstantial percentages were harder to pin down as income, and suddenly Bart's real income dropped suitably low. When it came time to settle on child support and a division of assets, Bart's income and their assets appeared modest. It was all quite common divorce protocol. Lesson one any lawyer will tell you: Hide your assets.

She gave up the fight at that point because she wanted out of the marriage immediately. Her lawyer cautioned her. "If you're in a rush, you're not going to get as much. It takes time to uncover the hiding places. It's a big mistake to take the first offer." But she didn't want to spend months in court haggling. She settled for half the equity in the house. Bart wanted to sell their suburban home and move into a river-view penthouse downtown. It was fine with her; she couldn't afford to keep up the house alone, anyway. And since he was eager to sell, that money was available to her swiftly.

The years since the divorce had been a struggle, starting over again, but she wasn't afraid of hard work. She knew she'd make it somehow, although bankers were no more liberal in their loan policies than they'd been in the past. But after dogged knocking on doors, Molly had gotten a small first loan and, with some help from her parents and her share of the house money, had managed to accumulate enough capital to put a down payment on an old factory that had been sitting idle for years. She and Carrie had moved into a half floor of the old building, both to save money and so she could be near Carrie when she worked late on the weekends. Eighty percent of the building was rented now, the wholesale showrooms were exquisite, their anchor restaurant in the atrium was on a reservations-only status as of six months ago and her future looked to be financially solvent in under ten months.

So head south, Molly thought, turning onto the freeway entrance. Pick up your daughter at Mom and Dad's, and you'll still be home by 8:30. Not too late at all.

It was only five miles from the motel to Ely Lake, and every argument against stopping there had been laid out and swiftly discarded by the time the exit sign appeared.

"Oh, what the hell," she murmured in a soft explosion of breath and flipped up the turn signal. Hers had never been a rational temperament, anyway; she was defenseless against her quickening emotions. At least with Carey Fersten that had been the case. She had shivered once and said "yes" to his innocuous invitation to a movie years ago, and today her feelings were as turbulent, flaring like a pennant in the wind. She wanted to see him again. Her susceptible emotions were mercurial, unsettled, but blatantly transparent. She wanted to see his dark seductive eyes again, wanted to see if a glint of recognition, of arousal would gleam in their smoky depths. Youthful moralizing and parental pressures were gone now;

no agonies or aching anguish of right or wrong, should or shouldn't, remained. She wanted to see him and, one way or another, put a ghost from her past to rest.

After parking her car in the graveled parking lot near the stone pavilion, Molly walked to a large white trailer with Golden Bear Productions painted boldly on the side and knocked on the door. She was told by the young man who came to the door dressed in a sweater, jeans, and a baseball cap, that Carey Fersten was filming down by the beach, they were racing the setting sun, and please don't bother him.

She hesitated at that point, not brave enough to incur the censure of an entire crew busily engaged in a losing contest with the light. Returning to her car, she sat cross-legged on the hood and debated, with increasing cold feet whether this was a sound idea. Not cold feet. Terror. It had been years, after all, with crowds of attractive, worldly women dogging his heels since she'd known him; she might be getting herself into a potentially embarrassing situation. Carey'd probably look at her and say, "Who?" She'd make a complete ass of herself.

It was, she decided suddenly, much too stupid a move, even for someone as incredibly rash as she. Dropping her long, khaki-covered legs over the side of the fender, she slipped to the ground and turned to get back into the car.

She heard the familiar voice before she saw him. Inexplicably, even after all this time, the low resonance was capable of causing her pulse to flutter. Its measured tones were explaining to unseen listeners, "We've still sun *above* the beach. Let's finish with the festival scene before we pack it in tonight."

A breathy female voice protested, "I'm getting hungry. How long are you going to keep shooting?"

Carey's voice, overlaid now with a touch of impatience, slowly replied, "If you're hungry, Tina, there's food in the trailer. We shoot till the sun goes down."

And then Molly saw him cresting the rise of the path from the beach, surrounded by people hurrying to keep up with his brisk stride. The saffron rays of the late afternoon sun caught in his pale hair like gilded mesh, and as his lean, broad-shouldered form emerged fully over the ridge of the slope, shirtless, barefoot, clad only in worn jeans riding low on his slim hips. Molly decided that he was altogether too handsome and always had been.

In the next split second she knew her nervy impulse was all wrong. They didn't have anything in common any-more . . . never had with their disparate backgrounds . . . outside the passionate wanting. The scion of aristocracy was an international celebrity now, a lover of endless chichi women, eons away from one of his youthful flings. At best, they would exchange banal civilities, at worst . . . she didn't care to contemplate *that* humiliation.

Molly already had one foot inside the car when she heard his deep voice cry, "Molly? Molly Darian?" The words held a question. And before she'd returned her foot to the ground, he was running toward her, shouting her name.

Her breath caught in her throat as she stepped out of the car and the years dropped away. Impossible. Ridiculous. It can't be. Disbelief tumbled frantically through her brain, but in seconds he was standing before her, clutching her hands in his and, like so many times, so many years ago, whispering, "Honeybear," in that incredible sexual rasp that always tore through her senses. Looking into the dark eyes lightly roam-ing her face, she saw the unsettling, smoldering possession that roused as acutely as a thousand caresses. "How long can you stay?" he murmured, intense as always, single-minded, oblivious to past and future.

Molly finally found the breath to speak under his devour-ing gaze. "An hour or so. I'm on my way home."

"Good," he said softly. He didn't ask where home was or where she'd come from. Only the short, clipped utterance, its meaning infinitely more complex than the single word. She looked exactly the same, he thought, his heart pumping as if he'd run ten miles; the woman from his dulcet memories, as though he'd only left her a minute before. A rush of sensation—more than that, *sentiment*, heavy as Irish lace, sweet as ripe papaya, unfamiliar but wonderful—innundated his mind. When he was with her he always felt as though the world had been washed fresh and clean and its bounties were his to enjoy. A childlike delusion, fascinating in its intensity.

Her blond hair was still long, touching her shoulders, the natural curl softly frizzed as he remembered it in wisps around her face. He wanted to touch it lightly, as if testing the buoyancy of gossamer, then slide his fingers through it. He wanted to grip her head possessively and pull her close to him so her tall, slender body was pressed tight. Her lapis eyes in the perfect oval of her face were wide and startled, only inches away from him. He wanted to lean close and, just before his lips touched her soft, full mouth, he wanted to whisper, "You're mine. You've always been mine. I don't care about husbands or boyfriends or acts of God."

It was a feverish, mad feeling, an aberration in a man noted for his solid pragmatism and self-control, and he fought the overwhelming impulse to blurt out the Neanderthal phrases. Fought it down, locked it away, and decided in the next moment of sanity he was just unconditionally glad she was here. It was the first miracle to occur in his life, and with a twinge of guilt he reconsidered his insensitivity to religious experiences. No more. He winked at her and murmured, "The earth moved."

The crew following him had come up by now and were gathering round. Dropping one of her hands, he turned to them and in a businesslike voice said, "That's it for today. See you all tomorrow at 8:30." He still held one of Molly's hands in a tight grip, as though she might disappear if he loosened his grasp. His tall body dwarfed her, but with a feeling of protection rather than intimidation, and his familiar presence warmed her.

The response was a garble of protests, which he countered until only two people remained: the young man in the baseball cap and the tall redhead. "Christina," Carey said politely, "Allen will drive you to the motel. I'll be back later."

Christina scanned Molly with icy eyes, noted the held hand with a black look, and replied in a throaty, pouting tone, "When later?"

"Later, later. I don't know. Have supper with Allen." Looking significantly at Allen, he added, "Drive carefully." Allen winked behind Christina's back, purposefully took her arm, and marched her off.

Turning back to Molly, Carey recaptured her other hand, pulled her up to his bare chest and, looking down at her from disturbingly close range, murmured, "You don't know how many times I've thought of you since that summer."

"Have you really?" It was gauche, she knew, and the words had come out oddly hushed, but only inches away from his body and his piercing gaze, any attempt at sophisticated repartee was lost in an overwhelming sense of awakening. How could he still do this to her after so much time? He made her feel that life was endlessly exciting and intoxicating.

But when he whispered, "Really," and bent to kiss her, Molly suddenly pictured herself in a vivid freeze-frame image as another adoring female in an endless parade of people who loved him. People just do, Molly thought. They loved the energy, the fascinating, charming vitality.

Although her hands were still tightly held in his warm grasp, she pushed against his chest, taking grudging exception to her mental image and his casual ardor. Torn between ferocious desire and pent-up cavil, she perversely asked, "And how many times have you used that winning turn of phrase, Mr. International Director?"

He stopped, lifting his head when Molly forced him back. Looking quizzically at her, his rugged brows raised, he answered, "Since there hasn't been a 'that summer' with anyone but you, it's a virgin line. Something wrong?"

"Don't you care to know where I came from or where I'm going or what I've been doing for the last ten years?" Her blue eyes weren't the typical placid blue that blond hair demanded, but a rich, deep cobalt, touched at the moment with small storms like potent gusts off the coast. Too many pictures of Carey with too many magnificent women for too many years fed her testiness.

A tilted half-smile appeared and the tenseness infusing his body diminished. "Sorry, Honeybear. It was such a miracle to see you again, I wasn't going to take any chances of dissolving the mirage with cold, hard questions. I wanted to kiss you to see if you were real or only another creation of my wishful thinking." His smile widened. "You must be real. Your fiery temper has survived intact, I see. Remind me to keep wine bottles out of your reach." Her defiance melted, and they both laughed at the memory of the flare-up on a long ago summer night.

"I'll have you know I bear the scar to this day. It's given me lots of mileage over the years. I don't mention that a sweet as honey young woman swung at me with a wine bottle and my hard head broke the blasted glass. Detracts from my macho image to be bested by a mite like you. So, okay, Honeybear, tell me where you've been all this time, and then I'll kiss you. Come on, sit down on the wall here and we'll watch the sun go down. Fill me in." And he swung her up on the stone wall, his hands warm around her waist. Leaning against the irregular masonry, he listened patiently while Molly, in a deliberately casual tone, gave a rapid and highly edited account of her life to date.

"Divorced," he said thoughtfully when she finished. "Love to hear it, although having you appear after all these years, I wasn't about to quibble over marital status. I tried to find you once a few years ago, but I didn't know your husband's name, your folks had moved out of town, Linda's parents were gone, too, and I never did know where Georgia lived. I came up against a blank. When women marry, they can drop out of sight pretty easily."

It warmed Molly's heart that he'd tried. "When was that? When you looked," she asked.

"I don't know . . . probably four or five years ago. Life had been pretty hectic for a while; I was vacationing with my Dad and just wanted to see you. Everything's supposed to be progressive nowadays—anyone can be friends—so I thought, married or no, I could drop in and say hello."

"I wish you had."

"Since I struck out on that attempt, *I'm* glad as hell you stopped by. Can you stay with me now?" He asked the question in a conversational tone.

Molly scanned his hard body casually braced against the wall next to her, took in the bold, beautiful face, the coarse, sun-streaked hair and she tried to reconcile the familiar image with the international jet-set celebrity director he'd become. She also tried to decipher the meaning of his simple question. "What do you mean, *now*?" she quietly asked.

"Now as 'from now on.' Ten years is a long time to wait, and I'd rather not wait any longer."

"You haven't exactly been waiting alone."

"Well, neither have you."

"I think your scorecard, at least according to the glossy magazines, totals considerably higher than my one-and-only husband."

"How long have you been divorced?"

"Two years."

"And there's been no one else?" A skeptical edge had crept into the bland question.

"No one appealed enough."

"You fascinate me, Honeybear," he said teasingly. "You mean it's all for me?"

"*It* is not for anyone. We live in liberated times, Carey Fersten. My life's my own, my body, too."

"*Pardonnez-moi.*" His dark eyes sparkled. "Perhaps Ms.—" He waited for her to contribute the name he'd never known.

"Cooper. But I use my maiden name now."

"I wish I'd known Cooper five years ago and now that I do, it doesn't matter, so Ms. Darian, perhaps you'd be willing to share some of your"—his eyes slowly slid down her body—"liberated sensibilities with me. If I appeal of course," he added, smiling. "Am I going too fast?" His gaze was back on her face and while he spoke with lightness he was impelled by emotions he couldn't control. He couldn't have slowed down if he wished and it required all his self-control to keep from carrying her off to his bed.

Yes, Molly thought, considering this is the first time I've seen you in ten years, and no, because she was honest enough to acknowledge she'd wanted him ten years ago, all the time between and now. "You always were fast," she said instead, smiling back, thinking Paradise had materialized right here in the gravel parking lot of Ely Lake park.

Carey exhaled the breath he'd been holding. "Back to square one, then, Honeybear. Can you stay with me now?"

"Stay with you?" She knew she was sounding obtuse or retarded or coy, but much as she wished to jettison her entire life on the spur of the moment, she had to consider her daughter who was waiting for her in the Cities, her business which didn't operate without her and, equally important, Carey Fersten's vagrant and capricious life. Including one impermanent wife and possibly ten such invitations to ladies a week.

"Stay, as in walk, talk, eat, play." He paused, took a small breath. ". . . Sleep with me. Can you?"

A heated rush tore through her senses, but she couldn't— just like that—like picking up Boston cream pie in a cafeteria line. "Not now," she said, her ambiguity a blend of logic and wanting. She was careful not to say no.

He frowned. It wasn't the answer he wanted. "When?" he asked, very quietly, not forcing too hard, but wanting to know if there'd be a "when" so he could last till then, only breathe small breaths and last till then.

"I don't know." Was it because she was afraid of being a

number—that old girlfriend, what's her name—who stopped by during filming. She was questioning his sincerity. "I *have* to be back in the Cities to pick up my daughter and I've an appointment with my banker in the morning." The truth intervened to mask her uncertainties.

"Tomorrow then?"

"I'd love to, but . . ."

"But?" His query was very soft. He wasn't used to refusals.

"Look," she said, hearing the small touch of resentment in his voice, deciding to be frank, "you walked into my life once and tore it apart. I don't know if I want a repeat performance . . . If I can handle one."

"You were the one who married that summer, not me." His voice was controlled but he'd never completely gotten over his anger.

"The wedding had been planned for months."

"Not my idea of a reason to get married."

"I was young."

"That, at least, is a reasonable excuse."

"You never mentioned anything more permanent to me." After all these years did she want an apology?

"Damn right I did," he said, and for a flashing moment he felt young and uncertain again. "It just wasn't good enough."

"It was vague as hell and you know it."

"You were nothing but a bundle of contradictions—flighty and uncertain, persuaded it could never work. That's what I remember. You only saw me between visits from your fiancé who was away at school, and even then I had to beg like crazy because you were so guilt-ridden. 'What will my parents say? What will Bart's parents say? They're such good friends.' " His voice mimicked the words he'd heard so often. "I wasn't," he went on in a cool tone, "getting reassurances about you wanting me, either."

Molly's eyes widened. "None?"

"Besides that," he hastily murmured.

She smiled at the correction and sighed softly. All the

years of unrequited love vibrated through the gentle sound. "Oh, I did," she slowly replied, "I wanted you . . . in every way. But all the pressures of the wedding—"

"And I didn't fit into the plans."

She mutely shook her head. "You weren't even from the same world. And you never said anything about *us*—not voluntarily. Why didn't you talk about *us*?" she whispered.

Carey looked at her downcast eyes and tightly clenched fists, then took her hands in his and soothed the backs of them with gentle brushing movements of his thumbs. He glanced past her shoulder to the blue lake spread serenely below them, as if its serenity would somehow calm the tumult in his mind. "I don't know," he murmured, thinking of all the years he'd searched for Molly in other women's arms. "All sorts of mixed-up reasons . . . fear mostly, I suppose. I'd never really thought of marriage and maybe I figured you'd change your mind about marrying Bart and I wouldn't have to consider it, right then. We could just *be* together . . . but the days kept ticking away . . . until they were gone. You'd never talked about marriage either except—that last night— and when you didn't accept my offer of marriage . . ."

She looked askance at him. "That was something to accept? The 'I suppose . . . if you want to . . . I guess . . . maybe . . . if you give me some time'?"

"Christ, I was young, too. I don't know why I said everything wrong. But I did." With a visible effort, he seemed to shake away the memories and his fingers twined strong and hard through hers. "All I know is that's past . . . it's over. About now," he urged. "Can you stay with me tonight? Is that clear enough, Honeybear?" His glance was direct and imploring.

"Oh God . . . I *have* to go back. My daughter, my parents are—"

"Can you stay *awhile*?" His eyes were velvet soft and expectant as they always had been when he looked at her. Those breathlessly artful eyes, she thought, had the capacity to enter her soul.

Molly smiled at him, at the warmth and contentment washing over her, at the quizzical smile he was directing at her. "For a while," she said.

"I'll settle for that," he said quickly, like someone who'd had their hand over the buzzer on a quiz program, and, lifting her down from the wall with a light swinging motion, set her on her feet. "All the other Byzantine intracacies can wait," he added with a grin, feeling as if divine grace had offered him a chance to relive his life. And he wasn't going to fuck this up.

Very politely, calling on all the courtesy he'd been taught and had acquired in the past thirty-three years, he said, "Come into my trailer. You can tell me all about your daughter and your new business, we'll have something to eat, we'll talk. And this time we're old enough not to be quite as stupid . . . We'll work something out."

She grinned, his solicitude charming. "You're awfully cute."

"And you're way the hell past 'cute', Honeybear," he said very, very softly. "You're a miracle of the heart, a million wishes fulfilled. And I'm seriously thinking about locking the door once I have you inside," he finished in a whisper.

But he didn't because he was treading uncharted second-chance-in-life ground and reading the road map with caution. He said instead, the asterisk on his internal map denoting, **GO SLOW, TRAVEL WITH CARE**. "Why don't you call your daughter first so she won't worry. Tell her you'll be a little late."

Molly hesitated. "I can't stay very long . . . I don't have to call."

"This time I won't let you go so easily," he said, handing her the phone. "Call."

After speaking to her mother, Molly said, "Put Carrie on, will you, Mom? I'll explain to her that I'm running late and

I'll pick her up at your house in the morning." With her back to Carey, Molly didn't notice the startled look flicker across his face when she asked for her daughter.

After Molly hung up Carey challenged, "I thought you said your daughter's name was Charlotte Louise."

"It is, but I call her Carrie. Char never appealed to me for obvious reasons, and Lottie always reminded me of a nineteenth-century tart. So . . . Carrie."

"How old is she?"

"Eight."

"And blond like you?" he asked more casually than he felt. Although he'd never met Bart, he knew he was dark-haired.

The eyes that met his were open, calm, proudly maternal. "Not exactly . . . quite a bit lighter. Pale, Nordic, more like yours, actually."

Still no subterfuge Carey noted, and before he could ask the question that was bringing the adrenaline peaking in his nerve endings, Molly teasingly added, "Don't go getting a bigger ego than you already have. I *did not* name her after you." And all the subconscious vaults Molly had securely locked years ago remained, through practice, secure.

While a suffocating sense of déjà vu and subliminal fantasy held sway in his mind, Molly went on, "The name's only a coincidence. She was named after my grandmother whom I loved very much, and the diminutive was a simple process of elimination."

"I see," Carey replied with the same deliberate control that kept cast, crew, and the elements of nature in ordered compliance, and he dropped the discussion. Too many major upheavals had occurred in the past hour to add another unsettling speculation to an already overtaxed mind. Relax, he thought. There's plenty of time . . . for that. "Since you don't have to rush off," he said like a congenial host, not a man whose life had just been turned upside down, "why don't I fix us something to drink or eat? Or would you rather go somewhere?"

"This is fine," Molly replied, glancing around the tastefully decorated interior. It was the room of a successful man. Elegant but solid furniture. Lighting carefully designed to be both warm and unobtrusive. Some small, illuminated paintings. It was lived in, not cold like modern decor could sometimes be, but warm and relaxed. His desk was littered, a pair of riding boots were tossed in the corner near the door, and a splash of red carnations was casually spilling out of a clear glass vase on a small table.

Carey was quickly picking up a variety of clothes that had been dropped and draped on the furniture. Rolling them into a ball, he tossed them behind the couch.

"Still neat," Molly remarked with a smile.

His head swiveled back around and he winked. "You gotta have the touch."

"If you're that good about the cooking, maybe I should help you . . . or do you really know how to cook?"

"Sort of," he answered, his grin infectious. "Remember the fettucini I made at my apartment on Third Avenue?"

It was incredible how perfectly it all remained in her mind. "I remember," Molly murmured, and every wall, corner, picture, and chair of the tiny apartment Carey had rented above Mrs. Larsen's house came back in a warm rush of pleasure. It was there Carey had made love to her the first time . . . on the old iron bed on a warm spring night in April. He'd sneaked her up the outside staircase, past Mrs. Larsen's kitchen window, hoping his landlady wouldn't hear because she had strict rules about "female" guests. The bed was big and soft; they'd whispered in the dark room; only the light from the streetlamps had shone through the opened windows.

He'd undressed her with shaking hands, this young man who'd survived the horrors of Vietnam with unflinching boldness, then carried her across the patterned carpet and placed her gently in the center of his bed. She'd watched him undress. His movements were hurried, swift, shoes kicked off, his shirt pulled off male-fashion, with one sharp tug over the back of his head. She still remembered the play of golden light on his lean, muscled shoulders and curved torso, waist, and hips, as he stepped out of his jeans. Aroused and urgently ready, his maleness had brought a small gasp from her.

"I won't hurt you, Honeybear," he'd whispered as he lowered his strong body next to her. "I'd never hurt you."

"Drink first?" Carey asked, moving toward the compact, chrome kitchen. "Coffee, tea? Wine? Scotch?"

And Mrs. Larsen's rented room abruptly changed to an ultra-luxurious trailer-studio, all burnished metal and pale wheat wool and Bauhaus functionalism. "God, no," Molly replied, shaking her head, "no wine or scotch. We were at the Holiday Inn drinking until four this morning. By the way," she added, noting that his rangy frame limned against the entrance to the lighted kitchen hadn't gained an ounce, "I saw you walk in with Christina around three A.M."

"If you're hung-over," he said, as if she hadn't mentioned Christina, "you have to try my famous 'morning after' remedy."

"What's that?" Molly asked, somehow pleased he hadn't wanted to talk about the woman. And suddenly, all sorts of rockets began detonating in small, heated explosions through her senses when she recalled with a startling vividness what Carey was like "the morning after." His remedy in those days hadn't been a drink. The memories were so real she could almost feel his hands on her body.

"Tried and true formula," he casually replied. "Orange juice, honey, tonic water, and a little champagne." If he felt the charged memories in the air, he was deliberately ignoring them. "Absolutely foolproof," he declared, already pulling bottles out of the refrigerator. "Sit down, make yourself at home."

In short moments, the drink was prepared. It was marvelous, she thought, taking a sip—crisp, cold, sweet. Slipping his arms into a shirt that had escaped his cleaning because it was a part of the litter on his desk, Carey dropped onto the couch opposite her, slouching low along the wide cushions. His shirt was unbuttoned, his long legs stretched out so they almost reached Molly's chair. As they talked, his arms were lightly crossed on his muscled chest and he looked at her in that same brooding way, so achingly familiar it seemed she'd seen him just yesterday. He'd always listened to her that way, intense, concentrating, as though he were watching, not only listening, but watching the words come out of her mouth.

The lamplight caught the modeling of her classic cheekbones, accentuated the shadowy dark blue of her eyes, underscored the fullness of her bottom lip, highlighted the pale yellow of her linen blouse. Her breasts strained against the light fabric, the outline of her nipples tempting jonquil buds.

Carey shifted his position slightly, his body warming too fast, her nearness too provocative. He concentrated on the conversation, wrenching his mind from the sensual feeling bombarding his brain.

They quickly, casually, covered the how, what, and where questions, the physical details of their lives in the intervening years, carefully avoiding the interior shots, the close-up exposures revealing emotions, hopes, and dreams. Molly was saying, "So when the reunion came up, I was—"

"Come here," Carey said, so quietly that at first she thought she'd misunderstood. Her sentence remained unfinished, her expression inquisitive. "Come here," he repeated.

"No," she answered when she was sure what he'd said. "No." Her refusal was almost a desperate whisper.

"Please?" he pleaded softly and held out his hand.

She gazed at him for a long time, at his eyes, those gorgeous black eyes staring straight into hers, at his hand, strong, sure, well-formed, only a yard away.

"Please," he said again, and after a moment of taut silence, he exhaled a rush of breath. "God, Honeybear, do you know how long it's been since I held you last?" His voice was hushed, with a quivering thread of undisguised longing vibrating in the deep, rich tone.

"Nine years, nine months, twelve days, seven hours," she whispered and rose to go to him, no more able to deny him now than in the past.

CHAPTER 18

Their fingers touched like a bridge between poignant memory and hope, and he pulled her into his arms, folding her against his chest, her head cradled with the gentlest pressure close to his heart. She heard the quickening acceleration of his heartbeat through the muscle, sinew, and bone of the honed athletic body that had altered so little. He held her lightly, tense and rigid despite the tenderness of his embrace while a warmth and wonder inundated their souls. It was as if time had been turned back, all the pages of the calendar in some bizarre time warp had flipped backward, and they were transported to an enchanted long-ago summer. He felt the warm tears first, and then looked down at her, lifting her face gently with a crooked finger. "Don't cry, Honeybear," he murmured. "We're together." His lips touched her eyes, lightly kissing away the tears, his fingers reaching up to slide through her golden hair. "Oh, Honeybear," he groaned, "I've missed you so." And his hands slipped to her shoulders, tightened, almost hurt as he covered her mouth with his, tasting her lips and the sweet interior of her mouth with a desperation that would have startled any of his current friends and lovers. Carey Fersten was never a desperate man.

Molly's hands smoothed over his pale hair, moved down over the powerful muscles of his neck, glided laterally and clung to his solid shoulders while she cried tears of joy, her mouth welcoming his fevered urgency. And when the first powerful demand to feel and touch and know for certain had diminished, they nibbled between soft sighs and giggles, delicately exchanging low murmurs of pleasure.

Long moments later, Carey drew back enough to look into Molly's face, his dark brows slanted in raven-winged swoops over deep-set smoky eyes that always had the power to melt her at a glance. "Welcome home, Honeybear." His smile was warm, tender, soul-shattering. "No more tears . . . never any more tears for us."

Feeling enchanted, content, as if she'd arrived in a safe fjord after a calamitous stormy sea, Molly raised tear-splashed lashes. A blissful radiance filled her eyes as she murmured, "Sure as ever."

"Not as ever," Carey whispered, his glance smoldering. Molly's cheeks were brushed with a rosy glow, her lips reddened to bright cherry by his bruising kisses, her mouth slightly open as though the warming pleasure coursing through her needed release. "But older and much, much wiser," he added, lowering his head to recapture the passion her melting lips offered, "and damn sure, this time." His breath was warm on her lips, his mouth brushing a seductive caress back and forth as he eased her down on the couch, his hands insistent on her body, arranging her carefully beneath him.

His fingers moved to the buttons of her blouse. Between tantalizing kisses, between gentle nudges of his lean hips which enticed with the magnitude of his need, he deftly opened her lemon-colored blouse. Deliberately sliding the fabric aside, he exposed her full breasts, the slender curve of her rib cage, the unmistakable arousal of her peaked nipples.

He touched one begging peak with a delicate fingertip and watched its swelling response. Molly felt the cushioned couch under her melt into mythical, pink-tinged olympian clouds, felt the spiral of flame spin downward to the throbbing center of her trembling senses. And when his slender hand moved to her other breast, his warm palm rubbing its crested point, she moaned a low, purring sound.

"You haven't changed," he breathed in a husky tone. He glanced down at her gently undulating hips, and his hand moved to the waistband of her slacks.

Suddenly, she saw herself as naive and vulnerable, a prey to his expert seduction. How could she, she anxiously thought, when every rational argument decreed Carey Fersten not only unreliable but inconstant? He was hardly the kind of man who offered a stable future, despite the honeyed words. He hadn't been years ago and certainly wasn't now, with his star status. She felt foolish, confused. "No." On impulse, she pushed him away. "No, please don't."

Raised on his elbows, he gazed down at her. Her eyes, full of entreaty, held his. "I want to," her voice shook, "and I don't want to. Do you know what I mean?" she inquired with candid honesty.

His body tense, he exhaled slightly. "No," he said. Balancing on one elbow, he covered her hands pressing against his chest. His eyes were pitch-black with desire. "You told me that once before. Remember?"

Molly nodded mutely, her breath shallow and labored.

"And do you remember what I did then?" His voice was hushed, shaken.

Her eyes were large, infused with sudden tenderness.

"I told you what holding you did to me. I told you how every touch of your small hands set me on fire. Touch me. Touch me again, now, like you did then," he implored, pulling her hand downward, "and you'll see the power you still have over me . . ."

She hesitated, but in her mind's eye she saw the hard length of him, and a shiver raced up her spine. "Could I take this a little more slowly?" she asked on a long exhalation of breath, trying to deal with ten years of longing and instant gratification simultaneously.

"As slow as you want, Honeybear."

"I'm sorry." She felt guilty somehow for her green uncertainty. "I want you very much," she added in a whisper.

"I know." She didn't have to tell him when their heated bodies were talking in their own fervent dialogue. "You're my sweet and earnest virgin," he whispered back, lying over her with his erection hard against her stomach, their naked chests only inches apart, her hands trembling in his.

"I thought I was more blasé."

"I'm glad you're not. I know half a world of blasé people, but I don't know any sweet and earnest virgins." His grin was intoxicating, like a drug that touched your senses, curled into your nostrils, drifted down the back of your throat so you could taste its offered pleasure.

"I'm too old for trepidation," she murmured, trembling.

"You're forever young to me. I'm feeling sensations—" He stopped to swallow, staggered by emotions he would have written off as mawkish sentiment two hours ago, seeing Molly as he had the first time . . .

His hand still covered hers, the heat of his palm so much warmer than her skin. "Do you remember what you used to call me?"

Tiger, tiger, burning bright . . . she silently recited, seeing Blake's potent icon, its animal spirit boldly evident in Carey's burning eyes. "Tiger," she whispered, and the softly uttered name brought back every bittersweet memory of her youthful love. It brought back warm summer nights at the lake, lying in Carey's arms. It brought back the scent of wild roses and pine trees and crushed meadow grass. It brought back a rumpled bed in the moonlight, a strong young body holding her, filling her, teaching her about love and pleasure and fierce contentment.

"And do you remember," he went on in a low voice, "what I said at the very last, after you'd whispered that to me?"

A hot rush of pleasure stabbed through her body, and though she didn't answer, her eyes told him she remembered.

His words were hushed, just as they'd been when his young body had hovered above hers on Mrs. Larsen's rented bed. "Try and stop me," he said.

After that she was lost. Reaching up, she pushed his shirt from his shoulders. He helped, and with two impatient shrugs it was off completely and sliding to the floor. Molly's hands were trembling when they touched the zipper of his jeans. His hands covered hers, sliding them down over the strained denim. Pressing against his maleness, feeling the hard desire, the enormous size, she whimpered in shivering excitement. Carey's eyes closed for a brief moment, his breath in abeyance, then he swung up from the couch in one swift movement and stood. In a few seconds he was stripped to the naked beauty that always reminded Molly of sheer male strength. She caught only a glimpse of his marvelously made body, his maleness so rampant it hugged his belly before he was back beside her, unbuckling her belt, undoing buttons and zippers, slipping off her shoes, slacks, lace panties, all with a quiet haste that beat like drum rolls, that spread a fiery ache of anticipation through her.

"I'm not doing this right," he murmured as he eased over her and lowered his body, an expression of intense concentration drawing his dark brows together. His hand was already reaching to touch her, to make way for the urgency that was exploding inside him. "But I can't wait," he whispered, this man known for his skill as a lover. His breath was hot on her lips, his rigid arousal forcing its way into her soft, warm body. "God, Honeybear," he groaned and thrust forward with a fierce, uncontrolled madness.

Molly cried out, passion flaring, and she arched up in ancient welcome as he filled her deeply, crushing her in an embrace that spoke of harsh need and restless homecoming. In mere seconds she felt him begin to shudder, felt his initial movement of withdrawal. "No," she cried softly, her hands strong against his arching back. "Please stay," she whispered, reaching up to kiss his mouth, his cheeks, his strong jaw.

"I can't," he moaned, knowing she was wrong, knowing he shouldn't stay, knowing with the exception of a few youthful moments of reckless passion with her, he'd always been careful. Since Vietnam and Agent Orange, since bouts of nausea and intermittent periods of nerveless fingers and toes, he'd forced himself to be careful.

"Yes, you can," Molly breathed. "Stay . . . don't leave me . . ." Her words were full of lush invitation and searing want, they were words for now and for the past. She looked up at his face in the lamplight, his eyes stark with strain, the predator's gaze softened by need, and she felt as though it were she who were the possessor, not he. It was a primeval emotion, a female feeling of triumph that defied explanation.

It was too late by then—moments past any rational decision.

She felt his unchecked trembling, the first small orgasmic spasm. This time when her demanding hands urged him closer, he capitulated, crushing her savagely close, grinding into her, pouring out his pent-up white-hot climax.

"Damn . . ." he breathed softly when it was over. His body still covered hers, impaled her, his face buried in the curve of her shoulder.

She was smiling in a way she'd forgotten existed, stroking his back, lazily sliding her hands down the heavy muscles bordering his spine, touching the smooth dip in the small of his back where pale, silky hair formed a swirling pattern. "It's all right."

His head lifted, dark brows creased into a mild scowl. "It's not, and you know it."

"No problem," Molly said, moving her hips gently. Feeling his reaction, she smiled again.

He looked down at her face, contoured with the rosy flush of passion, and his scowl disappeared. "You're still the same." A lopsided smile creased his cheek. "Still demanding."

"You haven't changed, either," she replied, a teasing light in her eyes, "except maybe a little more . . . impatient."

"Sorry about that."

"How sorry?" Her slim hips moved again with the requisite response.

"About two-minutes-more sorry," he answered in a husky drawl.

"You always were reliable," she announced graciously with an impudent, seductive smile.

His mouth quirked and his eyes crinkled in the corners. "I recall you commenting on that before."

Gently arching upward, Molly wrapped her legs around his waist, pulling him close. She felt the full length of him surge, strong and hard, deep within her waiting body.

His smoldering glance held her in a current of understanding. "This time, Honeybear, you can have as long as you want." He said the words slowly in time with the driving motion of his lower body, his rich voice promising fulfillment. "You tell me how long you want."

"A day, a week, a hundred years . . ." Molly dreamily murmured.

He began leisurely, as if the hundred years were beginning that moment. Teasing her, pleasing her, lightly kissing her, nibbling on her lips for an infinite amount of time, he whispered seductive words, words that shamelessly stroked the delicate mind centers of sexuality. With languid abandon she followed him or led him where she wanted to go. But he wouldn't allow her to order the pace, to order his strokes or hasten the excruciatingly disciplined pauses, or keep him deep inside her so it would be over too soon. He knew what she liked, he remembered as if they were both back in his bed at Mrs. Larsen's. He remembered, so he ignored her protests, whispering, "No, Honeybear, wait . . . wait." With infinite skill he brought her pulses beating to such an intensity that when she climaxed she sobbed great, panting sobs of release. Then—fainted.

She had always been a spendthrift with her body, generous, reveling in the hurtling temptations of passion, wanting things too fast, he thought, wanting everything right now, wanting him. Thank God.

He put both his arms around her slim body, rolled over, and lifted her into his arms. She woke in a few moments, cradled against his body. He was stroking her hair, cuddling her. And when he saw her eyes flutter open and look up at him, he grinned at her and said, "Gotcha."

She clung to his smiling warmth and strength, giving herself up to the joy of realizing that Carey Fersten, whom she'd never stopped loving, was holding her and kissing her and telling her the world would be right. Blotting out all thought, she abandoned herself to an incendiary happiness.

He queried her later with that essentially pragmatic side of his nature about the "no problem" comment. "On the pill?" he asked. Rarely permitting himself to surrender so completely, he was now troubled with his carelessness. "No?" he apprehensively uttered at her negative headshake. "Has your body altered into some regular schedule now, that you can so assuredly say, 'no problem'?" he asked, startled and newly suspicious.

"Sort of."

"What the hell does that mean?" he urgently demanded. She was half-turned into the curve of his chest and arm, and he lifted her within inches of his serious face.

"It means I think so. It means I'm more or less regular. It means I haven't slept with anyone for two years so I'm not totally certain if the regularity is regular or only that it hasn't been put to the test."

He looked incredulous. "You're joking," he said in a disbelieving voice. "You were joking before, right? Look," he went on with a quick shrug, "it's none of my business, really."

She slowly shook her head. "No joke."

His brows arched in astonishment over narrowed eyes: "Not you, Honeybear." Not only recent events but carefully preserved memory fostered his incredulity. "Don't expect me to believe that," he crisply added.

Molly shrugged, innocent of deception, calmly acceptant of her own idiosyncrasies. "They have to appeal. I told you and I mean it. And appeal is mystical, esoteric, an inexplicable feeling with *me* as the only authority."

"They?" he said with territorial maleness, his black on black eyes piercing, jealous and edged with worldly cynicism.

"He," she corrected, knowing even with Bart it had never been like it was with Carey. But she wasn't foolish enough to inform him of that fact. "He," she repeated. "Don't get agitated," she teased. "I always take men one at a time."

"That's reassuring," he mocked. "But not for what—two years?" His skepticism was blatant.

"Nope."

And that single word inexpressibly gave him more pleasure than a thousand Cannes Film Awards. He didn't realize how moral he could be.

"Unlike you," Molly returned. And despite her best intentions, an edginess came through. "Your prowess with starlets, models, Italian countesses is world news. Wasn't there a Berber beauty at the last location in Morocco? You see how busy the paparazzi are keeping us titillated Stateside."

His own good mood restored, Carey reached out to smooth away the hostile line between Molly's pale brows. "Honeybear, I don't care about all those women. They're just *there*. It goes with the business."

Mild affront greeted his casual disclaimer and too many photos over too many years colored her reply.

"Don't try to tell me there's no enjoyment in all that adulation."

"They all want something," he said, speaking deliberately. "Most of them, anyway," he added, "and it's not necessarily me. They'll go after anyone who can give them a role, a job, a chance in a film. A lot of those beautiful women have been trained from birth to sniff out the scent of power. Understand?

But no one has ever come close to touching what we had. You've always been in my heart, my soul, in hidden corners of my mind."

"Tell me about Sylvie," Molly said with impudent bad manners. Until today she'd never allowed herself to deal with the jealousy that had eaten at her when she first saw the wedding pictures splashed across the tabloids. The timing had been disastrous. Bart had just moved out of the house the month before for the first of their trial separations.

Carey grimaced. "A very bad mistake," he said with rue in his voice. "I should have known better; but I'd turned thirty . . . thought maybe I should consider settling down. She'd moved into the villa and was . . . well, insistent."

"And you married because some pretty German countess was insistent?"

"No, not really. If that was the case, I'd have been married any number of times. But don't forget, love," he added to forestall the flashes of fire in her eyes, "insistence does play a role occasionally. Remember Bart? Hmmm?"

"Touché," Molly admitted, her temper deflected by the reminder.

"You lasted a long time. What—six, seven years?"

"Eight. I was dumb. Stubborn. Believed in marriage till death do us part. And then there was Carrie. She needed a mother *and* father. Or at least I thought so."

"What finally changed your mind?" he asked curiously.

Molly sighed. "The proverbial straw was when one of his girlfriends came over to the house to return the wallet Bart had 'forgotten.' He told me he was going out of town on business. Arizona in winter. The girl had a beautiful tan. At that point, I decided Carrie would have to make do with a one-parent family, anxieties or no anxieties. It was better than having a murderer for a mother."

"I'm sorry," Carey said quietly. "I wish I could have been there to help."

"It probably was better I went through it alone. I grew up

beaucoup fast. Finally recognized the frustration as counter-productive, started shifting priorities and revising my notions of marriage to more accurately reflect my reality, not someone else's. I learned to take care of my own life and enjoy the freedom. It was, as they say, educational."

"And Bart?"

"Bart who?"

"Does your daughter miss him?"

"He was never home much."

"Oh," Carey said, startled. "I'm sorry."

"Don't be, or I'll have to be sorry for you and Sylvie," Molly responded pertly.

Carey broke into a grin. "That would be a great waste of emotion."

"Ditto, in my case. Underlined, exclamation points."

"Do you think we made a mistake somewhere down the line, Honeybear?"

"I'd be inclined to conclude perhaps our judgment in spouses had a flaw or two," she agreed with an easy smile. "Although," she went on, her tone less facetious, "my marriage wasn't so different from others I knew. None of my friends adored their husbands. No one thought marriage was made in heaven. We all agreed that marriage was a mutual compromise, a great deal of hard work and an occasional sweet, tender moment in a hectic schedule. All the men had their flings, and lots of the wives did, too. That was life. We were mature adults. We read the statistics on marital fidelity and understood life's passages. I didn't expect to have a marriage different from anyone else's. But . . ." She seemed to reflect for a moment, considering.

"But what?" Carey inquired, wanting to know everything about the years he'd missed: how she felt, what she cared about, how she lived. He stroked her back, for the pleasure of feeling her warmth, for the reassurance.

She propped her chin on the flattened back of her hand, gathered comfort from the solid feel of his chest beneath her palm, and tried to explain her coming of age in America. "I finally decided," she said very softly, "I wanted more. *More*, in capital letters. It wasn't a sudden revelation. Just a small germ of an idea that grew and wouldn't be set aside. I realized in the slow evolution of this concept that I didn't care what other people were settling for—the house in the right neighborhood, the new cars, boats, vacations, memberships in the clubs that mattered, the trade-offs for the void in their marriages. I didn't want to be in a marriage that was just okay. Even being alone, I decided couldn't be any worse than 'just okay.' And hell, I thought, it could be a whole lot better. At least I wouldn't be running into any more girls with winter tans returning my husband's wallet."

"Was it better?"

"It was great. It was hard work and scary sometimes when the money was low, but independence is primo."

The warm glow in her eyes was just as he remembered. She was so intensely alive that other women seemed pale in comparison. He used to go through the intellectual games occasionally when his spirits were disastrously low, because thinking of Molly was like popping a pleasure pill. And he'd mentally catalog all her charming assets: her radiant beauty; how she could make him laugh; the way she felt when she clung to him, lush as silk, hot and wanting him with a ferocity that matched his own. And her smile. It was the eighth wonder of the world.

"How independent has your independence become?" he asked cautiously, remembering her fierce streak that had generated many clashes that summer when his own independence met hers. They'd never quite learned to deal with it then.

"I'm not eighteen anymore," she said and looked him straight in the eye.

"In that case, a quick refresher in the Queensberry rules might be in order." One dark brow rose in provocative challenge.

"Is that the sound of the bell?" she asked, but her eyes were amused.

"We'll have to see how much you've learned in ten years. How many rounds can you go now before I win?"

"What makes you think you'll win?"

"I always win," he murmured. Her eyes were emitting little sparks now, so he touched her cheek with a caressing finger and whispered, "Used to win . . . And," he said with a grin, "in the interests of future universal harmony, I'd better see that you get home, for your mom and dad and Carrie." He glanced at the clock. "We'd better fly."

"What about my car?"

Junk it, I'll get you a new one, he thought. "Someone will drive it back," he said instead.

"Someone?"

"There's about two hundred people up here on my payroll. I'm sure one of them has a driver's license."

"What if I say I'll drive myself back?"

Carey smiled. "I'd forgotten how difficult you could be. Don't you like to fly?"

"I'm used to running my own life. You get a taste for it, like rattlesnake meat." She slid away from him and sat up.

"Okay, okay, no problem . . . I'll drive back with you and Jess can fly down and pick me up."

"Carey!"

"Hey," he responded, wondering what he'd said wrong now. "I'm being understanding as hell. You make your own decision."

"From a list of your choices?" Molly asked testily.

"Look." His voice was quiet, his glance placid. "Arrange it anyway you like, only I'm staying with you until you get home because I don't want to miss a minute of our first night together in ten long years. In the morning I've got to shoot come hell or high water. Delays cost eighty thousand a day. *You* have to work tomorrow, you already primly informed me; your daughter needs you; your mother and father expect you and your banker, who holds your note currently up for renewal, wants his interest money. Only until tomorrow morning, I'm going to stay with you. Now, should we try and eat quickly before we leave? You haven't tasted my fettucini since I learned how to cook and I love you no matter what you say, but keep in mind I outweigh you by at least ninety pounds when you decide how to respond."

"You love me?" Molly said so softly her words wouldn't have carried another inch.

"Always have," he said, equally softly.

"I wish I would have known . . ."

"I know, Honeybear . . . It's been the longest ten years of my life. But," he went on briskly, shaking away his melancholy and reaching for her, "the next hundred are going to be great."

As it turned out, they were chauffeured down to the Cities in Carey's limousine while Molly's car, driven by one of Carey's numerous employees followed behind.

Isolated in the plush darkness of the backseat, Molly and Carey watched the late show and the late, late show, seated hand in hand, kissing occasionally or just squeezing each other's hand in a message of contentment.

The sun was rising when they reached Molly's.

"I'll call you tonight," Carey said. "Don't go away."

"You're going to be late getting back."

He debated his answer for a moment. "Jess is waiting at the airport."

She grinned. "I can see it's going to take awhile to whip you into shape."

His brows rose and fell like Groucho Marx. "I'll hurry back."

And they were both giggling when they kissed good-bye.

CHAPTER 19

Monday started out well in a haze of tumultuous feeling. Carrie was brightly vivacious all the way to school, interested in her mother's weekend, full of details of her own visit with Grandma and Grandpa. Molly's employees welcomed her back warmly with a hand-painted banner over her office door. She had never missed a day of work before. And, to top it all off, one of her largest accounts decided to redo their executive offices. It was the key to solvency; the commission and profit would bring her company solidly into the black by the time the project was completed. So when Molly faced Jason Evans across his polished walnut desk at precisely eleven, she greeted him buoyantly.

His response was less enthusiastic, but she didn't notice, insulated by her own special happiness. "This may be the last time I have to renew the note, Jason. United Diversified just came through with a marvelous contract. By December—February at the latest—I should be in the clear."

"I can't renew the note, Molly."

"Do you realize what that means to my company? It's only been two years since I put together financing and—" The apprehension showed in her eyes first. "What did you say, Jason?"

"I said I can't renew the note." Picking up a pen, he tapped the point lightly on his pristine desk blotter.

"Seriously?" Molly's stomach tightened convulsively. "Why not?" Panic was accelerating her heartbeat; she could feel the added flurry tingle through her body.

"The interest rates are going up on short-term notes."

"So rewrite it. I don't mind paying higher interest for a few months." She waited for the answer with the terrible feeling that her life depended on it.

Setting his pen down, Jason moved it precisely in line with the edge of his desk. This martinet was concerned with symmetry when her business was at stake, she thought bitterly. "I can't," he said, not quite meeting her glance. "We're not going to be writing short-term notes anymore."

An awful, sinking feeling overwhelmed her. "Does Bart have anything to do with this?" she asked suspiciously, carefully watching Jason's face. He wouldn't give her an honest answer if Bart was involved, but maybe she could read something from his denial. Although not close friends, she'd discovered during one of Bart's infrequent visits that they'd been fraternity brothers in college.

"Of course not," Jason replied, adjusting his perfectly arranged tie.

"Don't of-course-not me, Jason, not after last time. Bart's little dealings through First National and Chip Ballay cost me a business, and you know it." It annoyed her how the old-boy network supported each other exclusive of their employers, like a well-ordered, smoothly run mutual aid society.

"That was all perfectly accountable."

"But not ethical, and you know it," Molly snapped.

"I'm sorry, Molly," he said in a tone that was bland and hardly sincere. "Maybe some other bank could give you an interim loan. My superiors are on my case. We've renewed this four times now."

"I'll be able to pay the balance by the first of the year.

Can't you tell them that?" She bit hard on her bottom lip to stop the tears from filling her eyes.

He only shook his head.

Composing herself with superhuman effort, Molly heard her calm good-bye, heard her reasonable voice telling Jason she'd call him by Friday and then in numbed panic she spent the next hour walking the downtown streets frantically totaling her assets, re-arranging payrolls, operating expenses, accounts payable and receivable in an attempt to come up with the two hundred thousand dollars she needed to pay off the note. Jason could suggest interim financing all he wanted, but if it was so easy, why the hell didn't *he* give her the interim financing. All she was asking for was another six months. You work for years to make a dream happen, work and sacrifice and work some more, nights, weekends, holidays, and then zap—a banker's reality.

Returning to the office, she spent the afternoon with her assistant Theresa, going over expenditures. But everything was cut to the bone already. They had enough coming in to cover monthly expenses, but not enough to cover an extra two-hundred-thousand-dollar note, not until United Diversified's offices were finished and billed out. At four o'clock she left to pick up Carrie from school and tomorrow she'd simply begin with the other banks. If she talked to them all, perhaps someone would advance her the money. Her building was mortgaged to the hilt but she was beginning to see small profits at the end of the month and once the last empty spaces were leased, she could anticipate a healthy financial statement.

But that eventuality wasn't today and after Carrie was put to bed that night, Molly indulged in a bout of crying self-pity—her responsibilities overwhelming her. As if being a mother, employer, and lease-holder to seven and a half stories of distributors wasn't enough, now, in addition she had to take on Midwest Metro's adjusted policy on note renewals as though it were a matter of accumulating enough dollar bills to fill a cookie jar. It wasn't dollars though, it was two hundred thousand impossible dollars and even thinking of the sum made her stomach constrict. Oh God, she dreaded tomorrow with the necessary calls on the banks. But what she dreaded more was the possibility of losing her business. The anxious fear crept in and filled her mind.

When Carey called late that night after shooting, after the editing, after Christina had been politely sent to her own room, he almost immediately asked, "What's wrong?"

"Nothing," Molly said, valiantly trying to disguise her misery. "Too busy a day at work, that's all. How did the shooting go?"

"Great. The weather cooperated. We're almost through with the midsummer scene. Probably Wednesday we'll finish, and I'll give everyone a couple of days off and come down. I'd like to meet Carrie, see your business, take you to dinner, all those domestic details I've missed in your life."

"I told Carrie I'd met an old friend at the reunion. A dear old friend. She's looking forward to seeing you. When I told her you were a movie director, she asked whether you could get her a date with Chachi from *Happy Days*."

"Tell her I'll check it out."

"And then Theresa my bookkeeper thinks you're the hottest thing to come down the pike, and Georgia called early this morning—"

"What's wrong?" he repeated, interrupting the brittle elan. "Tell me."

"Nothing serious. Business stuff. It'll smooth over." Molly hadn't perfected a gift for dissembling, and her answers were far from convincing.

"The note?" Carey asked.

She gulped in astonishment. "How did you know?"

"Movies, even modest movies, cost millions, love. I've

dealt with enough money brokers in my life to anticipate trouble. No renewal?"

"Right," Molly dejectedly replied.

"I'll give you the money."

"We went through that last night. I can't take money from you. I'm going to the banks first thing tomorrow. Jason suggested an interim loan, only for a few months. There shouldn't be any problem," she finished with a forced lightness. She didn't want to take Carey's money. After her bitter experience with Bart, she was wary of some man saying "you couldn't have done it without me." She wanted her independence. Needed it. It was doubly important to her after having broken out at long last from her closed-in no-win marriage with Bart.

"Is that the banker you were talking about last night?" Carey asked. "The one at Midwest Metro. Jason Evans?"

"None other," she replied, surprised at his memory for detail. "But enough dismal business," she quickly went on, determined to shift the conversation from something that could cause an argument. Last night, Carey's mouth had clamped tightly shut when she'd refused his money, and she knew that expression from past experience. "Did you miss me today?" she murmured in a wonderfully fey voice that reminded him of splashes of sunlight.

"Did Byrd want to reach the North Pole first?" he replied in an amused drawl.

"That much, hey? Thanks."

"You're entirely welcome. It was a pleasure thinking of you, remembering you, remembering us, wondering occasionally how a relatively sane man could have been so stupid for so many years—"

"You're glad I stopped by at Ely Lake, then?"

There was a sudden silence, and for a moment Molly thought they'd been cut off. "Yes," Carey said very softly, "I'm glad." A hundred times that day, he'd been struck with terror when he thought how close he'd come to missing her—again.

"Good," she replied with pleasure.

"I'll call you tomorrow. And if all goes well, I'll be down Thursday."

They hung up on whispered good-byes and silly love words murmured in childish accents that would have shocked anyone familiar with Carey Fersten, film director. But they had their own private world and always had, a world of pet names and lispy silliness and warm, undiluted happiness.

Three minutes later, Allen was summoned to Carey's motel room. Waving him to the phone before he was completely into the room, Carey said, "Get me George. It's important."

"He's on vacation for two weeks," Allen reminded him. Carey's principle accountant had carefully explained his schedule before leaving, tied up any loose ends with Carey personally, and been wished a bon voyage.

"Get me one of his assistants, then," Carey said impatiently.

"Problems?"

"Nothing they can't handle."

"Care to wait till morning? It's midnight in New York."

"If I wanted to wait till morning," Carey said in a monotonic voice, dangerous in its blandness, "I wouldn't have dragged you out of Valerie's bed. I want someone at CRT in New York," he directed, his syllables rapid now, "and I want two hundred thousand dollars at Midwest Metro at nine o'clock tomorrow morning, care of Jason Evans." Allen immediately paid careful attention to all the details because Carey was rarely demanding. This must be important to him. "Don't use my name," Carey went on, "use the name of one of our corporations. I want the note paid in full and I want CRT to speak to someone in authority at the bank concerning the payoff instructions. Ms. Darian is to be informed there's no further problem with her note and she'll receive the renewal papers in ten days or so. She is to be informed with a maximum, stress *maximum*, of discretion and no details. I'm sure George knows someone on the board at Midwest who can authorize this discretion. I'd like to wring that prick Jason Evans's neck for making Molly uptight over this goddamned note, but for now we'll bypass the asshole. I don't trust him; Molly said he might be friends with her ex. If she doesn't think she's going to get the renewal papers for a few days, it'll give me time to talk her into my loan. Right now she needs her money problems solved. She and I," he said in a level voice, "can argue the details later."

"The lady won't take the money?"

" 'Pride,' she says. 'Won't take it,' she says."

"Pride," Allen repeated very slowly as though the word came from a foreign language. "Interesting concept," he added with an ironic smile. "Is she left over from some ice age?"

"She's a throw-away-the-mold, one of a kind," Carey said grinning. "She's the best." His eyes went to the phone, then to the clock. He wanted to call and tell her to sleep tight—Jason Evans was getting a kick in the ass tomorrow. But no way would that work. He turned back to Allen. "Got it now?"

Allen nodded.

"Report back to me after you hear confirmation from the bank." Suddenly he stretched out his hand and smiled. "Sorry, Allen, for getting you out so late at night, and thanks in advance."

Allen was at the door when he turned and said, "This one's really different, right?"

Carey looked up, his hand about to reach for the next day's script. Lamplight shone on his gilded head, softened the stark angles of his face, muted the predatory eyes. His thick lashes came up, and his direct gaze answered before his voice did. "She's the girl I left behind. And even though she doesn't know it, she was in every film I ever made. Yeah," he said softly, "this one's different. She's the first one, and . . ." a smile flashed across his face, "the last."

"Sounds like congratulations are in order."

Carey laughed, a carefree, boyish sound Allen had never heard. "Thanks. A little premature. I haven't officially asked the lady yet. But thanks, anyway."

When Carey called Tuesday evening, a very different tone of voice greeted him. "My Honeybear sounds happy," he remarked, stretching out on the hotel room bed.

"The understatement of the century. They renewed my note, after all! Jason called early this morning. Can you *believe* it?" Joyous spirits were in every animated word.

"Amazing," he replied calmly.

"This, Carey, my sweet, means I and my business will be totally solid by the end of the year, thriving and out of debt. It was like some *miracle*!"

"Probably more like a calculated business decision," Carey said. "That Evans fellow probably had second thoughts after he had time to sleep on it."

"Do you think so?" Molly queried. "It doesn't sound like Jason. Do you think I should call him back and ask him?" she went on, uncertainty coloring her voice. "This morning I didn't ask any questions. Just said, thanks, and *hallelujah*!"

"I wouldn't," Carey quickly interjected. "Hell, it's only business with those guys. No sense in questioning their motives. Bad for their karma. No, my luscious long-lost lover, ask me instead how the shooting went today."

"How?"

"Terrific and finished."

"Finished! You *finished* the midsummer scene? That's a day early!"

"My accountants sounded almost as pleased as you. Remember, I had the very best incentive. Rode the crew like an overseer."

"So when will you be down?"

"Tomorrow, late afternoon probably. I have some editing

to do tomorrow morning. Tell Carrie she can pick out the place to eat tomorrow night. I'm looking forward to taking her and her mom out to dinner."

"You always did like kids, didn't you? I remember you helping me baby-sit a few times, and the kids always liked you best. You should have had some of your own."

The silence was abrupt.

"Oh, God, I'm sorry," Molly apologized. "I forgot."

"Don't apologize. I shouldn't react that way. You'd think after all these years," he finished with a small sigh, "I'd be reconciled."

"The government's still stonewalling it on the Agent Orange birth defects, I see," Molly hesitantly said, wondering if it was better or worse to talk about it.

"Along with all the other side effects. No one's ever going to admit fault and that's why the vets have taken it to court. At least it'll be out in the open there and the facts will be on record.

"In the meantime, I've seen Jim Hill's daughter and Leroy Gazinski's son and I'm not taking any chances, regardless of the government's assurances Agent Orange is harmless."

"I suppose you're being sensible." She didn't dare ask what problems the two children he mentioned had because his voice had broken when he spoke of them.

"I'm not being sensible, I'm terrified of the consequences . . . and sometime when you have a couple of weeks I'll fill you in on my outrage," he said harshly. "But let's not ruin my really great mood with this conversation. So—tell me what you want to do when I come down. We could take Carrie shopping or go to the zoo, or both, or something else. What do little girls like to do?"

"She's not fussy. How long can you stay?" Molly understood his anger, his reservations, and his need to set it aside.

"A couple of days this time. We have to talk," he said seriously. "Which reminds me. Do I reserve a hotel room or can I stay with you? What exactly is the protocol involving moms with eight-year-old daughters?"

"I want you to stay here."

"Sure it's okay?"

"This is a very progressive, liberated woman you're speaking to."

"You're sure?" He still sounded uncertain.

"Besides, I've a spare bedroom for you."

"Is that how you remained celibate for two years? I warn you, I sleepwalk at night."

"Sounds marvelous. My room is directly across the hall."

"How very convenient."

"I thought you'd like it."

"Are we going to play games?"

"I don't know if I can remember any."

"I'll remind you."

"You're probably thinking of Italian countesses or the French model, or—"

"Honeybear," he broke in, his voice caressing, "only your games are unforgettable."

"Your reputation's showing, Carey Fersten," Molly replied. "You're way too smooth for a small-town girl like me."

"My reputation's much overrated," he retorted mildly.

"You mean you really haven't slept with every woman between eighteen and forty in the world?" But under her bantering was a very real jibe.

"Sweetheart, give me a break."

"Really?" His voice was so sincere she began to doubt all the stories.

"Sure. I swore off eighteen-year-olds a long time ago."

"Carey Fersten! I'm going to beat you!"

"Now we haven't tried that before—that's more British boarding school background—but what the hey, if you want to . . ."

"You're a libertine."

"And available," he murmured. Her jealousy warmed the

heart of this man whose heart had remained untouched for a decade.

"Damn you, Carey! I don't want to be one of a cast of thousands passing through your bedroom." Her resentment was real this time, heated and fiery.

"I burned my bedroom Rolodex this morning. The stench was spiritually bracing."

"You did? For me?"

"Of course," he said mildly, "you're my Honeybear."

From that point the conversation became scandalously amorous. Within minutes of hanging up the phone, Carey, prompted by a healthy libido, decided the editing could wait for a day or two. Leaving Allen with a few crisp orders, Carey was airborne in twenty minutes, copiloting the Lear, only thirty minutes away from Minneapolis/St. Paul International.

CHAPTER 20

While Carey was cruising high above the cumulous clouds obscuring the green midwest landscape below, Molly was having a heated telephone conversation with Bart.

"I'd like to come over to see Carrie," he said in that demanding tone that always grated on her nerves.

"I told you to give me some warning on these visits."

"That's why I'm calling first."

"That's not what I had in mind," Molly replied sardonically. "A day or two, not minutes."

"Come off it, Molly. If you're not busy and Carrie's not busy, why be pedantic?"

Molly thought of her daughter and sighed resignedly. "She rode her bike to the corner store and won't be back for half an hour or so. I suppose you could come over then."

"Great, I've missed her."

"You haven't seen her in six months, Bart," Molly said dryly.

"Well, I missed her today."

"In that case, I suppose we mustn't be obstructive," she said with elaborate sweetness.

"That would be sensible."

Bart's visit wasn't prompted by paternal affection, but rather by a hellish curiosity. At the club that afternoon, after his racketball game, he'd run across Jason Evans and heard a fascinating bit of information. "Molly's picked up a damn rich friend," Jason had archly declared.

When Bart had asked who, he'd shrugged.

"Beats me. Some corporation . . . no names. All very discreet. Two hundred thousand dollars discreet. Your ex-wife is now totally out of debt."

"Very interesting," Bart had said.

"I thought you'd like to know," Jason had replied, a locker-room leer on his face.

Bart deliberately arrived before Carrie returned, intent on discovering the wealthy new "friend" who'd entered Molly's life. With that kind of money it wasn't an anonymous donor. His visit was fueled by nothing more than rabid curiosity—not necessarily malice. He'd always been the type to go through people's desk drawers and medicine cabinets. Insatiably nosy.

After a long, busy day, Molly had changed into a cotton caftan and was lounging on the couch, a glass of wine in her hand when Bart arrived. Out of an inherent politeness rather than any desire for is company, she offered him a drink while he waited for Carrie to come home.

Bart immediately launched into his probing catechism.

The evening sunset heightened the streaked gold of Carey's hair as he pushed open the wooden garden door at the entrance to Molly's home. Walking into a small, colorful English-style garden incongruously growing against an eight-story factory building, he strolled up the serpentine brick path to a carved front door. Near a lush, wandering wisteria which looked as though it had been framing the doorway for at least a century, a young girl was settling her bicycle into its wrought-iron stand. In a few steps he was close enough to say, "Hi, is your mother home?"

Her long pale hair swirled across her shoulders as she turned. A small, straight-nosed face with wispy brows and lacy lashes framing enormous dark eyes lifted from her task. The faintly slanted eyes, like an eastern princess from long ago, studied him.

A dozen searing questions streaked unanswered through his mind as he gazed at the young features so shatteringly familiar, like a miniature mirror-image softened by childhood and femininity. And for a moment, his heart stood still.

"You must be Carey," the young girl said, looking up into Carey's startled face. "We both have the same name. Though Mom said the spelling's different for boys and girls."

His composure restored, Carey managed a smile. "Just a couple of letters different, I guess. Here, let me take your package," he offered. He willed himself to stay calm, but his hands tightened convulsively on the box when she handed it to him.

"Don't squeeze it," Carrie warned. "The ice cream bars get mushy by the time I bike back. I better carry them," she added decisively, noting how his large fingers were making indentations in the cardboard box. She took the package and said, "I thought you weren't coming till Thursday. You're cute," she abruptly stated, then twirled and pulled open the door.

Before he could reply, she was through the door. "Come on up," she sang out. "Mom's in the living room." And she raced up the stairs.

He stood there for a moment contemplating numerous other possibilities that would reasonably explain the staggering likeness, other than the one burning in his brain.

And failed utterly.

He wanted to cry, but a dangerous fury related to deception, lies, and impossible hurt, damped the impulse.

He took the stairs two at a time.

With a minimum of courtesy, Molly had been dodging Bart's questions. "Look," she finally said exasperatedly, "if this is going to be twenty questions, why don't I excuse myself and you can wait here alone until Carrie returns." Rising from the Chinese silk couch, she started across the room.

Quickly setting his wineglass down, Bart reached out an arresting hand. "Hey," he objected, his fingers tight on her wrist, "sit down, relax. No need to get huffy."

"No *need*! Jesus, Bart, how would you like it if I started at the top of a list of questions and ran through them; all, by the way, directed toward your amorous partners."

"Okay, okay, sit down. I'll stop. Just curious, that's all. I saw Jason today and—"

"What about Jason?" she coolly inquired, tensing with a bitterness she'd thought long gone. "So help me, Bart, if you're sticking your nose into my business again, I swear—"

"Temper, temper." He pulled again on her wrist. "If you're nice and tell me a few things, I'll tell you what Jason said."

"Go to hell."

"You never did know how to argue reasonably, Molly." He was smug from the sleek blackness of his hair to the white leather of his court shoes. His neatness annoyed her. He was dressed casually, having come over directly from the club, but he managed to look as though his sweats were pressed. And there wasn't a mark on his white sneakers. She didn't know why his fastidiousness provoked her, but it was probably because he'd complained about her messiness. If she'd only had sense enough to live with Bart before she'd married him, it wouldn't have taken more than a week to know how incompatible they were—parents or no parents, wedding or not. There's nothing like the cap-on-the-toothpaste argument to open one's eyes to marital discord.

He had always been tremendous fun to date, the life of the party, entertaining, and funny. It wasn't until they were married that she'd realized there was another personality beneath that stage facade. A person who was always right. A person who thought of himself first, last, and always; a man whose ambition was a consuming passion. Men like Bart wanted wives and a child (one was enough to complete the image of "family"; no sense in going overboard) as accoutrements to his life. It completed the picture. A successful man needed a family. Single men past a certain age were slightly suspect, not normal somehow.

So she and Carrie were the required actors in the scene: house, wife, child. Wave to Daddy when he leaves for work. Give him a kiss and a straight scotch when he comes home after a hard day at the office. Fade out . . .

Bart was also a nag. And that finally had driven her over the edge. The house wasn't clean enough or the yard was mowed clockwise instead of counterclockwise. "Don't bitch at me," Molly would say. "Bitch at the maid or the yardman."

"Do I have to take care of everything?" he'd scream.

"If you want to complain about their work, you'll have to do it yourself," she'd reply.

Or Carrie's bike was in the driveway and he had to drive around it.

Or the pool man had the unmitigated gall to miss three leaves floating in the pool.

Important things like that upset the symmetry of Bart Cooper's existence.

And if Molly had a penny for every time Bart had said, "Why can't you hang up your wet towels; it only takes a second," she would have been a millionairess. She didn't like to pick up her bath towels; she liked to toss them on the floor; she liked to walk on them. She picked them up later, but later wasn't good enough for Bart. Neatness was his religion. God help him. He was doing extremely well though, come to think of it. Was it possible God was a neatnik, too? Maybe she was on the wrong side of a philosophical issue and hadn't realized the direction of her life was being manipulated by a vengeful deity whose all-seeing eyes noticed dust bunnies under the bed.

But none of the differences had mattered when she found herself pregnant so soon after their marriage. And the arguments had never stopped. Just like now.

Dislike for his petty nastinesses came flooding back, and she stood rigid in his grasp, her eyes scathing. "Let me go."

"Soon," Bart grated, angry now, apparently thwarted in his quest. "Sit." He jerked her down so she fell awkwardly across his lap.

As Molly was struggling in his grip, a familiar voice with a coldly reined-in courtesy said, "Pardon me. I'll come back at a more convenient time." Carey was wearing a linen jacket with stylish slacks and a shirt with intricate pleats down the front. The pale colors contrasted with his dark tan and hard masculine features. He didn't move, not a muscle, except his eyes, which took in the two wineglasses side-by-side on the glass coffee table, and the two figures entwined on the couch.

"Carey!" Molly cried, terrified at the diamond-hard coldness in his eyes.

But he was walking out of the room already, and only narrowly missed colliding into Carrie who was running in from the kitchen. Steadying her with his hands, he bent over and briefly whispered to her. Then, straightening, he strode down the hall. Molly heard his light tread running down the stairs. Then the slam of the door.

"Damn you, Bart. Look what you did now," she exclaimed, untangling herself from his grasp.

"Who the hell was that?" he rebuked. "I like the twin names. Enlightening." And the gray eyes he turned on Molly were flinty hard.

"Carrie, go to your room. Daddy and I want to talk," Molly hastily interposed before anything more was said. After Carrie left she turned on Bart, her expression indignant. "Now do you have something to say?"

"I don't know who the mysterious blond stranger was," he sneered, "but looking at the remarkable resemblance to your daughter, I'd say, he's someone a helluva lot closer to you than I ever was."

"You're insane," Molly snapped.

"Hardly, and not blind, either," he curtly retorted. But then his voice changed into a taunting sweetness. "Here the little wife I thought so prim and sexually unawakened has a skeleton in her very own closet. My congratulations. You carried off the demure facade winningly all those years. And the offended wife at divorce time. I wish I'd known Mr. Blond Fashion Model before you took half the equity in the house. By the way, child support payments stop as of this minute."

"Bart, you don't know what you're talking about. Carrie's your daughter."

"So I always assumed—until her twin just walked into this room."

"She was born nine and a half months after we were married."

"So?"

"I was true to you all our married life," she protested, her temper rising.

"Commendable, I'm sure," Bart said, the sarcasm in his voice denigrating. "Although under the circumstances, hardly believable. Come off it, Molly. I don't care. I don't care about anything you do or did."

"That at least is the truth," Molly replied, her eyes smoldering with resentment. "Why don't you leave now? I'm not up to any more of your pleasant company." And she stood, waiting for him to go.

"Who is he?" Bart asked, leisurely unfolding himself from the sofa.

"Do me a favor. Get the hell out of here."

"Is he rich?"

"I don't know."

"He looks rich," Bart said mildly. "That haircut cost at least a hundred dollars."

"He cuts his own hair," she answered, her control dangerously near to breaking.

"He looks vaguely familiar. Carey who?"

"It was wonderful, as usual, Bart. Stay away longer next time," Molly said, pushing his unresisting body toward the hallway.

"I'm glad you found a rich one again, Molly. You're going to need someone rich to bail your business out from time to time. Women weren't meant to be business *men*."

If looks could kill, Bart would have been a puddle on the hall floor. Undeterred, he turned his sleepy eyes on her and smiled, "Ciao."

"Right, ciao, Bart, and sayonara and write if you get work, preferably in the nether regions of the Amazon." Keeping a tight rein on the hysteria cresting when she thought of Carey's basilisk expression, Molly pressed her temple against the doorjamb after Bart left and slowly counted to fifty. Carey wouldn't walk away without an explanation, would he? Good God, would he? But his chill eyes haunted her; she knew him so little. And what she *did* know had been transfigured into this world-class luminary. However, she'd have to deal with all the confusion and doubt later. Carrie needed some kind of explanation now.

Seated on the bed in her daughter's room, she explained that both Daddy and Carey had left, but—and at this point, she crossed her fingers unobtrusively to negate the fib—they'd be back.

"I know," Carrie agreed. "Daddy always comes over on my birthday, and that's only a few days away. And Carey whispered he'd come back to see me. Did you and Daddy have another fight?" The question was posed casually, as if she had asked whether her mother thought it would rain soon.

"Well, sort of."

"You two should learn to communicate better."

"Thank you, Dr. Freud."

"Then I wouldn't have to suffer loads of childhood

anxieties. I read Judy Blume and know every childhood anxiety in the whole world."

"In that case," Molly said with a fond smile for her precocious daughter who absorbed life like a sponge and treated it as mundanely, "I'll try to 'communicate' better with your father and save myself thousands of dollars in therapy for you."

"You gotta learn, Mom. Just smile and nod your head with Daddy. That's what he likes best. He never really listens, anyway. That Carey guy sure looked mad," she went on in the same breath as though the two thoughts weren't mutually exclusive. "Doesn't he like you sitting on Daddy's lap?" Her innocent dark eyes opened wide in inquiry.

"You tell me. You seem to have the world figured out," Molly teased, her mood lightened by her daughter's prosaic outlook on humanity.

"Well, Tammy says her mother's new boyfriend is really jealous of Tammy's dad. They had a big fight one night when Tammy's dad came over to the house to fix the filter system on the pool. Are men possessive, Mom? Tammy says they sure are."

Molly laughed. "I don't know, honey. Some men are; some women are, too. It's not a gender-based feeling. Come on, you'd better get ready for bed. Only two more days of school before vacation, and you have tests both days."

CHAPTER 21

After Molly had tucked Carrie in for the night, she went into her studio and tried to concentrate on a floor plan for the new office for United Diversified. Her mind was blank except for a disastrous feeling of loss. Would he come back? Was Carrie right? Or was he only being kind to a child, something very like the man she'd known? Should she call him? But where? Tonight was impossible; he wasn't at the only number she had for him. Damn, damn, damn, she cried. Why did Bart have to come over *tonight*?

An hour later the floor plan was beyond redemption, hatched and crosshatched with a multitude of revisions and revamping. Tossing aside her pencil, she snapped off the swivel-necked lamp on her drafting table and slid her chair back. This would have to wait till morning. She couldn't concentrate with the current state of her emotions.

He'd been walking since he left the apartment, anger and resentment in varying degrees forcing his long stride. He could have kicked himself. First for acting like a young schoolboy, jettisoning everything—the editing, the 220 people costing him salaries even though they weren't filming—all because some woman talked amorously on the phone and he wanted her. And then to find her with another man. He stopped at a park bench facing a quiet lake and shrugged out of his sport coat. Elbows on knees and chin in hand, he contemplated the emotions tearing him apart. Having Molly back was like stepping into the past with all the old needs and desires.

And as if that weren't enough, Carrie was there, demanding resolution in the turmoil of his thoughts. He didn't know how old she was. He didn't know her birthday so he couldn't make exact calculations, but there was no question: Carrie was his daughter. Joy washed over him like applause. A healthy daughter. A miracle, a gift he'd never dared hope for. He cried, helpless to stop the tears. For nine years he'd been a father and not known. While he was trying to forget Molly, Carrie was drooling, and gurgling, and learning to sit up. She had learned to walk and talk and sing nursery rhymes without him. Her "father" had taught her to ride a bike while he had been practicing self-destruction in Yugoslavia. Someone else had taken her to her first day of kindergarten and bought her her first sundae and held her close when she woke up at night with bad dreams.

She was beautiful.

And I'm her father, he thought.

And was never told.

He and Molly had some talking to do.

Leaving the park bench, oblivious to the jacket tossed across the slatted seat, he started to retrace his route to Molly's.

Molly was halfway down the hall to her bedroom when the phone rang. Rushing back to her desk, she breathlessly picked up the phone and said, "Hello."

"May I come up?" Carey asked brusquely.

"Yes, where are you?"

"On the corner in a phone booth."

"Where've you been?"

"Walking."

"I'm sorry about Bart."

"I'll be there in two minutes," he declared, ignoring her apology. "I want to talk to you." He sounded grim.

Greeting him at the door, Molly led the way upstairs into the living room. He didn't touch her, hardly looked at her. Only said, "Hello," in the polite tone of a stranger. Apprehensively she watched him stalk across the room. She'd seen him go into a cold rage once when someone had challenged his control over his life, and she was uncertain how deeply the scene with Bart had affected him.

Sitting down, she invited him to, but he didn't. Instead he paced to the bank of windows facing the city, briefly looked out, then restlessly moved back toward her. "Would you like a drink?" Molly nervously inquired.

He shook his head, skirted the end of the peach silk couch, and strode back toward the windows.

"Something to eat?" she queried into the deathly silence.

Stopping, he spun around and stared at her as if she'd lost her mind. His mouth opened, then shut again in the same hard, determined line. His pale hair was ruffled, as if fingers had repeatedly raked through it. The sleeves of his shirt were rolled up to his elbows; he no longer had on the cream linen sport coat.

"Would you sit down, at least," she said forcibly, his restless stride making her increasingly nervous. "You're pacing like a new father." It was not a good choice of words.

His shoulders stiffened. Stopping abruptly, he walked over and dropped into a chair near Molly. "So who was the man you were playing with when I walked in?" he accused her in a hard voice.

"I wasn't *playing* with anyone. The man was Bart, my ex-husband, whom I despise. We were *arguing*," she answered coldly, responding to the injustice of his remark.

His eyes which had been studying his steepled fingertips, flashed upward and pierced hers like lasers. "You could have fooled me." Although his voice was flat and passionless, the muscles in his neck were rigid.

"Don't get authoritarian with me, Carey Fersten. I'm not eighteen anymore, and I don't care if you're used to pulling rank on half the world." Spreading her arms along the back of the couch, she straightened her spine and added, "I don't give a damn how important you are. But to clear your suspicious mind, I kicked Bart out right after you left. Supposedly he'd come over to see Carrie, but kept trying to pry into my private life."

Carey relaxed fractionally. "Really?"

"Cross my heart," she said. "Is that good enough, or would you like a blood oath?" The flowing white of her robe against the silky peach couch set off her golden-haired beauty like a framed portrait. Her long hair glistened, her rich blue eyes stared directly at him, her cheeks were touched with a rosy blush of anger. She was too beautiful for any other man to touch. An inexplicable feeling from a man who until now had calmly accepted the more liberal modes of human relationships.

"I'm jealous as hell, Molly," he said quietly, his familiar, brooding eyes gazing at her. "It's a novel sensation, but damnably real."

"Coming from the darling of the international jet set, I suppose I should be flattered."

"Don't believe all the hype. I lead a quiet life, and I'm not trying to flatter. It's God's truth."

"Thank you, then," she replied stiffly.

"You're welcome," he answered, equally unyielding.

They sat facing each other in the golden glow of silk-shaded lamps, across a short distance of pale green Imuk carpet crafted a century before they were born. Although his long legs were sprawled in front of him, Carey's posture was tense, adversarial. The lamplight burnished his pale hair like gold brushwork on eleventh-century gospels. His bronzed face was angular, cautious, his dark eyes compelling like some pagan god. After a short, spare silence, Carey said, "Why didn't you tell me about Carrie?"

"I know what it looks like," Molly replied, understanding his question although it was ambiguously worded. Dropping her arms to unconsciously clasp her hands, she went on, "but Carrie isn't—"

"That child is mine."

"No!" Her exclamation was filled with disbelief and poignant pain. "Oh, Carey," she cried, her glance anguished, "don't you think I wish she were? But it isn't true."

"Why not? The last time I was with you was only a few days before your wedding."

"Two weeks before."

"Twelve days," Carey said in a voice scarcely above a whisper, "to be exact." Molly's wedding date was etched on his heart, and the years had never erased that pain.

"But I had a period after that," she explained. The bizarre turn of conversation clouded the sequence of events that had until a few moments ago, seemed logical and clear.

"What kind of a period?"

How did he know, she wondered, looking at him with trepidation. Even though it had all happened years ago, she knew the answer as though it were yesterday because it had been so unusual. "Only slight bleeding," she whispered at last.

"It looks as though you were pregnant with Carrie when you married," he said. "You never had a period, after all." His gaze captured her blue eyes and held them in a glance that demanded an answer. "Did you?"

"I don't know. It was years ago," Molly dissembled, trying to avoid the collision course facing her, too confused now with complex emotional conflicts to want to come to terms with the unbelievable idea Carey was so relentlessly pursuing.

"All you have to do is look at her and you'd know."

He was right. The physical resemblance was the most

telling argument, the most damning evidence. Carey and her daughter were so remarkably similar, she marveled at her obtuseness all these years. "It can't be," she declared with a stubbornness that still clung to the tenuous substance of her own misplaced convictions. "Carrie was born too late. She was born almost ten months after the wedding."

"My mother's pregnancy was close to ten months. It was a family joke, how I didn't want to leave the security of the womb."

"No, don't say that," she pleaded, her eyes huge and liquid. "It's too unreal." Covering her face with her hands, she sat there trembling. "It's not the way it happened," she whispered, looking up. She was holding back tears, the struggle visible on her face.

He only said, "Thank you for giving me a daughter." And then, uncurling himself from the depths of the chair, he walked over and lifted Molly. He held her protectively in his arms, kissing her tear-streaked cheeks, murmuring, "I love you, Honeybear. I always have. Always . . . always . . ."

Nestling close, she clung to him like a small child clinging to the only security it's known.

He whispered his love and brushed his warm lips over hers. "I'm going to take care of you both," he murmured.

Molly lifted her head from his shoulder and gave him the beginning of a smile. "I can take care of myself . . ."

He smiled back. "Well, I can kiss away the tears while you're taking care of yourself, smartass."

"Deal," she whispered.

"Now if you'll tell me," he murmured, glancing over her head to assess the direction of the bedroom, "where the spare bedroom is, I think I'll turn in for the night."

"It's early," she teased, licking his chin.

"Fatherhood is exhausting." He winked at her. "Arguing with the mother of my child is what's exhausting," he amended, starting down the polished parquet hallway.

"I'm not accomplished," she whispered, thinking of all the women in his past, "like all . . . all those—"

"I don't want that, Honeybear," he murmured, crossing the threshold of the bedroom. "I just want to feel your warm body next to mine, feel the woman I love in my arms, touch your sweet face. I don't want accomplishments, sweetheart, only you, my Honeybear, the mother—" his voice grew ragged "of my child." It frightened him how helpless he was to the deep emotion he'd thought long vanished.

"Promise me something," Molly said, her arms tightening on his shoulders.

"Anything."

"Keep your girlfriends in the closet."

He set her on her feet and placed his hands very gently on her shoulders. "No girlfriends," he said, his dark eyes solemn. "I'll promise that instead."

Her eyes shone with happiness, and he smiled because she meant to be practical and civilized but was as jealous as he.

"I don't want any other woman. I'd be a fool to waste my time. I'm holding *you* every night . . . and every day," he added emphatically, "until we're ninety-two."

"And then what happens?" she teased, sliding her arms around his waist.

"We start on the second ninety-two years."

Molly's eyes filled with tears. "Sometimes I'm not as strong as I say I am."

"That's what I'm here for," he whispered, reaching up to brush away a tear. "I'll take up the slack when you're too wacked out to be strong."

"Like now. Oh, Carey, everything's happening too fast," Molly cried. "All I know for certain is I love you. The rest—" Panic was closing in. "Tell me the rest will be fine," she softly entreated, overwhelmed by the sudden changes in the fabric of her life.

His life had been full of attractive people and congenial events, visited by success, insulated by wealth. Not in a grandiose way, but with a security he'd never had to question. What makes one person so special to you that life dims without them? He didn't know the answer. But only Molly could evoke this happiness, and until now he'd never comprehended the extent of his own sadness. He needed her.

"I love you, Honeybear," he whispered, "more than anything. And everything's going to work out. From now on," he vowed, "life is going to be perfect. Guaranteed."

CHAPTER **22**

The following morning in Rome, Shakin Rifat was seated at his desk an hour earlier than usual. Even for a man trained to give away nothing in his expression, the fire of triumph couldn't be disguised. He was leafing through a dozen black-and-white photos taken with a telephoto lens, developed in a private jet that flew across the Atlantic the previous night and landed at the secluded airstrip thirty miles north of Rome an hour after daybreak.

The photos were of a blond man talking to a young girl with shoulder-length hair. The sequence of shots showed her placing her bicycle in an elaborate stand, then handing the man a package, only to take it back in the next two frames. Both subjects had the same color hair; both subjects had winged black brows; the similarities had been definitively cataloged by Shakin Rafit, his gratification heightened with each enumerated resemblance. Nose, eyes, chin, the same subtle curve of upper lip. The child was a girl, of course, so the strength of form was modified, but in a way, a girl was much better for his purpose. A father would do anything to save his helpless young daughter from harm.

Shakin pushed the photos into a neat pile, a gold signet

ring on his left hand catching the light, then leaned back in his chair, a satisfied smile on his dark, aquiline face, a quality of animal assurance in his relaxed posture.

At last he had a way to put pressure on Egon.

Leisurely reaching out, he rang for his secretary. When the young man walked in and noted Shakin's satisfied smile he said, "The photos were pleasing?"

"Very. Mete told you?"

"Only that the young girl appears to be—"

"*Is*, Ceci . . . no question about it. How soon can you get the team ready?" Ceci Kiray had been aide-de-camp to Rifat in Turkey's First Air Corps prior to General Evren's takeover in 1980. With inbred military custom and a deferential nod of his head, Ceci silently asked permission to sit. Less punctilious than his young subaltern, Rifat casually waved him into the chair facing his desk. "I'd like to move on this as soon as possible, Ceci. A large shipment of gum base is coming out of Turkey next week, as you know, and our operating capital will be nicely maximized after the sale to the French chemists. You also know how desperately Brazil wants the prototypes for the new weapon. Señor Jorge has been calling daily. It's an opportune time with our war chest in good order to step into the arms manufacturing business."

"Jorge is amenable to a percentage cut?"

"He'd prefer buying the technical data outright, but I'm not so inclined. Everyone wants this prototype. All the third-world nations currently producing arms under license will pay for it. But Brazil will pay the most. Have you ever been to Rio?" Rifat leaned back in his chair and looked at his secretary who still bore the stamp of a hardened officer beneath his tailored suit and custom-made shoes. "You'll like it," Rifat continued with a smile, answering his own question, aware of Ceci's postings over the last ten years.

"What sort of timetable will you give to Colonel Jorge?"

"That depends on how soon you can kidnap the girl."

Ceci shrugged dismissively. Mete had filled him in on the

disposition of the apartment and inhabitants. "Two days at the most once we arrive," he said casually, "but I'll need a week to ten days to round up my team. Reha's in Marseilles arranging for the delivery of the gum base, Husameddin's in Athens finishing the arms transfers out of Bulgaria, and Timur's back in Kemer burning away the days and nights in a state of seminudity at the Club Méditerranée."

"Austerity has never been Timur's strong suit."

"But since he flies anything that lifts off the ground . . ."

Rifat smiled. "We indulge his vices . . ."

"Or do without him." Ceci smiled back, a younger version of Rifat, perhaps a trifle more elegant in his double-breasted banker's stripe suit, the twenty years difference in their ages distancing Ceci as well from the more brutal circumstances of Turkish military life.

Rifat nodded in agreement. Although Rifat's Turkish father's military background had bred an austerity in him that looked askance at hedonists like Timur, he recognized talent when he saw it. Timur had been a genius with aircraft from the first day of flight training. Under Rifat's expanded aeronautics program during his command, Timur had risen swiftly through the ranks and come to Rifat's attention not only for his flawless performance but for his imaginative maneuvering in all the NATO wargames.

In September, 1980, when Evren won the scramble for power among the generals, when Rifat's faction lost their bid for control and found it prudent to depart Turkey, Timur had chosen to align himself with Rifat even in defeat. "My mother is Armenian, too," he'd said before offering his services to Rifat, but he had had other more practical reasons, as well. Evren's military coup meant a return to reactionary principles and a suspension of all political activity. And while his mother's Armenian heritage was a consideration in a conservative military regime that traditionally treated Armenians as déclassé, Timur's reputation as Turkey's best pilot would have overridden the deficiencies in his background. At base though, Timur was interested in a grander lifestyle than that afforded by a colonel's pay. He had a taste for casinos, beautiful women, and fast cars—vices that required the kind of money Rifat paid. And danger had always exhilarated him. While supersonic aircraft and wargames sharpened that sensational flare of excitement he thrived on, they couldn't compare with the life and death reality of Rifat's outlaw world.

"How long would you say," Rifat inquired with a chilling smile that often appeared when he oversaw the "interrogation" of the assassins General Evren periodically sent out to kill him, "after the kidnapping before Charles Fersten appears at Egon's demanding he cooperate with us?"

Ceci's smile appeared again. There was gratification in a well-conceived assignment. "Since he flies his own plane at times . . ." his strong hands slowly aligned themselves across his trim stomach, satisfaction audible in his voice, "a matter of hours I'd say."

"At which point we no longer have to deal with the erratic Count von Mansfeld. Directives will be given to Egon so he understands once he orders the weapons and blueprints released from his munitions factory, Mr. Fersten will be conveying them to us."

"Until then, Egon is the weak link." Ceci grimaced, insensitive to the forms of paranoia motivating Egon's drug use.

"Unfortunately. But once von Mansfeld has the prototypes ordered from his research facility, Mr. Fersten will better suit our purposes. He's seen more than the calibrations on a hypodermic syringe and the inside of Regine's. He's a seasoned athlete and an intelligent, practical man who served in America's war in Asia and survived. Unlike Egon, who's apt to disintegrate at the first sign of stress, we can depend on Charles Fersten to pick up the weapons and deliver them to us . . . for his daughter's sake."

"How necessary *is* Egon?" Ceci's voice was low and muted.

Rafit answered in an unhurried tone, as if he were describing an ordinary protocol in an ordinary businessman's schedule. "Only he or his sister the countess are able to order the weapons released. Von Mansfeld Works is, after all, a family-owned business, appearances notwithstanding." Before his secretary could articulate the obvious question, Shakin straightened from his lounging posture, placed both hands palm down on his malachite desktop, and deliberately said, "*She* is more unstable than her brother. At least with Egon the only emotion we have to deal with is fear. He's considerably more tractable. So we need him . . . at least temporarily."

"Very well," Ceci quietly replied, the matter settled. "I'll leave tomorrow to arrange the safe house while the men come in from the field."

"Once the girl is abducted, send me a message and I'll see that Egon receives his instructions."

"While I relay the necessary directions to Mr. Fersten."

"Precisely." They could have been discussing the weather, for all the emotion displayed.

Rising abruptly, Ceci stood with his natural military correctness and asked, "Will you be accepting Colonel Jorge's call today, then?"

General Rifat implicitly trusted Ceci's competence. He'd never failed him and, while normally not optimistic, normally a very prudent man who anticipated each possibility of reversal in advance, he uncharacteristically fell in with Ceci's prompting. Glancing briefly at the photos spread before him on the desk, he thought: How convenient. "Yes, today I'm in to the colonel. We're about to add a new legitimacy to our entrepreneurship."

"Indeed," Ceci said with a faint curve of his mouth. "Less tainted than the business of paying back other people's debts of vengeance." Rifat's men were for hire . . . and to those in the world wishing to remain aloof from terrorism, for an appropriately large gratuity, their conspiracies could be executed, quickly and quietly.

"More respectable," Rifat pronounced the words with a

fastidious inflection, "than brokering the arms passing between belligerents. Although," he went on with the merest of sighs, "I ask myself occasionally, Ceci, when a rare philosophical mood strikes me, why it's acceptable for some to sell arms and not others?"

"You mean the deceit of defining arms sales as 'maintaining national security'?"

"That wonderful, benign phrase was what forced the third-world nations into the arms business in self-defense; they were being held hostage to powerful nations' whims of diplomacy. Although the small nations' inroads into arms manufacturing is tolerated, because they don't put enough product on the market to matter."

"While the large nations maintain the fiction of 'national security' as a motive because they're selling to *everyone*, and even a five-year-old knows that's unethical," Ceci said.

"But if you're an independent broker, you're cutting into some country's profits, so you're criminal."

"When in fact it's simply an interpretation of whose bottom line is losing money to people like us. And all the noisy rhetoric and byzantine definitions are simply so many words—a smoke screen to hide all the profitable transactions and deceit."

"Ah, yes, deceit . . . life's basic ingredient, along with the profit motive." The general began stacking the photos with swift precision, impatient suddenly with the false righteousness so prevalent in arms sales. "Luckily my brief fits of piety are rare," he briskly said, looking back up at Ceci. "I look forward, then," his eyes were devoid of any trace of sentiment, "to confirmation—say in ten days—that the girl is in your hands."

"Perhaps two weeks. But Minneapolis is a quiet city, insulated by its geography, untouched by terrorist alarm." Ceci's tone was lazily confident. "The assignment will be without obstruction."

CHAPTER 23

Late that night in the warm shambles of the bed, restfully content, Molly and Carey talked. Carey wanted to get married immediately. He had a film scheduled in Australia next, and would be gone a year. He wanted them to go there as a family.

"My business . . ." Molly said. "A whole year?"

Lounging on his side, he reached out to touch the gentle curve of Molly's waist as she sat beside him. "Get someone to watch it for you."

She looked at him incredulously. Watch it? Did he think it was a Springer spaniel? "I can't," she said. The Design Center was her baby, had been her sanity, her passion, her pleasure for six years. And now, this second launching was only coming into its own. He couldn't ask her to simply walk away and leave it, and she told him so.

He stared at her in the soft, illumination of the bedside lamp for one of those long, brooding moments, and then replied, "You're right, Honeybear. That was selfish of me. We'll resolve this somehow."

And Carrie needed some time to get to know him, she added. Even though he was her natural father, she couldn't abruptly marry a man her daughter had seen for the first time a few hours ago.

He rolled over on his back then, raked his fingers through his hair, and lay, arms stretched above his head, staring at the ceiling. After long moments, he finally spoke, his voice calm, though his eyes were electric, charged with his own special kind of raw energy. "Okay, Honeybear," he said quietly. "We'll do whatever you want, but I'm marrying you this time. One way or another. You work out the details, the scheduling. Just let me know where and when." He smiled then, mitigating the intensity of his gaze, softening the harshness of his features. "You're the boss, ma'am, on all the wedding arrangements."

"If it wasn't for . . . my employees," Molly murmured, "not to mention the mortgage payments," she added in a small apologetic voice, suddenly aware how contrary the tenor of her refusal. "And the Midwest Wholesalers Show scheduled for August, I'd race you to the altar," she finished in a whisper.

"I know, sweetheart." His voice was soft, matching the dark splendor of his eyes. "Forgive my impatience, but after ten years—" He sighed, the hard muscles of his stomach rippling in a tiny flurry of movement. "Oh hell . . . come here." His large hand circled Molly's wrist, and he tugged gently. "We'll iron out the timetable later."

He held her in his arms, and she wondered how she'd survived so long without him. Too much had happened too swiftly tonight to unravel all the complexities. It was enough to hold Carey close and know they had a future together; it was enough to simply feel the warm, tangible, blissful security. Molly fell asleep to the slow, steady rhythm of Carey's heart beneath her ear, like a gentle lullaby.

Restless and vigilant, his passions too ardent, Carey lay awake, wanting to document and store away the precious sweetness, the sight and feel of the only woman he'd ever loved. Unlike the previous years of his life in which time and people were squandered, in which weeks and months were laid waste in lavish spendthrift destruction, tonight he was collecting and preserving the beauty and fullness of this feeling called love.

Tonight he'd become a father, too, a thought that infused him with a riveting excitement. And several times during the night he softly spoke the words aloud into the hushed darkness. "I have a daughter," he'd murmur, "just down the hall . . . in this very house," he'd add to reinforce the reality. And he'd grin from ear to ear—no matter that he cautioned himself to anticipate less delight from his daughter when she discovered that Bart, the only father she'd known, had been replaced by a virtual stranger. No matter that he knew the possibility of rejection existed, that bonding delayed for almost nine years was a serious neglect, that his meager knowledge of fatherhood could be written in less than ten words. But he grinned in the quiet darkness, immune to problems tonight.

From time to time he'd gently stroke Molly's tumbled hair or touch the flushed softness of her cheek and whisper, "I love you, Honeybear." And his smile would reappear, his happiness would surge, the kind that inspired poets and songwriters to compose metaphors about tropical nights and trips to the moon on gossamer wings. And elation kept him awake all night, a happiness so profound he reached out once to touch the bedside table. The wood was solid beneath his fingers. This was not a dream.

As the dawn sky lightened, he watched the grays change into color, sensitive to the minutest transformations, feeling like a man experiencing his first sunrise. And as the glow of the sun first slipped radiant tendrils over the horizon, bathing the summer morning in a shimmering rose, Carey kissed Molly softly near the pulse of her temple, and murmured, "I'm never going to let you out of my sight."

He repeated the sentiment again, immediately after she woke.

Actually—not immediately.

First he told her he loved her more than the President loved macaroni and cheese, and *then* he said he was never going to let her out of his sight.

Smiling up at him drowsy-eyed as she lay with her cheek resting on his chest, she murmured, "Thank you for loving me *obviously* beyond reason, but never letting me out of your sight doesn't sound very practical."

"So I'm not a practical man." There was a seriousness to his voice under the smiling answer.

"Perhaps we could negotiate the finer points of 'never,'" Molly said, the twinkle in her eyes joyous, "to allow us both an opportunity to earn a living."

"Don't have to earn a living," Carey growled, half in jest, half in earnest.

"And then again," Molly replied, "some of us weren't fortunate enough to have been born counts."

"And then again," Carey murmured very low, looking down at her from under his thick, dark lashes, "some of us will soon be countesses."

Molly sat up abruptly in resentment. Carey had triggered her damnable touchy pride that had been trampled on so recently by the master trampler—Bart Cooper—and was still bruised and sensitive. "Are you implying that's enough?"

Carey's eyes opened a fraction wider, surprised at her sudden withdrawal and equally unexpected nettlesomeness. "No," he said after a short time, having surveyed the faintly irascible woman beside him. "I didn't mean to imply anything of the kind." His self-esteem had never rested on his parentage.

"Good," Molly crisply retorted, "because I don't care if I'm a countess or not." She moved back another small distance as if unconscious prelude to her next statement. "But I do care *very much* about not losing my identity or independence."

"How independent do you have in mind?" he asked, not altogether sure he was progressive enough to accept some of the newer social mores where couples worked and lived apart. He was rather of the predisposition at the moment after so many years apart to keep Molly under lock and key. Rapidly discarding his moment of anachronistic irrationality, he segued instead into his most diplomatic tone and in softly reassuring words added, "I don't *want* your identity, Honeybear . . . only your love."

Whether it was his diplomatic words or his soothing voice or the outstretched hand he offered her, Molly smiled suddenly, then sighed. "I guess I overreacted," she quietly said, and touched his open palm lightly in a tiny, tentative gesture that conveyed both her love and uncertainty. Paradoxically at that moment she seemed very vulnerable, like the Molly he'd known long ago, but also imbued with a quiet, resilient strength developed in the years he'd been away.

Carey didn't make any sudden moves, although his fingers ached to close over hers and pull her close. He understood her struggle for independence better for having known her in her youth. Unlike Molly, *he* would never have married someone simply because the invitations had been mailed out, but she had for all her own reasons and with the ache of their youthful parting a never-to-be-forgotten pain, he quietly said, "You didn't overreact, Honeybear. I was using the wrong words. They were thoughtless, flip, and irrelevant, okay?" He had never apologized to a woman before outside of the casual disclaimers normal courtesy required; he had never seriously questioned his own selfishness. His dark eyes were trained on Molly's face as if gauging the success of his apology. "Although," he went on slowly, his explanation as much for himself as her, "my feelings are relevant . . . and powerful." His voice was very low, as though he held those powerful feelings in check. He didn't dare tell her how intensely he needed her, how he loved her with proprietory indiscretion. It frightened him at times . . . that sort of urgent wanting. And Molly's newfound freedom might be too fragile to stand the unleashed assault of his compelling need.

"If my divorce hadn't been so ruthless . . ." She smiled ruefully. "It left scars. Sorry."

Very slowly Carey's fingers closed over Molly's small hand. "I'm sorry, too." And he was. For not being there to protect her from Bart Cooper's predacious demands.

"That's why my independence is so important to me. I want to be in control of my life." She was still sitting straight-backed and assertive, but her beautiful nude body gilded by the morning sun was blatantly distracting, an ultrafeminine assertion of supple curves and yielding softness. "And I'm probably overexaggerating this all out of proportion."

She was talking to a man who had had the opportunity to indulge his independence most of his life. "I hear you loud and clear, sweetheart." One tanned shoulder rose in a negligent shrug. "Look, you can have a prenuptial, nuptial, post-nuptial contract down to the color of the bath towels if it'll make you happy. I don't want to take anything away from you, Honeybear, I only want to give." He was offering her carte blanche with a mild, gracious courtesy.

He lay powerfully lithe on her bed, undisturbed by her exacting requests and less than eager assent to his marriage plans, relaxing against the turquoise striped sheets as though he hadn't been absent from her bed for ten years. His muscled, athletic body was dark, tanned by the same sun that had shone on her but in other faraway places. She had only just found him again; it was sheer folly to make demands. He was too wonderful to chastise. Perhaps she was a fool to inflict her high-strung requirements on this golden-haired, dark-eyed, attractive man. "I don't deserve you," Molly murmured, touched by his compassion, her eyes glistening with emotion.

"Yes, you do, and I deserve you. We deserve each other after ten bloody years of sacrifice to some damn god of misrule who sent those wedding invitations out before I had a chance to make you mine. But I'm going to make you mine *this* time, Honeybear, if it takes a bushel of sweet-talking and every écu in my Swiss bank accounts."

"Why are you being so accommodating?" Her question was half-teasing, laced with suspicion left over from all the glossy pictures seen of Carey Fersten with the beauties of the world.

"I'm always accommodating," he murmured in a deep growl which offered potentially diverse choices.

"Is there a catch?" Her teasing was lighthearted now, all weighty concerns over identity and independence discarded. "Is there a payment due for all your congenial accommodation?"

"Not anywhere on God's green earth, sweetheart," he cheerfully replied, and then his dark lashes lowered so that he looked at her from under their lacy fringe. "At least," he whispered very low, "nothing you can't handle."

Joyous and full of laughter, she fell on him and he welcomed her with open arms, his heart spilling over with love. Tumbling like young puppies they exchanged teasing kisses and words of love until their kisses altered, leading to other, more time-consuming pleasures.

And it was sudden shock that brought her sitting upright from soft layers of lethargy an hour later, the harsh buzzing of the alarm followed by shock. "Yipes," she cried. "Carrie's breakfast!"

It was Carey's first startling introduction to fatherhood.

CHAPTER 24

After a quick shower, Carey tossed on some clothes and padded barefoot into the kitchen to join Molly and his daughter for breakfast. As he stood just inside the doorway, Molly introduced him.

"Honey, this is Mom's friend Carey Fersten. Carey, this is my daughter. She has pierced ears."

Carey shifted his glance from his daughter back to Molly, surprised at the small shadow of contention in the last two words. "And you don't," he quietly said with a smile, the taste of her earlobes sweet recent memory.

Molly had always resisted putting holes in her flesh, and had played guardian over her daughter's earlobes, as well. Or had tried to. And while she'd raised Carrie to be independent, it often disconcerted her when she was. "She's so young," Molly replied, sounding petulantly youthful herself for a brief moment before her jeunesse dorée expression altered to one of resigned motherhood. "Carrie tells me pierced ears are de rigueur for eight-year-olds," Molly added, her voice warm with affection as she looked at her daughter.

"Are you dragging your mother into the twentieth

century?" Carey inquired, his glance returning to his pale-haired daughter who was calmly gazing at him.

"Mom's kind of old-fashioned sometimes. She used to live in a small town," she added, as though that explained her mother's conservative spells. "You came back," Carrie said in the next breath, changing topics with childlike ingenuousness. "I knew you would."

"Said I would, didn't I?"

"Yup." And she shoveled another spoonful of Cheerios into her mouth. "Did you and Mom make up?"

Molly blushed. Carey smiled and said, "Yes, I can never stay mad at your Mom."

"Gonna be here tonight when I come home from school?"

"Really, Carrie," Molly interposed, embarrassed by her daughter's forthrightness.

"I'm visiting for a couple of days. Want me to pick you up from school?"

She nodded. "And you can drive me there in two minutes, if you want." Carrie cast a rebuking glance at her mother. "You overslept, Mom. I'm going to be late, and Theresa's going to wonder why you haven't checked in downstairs."

"It's my fault," Carey explained. "I kept your Mom up late last night . . . talking." The warm hue on Molly's face was the exact shade of the rosebuds on her bathrobe, and Carey tried to remember the last woman he'd seen blush.

"So?"

His daughter's pointed inquiry brought him back to earth.

"I'll drive. You don't have to drive, Carey," Molly rapidly declared, disconcerted by her daughter's presumption.

"I'd love to," he replied. I'd love to, he thought, love to drive "my daughter" to school—a simple, ordinary act he'd considered forever denied him.

With a hesitant, "Are you sure?" to which she received a firm, "Yes," Molly excused herself to get ready for work.

"Do you really make movies? On location? With big

budgets and extras like from . . . people you know?" His daughter's eager tone reminded him of his own voice when he was asking for his first car, years too early.

"Are you really nine?" he asked, amusement rich in his voice. Even with his limited acquaintance with children, she struck him as wonderfully precocious.

"Eight and seven-eighths."

Controlling an impulse to smile, he said, "That accounts for it, then."

"Are you going to drive barefoot?"

"Do you mind?"

"Georgia's boyfriend got a ticket for driving barefoot."

"Who's Georgia? Your mom's old friend Georgia?" he asked in the next flashing moment. "What boyfriend?" he asked immediately, as though he were guardian to a minor. Had Molly had boyfriends, too, although she'd denied it? Relax, Fersten, he cautioned in the next millisecond. This is not the middle ages. She is not your exclusive property. Oh, yeah? his possessive instincts dissented. Remember, these are liberated, progressive times, the logical voice inside his brain declared. And sense and sensibility lasted another millisecond. "What boyfriend?" he testily repeated.

"Her lifeguard boyfriend."

"Lifeguard boyfriend—as in beach lifeguard?"

"He's a little young for Georgia, Mom says."

She had looked at another man; he'd kill him. With Molly he had never been dégagé; irrationally possessive was closer to the mark. "How old is he? What's his name?" A trial lawyer couldn't have been more decisive.

"His name's Scott. He's eighteen."

He had to repress the urge to gasp, and immediately reminded himself that equality existed between the sexes, as well as between age groups. And if he was honest with himself, he had been known to escort a starlet or two in that nubile age group. Although he hadn't been sober at the time. "Has your mom dated Scott?"

"Mom?" Incredulity lit her wide eyes.

Immediately Carey's world righted itself. "She didn't date Scott."

"Mom doesn't date anyone. She's too busy, she says. Georgia says she's too uptight. Mom says Georgia had more leisure time, and when she has more leisure time she'll ask for an introduction to Mark. Mark's cute."

"Who's Mark?" His voice had that cutting edge to it again.

"Scott's friend."

"Another lifeguard?"

"I think so; he has a really great tan."

"I can see I got here just in the nick of time," he murmured in a tone very close to a growl. For a man who had prided himself on never experiencing jealousy, the green demons had surrounded him and were coming in for the kill.

"What?"

"We have to get out of here or you're going to be late," he improvised, the unknown Mark assuming a prominent position on his black list.

"You don't have to worry, you're cuter than Mark." Dressed in her pink denim pinafore, flowered blouse, lace-trimmed anklets, and pink leather hightops, Carrie looked too freshly angelic to be so perceptive. But she'd read the convoluted chaos of his mind, and after his first start of surprise he immediately thought, *What a darling child*. It wasn't simply that she was his daughter, she was darling in general. And he told her so after he thanked her for the compliment.

He did drive to school barefoot. Carrie asked questions nonstop, and when she paused for breath occasionally, he asked questions of his own. He wanted to know everything about his daughter, everything he'd missed in the years she'd grown up without him. And when she ran up the steps of the school, he watched her until she disappeared into the building, awed that he had a child, a precocious, beautiful, *healthy* child.

While Molly spent her day downstairs in the office, Carey

spent his time on the phone handling some of the editing preliminaries long-distance. But it was awkward and erratic, frustrating for him and for his crew.

"We need you here, Carey," Allen said. "I can transfer some of the calls, but not all of them. And when you operate the way you do—with no assistant directors—it all grinds to a standstill, boss."

"Ask me if I'm happy here in this apartment," Carey replied, immune to the mild censure.

"Don't have to. Bunnies of happiness are bouncing down the wire to me. The fights at the preliminary edits are reaching flash proportions, though. Hope you can make it back soon. Wishing you the greatest, boss, no offense, but when are you coming back?"

"William and Jock are at each other's throats I take it."

"You know their divergent *creative* impulses," Allen said with sarcastic emphasis. "They're about to name weapons."

"Shit. Do I have to do *everything*?"

"You always have."

Carey sighed resignedly. "Okay, I'll come back tomorrow morning. Arrange for Jess to be ready to take off at nine."

"Great! No offense, boss," Allen quickly added.

"One more thing." Carey hesitated.

"I already sent her back to L.A."

Carey grinned. "That must be why I pay you so well."

"We try, sir," Allen replied with mock modesty, "to earn our princely stipend."

Dinner that night was orchestrated by Carrie, newly christened "Pooh" to avoid the confusion of their names. Winnie the Pooh was her favorite stuffed toy from babyhood, and when the discussion turned to their similar names, the decision was simple.

"Some people call me Charles," Carey had offered in the event Carrie preferred her name.

"I want a nickname," his daughter declared from her spot between her parents in the front seat of the car.

"Should we discuss this?" Molly asked in that parental tone that always reminded her immediately after hearing her voice of a child psychologist dealing with a firebug toddler.

"I want a nickname. I want Pooh like a cousin to Winnie."

Molly looked at Carey over their daughter's head and lifted one brow in inquiry. "Sounds good to me," he said, his smile amiable.

"No discussion?" Molly had a tendency to over-verbalize. Carey, on the other hand, made decisions swiftly with a minimum of words. Apparently, his daughter did, as well. "Are we agreed?"

"Is this a town meeting?" Carey teased.

"Call me Pooh."

"It's not a town meeting," Carey declared with the faintest of smiles, experiencing instant bonding with his determined young daughter.

Carey had never seen a Chucky Cheese; the din was overwhelming. With the musical life-size toys and the raucous shouting of scores of children, conversation was impossible. So they ate their pizza while the decibel levels of a rock concert exploded around them. When they'd finished, Pooh took Carey into the game room next door. He was astonished with her expertise on the machines that lined the walls and formed aisles in the center of the enormous room.

"You must come here often," he said, watching her coordinate two levers with superb reflexes as a careening car went down the computer-style mountain road without crashing into a losing score on the screen. "You're pretty good."

"There's games in the hotel down the street from us. Mom lets me go there sometimes." Her concentration was focused on the lighted screen. "Wanna try?" She had accepted Carey with a casual friendship he found endearing, and he marveled at the assurance she exuded. She seemed to take the changes in her life in stride.

"I'll play this one next to you so you can keep racking up your score. Wouldn't want to upset the record you've got going." And for the next few minutes, father and daughter coordinated hand and eye, and set the machines humming.

Carrie ran out of tokens first, and she calmly surveyed Carey as he decimated a space army on the colored screen battle field. "You're pretty good yourself," she said with the calm delivery he found so surprising in a young child. Highlighted by the fluorescent green from his game screen, her pale hair framed her face in an ethereal, surreal quality, like an underwater image. The other-worldly image was so vivid, it took him a moment to respond to her question. "I had lots of practice," he finally said, remembering another surreal world of black violence and red death, remembering the base camps in Vietnam where playing the machines filled the endless morning hours when you were too hung-over to drink. He'd lived on Coke and Hostess Ho Hos those mornings, and had become proficient at the machines. For the next hour he and Carrie tested the two rows of electronic games nearest the dining room, enjoying a camaraderie based on mutual skill.

As they drove home, Molly said, "A person could feel like a third wheel real easy with you two pinball wizards doing your stuff."

"Teach you how," they both said in unison, and then laughed at their simultaneous response.

"I don't have time, although," Molly said with a smile, "I'd be *thrilled* to learn, otherwise."

Father and daughter looked at each other and raised their dark eyebrows. The dual effect was a devastating mirror image, and Molly wondered for the dozenth time why she hadn't realized Carrie's paternity years ago. They were so alike: pale-haired, dark-eyed and with smiles that began as grins, then grew into laughter. They'd have to tell her soon, she thought, but not tonight. It was too sudden. She wanted them to get to know each other better before the major announcement was made, although there was no denying their compatibility.

"Mom, you know you hate those games."

"I never said that."

"Did so."

"Well, I suppose I might have said it's not my favorite type of amusement."

"Right after Ping-Pong, you always said."

"She doesn't like Ping-Pong, either?" Carey inquired in mock affront.

"Hates it," Carrie replied with finality. "Mom's not much good at any games," she added, matter-of-factly, in the way young children had of explaining adult idiosyncracies.

"Oh, your mom likes some games," Carey said, catching Molly's gaze over their daughter's head.

"She does?" Carrie asked, her dark eyes intent on Carey. "What?" In her memory, her mother had rather systematically rejected all games, period.

And while Molly blushed, Carey replied, "Big people games."

"Oh, you mean like bridge and backgammon?"

"Don't you dare," Molly quietly warned as Carey's grin widened.

At her mother's warning, Carrie's gaze went from Carey to Molly and back again. "You mean mushy stuff," she declared.

"Could we change the subject?" Molly said, not as unflappable as her daughter.

"What do you want for your birthday, Pooh?" Carey inquired, angelic innocence prominent in his expression.

Carrie's interest was immediately diverted. "How did you know my birthday's coming?"

"Er—" the twinkle in his eyes was boyish and light-hearted, reminding Molly of the young man she'd once known before the "international director persona" had taken precedence. "Your mom and I discussed your birthday last night."

"*Thanks*, Mom." Carrie's head swung back toward Carey. "Can you get me a date with Chachi from *Happy Days*?"

"Charlotte Louise, for heaven's sake!"

"Something smaller, huh?"

"I'm sorry, Carey, I thought I'd taught her some manners." Molly's apology was part rueful but only mildly serious; after nine years she was familiar with her daughter's frankness.

"Hey, it's all right. I asked her, and it doesn't have to be small at all, Pooh, only not Chachi just yet," he said with conspiratorial delight. "I don't think your mom would approve of you dating. Why don't you make a list when you get home and we can avoid the frown forming on your mother's face."

Tardily remembering her manners, Carrie said, "You don't have to buy me anything. I mean, if Mom—"

"I *want* to buy you a present, and your mother doesn't mind. *Do* you?" he said with unmistakable emphasis.

Molly sighed, knowing she was the only voice of moderation between father and daughter's cheerful insistence. "No, I don't mind, but I'd like Carrie to—"

"Remember her manners. Okay. Make the list a polite list, Pooh," he said kindly, "and everyone will be happy." It was going to be an incredible, exhilarating experience to go birthday shopping for his *own* daughter. Something like a bona fide twenty-four-carat gold miracle. And after all the tragedy of birth defects he'd seen in the offspring of his platoon members, a beautiful, healthy daughter of his own was heart-stopping jubilation. As she sat between them with her hands in her lap, he quickly surveyed the five perfect fingers on each of her hands and thought of Denny's baby boy who was missing all the fingers on one hand. Then a swift perusal of her Reebok-clad feet assured him no deformities existed. Lloyd's baby girl had had six operations on her clubfoot before she was three. And Carrie was free of the other birth defects attributed to Agent Orange too. Thank you, God.

Why them and not me? The question silently looped through his mind . . . Why, why, why? Maybe he'd been in the hospital when his platoon had been most heavily sprayed; maybe the damn purple heart had saved him from the moonscape they'd all talked about at Ashau when they'd bathed in the bomb craters. Or maybe pure luck had kept him out of the most toxic areas just sprayed for "mosquitoes."

The Vietnamese birth defects had been reported very early in the Saigon papers, but the military administration had called it VC propaganda. American servicemen had been told the spraying was harmless to humans and animals. Another instance of war contractors placing profits over people. Legal research of the chemical companies after the war had proven they'd known about dioxin's deadly consequences as early as 1957. Carey always had the urge to kill when he thought of the chemical companies' derivative sovereign immunity defense which argued they had been employed by the government as war contractors and, like the government, couldn't be sued. The defense so often used by war criminals: "We were only following orders."

Brushing a hand over his forehead, he forced away his black thoughts. Count your blessings, he reminded himself. But a twinge of guilt colored his own happiness. How lucky he was and how unlucky so many of his friends were.

"Headache?" Molly inquired, their daughter deep in thought as she mentally cataloged her birthday list.

He smiled. "Hell, no . . . too much happiness," he said softly. "I'm not used to it. But," he added with a small smile, "I'm damn well going to enjoy *getting* used to it."

"You're glad I stopped at Ely Lake to look you up?"

"Do fish swim?" he said, glancing at her with a quick lift of his eyebrows and a flashing grin. "I'm considering shackling you and Pooh to my wrist. *That's* how glad."

"That's pretty glad," she teased, "for an independent man."

"What time is it?" he murmured in return, insinuation clear in his voice.

She looked at the dashboard clock. "Almost nine."

"Good."

"It's too early," she warned.

"When."

"Bedtime's at nine-thirty."

"I think I can wait."

"You have to."

There was a moment of considered silence before he said, "Maybe . . ."

"Carey!" Her whisper was hushed, but in the single breathy word, beneath the small indignation, was piquant anticipation.

"You make the hot chocolate, and I'll do the bedtime story." Urgency threaded lightly through his words, but then his expression changed, his dark eyes surveying the young girl between them and he very quietly added, "May I?"

It was the first time in his life he'd ever tucked a child into bed, the first time he'd told a bedtime story, and the first time he'd had to fight back tears since Dhani MacIntosh. Molly was in the habit of telling an extemporaneous story which drifted off on tangents like an *Alice in Wonderland* narrative. So Carey picked up the plot and added some creative color of his own with wizards and princesses and a quest for a treasure in emeralds.

"Thanks, Carey," one sleepy young girl murmured as the chapter ended, "you're nice."

He wanted to crush her in his arms and tell her he loved her, tell her he was her father, map out their entire future together, but Molly wanted to proceed more slowly until they knew each other better. Instead, he said, "You're nice, too,

Pooh . . . the very nicest little girl I know." Bending low, he kissed her lightly on the forehead. "Sleep tight."

She was staring thoughtfully at him when he straightened, her face framed by the pink-flowered pillow. "Your eyes are a lot like mine."

The plain words hit him like a jolt, and in a flurry of mental activity he discarded the first dozen unsuitable answers that came to mind. "Lucky me," he finally said.

"And you play a mean game of pinball." She spoke the words with a quiet gravity, and he had an irrational sensation he was being graded. An overwhelming feeling of panic assailed him, fear that he would somehow fail this young child's test. He desperately hoped that she would not dislike him once she knew the truth. She meant too much to him.

He smiled. "You and I'll have to teach your mom someday."

Her little nose curled up. "She won't."

"Maybe we can coax her to come to London. My house there has a room full of game machines. We'll tell her she can have tea with the queen," he teased.

"She'd like that. Could she really? I know you're teasing, but *somebody* has tea with the queen 'cuz I saw a picture once with everyone in big hats outside a red brick mansion. Mom would *die* of happiness. Why do you have a house in London?"

"Because my dad had one, and now I've got it. I can't promise the queen, but I can line up a duchess or two if we can convince your mom to come."

"Hey, way to go . . . we'll work on her together." Her eyes were alight.

"I'd like that," Carey softly said.

Molly drove Carey out to the airport, and for the first time in her life she encountered paparazzi upclose and personal. A crowd of photographers were stretched out along the chain-link fence surrounding the airstrip for private planes. The scene reminded her of all the telecasts she'd seen on TV for visiting dignitaries or rock stars or the astronauts returning from some space mission. It was unnerving. As they stepped from the car the crowd seemed to surge into the fence, and dozens of shouted questions sailed across the twenty yards of tarmac.

"What's her name?"

"Is she American?"

"Is she going back with you?"

"Is she why you shut down production?"

"Hey! Turn this way, lady!"

"Would you call this one serious, Count?"

"How serious?"

Ignoring the uproar of questions with a calm based on years of experience, his arm protectively around Molly's waist, Carey guided her away from the clamoring photographers to the sanctuary of the hangar.

"Carey!" Molly whispered, the turbulence of sound following them inside. "Does this happen *often*?"

"Ignore it," he replied casually, used to deflecting the attention aroused by his looks, wealth, and reputation.

"*Ignore* it?" she inquired with mild incredulity. The swell of noise followed them into the quiet of the hangar like a thin wave of haphazard exclamation marks. "How does one become that blasé?"

"Practice."

She looked up at him in astonishment. "How long does it take," she quietly asked, a private person in an increasingly public world of instant telecommunications and computer trail dossiers, "to practice up?"

Glancing down at her, he smiled. "Thirty-three years," he said. "Don't worry, I'll have someone bring your car in here so you won't have to see them again. Oh, shit!" he swore, and pushed Molly behind him just as a flash exploded from close range. "*Jesus*! Paolo, don't you ever give up?"

The short, stocky man dressed in mechanic's overalls shrugged negligently. "Smile, Count," he said in heavily accented English, "and bring out the signorina so your fans can see her face, per favore."

"One of these days, Cerelli, you're going to lose your teeth." All the blandness was gone from Carey's voice. "Out of here, *dammit! Now!*" And Mr. Cerelli only snapped a half dozen more shots of Carey angrily striding toward him before prudently turning and fleeing.

"He's resourceful," Molly said with a touch of irony when Carey returned.

"He's a pain in the ass," Carey growled, watching the retreating figure.

"You must be profitable for him."

"Hell, yes, but with Cerelli it's the damn challenge more than the money. I'd be happy to pay him double what he makes to stay off my back, but the bastard's refused. And like some goddamn ferret, he shows up anywhere!"

"Like at the Rembrandt Hotel?"

Carey's head snapped around.

Molly lifted her brows.

"Christ," Carey muttered, "that picture must have been in every paper in the world."

"Serves you right, keeping married duchesses out all night."

Carey groaned. "Could we drop the subject?"

"I, on the other hand, have been quite virtuous," Molly replied, mischief and a touch of resentment blending in her voice.

"Have the last ten years been a contest?" Carey asked.

"It appeared as though *you* were attempting to set records."

"Are we having a fight? Because if we are, let's fight about something more interesting." It was the primal masculine response to discord in general and inquiries into infidelity in particular.

"Weren't *they* interesting?"

Carey grimaced, considered briefly, and said, "Not particularly. Any more questions?" By now there was a certain terseness to his responses.

It fell, however, on the fearless ground of Molly's pride. "Only one," she crisply replied. "Could you keep Cerelli away from me? I don't care to be in every paper in the world as your latest fling."

"Okay. I'll have both his knees broken."

"No!" she exclaimed. "You wouldn't, would you?" she finished, contrite and confused and feeling slightly out of her depth.

"Look, honey, I'll do what I can, but seriously even broken knees would only slow him down for a few weeks. Now," he said "can we *not argue*?" Pulling her into his arms, he softly murmured, "Personally, I've never been happier in my life. And if the future goes according to my pollyanna plan, I intend to make you equally happy. Okay?"

His arms held her tightly, and she had to arch her neck to look up at him. It was cool inside the cavernous hangar, undisturbed by the morning sun held at bay outside the large open doors. For a moment she felt as though they were in some ancient pagan temple.

"Okay," she murmured without further thought. Suddenly discord seemed trivial. Her smile was strong enough to banish images of a dozen irritating Cerellis.

"I'll be back as soon as I can," he whispered, not wanting to leave.

"When?" she asked, not wishing to relinquish him, either.

"Tomorrow . . . the next day." And then Allen's insistent reminder overrode his own potent wishes, and he amended, "Probably a couple of days. Do you want to come back with me?"

"Can't," she breathed just before his lips brushed hers.

"I'll try and wait two days, then."

"Why wait?" It was a breathy invitation, a flirtatious

promise from a young woman who had until very recently relegated her own sexuality to a future place on a future list of future leisure time.

Carey's head came up, and his sweeping glance took in the quiet dim, interior.

"I haven't done it in the backseat of a car since that night at Lake Fourteen," Molly teased, reaching up on tiptoe to nibble his earlobe.

Bending his head, he kissed her very hard. He'd also remembered that night, had recalled it fondly countless times. "Let me show you," he said a moment later when his mouth lifted from hers, "the inside of my plane."

"*That* is the smoothest line I've ever heard."

"You're the only one who's ever heard it."

"I find that charming," she said, her chin resting on his chest.

"And I find you irresistible—Excessively so at this exact moment. Damn the photographers." And, sweeping her into his arms, he carried her to the gleaming jet parked outside.

An hour later, Carey flew back to northern Minnesota and Molly drove home to face her busy schedule at the office. There were fewer photographers now; most had grown tired of waiting, and had left. So Molly didn't notice the gray sedan in the traffic behind her, following her on the freeway back into the city. Nor did she notice the man across the street from the Mart parking lot hastily fit a telephoto lens on his camera and run through twenty shots as she left her car to enter the building. From his vantage point near the wooden fence of Molly's small garden and yard, Paolo Cerelli noted with surprise and pleasure, the young girl walking toward the garden gate. An artist beneath his lucrative commercial profession, he immediately recognized the resemblance to the man he'd come to know intimately through the lens of his camera. "She's quite beautiful," he murmured over the hum of the automatic shutter. "Like her father," he added. That explained why production had been shut down so suddenly.

Cerelli had been following Carey for nearly a decade, since he'd appeared as the barefoot boy director—everyone's darling at Cannes—with his first full-length film and walked off with the prize. And Cerelli knew how serious Carey was about his movies. Once production began, he was thoroughly dedicated, even in his enfant terrible stage when women and drugs were taking a great deal of his time. Even then, the cameras rolled every morning with the young director on the set bright and early doing his job. Nothing had ever interfered with Carey's film-making. Until now.

After the pale-haired girl disappeared into the garden behind the fence, Paolo packed up his film and drove to the airport. He was anxious to express his newest photos to the sensational news magazine that paid him so well.

CHAPTER 25

Ceci had contacted his team by phone and passed on his orders in a cryptic code impenetrable to listeners. With the specialized surveillance equipment throughout the world, no one relayed sensitive information in open language. Everyone was listening to everyone else, the modern-day Maginot Line of self-defense encumbered by its own informational bulk, just as its predecessor was by its static concrete.

All the men collected from various points on the Mediterranean were to be in Paris in a week. There they would meet in a safe house near Orly and confirm the required procedures for kidnapping Count Fersten's daughter. Ceci was flying up with all the necessary bank account numbers to finance the venture. The men expected half-payment up front deposited in their Swiss accounts prior to the beginning of the mission.

Deraille had only to travel from Marseilles, so he had arrived first, followed by Reha from Athens. They were still waiting for Timur Makal, but he was always the last to arrive, loathe to leave his gambling and women. Since the deadline for their meeting was noon on Thursday, Kemal "Ceci" Kiray expected Timur to arrive just under the wire, as usual.

His entrance was as expected. At 11:45 there was a small flurry of flying gravel in the curved drive, and a black Porsche Targa came to an abrupt halt. A minute later, he stood in the drawing room doorway. "I drove all night from Vienna," he said, and his eyes were dilated from the amphetamines in his blood. But he always appeared with a beaming smile, like an uncontrite young boy.

"Was she pleasant company?" he asked, indicating the peony pink lipstick stain on the coarse silk weave of Timur's putty-colored jacket.

"They're all pleasant company," Timur replied with a negligent glance at the pastel souvenir of his beautiful companion. "If she hadn't been so pleasant, I wouldn't have been so late."

"You're an irresponsible boy."

"But a lot happier than you, eh, Ceci? And ready to fly you wherever you're off to." He moved toward the liquor table to pour himself a drink, undeterred by Ceci's mild censure.

Both Deraille and Reha were familiar with Timur's nonchalance, though they were as different from him as day and night. Deraille was a small, dark Corsican who'd spent most of his life in Marseilles and was the very best in his line of work. He was a specialist in surveillance, and could reconnoiter the movements of an intelligence chief within the confines of his own safehouse. Rifat had first heard of him when the Cypriot Prelate had been assassinated in his isolated monastery cell. Bernard Deraille had found the way in. That job had taken him a methodical three months to reconnoiter . . . his longest ever. But the political ramifications of the murder were still being felt in Cypriot politics.

"Hey Deraille . . . killed any priests lately?" Timur inquired with another of his charming smiles, holding up a glass of the pear liquor he favored.

"I'm saving myself for the Pope, now that the Bulgarians botched the job," he replied, his teeth flashing white against his swarthy skin.

"In that case, I won't bet a sou on the Pope's life. You're the best, Bernie." And he drained the glass in one long swallow.

"I know," the wiry Corsican replied matter-of-factly. He'd been the best for many years; false modesty did not figure prominently in his psyche.

"And Reha," Timur went on lazily, setting his glass aside with precision. His finely tuned nervous system was singing. "I hear a prominent Athens shipping magnate died in his Mercedes outside a small taverna. Are the arms transfers out of Sofia finally cleared up?" Timur's smile was angelic.

Reha only grunted. He lacked a sense of humor and had never appreciated Timur's whimsy. A former Turkish olympic heavyweight wrestler, he'd been cashiered out of the army after breaking one too many heads, then saved from prison by Rifat. A brute of a man with no neck or remorse, he was Rifat's most dependable bodyguard and assassin.

Dropping into a tapestry armchair, Timur lounged, all dark-haired, dark-eyed, lean elegance. Contemplating Ceci over the hands propped idly under his chin, he said, "I suppose we gear up at the crack of dawn tomorrow."

"You're restricted to the flat tonight," Ceci replied. "Departure is 0500."

Timur groaned. "You're a sadist, Ceci. Why can't we lift off at a respectable hour?"

"Because my dear Makal, there are fewer people around at 4:30 in the morning to see us load the necessary supplies on board."

Timur sighed, his dark eyes half-lidded. "Where are we going?"

"Minneapolis."

His eyes widened in inquiry. "Where?"

"A city in the center of the U.S." And then Ceci laid out the details of the kidnapping.

CHAPTER 26

During the following days Carey often flew down late at night, but he arrived and left as discreetly as possible. He had warned off as many of the photographers as his clout allowed; those on location understood—if they wanted to stay through the filming—that his private life was *private*. So it wasn't until well into the next week that Molly was faced with the sudden appearance of two photographers as she and Carrie walked through her garden gate, about to spend the afternoon at the beach.

Retreating hastily, she slammed the gate in their faces, locked it, hurried Carrie upstairs, said, "Wait one minute. Mom has to make a phone call," and dialed Carey's number.

"Could I speak to Carey, please?"

A male voice replied, "Sorry, Mr. Fersten's not taking any calls."

Her temper flared. The photographers were a disagreeable surprise, but she'd mostly wanted to seek advice from Carey, or ask if he knew who they were, or if he could dislodge them. She had a gut level problem about living her life on the photo section of some gossip newssheet. But coming up against the Hollywood celebrity he-doesn't-take-calls wall brought all the abrasive elements of Carey's life strongly to the fore. "Would you," she carefully enunciated, controlling her urge to let the temper in her voice show, "leave him a message."

"Sure, honey, but it won't do you any good. He doesn't return messages. Look," the voice was clipped and business-like, "if he told you he'd do you a favor, he will. The man's word is good. And if you don't know him, I'm sorry, babe, there's just too many of you calling."

Images rolled in accelerated fast-forward motion through her mind, and all the women in Carey's life appeared in blurred technicolor. "Tell him," she said, icicles hanging from each word, "Molly Darian called."

"Oops. Put you right through. Sorry, but I usually run interference for Carey. No hard feelings . . ."

And she heard the ringing of the extension.

"Golden Bear Productions."

"How many people does he *have* running interference?" Molly asked.

"Could I help you?" Allen said. If Joey had put the call through, it was someone worth being polite to, regardless of the sarcasm.

"This is Molly Darian. I'd like to talk to Carey, *if* he has time for one of the *many* women calling him," she crisply replied.

"I'm sorry, Molly, he's out in the middle of the lake on a barge filming. Could I have him get back to you?"

The man's voice was too smooth, too soothing, as though he'd run through this number endless times. "Tell him I've two photographers camped outside my door. It's extremely annoying, and if they're not gone *very* soon, I'm never talking to him again." Her statement was partly rhetorical, but a real anger colored her words when all the old jealousies resurfaced at the thought of Carey being bombarded with female callers. In all the idyllic happiness of their reunion, somehow she'd lost sight of the fact Carey lived another life outside her world. A life where he was sought after, panted after, seen as an enviable prize by beautiful women everywhere.

I value my life, Allen thought. *Let her tell him herself.* "He'll call you as soon as he's off the lake."

"Do me a favor." She couldn't keep the snappishness out of her voice, wondering how many times other women had been put off by that calm tone telling them Carey would call them back.

"Sure, Molly, anything."

"Tell your boss, if these photographers aren't away from my front door and out of my life—" She paused, realizing how shrill she sounded. "Sorry," she said, "I'm not used to this—"

"Carey will take care of it," Allen said in the reasonable voice he reserved for distrait wives, carping producers, and IRS officials. "Trust me. Just as soon as he's back on shore."

"God I hate this." Molly's voice had begun to rise again. "He's notorious, you know. Not only famous, but *notorious*, dammit."

God in heaven. She just discovered that? In his position, however, Allen knew how to dodge a confrontation. His pacifying retort came automatically. "I'm sure Carey will straighten everything out. I'll have him call you." But Allen also knew better than anyone that Carey Fersten was indeed notorious. Notorious for having a new woman on every location and in every city.

But this Molly Darian was different. That was obvious to him, to the crew, the cast, to anyone who'd seen Carey since she'd walked into his life. He was adjusting his life for her; he was forcing a relentless pace on the film, pushing the shooting schedule up so that he could fly off and spend a few hours with her. And this movie was his personal pet, the movie he'd waited all his life to make. Changing his life for a woman? No one would believe it. Not anyone who knew Carey before. You had to be here. Yeah, Molly Darian was different, all right.

She was the only woman Allen had ever seen who cost Carey Fersten a cool half million bucks. That was what the shut-downs had cost so far, and the accountants were screaming at him daily over the phone.

An hour later when Carey returned to the trailor, he received Molly's message along with a newly arrived tabloid emblazoned with headlines in twelve-point type screaming: **CAREY FERSTEN'S LOVE CHILD** over a series of photos showing Carrie walking home from school.

"Fucking Cerelli."

"None other."

"Shit."

"Molly called to tell you she wants the photographers making a home on her doorstep removed a little sooner than immediately."

Carey frowned. "She was mad?"

"I detected a twinge of annoyance," Allen said.

"And she hasn't seen this yet."

"She didn't mention it." And Allen thought of her final comment—that Carey was notorious. Soon she'd be in that same category herself. It went with the territory. "I'd ease into the subject if I were you."

"Diplomacy is required, then."

"Along with a running start."

Carey laughed. "Oh, hell, so what else is new." But it *was* new. For the first time in his life he didn't walk away from an angry woman pressuring him. A novel experience.

Molly wasn't like all the other women. Those headlines and Carrie's pictures would be public property by noon tomorrow. Molly would *have* to marry him now . . . very soon. A press conference was in order to announce the date and acknowledge Carrie. "We'll have to call a press conference."

"For—?" Allen tactfully inquired.

"Carrie's my daughter. I want to acknowledge her, and if I

can talk some sense into her mother, we'll announce a wedding date."

"The lady's reluctant?" After eight years of watching women try to entice Carey to the altar, Allen tried to disguise his astonishment.

"Not reluctant, but she wants time for Carrie and me to get to know each other."

"The *Star Inquirer* moved that scenario into fast forward."

Carey shrugged and smiled. "I'm not complaining." He picked up the phone. "Wish me luck," he said, "she's going to be pissed."

"Luck, boss, although you've had plenty of practice with irate females." And Allen knew if Carey set his mind to it, he could get most people to do what he wanted. Especially women.

"This is the only one who matters." Carey crossed his fingers and then waved Allen out.

After making her call to the film site. Molly had explained to Carrie that some of Carey Fersten's prominence had spilled over on them. She promised to take her daughter to the beach later, after the photographers were gone. Then she waited, restlessly and disturbed, wondering if her call would be returned.

She picked up the receiver before the first shrill ring had completely died away.

"Are you all right?" Carey asked, and she could feel the warmth of his concern.

"I'm fine," she replied, determined to remain composed. "But you heard . . . there're some photographers outside the gate. Can you get rid of them? Is that too much to ask?" Her initial anger had subsided in the interval between her call and his.

"I'll have some security guards hired and sent over."

"Guards? I don't like the sound of that."

"Just temporarily, sweetheart." *Until we hire the body-guards*, he thought, *once the national scandal sheet hits the streets.*

"They won't just leave if I ask them to, or if you ask them to?"

"It's a job for them, honey. They're not charitable institutions," he said with a temperance he was far from feeling, knowing the stormy issues confronting them. Wishing he didn't have to break the news, he said, "Are you sitting down?"

"That sounds ominous," Molly said softly.

"It's not dire, but serious. It's about Carrie."

What could possibly be dire? Molly thought with relief. Carrie was here with her, safe and sound in her own room watching *Love Connection*. "She's here with me, Carey, and perfectly fine."

Looking down at the front page article, at the bold head-lines and fair, young girl pictured, Carey swore softly under his breath before saying, "I received an advance copy of the *Star Inquirer* today."

"What could that have to do with Carrie? Oh, is there an-other one of those photos of you and some duchess? Don't worry, Carrie never reads those tabloids. And even if she did, she seems to accept your jet-set reputation without censure."

"It's not a duchess, Molly." His voice was deathly quiet.

"Well, whatever title, it doesn't matter, really . . . Carey, you're being overly concerned about something that couldn't possibly affect us, anyway." Molly was rushing along in a breathless flurry of words because Carey was too quiet, too starkly quiet, and she hoped to fill the awful void of silence. "Even if you are depicted in one of your notorious liaisons on the *Star Inquirer*, I'll discount it now that we've found each other again."

When she stopped for a moment to catch her breath, Carey said, "Carrie's on the cover, with the usual spectacular headlines."

"What headlines?" Molly whispered, struck with a terrible premonition of doom.

He read them to her in an even, modulated tone. The world was about to be introduced to Carey Fersten's natural daughter.

"Oh, God, no," Molly breathed, suddenly nauseous. Carrie hadn't even been told yet. And Bart, she suddenly thought, terrified. He was not a benevolent man. "Can't you *do* something."

"I've already checked with our legal staff. I can't sue; it isn't libelous."

"My God, Carey!" And for the first time she was struck solidly with the impact of full-scale public scrutiny. Carey may have lived his entire life in a goldfish bowl, but she hadn't, and it mattered fiercely that her daughter not be recognized and inspected by everyone standing in the check-out line at the supermarket.

"Honeybear, you don't know how sorry I am about this. I'd never want to hurt Carrie." The sincerity of his words held regret and comfort, his tender diminutive a message from the heart. "Molly, are you still there?"

She murmured some unintelligible sound, unable to articulate the overwhelming torrent of thoughts flooding through her mind.

"We have to do something before the paper is released. Do you hear me? Are you all right?"

"I'm breathing," she said. "Just barely."

"I know it's a shock, and I'm truly sorry, but we have to deal with this immediately. Allen and I agree we should call a press conference."

"A press conference?" He could have said a rocket launch and not been any more alarming.

"As long as everything's going to be public information by the weekend, we might as well acknowledge it in advance and arrest the titillating waves of curiosity. Allen will arrange all the details, and it'll only entail twenty minutes of your time."

"*I* have to be there?"

"You don't have to say a word. Allen and I will answer all the questions. Molly?" He could barely hear her breathing over the phone.

Dizzy, her stomach upset, Molly was resting against the headboard of her bed, visualizing dozens of klieg lights, scores of rude reporters, and her life spread out for all the world to see. How had her quiet life altered so suddenly?

"Answer, or I'm coming down," he threatened.

"I'm here." It was the smallest possible sound fiber optics could transmit.

"I'm sorry, darling . . . I'm so damned sorry."

His own mind was a jumble of unsorted chaos. He could only deal with one problem at a time: Molly and Carrie first; the film schedule second; then came revenge on the Cerellis of the world who didn't see the human lives behind the dollar signs. "The press conference," he firmly said, "is the only way to quash all the lurid speculation. I'll be there early tomorrow, and we can talk to Carrie before school. I was planning on coming down for Pooh's birthday, anyway." Just not before the day's filming was over, he thought. "Allen will schedule this thing for eleven. Okay?"

What could she say? No, I won't. No, I want to remain completely anonymous. I want our daughter to continue to exist in an insulated world. Stop the *Star Inquirer*, darling, for me. Instead, she reluctantly said, "Okay."

He was there by seven, driven over from the airport after an all-night session of editing. He was losing two more days, and Allen kept reminding him of the costs. But if he seemed remarkably composed for a bone-weary man it was because he was pleased to announce to the world he had a daughter he loved, and was eager to tell the media of his marriage plans.

Carrie was calmer than either of her parents over breakfast

when Molly nervously said, "We have something rather unusual to tell you, darling."

"I figured Carey was here this early for something, Mom," she said, leaning her chin into her cupped palm and watching Carey spoon the seventh measure of sugar into his coffee cup. "That's seven," she noted with a cheerful grin.

He looked up like a man waking from a dream, gazed into his cup, and pushed it away.

"Would you like a fresh cup?" Molly asked.

He shook his head, but noticed how her hands were clenched, white-fingered, in her lap. They were both scared by this placid little girl with her perfect chin cupped in her hands and her large, dark eyes moving slowly from one to the other.

"Would you mind missing school today?" Molly said after a fortifying breath to still the pounding of her heart.

"Are we going somewhere?"

"Well . . . no . . . but, well—" At a loss for words, she turned to Carey in appeal.

"Is it all right if I tell her?" he asked. Without waiting for an answer, he began, "I knew your mother years ago before you were born . . . and I loved her very much." He stopped for a moment, his dark eyes tender as he glanced at Molly, and his voice took on a note of poignancy. "But sometimes things don't always work out."

"So Mom married Dad."

"Yes, she did."

"I shouldn't have," Molly said softly.

"And that's why you got a divorce. Mom and Dad always argued," Carrie explained to the pale-haired man, dressed for a boardroom meeting, sleek and sophisticated at seven in the morning. "Did you get married, too?" she asked.

"Yeah," Carey said. "For a while."

"And you divorced, too."

He nodded his head.

"Just like *Dallas* or Lucy's mom and dad, or Tammy's—"

Molly smiled ruefully. "We're not shocking her sensibilities."

"Mom, you're more easily shocked than I am." It was said with the authority of eight years experience in the world, and her own special brand of assurance.

"Well, sweetheart," Carey went on, a small smile responding to her artless competence, "what we have to tell you *may* startle you, but I want you to know both your mom and I are very happy and love you."

"Can I tell Lucy about it?"

Molly instinctively began to say no, until she recalled the reason for this conversation. After tomorrow the entire world would know—Lucy included. "If you want to, it's fine," she said.

There was a lengthening silence, until Carey finally said very quietly, "Bart isn't your father. I am."

She sat upright, her placid pose abruptly altered as she looked at her mother for confirmation. When Molly nodded, her gaze traveled to Carey. "Bart isn't my father?"

Molly expected confused questions like: Why didn't you tell me? What does Bart have to say about that? How will it change things? Why did you wait so long?

"Carey's my father?"

She nodded again.

"You're my father?"

"Yes," Carey said, his heart thudding against his ribs, never in his experience so unsure and afraid. She was his only child, the child he thought he would never have.

Carrie leaned back against the painted kitchen chair, her hair like molten gold next to the swedish blue. Her small face was expressionless, and Molly thought for a moment how like her father she was, her feelings controlled and concealed behind the perfect symmetry of her features. And then her young face lit with the dazzling smile she'd inherited from her father, and she said, "Wow!"

"You don't mind?" Carey asked with a hesitancy which

would have shocked his entire entourage of friends and acquaintances. He was not a man of insecurities.

"It's great," his daughter said with feeling.

Then she glanced at her mother, a small frown furrowing her brow. "It's great for you too, right?"

Molly nodded. "Yes, the greatest."

Carrie's gaze flicked toward her father, her smile reappearing. "So when are you moving in?"

And the dire crisis both parents had dreaded with misgivings and doubts, with faint hearts and trepidation, was over.

They explained to her about the photos, the *Star Inquirer*, the press conference, and her only reaction was excitement. "My picture's going to be in the *Star Inquirer*? Wait'll Lucy hears. She'll die of envy. Can I be in one of your movies? If you're my dad, you can fix it up, can't you? Oh, wow, will Lucy just die. Me in a movie, my dad a movie director, wow! Mom, I'll have to learn how to put on makeup now. Lucky I had my ears pierced. Can I call her, Mom, can I, can I call Lucy?" And she ran off to tell her best friend her news.

Looking at Carey, her mouth quirked with amusement, Molly said, "It must be in the genes. She's as immune to public opinion as you are."

Carey smiled. "Indifference to society's judgment runs undiluted through fifty generations of Ferstens. Not to mention my mother's family, who consider themselves obliged to be outrageous."

"I'm the only one who prefers anonymity."

"You and Greta Garbo. That's it."

"I don't like people prying into my private life."

"They will, anyway, sweetheart, so why fight it?"

"It's embarrassing."

"Embarrassing that you and I love each other?"

"Yes, no, oh hell—it's not the whole world's business."

"The entertainment industry attracts that kind of fascinated interest, darling. You'll get used to it."

"I don't want to."

"On the other hand," he immediately said with a boyish grin, "they could live without knowing what you ate for dinner."

"Damn right they could."

"All right, we're agreed. No publicity."

"We can avoid the press conference?"

"*After* the press conference." Molly's face fell. "Darling, I want to acknowledge Carrie as my daughter. Do you realize how pleased I am to have a daughter? And if we announce a wedding date and explain briefly about our previous friendship, no one will be interested in continuing to examine us under a microscope. Everything will be out in the open. Trust me. It's the best way. If you run and hide, they follow like a pack of wild dogs. We'll feed them all the gossipy tidbits, and then that's it. They'll be satisfied. So when do you want to get married?"

"When do you have to leave for Australia?"

"Right after I finish this film."

"And you'll be gone for a year?"

He sighed. "I never realized, when I signed the contract . . . Damn. *You* can't really leave, can you?"

"Not for that long a time," she replied.

"Christ—our names should be Romeo and Juliet. Well, we'll just get married and worry about the rest—"

"Tomorrow, Scarlett?"

"Yeah. Hell, I'll fly back on weekends, or we could meet in Hawaii, or you take a week off, and then I'll take a week off."

Molly laughed. "With our luck, our flights will be canceled or delayed, and we'll miss each other somewhere over the Pacific."

"Fuck it. Let's just say when the film's finished, we'll get married. No matter what. How does that sound? That will satisfy me, and hopefully the insatiable press. And then I'll take some time off, and if you can manage to leave your nearly solvent business," he smiled a sweet, encouraging smile, "we'll check out married love as a lifestyle."

Molly smiled, content and happy and very much in love. "Sounds very nice. Am I allowed a temper tantrum or two before we reconcile our working schedules?"

"As long," Carey replied with a teasing light in his eyes, "as there's no wine bottle within reach." He rose from his chair in a swift, fluid movement. Somehow in his busy schedule he found time to keep remarkably fit. Buttoning one of the buttons of his double-breasted suit jacket, he said, "Now I'm off to get briefed before the press conference. Jess is waiting outside. Some security people are scheduled to be here this afternoon to keep the photographers at bay. Allen will send a car over at ten for you."

And in those short, terse sentences, he sounded very much like Carey Fersten, International Film Director. Despite his warm smile, Molly thought, despite the adoring look in his eyes, for a brief cold moment he seemed like a stranger.

CHAPTER 27

Carey was there to greet her at the service entrance of the hotel. Taking her hand, he drew her alongside him down several corridors into an elevator, then out again and into a small room several yards from the hall scheduled for the news conference. His full entourage was assembled: attorneys; business managers; publicity people flown in the night before; assistants; gophers; and some men looking suspiciously like bodyguards. Molly's uneasiness returned; she was an outsider in a smoothly run operation familiar to all its participants, save one.

There was no opportunity to talk in the crush of people determined to ask one more question or give one more word of advice. A cup of coffee was shoved into Molly's hand, and when she shook her head, Carey looked up from the document an expensively dressed man was explaining to him and brusquely said, "Tea. I told you Ms. Darian drinks tea. Take the coffee away." Then his eyes quickly scanned her pale face, his hand securely holding hers. "Are you all right?"

Molly nodded. In the flurry of nervous activity she couldn't tell him the truth. That she wasn't all right. She had the beginnings of a headache, and her stomach felt like a convention of butterflies.

"I'm sorry, Honeybear. This'll all be over soon." He squeezed her hand gently and forced his attention back to the man in the Savile Row suit who was pointing out another paragraph with a briskly tapping finger.

The tea appeared within seconds. In a glass, the way she liked it, with lemon and sugar. Carey had a very good memory. She watched him calmly absorb the attorney's instructions. He asked a few brisk questions, nodded in apparent approval at the answers, and then turned to the next of several assistants who issued further instructions. The tea was warm and soothing. Molly's stomach stopped dancing, and none too soon for the door opened abruptly and a man called out, "Camera time—three minutes."

Allen raced in. "You know what to do now," Carey said to him. "I don't want Molly upset with personal inquiries." He looked at Molly seriously. "If there was any way to avoid this, Honeybear," he murmured very low so only she could hear, "I would. Lord, you're pale. If you can't get through it, let me know and we'll just end it. I'm sorry, truly sorry, Honeybear, about all this hassle." His sincerity tugged at her heart; he seemed her young lover again, boyish, uncertain, miserable that he was hurting her.

Tears glistened in her eyes, and she saw him swallow hard when his glance met her misty blue gaze. She caught the hand he lifted to her face and said, "I understand. Don't worry about me . . . I'll manage."

"Okay, Honeybear." He smiled that heart-stopping smile. "It's you and me and twenty TV cameras."

Tightening his grip on her hand, he turned to Allen, hovering at his shoulder, and said, "Shall we?" And the entire crowd followed them into the bright lights across the hall.

The entourage unnerved Molly; it was like a royal court. Carey seemed to take it all in stride; when you walked out in public, forty people followed in your wake. He never opened doors, he never asked twice for a drink or for food. When he wanted something, it was there. When he didn't want something, it disappeared as rapidly.

In deference to the solemn occasion, he wore a suit, a navy linen Armani, his tie perfectly knotted, his normally bare feet shod in soft black kidskin. Some attempt had been made to set his pale hair in order, but the coarse waves fell in tumbled disarray by the time they mounted the small dais at the front of the room. He had tensely run his fingers through his hair one last time before entering the room.

Molly appeared at his side, slender, white-faced, her honey-colored hair shining on her shoulders. In contrast to Carey's dark suit, the apple-blossom pink of her voile shirt-waist seemed like delicate flowers against a stormy sky. He held her close to his side, his stance almost aggressive, as if he dared the world to hurt her.

At first the questions were vague and general: Where had they met? When? How had their friendship reestablished itself? When the kid gloves were tossed aside, Allen stepped in to thwart the more blatant queries. Once or twice Carey curtly cut off discourteous questions, saying, "I won't respond to that." But essentially his bearing was relaxed. He was at ease on the world's stage.

In twenty minutes all the necessary answers had been given, his replies couched in as general terms as possible. "Thank you, ladies and gentlemen," Carey politely said, "for your lively interest in my affairs. Thank you and good morning."

His dark eyes swept the crowd of reporters in dismissal, and then Molly felt his grip tighten. "Allen, the car," he ordered, his voice cracking with authority.

"What is it?" Molly asked, disturbed by the tone of his voice.

"Stay here." He unobtrusively motioned for his bodyguards, and three men quickly moved forward.

Oblivious to the cryptic gesture, Molly asked, "Why?"

"I'll be right back," was all he said. "Stay put." And he turned back to face the room. Near the rear door, not visible until the reporters had shifted positions at the end of the conference, was Rifat's ADC. Carey had seen him once at a party in Cannes. They'd exchanged banal phrases while Rifat overwhelmed the young actress in their party with his charm. Carey remembered the man's cool gaze, which didn't entirely conceal his hunter instincts. It wasn't a face one forgot. Oh fuck, oh shit. Rifat's man here in Minneapolis. His alarm set off danger signals in his brain. Molly was here, protected by his people. But Carrie was home alone, with only Lucy for company. And, spinning around, he began to run.

Glancing at his watch, Ceci walked as rapidly as possible without attracting notice, through the red-carpeted hotel lobby. In five minutes the kidnapping should be accomplished, although the sight of Fersten bolting for the back door was not reassuring. Had he spotted him? Pushing through the revolving door, faced with the possibility Carey suspected something, he sprinted for his rental car. He hesitated briefly before turning on the ignition. According to plan, after assuring himself Carey was at the press conference long enough for the men to pick up the girl, he was to proceed to the airport where Timur was waiting to fly them home. Deraille and Reha were to rendezvous there with the girl in twenty minutes. If he changed his plans now, he would miss the airport rendezvous.

Another moment of indecision, and he decided to adhere to plan. Surely Deraille and Reha would accomplish their task. She was only a young girl.

CHAPTER 28

His security men behind him, Carey ran down the corridors and burst out the side door, sprinting for his car parked at the curb. Wrenching the door open, he leaped inside. "To Molly's," he barked, and Jess began pulling away before the men behind Carey had caught up with him. Intent on his search for a weapon, he didn't look up when two of the security men threw themselves into the accelerating limo. He kept a small Beretta in the compartment under the seat and, pushing the sliding door aside, he felt for it. The feel of the cool metal was comforting, as if he suddenly had more control of his fear or at least an even chance with the Rifats of the world. Slipping the gun into his jacket pocket, he turned to the two men breathing hard beside him and said, "I saw Rifat's man."

Even in his worst nightmares he'd never considered having his daughter involved in Egon's asinine scheme, and he passionately hoped his emotional reaction was the *over*reaction of a protective father. He hoped Rifat's aide was simply out to involve *him* somehow in Egon's problem. They couldn't know about Carrie. Could they? The story had only hit the newsstands today; they'd have had to leave Europe yesterday to be here this morning. He hoped they didn't know of Molly and Carrie, although he wasn't naive enough to think Rifat's right-hand man was in Minneapolis to enjoy the summer lakes. At best, *he* was the object of their visit; and the worst, he dared not contemplate. "Go through the light," he ordered, and Jess accelerated to avoid another car bearing down on the intersection. The one-way street had only moderate traffic at that time of the morning, and Jess wove through the three lanes at a smooth ninety. He took the left onto Helseth Memorial Highway on two tires, and pushed the speedometer into the red zone when Carey said, "Step on it."

As they neared the Merchandise Mart, the police cars were obvious.

Four of them were parked out front as though they'd skidded on ice to stop.

And a fire truck was half visible around the south side of the building.

Please God, Carey silently prayed, his hand gripping the revolver, the safety already switched off, *she doesn't belong in any of this*. Shutting his eyes briefly, he drew in a deep breath and asked any god who was listening for help. When his dark eyes opened, he spoke in curt phrases to the men beside him. "They're Turks. Don't give them an edge. Shoot first. We'll work up the defense later. If they're here at Molly's," his voice was totally without emotion, "they're after my daughter, and I want them *dead*." His hand was on the door handle as Jess braked, leaving tire marks on the pavement. "If you have any problems with this, stay in the car. I won't take offense." And he was out of the backseat before the Lincoln came to a complete stop. Up the front steps in three loping strides, he dashed through the door and took the stairs because the elevators were too slow.

When he reached the second floor, the apartment door was open, the lock plate broken from the jamb, and he could see through the foyer and hallway to the light-filled living room. The apartment was empty, deathly quiet, and when he turned back to the men who'd followed him up, his face was set in a hard brutal mask. "Check out the apartment. I'll meet you downstairs."

His heart was pounding in his ears. Damn Rifat! Damn predators like him who took their bloody barbarian ruthlessness to peaceful people in peaceful regions of the world. If Carrie was harmed . . . he wouldn't allow himself to think of possibilities beyond that. But flashback images of maimed children in Vietnam filled his mind, and he swore to drive away the searing vignettes, swore his revenge on Shakin Rifat for coming within a thousand miles of his daughter.

His Beretta poised, he surveyed the second-floor corridor swiftly, and took the backstairs down. The mezzanine floor was as quiet as the second, but he was cautious when he opened the stairwell door into the corridor. Nothing . . . no one. And the absence of people was foreboding. Three offices on the mezzanine were normally busy with activity. A uniformed policeman stood near the main floor office when Carey eased the ground floor doorway open. One policeman and four cars outside. It wasn't reassuring. Where was Carrie?

The inside of his mouth was dry as it had been when he'd patrolled the jungles of Vietnam, never knowing if his next step was going to be his last. Taking a careful breath to calm himself, and at the same time reminding himself this was not Vietnam, death was not wholesale insanity in Minneapolis, he slipped his Beretta into his jacket pocket and stepped out into the corridor. He approached the policeman with rapid strides. "I'm looking for my daughter," he said. In a hurry to find out from this man where his daughter was or get past him in the least possible waste of time, he kept his voice impersonal.

The man looked him over with an appraising glance. "Who're you?"

"Carey Fersten; my daughter lives here. There're four police cars outside. Why?"

"Don't know anything about your daughter." The man

showed no emotion. Even his voice was a monotone without intensity or force, the audible expression of the principle: This is only a job. When my eight hours are over, I go home. I plan to live until retirement.

"Four black-and-whites?" Carey persisted.

"We answered a burglar alarm and a fire alarm. I was assigned to keep the office secure when the building was evacuated. Most everyone headed out back. The rest of them went down the basement 'cuz someone here saw two men running that way."

Carey felt ludicrously like a reporter. "No one's seen a couple of young girls?" Lucy had decided to keep Carrie company that day. A special treat for her birthday.

"Sorry, can't help you." And he looked at his watch.

Carey's pulse was still racing, but he turned away with a casual nod. Passing the officer, he sprinted toward the basement stairs. At least, he thought, the police were there. Even if Rifat's men had come . . . he paused with sudden alarm. They could have been here, snatched Carrie, and left already.

As though a computer had short-circuited in his brain, fragmented mental impressions raced through his mind: What the hell was that aide's name? Damn Egon and his drug habit; damn Sylvie for ever walking into his life. Could he shoot the Turks with the police around? Maybe Carrie was safe with Lucy, playing the video games at the Savoy Hotel down the street, maybe Kiray, *that* was his name, was only at the press conference as a precaution, keeping track of him to keep track of Egon. That was it. Right, God? Jesus, he was losing it. But he'd *only just found* his daughter, and she was more precious to him than he'd ever imagined possible.

How many years had he tossed off the casual disclaimer to the familiar question about children? How many times had he said: "The world will survive just fine without any more Ferstens." And all he wanted to do right now was find Carrie, wrap his arms around her, and weep with relief.

But in the next pulsebeat, he wanted to track down Rifat

and "neutralize" him, as the intelligence agencies so euphemistically put it. Was that a normal paternal instinct? Or perhaps an overprotective response nurtured by too many special assignments with Mac and Ant and Luger during the winding down of the Vietnam Era, as the Defense Department referred to the fiasco that would otherwise have to be acknowledged as a lost war. But for the first time since arriving back home, Carey appreciated the lethal skills he'd acquired with Mac, Ant, and Luger. He intended to use them on Rifat.

The basement was typical of turn-of-the-century buildings. Heavy, rough-cut stone served as foundation, and the musty accumulation of nearly a century worth of dirt, dust, and darkness struck him halfway down the stairs. The silence at the bottom of the steps unnerved him, as if the vast rabbit warren of dark corridors and walled sections had swallowed up four cars of policemen. And it reminded him of the tunnels in Vietnam.

He moved slowly down the narrow passageway, weighing risk against survival. His was the kind of caution developed in deserted VC camps where a booby-trapped map if picked up would blow you away, or a dead buddy would be detonated to go off when you lifted his dog tags. His Beretta was out front as he checked each room he passed.

A faint sound reached him; had he heard a child's voice—or was he fantasizing? Straining his ears, he waited to hear the high-pitched tone again. There.

Then men's voices, low and muted, joined the child's, the undecipherable masculine resonance turning into an occasional audible word—and then many. *Hurt*, he heard, and then *gun* . . . Yes, yes, yes, *a child's voice*, and the thunder of his heart intensified. He ran without caution, racing toward the human voices, no longer weighing the risks.

A door stood ajar at the end of the corridor, emitting a cool white fluorescent light in a neat geometric pattern on the floor and wall. Sure that his daughter was behind the door, he charged through it.

Across the room, a policeman squatted before a small, dark-haired girl dressed in yellow shorts and a DisneyWorld T-shirt, surrounded by several other uniformed men. His eyes quickly scanned the men. Seven police; there were seven policemen and Lucy. But no Carrie!

He couldn't catch his breath. A sudden chill struck him like an arctic gale, and he stopped dead as though he'd come up against an invisible wall. He was too late. Rifat had her.

"Drop it, mister," a gruff voice said. The statement was harsh, without room for discussion. When Carey refocused on the group near Lucy, he saw seven handguns aimed at his head.

Ignoring the guns, absorbed totally with the loss of his daughter, he said, "Lucy, what happened to Carrie?"

"Fucking drop it, asshole, or you're going to lose it."

I already lost it, asshole, he wanted to say, *you're too late.* And he blamed himself a thousand ways for not anticipating Rifat's treachery. She was in his hands. He couldn't breathe when he thought of his daughter at Rifat's mercy. A man without mercy. He was sick with guilt and despair.

"Daddy!" He heard her first, and his head swiveled toward the sound at laser speed. A small blond head appeared from behind a burly policeman's leg, and then a slender tanned shoulder. Followed by the whole beautiful sight of her looking like a summer rose in a pale flowered sundress.

Quickly setting down his Beretta, Carey dashed toward her. Scooping her into his arms he hugged her, gratitude and gladness rushing through him like the answered prayers of childhood. For long moments he simply crushed her to him, breathless and deliriously happy. Something moved on his cheek, and he reached up to brush away the wetness, thinking somewhere in the disconnected emotions of hope and fear and joy crashing through his mind, that he'd never cried in sheer happiness before. And he learned in those few moments of deliverance that his happiness was bound forever with this small child and her mother. It was not entirely news. After all, it had been the source of much of his former misery.

A polite cough returned him to the circle of policemen in the starkly lit room . . . *and* Carrie's breathy, high rush of words which tumbled out the moment he transferred her to a perch on his left arm. He wasn't about to set her down. He held her as if her security were guaranteed only in his arms.

"There were bad guys, like in your movies . . . these bad guys pushed in the front door," she excitedly disclosed, "but Lucy and I ran as soon as they started banging through the door."

"We took the backstairs," Lucy interjected, tugging on Carey's sleeve.

"And ran for Theresa's office," Carrie finished.

"But one of the scary guys came out of the elevator before we got there." Lucy's eyes were huge as she recalled their flight.

"So we changed our minds and ran for the basement." They couldn't talk fast enough, each finishing the other's sentences.

"Carrie pushed the burglar alarm at the top of the stairs . . . and the fire alarm down the basement."

"Then I headed for the old coal cellar Mom and I found last year. It's so dark back there, no one could ever see us. Not even the monster from *Friday the 13th*."

"And they didn't," Lucy breathlessly added. "But they sure were looking."

"They didn't talk English," Carrie offered. "Who are they?" she asked, confident that Carey would know.

"I'm not sure," he lied, not inclined to share his suspicions with the local police. Kiray's men were probably long gone, and his own security men could protect Carrie now that he knew Rifat's intentions. He didn't have a lot of confidence in the power of a Midwestern police department over a man who had outmaneuvered every intelligence agency in the world.

"Any idea who they *might* be, mister—"

"Fersten," he volunteered. "Carey Fersten. No, I'm sorry, I don't."

"Do you have a license for that side arm?"

"Yes, sir." His voice altered into that sincerity he'd found convenient when dealing with military officers and police the world over. "Were any of the men chasing my daughter apprehended?"

"Well, mister," one officer said quietly out of the corner of his mouth, reminding Carey of a young Humphrey Bogart. "It's possible these girls have seen one too many TV shows. If you ask me, I'd say childish imagination and hysteria. Either of these girls hyperactive?" he soberly inquired, switching to a concerned doctor role.

Hysteria *would* be a convenient explanation, Carey thought, eager to avoid further dealings with the police. Just as he was about to agree with the officer's interpretation, another policeman noted, "Someone busted that apartment door. No finesse. The jamb was in splinters."

All the men's eyes traveled to Carey's Beretta lying on the floor, and the spokesman for the group who was apparently an amateur actor, ominously said, "You *know* the guys chasing these girls?"

Shit. The hysteria theory was out. Now how much of the truth was necessary to appease them? As little as possible. Talk of terrorists and international arms dealers would provoke endless interrogation . . . not to mention all the auxiliary agencies who would race in to take a piece of the action. And in the meantime, Rifat was safely in Italy, anyway.

"It's possible my ex-brother-in-law was involved . . . an obsessive practical joker—"

"*This* was a *joke*?"

Carey shrugged. "He takes drugs, he's wealthy, and he's

got too much time on his hands. He shouldn't have come over here."

"From where?"

He could see they were all thinking Colombia or Jamaica. "Germany. His family owns the Von Mansfeld Munitions Works." His inclusion of Egon's last name was deliberate; he'd discovered at a young age that titled folk were like baseball stars or Hollywood actors, attractive celebrities treated with a combination of insatiable curiosity and awe. And Sylvie's name had been a star attraction in the tabloid story, as well as in today's press conference.

"You the guy on TV today?"

Bingo. And now we alter course away from terrorists and kidnapping. Carey nodded.

"And she's . . ." The man hesitated, slightly embarrassed when he recalled the headlines repeated on TV.

"My daughter."

"I suppose your brother-in-law thought it would be a good time—"

"To play one of his irritating pranks on me. He probably heard about the press conference. *Ex*-brother-in-law, by the way."

"Sylvie von Mansfeld's your ex-wife, then."

"Yes." He knew what they were thinking; he could tell by the smiles forming on their faces. Sylvie's early films had been well publicized, and her nubile young body was as familiar to the world as it had been to him. "We've been divorced for several years," he politely added.

"Just a prank, hey?" La Dolce Vita after thirty years in the press was an accepted reality. How many thousands of photos and sensational stories had been published throughout the world depicting the amoral and bizarre amusements of the leisured money class? While most people worked their way toward retirement one predictable day at a time, the beautiful people looked for ways to amuse themselves.

"I'm afraid so. Look, if I could make amends for your

inconvenience . . ." He turned on his most charming smile. "Say a contribution to some police fund? It's the least I could do for all your hassle."

And after a few more moments' discussion they traded business cards, Carey apologized one more time, and said his business manager would send a check. "Thank you very much for responding so promptly to my daughter's call for help." Carey and the two girls waved good-bye from the building entrance.

Theresa and the office staff were introduced to the two security men who would be, Carey said, "keeping an eye out for photographers."

Then Carey and the girls returned to the apartment, where he called Allen first, then talked to Molly, apologizing for leaving so abruptly. He explained that he'd recognized someone in the crowd. Yes, everything was fine, and he'd see her in ten minutes when Allen brought her home. The birthday girl, he reminded her, was waiting for the party to begin.

While Allen and Molly were driving over, he helped the girls prepare for Carrie's party, and then went into Molly's drafting room to make some calls. Although Kiray was probably halfway to Rome, Carey couldn't be sure another attempt might be tried. And if it wasn't Carrie's birthday today, he would have immediately removed her from any possible danger. The split second after he knew Pooh was safe, he had decided to take Molly and his daughter away to safety. Although his decision was firm, he realized diplomacy would be required when he told Molly.

Tomorrow morning he intended to bring Molly and Carrie north to his father's estate. Bernadotte had a sophisticated security arrangement to protect his home, thanks to all his old contacts in MI6. An intelligence officer attached to the British army in the last years of WWII, he'd never lost his love of gadgetry.

The most difficult task was going to be convincing Molly to leave her business for a time. Perhaps he could coax her with the idea of a family vacation in which he and Carrie could become better acquainted. He could already hear Allen screaming about overruns. "Fuck it," he muttered and called his father.

Their conversation was simple, but Bernadotte understood his son's purpose once Egon's name was mentioned. "By all means," he said, "stop by and see me."

Carey hadn't mentioned Carrie or Molly in the event the phone was tapped. He respected Rifat's intelligence. But Bernadotte knew from experience that Carey never called ahead to discuss his impending visits. Apparently something was in the air. When he replaced the receiver, he smiled and went to find his housekeeper. They were going to have houseguests. And if he interpreted his son's tone of voice properly, one was going to be a female houseguest. An unprecedented event for Carey.

In the few short moments since the police had departed, the entrance to the Merchandise Mart was awash with reporters who'd trailed Carey from the press conference. His abrupt departure hinted prominently at another story, and a crowd of reporters were milling about on the sidewalk. The two security men were hopelessly outnumbered.

When Allen's car pulled up, reporters surged over to it like a wave of curiosity. Allen and Molly alighted from the sleek black car, and the security men did their best to clear a path through the jostling throng.

"Did ya have a lovers' quarrel?"

"Hey, Allen, are you the lady's new escort?"

"Where's the little girl?"

"Is Carey here?"

"Has Carey skipped town?" He was not known for his faithfulness. The nasty barb was punctuated by the whirring click of camera shutters.

"Leave the lady alone, guys," Allen said as he shoved his

way through, one arm protectively around Molly's shoulder. "You heard all the news at the press conference."

"You gonna be able to keep him, lady, in your love nest?"

Molly's face flushed pink at the crude question and her temper began a slow simmer. Now instead of some duchess being chased from a hotel or a starlet photographed nude on a secluded Adriatic beach, *she* was the newest object of their attention. The situation was without precedent in her extremely normal life and it annoyed her. Because of Carey's reputation, she became an occupant of a *love nest*. Personally, she viewed her old factory turned Merchandise Mart as an energetic business employing forty some people, catering to wholesalers in the approximate neighborhood of a quarter million customers a year. Hardly the accepted connotation of "love nest."

Once inside the gate, Allen withdrew his arm. "Sorry, Molly. They must have followed Carey here."

"There're more photographers than ever. Is this normal for him?" She straightened the belt on her dress, which had been grabbed as she pressed through the crowd.

"He's newsworthy, I guess."

"His love life's newsworthy, you mean."

Allen wasn't about to touch that with a ten-foot pole. "The entertainment business attracts attention—unfortunately." He fell back on the platitudes.

"Carey Fersten's tastes attract attention even more." There was a distinct snappishness in the softly spoken words.

Allen gauged the distance to the door and straightened his baseball cap in a nervous gesture. Normally he ran interference with Carey's irate females, but Molly Darian didn't fall into the usual category of transient playmate. He was treading on very delicate ground. "Try and ignore the reporters, Molly. They just like to sensationalize everything."

"And with six nude starlets and Carey on a secluded Greek isle a year ago, sensationalizing is hardly required." He'd been smiling, damn him, his hair still wet from the sea, she remembered, looking athletic and capable, as if one girl or several were no trouble at all.

Allen opened the door to Molly's stairway entrance with relief. Clearly, she wasn't in the mood to be pacified, and in any event, that week in April would be impossible to unsensationalize, anyway. No one had slept for more than a few hours the entire week. Although, come to think of it, Carey had spent time occasionally brooding alone on a rocky cliff overlooking the sea. But then he'd never been one to appreciate female company for an extended period of time. Including his wife's. In fact, Sylvie's major complaint had been Carey's long, incommunicative periods when he'd refused to come out of his study. Who the hell would have, though, when Sylvie was in one of her moods? With her acid tongue, she could incite a saint to murder.

Enlisting in the marines and marrying Sylvie—Carey had always said they were the two major blunders in his life. "Which I survived," he'd say, "thanks to the grace of God and chemicals."

"Carey asked me to bring the birthday presents in," Allen said, opting for the coward's way out. The numerous presents could have been carried in by the driver, but leaving Molly now avoided discussion of Carey's lovelife. Christ, what was he supposed to say? "Tell Carey I'll be right up," Allen hastily said and escaped.

Carey was pacing before the windows facing the downtown skyline, his jacket and tie discarded, his shirt open at the neck, his sleeves rolled up. His energy always startled her; there was raw vitality in every fluid movement of his muscular body, as though leashed lightning lay just beneath the surface. When he saw her enter the room, his smile flashed in welcome.

"Darling, forgive me for rushing off. Everything's fine. Carrie's fine. Sorry about the press. How are you feeling?" He crossed the width of the room. Reaching out, he took her hands in his and looked at her with a quiet scrutiny, as though he hadn't seen her for years instead of merely minutes. Carrie's safe, you're safe, he thought, comforted by the warmth of her touch—and her presence. He relaxed completely for the first time since spotting Kiray at the back of the conference room.

"I'm feeling tense—and why shouldn't Carrie be fine? The press is obnoxious as usual, and I'm in a frame of mind that would prefer a soothing answer rather than the literal truth."

He bent to kiss her gently on the cheek. "I'll have the press cleared away soon, I'm sorry you're tense, and Carrie and Lucy are primping in their best eight-year-old fashion for the birthday party. I hope you don't mind—I invited Lucy to stay the night. She's Pooh's 'most absolute favorite best friend,' to quote a phrase." And he grinned with fatherly amusement when he recalled Carrie's excitement in adding Lucy to her family party. "Come, sit, relax, if that's possible after that press melee, and I'll soothe your temples or massage your toes or pour you a wicked belt of bourbon—whatever would do the most good for your strung-out nerves."

"A mild explanation of your abrupt departure would do, for starters," Molly quietly said, "and then if possible," she added with a smile, "a denial of all the past women in your life would go a long way toward invalidating the last question I was asked before the garden gate closed downstairs. 'You gonna be able to keep him, lady, in your love nest?' Feel free to lie." Pulling her hands away, she walked the few feet to her favorite overstuffed chair and collapsed into it, feeling as though she'd plowed the back forty in ninety degree heat with a single mule and a dull plowblade.

Oh shit, Carey thought. The reporters were just as diplomatic as usual. "You're the only woman in my life," he said, standing tanned and blond and handsome in the middle of her living room. "You've always been the only woman in my life. And, with the exception of a temporary case of insanity overcoming me during my brief marriage to Sylvie, I swear, I've never looked at another woman."

"Thank you," Molly said, her blue-eyed gaze veiled through half-lowered lashes. His powerful body was enhanced somehow by the stark simplicity of his white shirt and navy slacks. Larger than life, striking, he resembled some modern-day pagan god.

"Your servant, ma'am," Carey replied, the gentleness of his tone a contrast to the breadth of his shoulders, the primitive strength of his body. "I left the conference room," he went on, his dark eyes trained on Molly, "because I caught sight of a man I'd met once at Cannes. He shouldn't have been in Minneapolis." He hadn't moved, his stance as controlled as his quiet voice. "It's beyond his normal venue, so I panicked and came to check on Carrie."

Molly sighed. "I don't want to know this, do I?" Too much had happened in the last few days, too much public attention and rude questioning, too much upheaval in her life. Carey had brought his world with him when he'd reentered her life, and the turmoil and adjustments were peaking today.

"Nothing happened." His voice was reassuring, but he still hadn't moved and his posture betrayed his uneasiness.

"Was the man French? From Cannes?" A morbid curiosity overcame her fatigue and weariness. "Was he a reporter?"

"No."

"No? That's it?"

"Allen's going to be here any minute, along with Carrie and Lucy. Could we discuss this—" he paused and half smiled "tonight?" He'd need time to explain all the intricacies of his relationship to Egon. Time to decide what to reveal and what to omit. And most of all, time to determine whether he should explain the threat to Carrie. When she didn't protest, he walked over and touched her hand where it rested, small and pale, on the chair arm. "I love you, Honeybear," he murmured, squatting beside her chair so he could look into her eyes. "More than anything . . . and today's our baby's birthday. Give me a smile now, and I promise to zap all those reporters before evening for my Honeybear."

She smiled then, despite herself. "Seriously?"

"Seriously." And he meant it. He'd given orders to his security chief: No matter how many men it took, he wanted the entire block cleared by evening. When Molly looked out the window, *any window*, she was not to see a single reporter.

His security chief Matt Black had said, "You know they can file assault charges if we come on too strong."

"Let them," Carey replied, "we'll be gone early in the morning. All I need from you is one quiet night. Do what you have to do."

But before Molly could inquire further, Carrie and Lucy came running into the room, both dressed in party dresses.

"Mom, Mom," Carrie excitedly exclaimed, the jonquil ribbon in her hair bobbing as she bounced from one foot to the other, "you'll never guess what happened. Some men tried to get into the apartment, but we wouldn't let them in because you've always said, 'Never let strangers in.' And Mom, when we saw them through the peephole they were gruesome, I mean, all funny-looking like this." She pressed her cheeks back and stretched her mouth into a grimace. "So we ran away down the backstairs and rang the burglar alarms and fire alarms. And then the police came, and then Carey came. And we never saw the bad men again, even though they came down the basement looking for us."

Molly's fingers had tightened perceptibly over the chair arms as her daughter's recital unfolded.

"Carey told the police," Carrie went on, her eyes sparkling with excitement, "he's got a brother-in-law—"

"*Ex*-brother-in-law," Carey swiftly interjected.

Carrie took a much needed breath. "Ex-brother-in-law who likes to play jokes."

Molly's gaze quickly swung to Carey. "Jokes?" she murmured with a cool skepticism.

"It's Egon," Carey offered, as if the name alone was explanation.

"Connected with the man from Cannes?" Molly inquired in a tone that was a trifle too soft.

"Sort of."

"Carey Fersten, is this dangerous?" she asked.

"No," he quickly replied, his glance sliding sideways toward the girls.

"The policemen shook hands with Carey-er-Daddy," his daughter amended with a smile, "afterward. They know his wife."

"*Ex*-wife," he carefully amended.

"And everyone was friends," Lucy added.

Molly's eyebrows rose. "How nice."

"Look—" Carey began to say, only to be interrupted by a crashing sound from the vicinity of the hallway.

Allen stood holding two packages while the remainder of those he'd been carrying were scattered in colorful disarray at his feet.

"For me!" Carrie squealed.

At which point Jess came puffing up the stairs from the garden entrance ladened with more presents.

"Mom, *Mom*! Look at *all* my presents!" Carrie danced and hopped in delight, her eyes filled with joy. "Wow, wow, wow, *wow*!"

It was impossible not to share in her daughter's elation, impossible not to marvel at the pride and doting affection in Carey's expression. After all the years of Bart's blatant indifference as a father, a warm pleasure filled her heart. Maybe the reporters weren't so far wrong when they chose bizarre terms like love nest and love child. Carrie *was* their love child, conceived in love and adored. And with Carey in her home, busy with the girls and Allen and Jess in picking up the packages, his teasing making the girls giggle and laugh, maybe it was a love nest, indeed.

And a second later he was beside her, reaching for her

hands and pulling her up from her chair into the curve of his arm. "I'll never be able to thank you enough for giving me Carrie," he whispered, his mouth brushing her cheek, "if I live into the fifth millennium."

"I'm happy you're her father," Molly said, lacing her arm around his waist.

"Not as much as I," Carey murmured, feeling complete and whole for the first time in his life.

"Can I open them *now*?" Carrie screamed, disturbing her parents' idyllic moment. Carey turned with an immediate, "Yes," while Molly simultaneously answered, "After you blow out your candles."

"Yes, after you blow out your candles," Carey amended with a wide smile. "Now let's get this special nine-year-old's birthday show on the road." With a quick squeeze he released Molly. "Come on, Mom, our birthday girl's impatient."

Allen and Jess politely attempted to excuse themselves in the event they were intruding, but were coaxed to stay. The candles were lit on the cake, Happy Birthday was sung with boisterous cheer, and nine candles were blown out with a pinch to grow an inch.

After a consenting nod from her mother, wrappings were feverishly torn off and Carrie squealed, oohed, and aahed as she opened her presents. Carey had been calling orders into New York for days, not to mention the shopping he'd had Allen handle for him here in town. She received enough frilly dresses and play clothes to open a store, red cowboy boots with her initials embossed on the sides, a string of miniature pearls and tiny pearl earrings in an unusual golden shade (to match her hair, her dad smilingly remarked). There was also a baby doll from France with real hair, complete with doll wardrobe in its own matched set of Hermès luggage.

"Are you too grown up for baby dolls?" Carey inquired with an indulgent smile.

"Nope," Carrie replied, cradling the lifelike doll against her flushed cheek. "I've always wanted a brother or sister."

The portable compact disc machine with earphones was greeted with an ecstatic cry of delight, and the carrying case with a dozen discs was quickly perused. "How did you know all the cool bands, Dad?" Carrie asked.

"Even us old folks know one or two hot tunes, sweetheart," Carey replied, his hand covering Molly's on the lace-covered table, his dark eyes filled with delight. Last week he'd controlled his impulse to bring in a band from L.A. for her birthday, knowing Molly preferred a smaller celebration.

Molly had bought Carrie the canopy bed she'd always wanted, complete with ruffled buttercup-yellow bedcover. She'd slipped a picture of it into a card saying: Delivery tomorrow, Happy Birthday from Mom.

"Oh, Mom!" The swoon in her voice was reflected in her expression. "Thanks, thanks, thanks. It's exactly the exact one I've always wanted. Exactly!" And Molly realized how little control "parenting" had on the power of the gene pool. Her daughter viewed the world with unrepressed enthusiasm, which she as a mother had neither bequeathed nor imbued in her. Turning to Carey with a smile, she said, "She's like you."

Smiling back, he seemed to understand. "I know," he said.

And when their daughter saw the documents tied with pink ribbons making her the owner of her own two-year-old Arabian horse, the birthday proceedings came to an instant standstill, only to explode a moment later.

"My own horse, my *absolute own* horse! Where *is* she? When can I *see* her? *Who's* going to teach me to ride? Mom! Look! Look!"

"A *horse*. How wonderful," Molly said to her daughter, who was waving the papers in front of her face. When Carrie raced away to show them to Allen and Jess, Molly turned to Carey and said, "A horse?" in an altogether different tone of voice. "Here, in the city?"

"No, darling, it's up at my father's farm."

"Do you still race?" She had forgotten about his love of horses.

"Occasionally," said the only man in twenty-seven years to win the triple crown in steeplechase.

"Your dad can teach you to ride," Jess said, "and Leon can help out."

"Leon's *my* dad's trainer, Pooh," Carey explained. "He's the best teacher in the world. And as soon as you can, we'll go up north and see your horse."

"*Mom* . . . did you hear? When can we *go?*"

Allen and Carey exchanged glances.

"Whenever your Mom says the word," Carey replied, "we'll head north."

"Can Lucy come? It's summer vacation. Lucy, your mom will let you, won't she?" and in a quick succession of rapid fire dialogue between the young girls, it was agreed Lucy's mother might be amenable.

Molly merely smiled and said, "We'll see about going, darling."

The rest of Carrie's presents turned out to be riding gear: boots, a jacket, jodhpurs, a silk shirt, and a small velvet hat.

Carey thanked his lucky stars he'd selected a horse for one of Carrie's gifts; it gave him an excuse for suggesting a trip north and means for taking them to safety without alarming Molly. And his daughter was proving to be a great help in his plan.

She gathered up all her riding equipment and announced, "Lucy and I are going to try all this on now, and then we're going to learn how to ride. Right, Dad?" And in her inimitable fashion, assuming the world would recognize her onward motion as its own, she added before she and Lucy ran from the room, "I can hardly wait!"

Allen looked at Carey.

Jess looked at Carey.

Molly looked at Carey.

"It was a real nice party, wasn't it?" he said with a smile.

CHAPTER 29

While Ceci and his team were inside their plane, re-assessing their options in a mission gone bad, Sylvie von Mansfeld's private jet touched down on a nearby runway at Minneapolis/St. Paul International Airport. The man she'd sent ahead to locate Carey met her as she descended from the plane.

"Come along," she said, and walked briskly toward the Mercedes limousine parked conveniently near. "You can give the address to the driver," she added, stepping through the chauffeur-opened doorway into the car. After listening to Egon's recital of Rifat's handiwork, she had ordered a bullet-proof car, though she had little faith in such precautions. Sylvie was not only a bold woman, but a fatalist, as well. Men like Rifat didn't strike terror in her soul as they did in Egon's. She'd always been able to manipulate men, and even Shakin Rifat was a man under his formidable reputation.

When the investigator she'd hired attempted to join her in the backseat, she indicated with the merest nod that he should sit up front with the driver. When one's family owned the second-largest munitions works in the world, one learned the rudiments of authority in the nursery. And Sylvie had been born to command. "I'm in a hurry," she said to her driver. "This man will tell you where to go." And, leaning back into the plush seat, she crossed one leather-clad leg over the other, closed her eyes, and mentally rehearsed her dialogue with Carey.

Egon had received a phone call two days ago—a call from one of Rifat's minions, warning Egon not to leave the villa. Since then Egon had fallen off the wagon and started taking heroin again. Devious by necessity, he'd obtained the drugs without leaving the premises. Now Sylvie was here to try to talk Carey into coming back to help him. No one else could reach Egon when he was on drugs, and she knew a phone call to Carey would have been unsuccessful. He'd been adamant last time that it *was* his *last* time.

Should she plead, demand, reason? How best to approach Carey? she mused. A few years ago she would have been more certain, but he wasn't the same Carey Fersten any longer. He was *serious*, noticeably serious, a quality that hampered her familiar overtures. Thank God he cared for Egon. If all else failed, she'd resort to tears. Rasinsky had praised her dramatic weeping scene in the small Balzac film they'd done years ago. Now what were those lines . . . As she recalled first one phrase, and then another, the sentences began falling into place.

"He needs you, Carey, now more than ever. He's alone, desperately alone and in despair. If you don't care, I'm afraid this time he's going to slip away." The words began tumbling through her mind, with the pauses for effect, the exact moment the first tears welled up into her eyes, the gulping swallow to stanch the flood of weeping.

Her eyes opened, and she smiled.

Why hadn't she remembered the Balzac play sooner?

CHAPTER 30

Allen and Jess had excused themselves and left, promising to send a car sent round at six the next morning. Although Molly hadn't been persuaded yet, Carey was hoping she'd understand the need for precautions. The girls were in Carrie's room, listening to the new disc player, while Carey and Molly sat at the dining room table, smiling at each other over the shambles of the birthday cake and discarded wrapping, feeling like serenely contented parents.

"I always knew," Molly whispered.

"No you didn't." A lush smile accompanied the disclaimer.

"Well, I wished for it."

"Not as much as I."

"She even smiles like you."

"Like us."

"It's us, isn't it?" Molly wiggled her hand under his to feel the warm connection.

"Till the rocks melt with the sun." His large hand engulfed hers.

"You always liked Burns."

"I liked you a million times more."

"Only a million?"

He grinned. "Greedybear."

"For you."

"Good."

"Good, kiss me." And as their lips touched in a lingering silkiness, the pealing of the doorbell broke into the confines of the dining room.

"Don't answer," Carey whispered, his breath warm on her mouth.

"I always answer." And she tipped her head away.

"Why?"

"Why? Politeness, I guess."

"Not a good reason."

"This is Minnesota."

"An explanation, but not a reason."

"You're too blasé for me, darling." But after Molly went downstairs to answer the insistent ringing, she wished she hadn't.

A dazzling woman stood in her doorway. From the shouts of the paparazzi, there was no question that this was Sylvie von Mansfeld, Carey's ex-wife. And when Molly's eyes swept back from the jostling photographers to the luscious young woman, she was appalled and amazed. The young woman, was, if possible, more opulent in person than in any of the provocatively posed ads for her movies. Above medium height, very slender, wearing tight leather pants with a matching electric-blue silk shirt, she displayed a resplendent voluptuousness that would stop men in their tracks. Gazing at her, Molly was filled with horrified admiration.

"Carey," Sylvie demanded in only slightly accented English, abruptly curtailing Molly's astonishment, "I wish to see him." And before Molly could reply, Sylvie had swept past her and was running lightly up the stairs.

Molly lagged behind, since she had to shut the door

against the flashing cameras. She was in time, however, to see Sylvie run to Carey, throw her arms around him, and burst into tears.

Standing awkwardly stiff, Carey's eyes met Molly's over the gamin curls of his ex-wife. "Excuse us for a minute," he said, and walked her out on the terrace.

Molly heard his low, murmuring voice. Almost immediately Sylvie's strident, rapid tone broke in, this time in German. After that, Molly lost track of even the bits of audible conversation because Carey also shifted into German. Seconds later, a harsh "No!" from Carey was decipherable. Undeterred by the powerful refusal, Sylvie forged on in a curt rush of words. And then there was more weeping.

Feeling as if she were intruding, Molly walked into the living room. But even a room away, the sound of their voices drifted in, lowering occasionally so she only heard the murmuring inflection, rising as suddenly so each word was audible although the meaning was lost to her in German.

Carey was refusing.

Sylvie was insisting, demanding, and then abruptly pleading and crying at the same time. Her great, gulping sobs carried into the living room. Steeling herself to remain seated, Molly imagined Carey's ex-wife crying in his arms. He'd lived with her for three years, had wakened in the morning with her, had smiled at her over breakfast, had spent *three years* being a husband to her.

Did he still have feelings for Sylvie? she wondered. Good God, she was sex goddess to half the men in the world. He had to feel the normal male attraction to her. Suddenly Molly felt like a small, nondescript sparrow next to a bird of paradise. Regardless of what Carey said about their relationship, how could she compete with memories of a glittering woman like Sylvie? And right now, she was competing with more than memories. The little sex kitten of the eighties was wetting his chest with tears, and it would take a solid block of granite to resist those hiccupy whimpers. *Molly* was even beginning to feel the glimmerings of pity for her. The poor woman was definitely in distress.

A few moments later, Carey and Sylvie entered the room and brief introductions were made. Molly sympathetically remarked, "I'm so sorry . . . can I be of any help?"

"Carey's help will be sufficient. I'm sure we don't need you intruding."

"Watch it, Sylvie," Carey warned, exasperated at both her rudeness and implication. "I only said I'd call him."

"But, darling, I know you won't be able to resist the poor boy when you speak with him." Sylvie slid her arm through Carey's and tenderly explained to Molly, "Carey's always such a dear with our family; I just knew he couldn't refuse."

Carefully setting Sylvie a good two feet away, Carey replied, "A phone call doesn't require all this damn melodrama, Sylvie. Play your Balzac role for another audience."

"You remembered." She brightened with a tinsel glitter of feigned sincerity. "But of course, you always prompted me for all my roles."

"Jesus, cut the bull, Sylvie, or I'll have to put on my boots . . . You know damn well your drama coach did all the prompting."

But Molly interpreted Carey's responses as a touch too protesting.

"You always said you adored me in the Balzac play."

"What I said, Sylvie," and he was pronouncing the words with fastidious emphasis, his nostrils flaring slightly with his efforts to control his temper, "was I adored the Balzac play, and I liked your costumes."

"Such a sense of humor, darling." She swung around to Molly in a flash of electric blue silk, gleaming leather, and platinum hair. "He always loved to tease." Her voice was a catty purr. "Have you known him long enough to notice?" she inquired with malice.

"Actually," Molly said, "we spend so much time laughing,

I've missed two payrolls and Carey's cut three scenes from his movie."

"Ah, American humor," Sylvie retorted without a smile. "How droll. If nothing else," she said, insult obvious in her eyes as she surveyed Molly from head to toe, "she can amuse you, I suppose."

"*That* is enough, Sylvie."

"Darling, I meant it as a compliment. Dolly seems very pleasant. And so clever to own an entire building this large," she added, sarcasm dripping from every word. Her own inherited empire was valued at several billion.

"She at least bought it with money she earned herself."

"How industrious. Does she sew, as well?"

"One more word, Sylvie, and you can handle your brother's problems yourself."

"My lips are instantly sealed, darling. Egon needs you so."

"I'm sorry," Carey apologized as though Sylvie didn't exist. "She's a bitch."

"No need for an apology," Molly replied, tense and agitated. This glamorous striking woman, glossy with sheer physical perfection, probably owned more property around the world than the acreage of Texas. She didn't seem one bit insulted at being called a bitch. Wealth must insulate one from insult. And for the very first time in her life, Molly felt intimidated. How ludicrous her scramble for the down payment money seemed in contrast to Sylvie's fortune. She found herself gazing at Sylvie's earrings, the diamonds and sapphires large enough to choke on. Without a doubt, she forlornly decided, they were worth a dozen of her factory buildings. How does one compete against that kind of wealth and glamour? Put another tuna casserole in the oven? Damn, damn, damn, she was out of her league.

But just then Carey slid his arm around her shoulder and whispered in her ear, "I'll have her out the door in five minutes." And when she looked up, his smile was that special one she remembered from the summer dock on Fourteen when they'd dangled their toes in the water and argued about who loved each other more. He kissed her on the cheek quickly and, turning back to Sylvie, said, "Sylvie, sit down, don't say a word, and I'll call Egon and see what the hell I can do long distance."

"Excuse me, darling," he said to Molly with a small, encouraging smile. Moving toward the small desk under the window, he picked up the phone and swiftly punched in the numbers. He flashed Molly another smile as he waited for the transatlantic connection, and then, in rapid Italian, asked for Egon.

His spine went rigid, and his next few sentences were crisp, staccato questions. Two deep frown lines appeared between his brows, and Molly interpreted his dismay. Slamming the receiver down, Carey said, "He's bolted."

"You have to go after him." Sylvie's voice revealed the command she'd spent a lifetime cultivating.

Carey's gaze swung round to her, and he hesitated a brief moment before he said, "No."

"You *have* to," she cried, rising from her chair in a swift, vehement movement. "They're after him! You know they are! They'll hurt him!"

He knew as well as Sylvie did that Rifat was behind Egon's hasty flight. He hesitated in a moment of compassion. But he couldn't go—not when Carrie and Molly needed his protection, as well. He told Sylvie as much; He was responsible for a family now.

But she wouldn't listen to his reasoning. She didn't want to hear about anyone or anything standing in the way of his aiding Egon.

Even the revelation that he had a daughter failed to evoke her interest. She and Carey had never discussed having children since she'd had no intention of ever having any. And as far as Carey having a few children here and there: surely with his reputation with women, it was inevitable. She really didn't understand his extravagant concern for *one* child. "If you're worried about your family, hire guards," she casually suggested.

"I have."

"Well then, you're free to go."

"She's my *daughter*, Sylvie, do you understand? My *daughter*. And after ten long years, Molly and I are going to be married."

"I'm sure they'll be fine until you return," she retorted, not even glancing at Molly. "My plane is waiting."

"Read my lips," he growled, hot-tempered at her callousness. "*I'm not going*."

"He'll die."

"Maybe."

"They'll torture him."

He hesitated again because he knew as well as she did that they would. "Maybe."

"I hear Rifat likes to watch when they scream," she said, turning the screws.

"Jesus Christ, Sylvie, I'd go if I could. I can't, that's all." And a great wave of pity washed over him. Poor Egon. In too deep this time. And Shakin didn't care how he got those prototypes.

"Dammit, you *have* to!" Sylvie screamed.

"Have to what?" a lazy male voice inquired from the hallway. When Bart strolled into the room carrying his birthday gift for Carrie, he found himself the cynosure of three pairs of startled eyes. "Have I interrupted something?" he drawled, taking in the splendid but irate Ms. von Mansfeld, the equally irate Mr. Fersten, and a thoroughly horrified ex-wife who had never been party to a conversation in which human torture was discussed as though one were comparing sales prices on mattresses.

"Bart, you'd better come back later," Molly said tersely.

"I would if I could, darling," he replied with a flash of white teeth, "but Eldora Whitney wouldn't understand if her escort for the symphony reneged."

Up to his old tricks, Molly thought. A brief ten minutes for Carrie's birthday, and then off to more important things like escorting Minneapolis's wealthiest patroness of the arts. Eldora kept a stable of handsome young men as escorts, and she was generous with them, as well. Molly almost said, "And what accounts has she promised you?" but caught herself in time. She refused to lower herself to Bart's level. "In that case, why don't you go down to Carrie's room and visit with her there?"

After dropping the Walgreen's bag he carried on a nearby table, Bart was already halfway to Sylvie. When he spoke his eyes focused directly on her cleavage. "I don't believe we've met before. I'm Bart Cooper, Molly's ex-husband." His glance rose and he smiled. "Hello."

"Hello," Sylvie purred, instantly assessing the usefulness of an ex-husband to irritate Carey. Perhaps if he became incensed or resentful over a past rival, he might forget his very *new* sense of familial responsibility long enough to be persuaded to go after Egon. "How nice of you to come to your *daughter's* birthday. Carey was just telling me how *fond* he is of her. I'm Sylvie von Mansfeld, Carey's ex-wife. Isn't this cozy—a quartet of exes."

"I *knew* you looked familiar," Bart said, his smile cordial. "May I take this opportunity to tell you how much I've enjoyed your movies?"

"Thank you, making films is such a lark." Their dialogue could have been from a thirties film where both leads had slick hair and continental charm.

A lark, Carey thought irritably. What the hell role was that line from? Sylvie was a temperamental, sullen, always inadequately prepared "star" who insisted on preferential treatment every step of the way. A lark, indeed. Sylvie was every director's nightmare; she required a dozen takes for every piece of dialogue over two sentences long.

"Your joie de vivre shows on the screen," Bart complimented, his voice an octave lower for effect.

Along with everything else, Molly thought pettishly. "Bart, if you don't mind," she said to the man dressed immaculately in white linen like some colonial planter or Colombian drug czar, "I'm sure Carrie's anxious to open your present."

"I understand, you share fatherhood with Mr. Fersten. How delightful. One can almost envision a movie from the concept."

"A bedroom farce—French style." His smile was tight. "I was—I think the line is—the last to know, but hey, I'm a good-natured guy," he smoothly lied. Sylvie's presence had altered his intention to demand some monetary settlement. Bart Cooper bitterly resented being cuckolded, especially so publically. "When Carrie's birthday rolls around, I'm the first one to remember my special girl."

With the usual unwrapped present, this one obviously purchased at the Walgreen's down the block, Molly felt sickened by his hypocritical sweetness. Hopefully, it wasn't another Barbie doll like the last three birthday gifts he'd given Carrie, damn his indifference. She considered choking Bart until his fine white teeth turned blue. "Bart—" she reminded him, her voice low with frustration and rage.

"Am I in the way?" Bart asked.

"No," Sylvie said placidly, clashing with Carey and Molly's sharp, emphatic, "Yes."

"Actually, we were discussing a private matter, Bart, if you'll excuse us," Carey said, his voice carefully modulated. Whenever he saw Bart he thought of all the misery he'd caused Molly, and it took great self-control to remain civil. He also thought of Molly living with Bart for seven years, and feelings of jealousy overwhelmed him. "Molly asked you to leave . . . if you don't mind," he said, his eyes wintry as he motioned toward Carrie's room.

"In a minute," Bart replied, and turned back to Sylvie.

"I must insist," Carey said very quietly, struggling to maintain his composure.

Bart swiveled back slowly and lifted one dark eyebrow.

"Insist? Sounds like some chivalrous knight protecting his lady."

The air was palpable with tension.

"Oh, Carey's chivalrous all right," Sylvie cheerfully interjected, delighted to fuel the volatile situation. Maybe the woman would toss him out if sufficiently angered. Did she know his reputation for wildness? "Remember the young princess near Munich whose husband appeared unexpectedly at your private picnic? You were particularly chivalrous that time. The husband is very old, you see," she said, as though everyone was concerned with the details of the scandal, "and the princess likes to ride motorcycles and live dangerously. The summer afternoon temperatures didn't require many clothes, I heard," she went on, knowing Carey hated an audience for controversy, "and, well . . . under the circumstances, Carey felt obliged to defend the woman. It was all very romantic. Most men would have cut and run when Ludwig's touring car turned into the clearing. Gossip ran rampant for weeks. Marie told the story best; she's a cousin of mine and so sweet. I always thought Carey showed a remarkable sense of chivalry. Ludwig wanted to beat her."

Carey stood as if cut from stone, his dark eyes expressionless while Sylvie spoke. "Now if you're through," he said as she concluded her recital with a smug smile, "should you hear from Egon, tell him to call me."

"He may not live to call," she snapped.

"I'm sorry . . . if you'll excuse me." And he walked away.

Molly turned to Bart. "If you actually care to see Carrie for her birthday, you know where her room is." Her hostility was too intense to conceal. She looked very different from the woman in electric blue, her own dress a stark contrast as though the spring blossom pink was visual evidence as well of the enormous disparity in their lives. Suddenly uncomfortable in her own living room, she turned and followed Carey.

She found him in the kitchen sprawled on one of her painted pine chairs and looking grim.

He glanced up when she came in and ran a hand through his already ruffled hair in a slow, weary gesture. Sylvie's lacerating energy had apparently drawn blood. "I'm sorry," he said, "about the story and my unfortunate past. There's nothing else to say about Sylvie. She's a world-class bitch and that's it."

"She's pretty nice-looking," Molly said softly, seating herself opposite him at the kitchen table. *And there's a fortune sparkling in her ears*, she thought, looking at the kitchen curtains that should have been replaced last year.

"Who the hell cares?" he muttered.

"Bart does," she replied with a grin. When he heard the mischief in her voice he lifted his head and smiled wanly.

"Then he's welcome to her, with my blessing. What the hell did you ever see in—" he jerked his thumb in the direction of the living room, "him." Distaste was prominent in every word. Bart was everything he despised in a man— dressed as though he were ready for a photo shoot, haircut so trim the scissor marks must still be warm on his hair, and with that phony insouciance that always prompted Carey to clench his hands into fists to keep from taking a swing and cracking the slick facade.

"I could ask you the same about Sylvie," Molly replied, a hint of approbation in her tone, "but the answer's pretty obvious." She was much more warmly voluptuous in person— as though the two-dimensional screen neutralized her sun-ripened, perfumed *volume*.

"I was *not* sober. *I* had an excuse."

"Could we drop the subject?" Molly said with a sigh, unwilling to go into a topic they had rehashed on too many occasions. "I think we both agree we made a mistake."

"Lord, she puts me in a vicious mood," Carey growled, sliding lower in the chair. "When are they going to leave?"

"Now *that*, darling, depends on your handling of Sylvie.

Normally Bart wouldn't stay more than five minutes with Carrie—if he even remembers why he came here. On the other hand," she said contemplatively, "with anyone else but the world's sex kitten, I'd say Eldora Whitney and her millions would win out every time. However, Sylvie has her charms. Now that I think about it, you won't get me to bet on Bart leaving, one way or the other."

"There *is* Egon to consider, and Sylvie, despite her myriad faults, is loyal to him." Carey sighed, his mind in turmoil, his own loyalties strained in two directions. Molly and Carrie came first, of course, but his heart went out to Egon. He loved him, too, like one would a younger brother, and Egon was in horrendous trouble: His future was definitely in jeopardy. It was simply a matter of time before Rifat found him, and after that Sylvie could expect a ransom note with perhaps some portion of Egon's body as evidence of their sincerity.

When Rifat received the prototypes, he would profit for the next decade on every weapon manufactured. The profits in the arms industry had always been one of the great areas of capitalism. It was very much a matter of supply and demand, of pricing items to the limit of what the traffic would bear, and in many cases of selling to both parties in a conflict without scruple. The U.S. and Russia both understood the principles of free enterprise. They sold sixty-three percent of the arms manufactured in the world; and it was simply a matter of methodology to determine who was considered the number one or number two supplier of arms.

Always a sound businessman first, Rifat saw an opportunity to become involved in one of the most profitable businesses in the world. And poor Egon was the key, the man who would be used to help Rifat realize his ends. "She may not leave," Carey quietly said, thinking aloud. "Sylvie's persistent, if nothing else."

"Oh, she doesn't lack in the other departments, either, I assure you. Coffee? While you mutter your way through this?"

"No."

"Tea?"

He glanced up at her with a knit brow.

"Something stronger," she immediately suggested, her spirits pleasantly mellow now that Sylvie was *definitely* not a threat.

He smiled.

"Cognac?"

"Bring the bottle."

And Molly listened while he talked about the Egon he'd met the first summer in Yugoslavia.

"He sounds very nice."

"He is," Carey said, chinning the rim of his half-empty glass.

"How dangerous a position is he in?"

Carey shrugged, not willing to go into detail about Rifat. The less Molly knew of his involvement the better. He'd decided in the last several minutes as he talked to bring Molly and Carrie to his father's for safety as he'd planned, and then try to find Egon before Rifat did. He had to at least try to save him, or he'd never be able to live with himself.

But he'd do it without involving Sylvie. So after finishing his second cognac, he said, "Let's see if we can throw Sylvie and Bart out and enjoy what's left of Carrie's birthday." He wanted time, too, to discuss going north. Carrie's horse was the perfect excuse, and once there perhaps Bernadotte could help him convince Molly of the seriousness of Rifat's threat and talk her into staying.

With a promise to get in touch with Sylvie tomorrow, she was persuaded to leave, and Bart, practical man that he was, realized Eldora Whitney's promised account was decidedly more lucrative than an evening out with an international beauty, however enticing. Money came first with Bart. It always had.

"Do you or do you not feel a freshness in the air now that our guests have gone?" Carey asked with a wide grin.

"The stench of cauldrons bubbling has disappeared with

your ex-wife's departure, and the aroma of manure is retreating now that my ex-husband has descended the staircase in his planter's suit. I almost expected an overseer or two to materialize and say, 'Caught two more, Master, trying to escape.' "

Carey laughed. "He looked more like Tom Wolfe to me, he was so-o-o smooth. I was wondering where his orange tie and pink suede shoes were."

"Bart would die before affecting anything so lowly as a writer's style. Really, dear, consider, would any good club allow Tom Wolfe a membership?"

"Well, love, money talks. Sylvie has only a hundred-year-old title and wears blue leather pants or sometimes nothing at all and she belongs to some rather exclusive clubs."

"Bart doesn't have that kind of money."

"Oops . . . then he's blacklisted."

"Who's blacklisted?" Carrie asked, walking into the living room.

"Anyone with less than a million," Carey said, amusement in his eyes.

"That's us," his daughter cheerfully retorted.

"But not for long," her father replied.

"*Carey!* Don't talk that way," Molly protested, uncomfortable with his millions.

"*Mo-ther*," her daughter responded reproachfully, "it doesn't hurt to marry someone rich. Right, Dad?"

"And hey, I'm nice."

"There, you see, Mom."

Molly often felt she was the naive one and her nine-year-old daughter the seer of the world. "Thank you for pointing out my error," she said. "Should we check out Carey's bank account before we set a wedding date?"

"Don't have to, Mom, for sure he's got more than we do."

Carey held his tongue, not about to make a verbal misstep.

Molly would have liked to make some melodramatic

comment about pulling one's self up by the boot straps, her own financial independence too hard won to be dismissed next to Carey's millions. But she resisted the impulse and consoled herself with a small jab only. "Money shouldn't matter."

Carey had no intention of discussing the disparities in their incomes. "Why don't we change the subject?" he said with a smile. "My mother always said that when my father and I disagreed."

Molly's brows were still drawn together in a faint scowl. "Did it work?"

"She usually said, 'Let's go for a ride,' next which always did work," he replied in as neutral a tone as possible. He was walking a fine line here, needing to have his way about whisking them off while not giving the appearance of undue concern. "Speaking of riding," he murmured, his glance swinging to his daughter. "How would you like to go up north tomorrow and ride your horse?"

"Oh, Mom, *could* we?" Carrie pleaded, instant elation bubbling in her voice. "I just know I can ride! I really know I can! Think how many Black Stallion books I've read. I can practically do everything!" Doing a little dancing skip and a hop, she put her palms together and gazed up at her mother. "Say, yes, Mom—please, please, please, please, *please!*"

Carey smiled at the unrestricted vitality in his young daughter. "You're going to be a great rider." And he meant it. She had a natural fearlessness and competence, two primary components for world-class competition.

"I'll clean the kitchen for a month!" Carrie cried, "and my room too," she added, excitement flushing her cheeks. "And I promise to practice my piano every single night!"

"I'd like to go up tomorrow, if you could," Carey softly said, turning to Molly.

"Aw-w-right! Hear that, Mom? Two against one. *Hey! Lucy!*" Carrie's scream was deafening. "*Let's pack!*" And she was out of the room in two seconds.

"I'm not sure about this two against one," Molly muttered. "Should we talk about this?"

"It'll just be a quick trip," Carey lied. "She wants to go," he cajoled. "A day or two won't hurt your business, will it? And my father's anxious to meet you and Carrie. He'd be thrilled."

"Just for a day or so?" She debated the possibility of actually leaving her business when she never had before.

"Promise."

"Promise, promise?"

"Absolutely." Did a lie count when lives were at stake?

CHAPTER 31

They left at six the following morning. The street and sidewalks outside Molly's building were quiet and devoid of jostling newsmen, thanks to Matt Black's team. But he'd been right. It was going to cost Carey in lawsuits. Three of the reporters had screamed "sue your ass off" as they'd been hauled away.

That morning Allen contacted Sylvie at her hotel. He had a message from Carey: He'd try to find Egon as soon as he brought Molly and Carrie to a safe location. "Don't wait," Allen told her. "He said you should return home and he'll contact you in Nice or Frankfurt."

"What if I want to wait?" she said, her tone chill.

"Look, Sylvie, I'm not paid to argue with you. I'm delivering a message. But if you want some advice, I'd do what he says."

"And if I don't?"

"Hey, Egon's your brother, not mine."

"Damn him!"

"Jesus, Sylvie, he's doing you a favor."

"He always gives orders, never asks what I might want!"

Nothing else works with you, Miss Bulldozer Queen of the World, Allen wanted to say, but instead said, "Have a good flight home."

So that warm summer morning in June while Carey, Molly, their daughter, and her friend Lucy were being driven north to Bernadotte's estate, Sylvie was swearing her way through a hasty application of makeup after ordering her car brought round. If she knew where Bernadotte lived, she would have followed, but Carey had always carefully protected his father from Sylvie. As Bernadotte preferred tranquillity, he and Sylvie would not have mixed well.

"Ordered home like some underling, damn his arrogant ass," Sylvie muttered, throwing toilet articles into her overnight bag. She was dressed in an Yves St. Laurent nautical-theme slacks outfit, and looked as crisp as her temper in starched white and military blue braid. "And now I'm supposed to wait by the phone. I can't stand waiting . . . I *hate* it!" she breathed hotly. But her frustration was provoked not so much by the order as by the fact she had to obey or lose her best chance of helping Egon. She trusted Carey implicitly in this situation, unlike any hired investigators she might employ. No one understood her brother better than Carey; he seemed able to anticipate the direction of Egon's erratic thought process. So she sulked and muttered and swore under her breath, but she left because she needed Carey's help.

In Rome, Rifat had just received a cable from Barcelona. It was early in the afternoon, and the palazzo housing his office was cool, despite the high temperatures outside. His temperament was cool, as well.

The cable was encouraging after Ceci's unsuccessful mission, followed by the news of Egon's disappearance.

ON HIS TRAIL. NEAR RR STATION LAST NIGHT. POINTS LEFT BEHIND.

Egon would not be at his best on drugs, Rifat mused. A pleasant thought. He anticipated a speedy capture.

CHAPTER **32**

W hat's going to happen to Egon?" Molly asked after watching Carey silently contemplate the view out his window for the last twenty minutes.

He shrugged, too troubled to respond. Another five miles of suburban sprawl passed by as he tried to organize the turmoil in his mind . . . the major obstacle of Molly and her expected resistance, the overwhelming rush of emotion when he thought of how close Rifat had been to his daughter, the waves of fear and pity for Egon. And then, with an intrinsic decisiveness that was based more on feeling than logic, he decided now was as good a time as any to tell Molly his plans. Carrie and Lucy were in the front seat, happily chatting with Jess, and he hated keeping Molly in the dark. Taking a breath, he turned to her, his fair hair brilliant in the morning sun, his dark eyes watchful. "I'm going after him."

The words she'd been afraid of since Sylvie had appeared. She tried to repress the shock waves of anxiety. "Isn't that dangerous?"

"Not really."

"It's dangerous," she said, answering her own question. "You could be killed."

"I won't be killed," he said, his tone even.

"Or tortured." Molly's voice was beginning to take on the intensity he wanted to avoid.

"Look, darling—"

"I'd appreciate it," she said very softly, little daggers of anger underlying the gentleness, "if you didn't use that phony darling stuff with me. I'm not your ex-wife who responds to darling or bitch or apparently anything else you care to call her."

The subject has veered off track, he thought, but he preferred her frustration be directed toward Sylvie rather than toward him. "Of course. Forgive me."

"And don't be contrite just to avoid an argument. Dammit." She exhaled in a great sigh, knowing how childish she sounded. But *death* and *torture*? *How did she and Carey end up in this mess?* "Why are we even *having* this conversation? I shouldn't know a man who knows *terrorists*—or whatever you call people who try kidnapping little girls. And don't give me any of that crap about Egon's pranks, because I wasn't born yesterday. This car has bulletproof glass; I heard Jess tell Carrie. Jesus, *bulletproof glass*! What the hell is happening to my life? Terrorists shouldn't be any closer than the damn newspaper headlines."

"And they won't be," he said in the heated silence. "You'll be safe at my father's."

"Safe," she breathed in almost a whisper, turning so her body was directly facing his. "What the hell does that mean?"

Carefully Carey answered, "I'd like you to stay up north until I find Egon."

"This isn't a little jaunt to see a horse, is it?" She hadn't regained her voice, and her hands were clenched into fists.

"No."

"What if they kill you?"

"They won't."

"They could."

"They can't."

"You're not some invincible superhero."

"I'll be careful."

"Are you the *only* savior Egon has? Good God, with all their money, surely someone else can go after him. Carey, I'm not used to men trying to kill my daughter." She took a deep, steadying breath.

He thought about lying and saying they wouldn't have killed Carrie, but he couldn't bring himself to mouth the lie. More likely than not Rifat would have killed both girls, once their usefulness was over. Sending them back could have jeopardized him in too many ways, and he'd never have taken the risk. An ex-general, Rifat dealt in abstract numbers and equations based on human lives: How many would it take to achieve his goal?

"She's safe now," he said, avoiding all the lies and unpalatable truth.

"You keep saying that, but for how long and at what cost? And what about Lucy? Is she permanently a member of our household now, or can she ever return to her family? *When* will the danger be over?" Her anger cracked across the small distance separating them like a series of whiplashes.

When Rifat's dead, he thought, but said, "Soon."

"Jesus Christ," she exclaimed, "soon? What the hell does that mean. Soon in contrast with the current ice age in the arctic, or soon as in the life-span of a fruit fly? I have a business to run. My daughter has a life to live. *I* have a life to live. And maybe we don't want to live it in the fishbowl glare of publicity and terrorist threats. I hate fishbowls. I hate publicity. I don't even like to fill out anonymous questionnaires, for God's sake. I don't know if I can stand this, Carey, do you understand? I don't honestly know if I want to be the wife of a goddamn sex symbol who has people *gunning* for him!"

"Calm down, love."

"I don't want to calm down. I want to scream the roof off this bloody bulletproof car. And that's another thing. Is your father set up for sudden guests arriving in *bulletproof cars*?"

"He knows you're coming to stay awhile, and is extremely pleased."

"*He* knows we're coming to stay, but *I* didn't know. Awhile? How the hell long is that?"

"Jesus, Honeybear," Carey said, exhaling softly. "Relax a minute."

"I don't *want* to relax when my daughter and I are about to become hostages and my fiancé is about to go out and trade gunshots with some goddamn troop of terrorists. You know my life was *peaceful* before you came back into it. Prosaic and dull and *peaceful!*"

"I'm sorry. I wish I could explain what Egon means to me." His relationship with Egon eluded simple explanation, though even that would be useless considering Molly's current frame of mind.

"Does he mean more than Carrie and me?" It wasn't a fair question. It was one of those bitchy questions, the kind lawyers asked in criminal trials when they wanted only one answer. But even while she logically understood, emotionally she required one, single do-or-die answer.

"No, he doesn't," Carey said. His hands tightly clasped, he crossed his legs to ease the stiffness in his spine and leaned back against the dark leather seat. The planes of his sculptured face were vivid in the shadows. "But he's very alone in the world," he added, his voice soft, trying to explain and appease at the same time. "And if I can help him elude Rifat, I have to. Rifat's . . . methods," he omitted the word torture, "would create an uncomfortable situation."

"Why don't you just say torture," Molly rebuked. "That's what you mean, isn't it?"

Carey sighed and ran a hand over his brow. "I don't want to argue with you. If I could let Egon go down the tube and live with myself afterward, I would." He'd kicked off his sandals and was barefoot, looking very young and wholesome in his khaki shorts and T-shirt. His pale hair was highlighted by the sunshine streaming in through the back window. "Could we work out some compromise on this so we don't have a knock-down-drag-out fight over something I don't have a lot of control over?"

"Why can't Sylvie *hire* someone to find her brother? She could sell her damn earrings and hire a battalion."

"No one knows him as well as I do."

"Surely *she* must."

"Not really."

"So you were his father confessor?"

"No," Carey said very softly, "I was his friend."

Retreating into the opposite corner of the large backseat, Molly pulled up her legs and wrapped her arms around her knees. "Dammit, Carey, you're disrupting our whole life," she said. "Taking us away from my work and home, bringing us in contact with killers I thought only existed in books and movies." Her voice wasn't angry anymore, but a tightly leashed tension imbued her low tone. "It isn't fair. I'm afraid for Carrie's future, and I don't want to feel sorry for Egon."

"But you do." Carey's dark eyes were as tender as the quiet resonance of his voice. She looked very small in the corner of the enormous backseat, and even in a strapless sundress that should have made her look sophisticated, she looked sixteen. Maybe it was the green papier-mâché frog earrings dangling halfway down to her shoulders, or the silky blond hair draped across the curve of her collarbone, or maybe it was her beautiful, pouty bottom lip. He couldn't resist her. Leaning across the expanse of black leather separating them, he reached over and brushed her pink lips with his fingertip. "And I love you for it."

"We could lose *everything* after only finding each other again," Molly whispered, still not looking at him. "I guess I'm feeling sorry for myself, and angry that it's happening. But you can't let him die, can you?"

He stroked her shoulder, his hand drifting slowly down her arm to cover her interlocked fingers. "I think I know where he's headed, so I've an advantage over Rifat," he said.

"And if I'm lucky, I'll beat him there." He smiled a little then, feeling a twinge of his old, familiar luck. "I could be back here in two days."

"And safe?"

Guardedly he said, "And safe."

"What would you say if I asked to come along?" She turned toward him suddenly and quickly added, "Just listen first."

He swallowed the refusal he was about to utter.

"I know you want Carrie and me to stay at your father's while you go off to find Egon. I also know there's danger involved. But don't you see, it's infinitely worse waiting for you, not knowing where you are or what's going on. After all these years of *not* having you, at least if I'm with you, I'm *with* you. And if you know where Egon's going," her face had brightened, "we might be back before the men after him even pick up his trail."

If he revealed to her the danger in finding Egon, she'd freak. But if it wasn't dangerous, he had no excuse for leaving her behind. "You have to think of Carrie," he said. "She and Lucy need you."

"Not for only two days, certainly not after she sees her horse. Carrie's been horse-mad for years. She won't mind, really. She'll push me out the door, I know, because she's always telling me I'm too protective, and she knows I'll be biting my fingernails and saying, 'Be careful,' the entire time she's riding." Her rush of words came to a halt. With the tiniest lift of her chin, she added, "She's strong like you. She'll be fine, so I'm coming with you."

"Egon doesn't frequent the same spots a church group would."

"Pul-eese . . . it might be different vices, but after Bart, my eyeballs are not virgin, believe me."

He wasn't going to touch that one. Bending close, his lips brushed her cheek. "I'll bring you a present."

Her blue eyes took on a stormy cast. "Do I look like I'm ten?"

"Yes," he said with a grin. He'd relaxed.

"Let me reword that. Do I look stupid?"

His smile was rueful now. "No," he murmured, "but you can't come along."

"Oh, well, it was worth a try," she said, a shade too readily for comfort.

"I mean it," he said, assessing her with mild distrust.

"Of course, dear, you're right," Molly agreed with a smile, aware futher argument was useless. And yet, fully intent on accompanying him, she felt very brave, like Wonder Woman in full regalia. Maybe proximity to Carey Fersten promoted bravery. She'd jettisoned her prudence that summer she'd spent with him before her wedding, too. "I'm sure I'd only be in the way." Unclasping her hands, she laced them on top of her head, immediately distracting Carey from his apprehension over her abrupt capitulation. Her breasts swelled in lush provocation above the bodice of the green flower print dress.

"I don't suppose," he murmured, his eyes narrowing against an invisible wind, "we could close off the front with the girls up there. What would they think?"

"They might think we wanted some privacy. I don't suppose they'll die of shock."

"In that case, some privacy would be real high on my list of priorities, Ms. Darian." His gaze traveled slowly up her slender body, lingering gently on the rise of her breasts, then languorously lifting to meet her eyes.

"Let me take care of this, Mr. Fersten," Molly said, delight in her voice. "How long do we have before we reach your father's?"

Glancing out the window, Carey replied with a heated glance, "Three and a half hours."

"How nice, since I feel a sudden fatigue. I think I'll tell the girls to keep down the giggles; we're going to take a nap."

And when she did, Carrie turned around, pressed her

nose against the glass divider, and said, "Sure, Mom, I know what you guys are going to do. You're going to kiss."

Under his tan, Carey flushed to the roots of his hair.

"You're blushing," Molly whispered.

"She's my daughter," he whispered back. "I'm embarrassed."

"She's only teasing. Relax."

"Sure?"

"I'm s-o-o-o tired," she breathed, running her fingers down his muscled arm.

"See that we're not disturbed, Jess," he said crisply. Shutting off the intercom, he pushed the control that slid solid divider panels over the glass partition. Turning back to Molly, he murmured, "Have I told you how sexy you look when you lift your arms in that dress?"

"Like this?"

With another swift gesture, he flipped the switch controlling the window tint, and they were shut off from the outside world behind black glass. "Exactly," he whispered, touching the soft fullness rising above her strapless top. His bronzed fingers drifted over the satiny mounds, back and forth with a delicate languor she could feel warming her blood. His hands slid down the deep vee of her cleavage, and then further still until they slipped under her breasts and lifted them free of the constraining top. "I'm so glad you decided to take a nap." His voice was velvet, like his touch.

"A three and a half hour nap," Molly whispered. "I hope you don't mind."

"Oh, I don't mind, Ms. Darian," he murmured, bending low to caress the tip of her nipple with his tongue. "I've always found long naps fortifying."

"Like Ovaltine," she whispered, tremors of desire racing downward from his teasing mouth and lips and tongue.

"Not exactly," he breathed, and gave her a small bite.

She trembled, shivers of pleasure fluttering down to her toes and stirring the first small flame of passion deep inside.

She'd never last three hours; she responded to him too readily, too extravagantly. Her nerve endings would be flayed in an hour, charred beyond recognition.

"Slow down, Honeybear," Carey whispered, unzipping her dress, replying to her as if he could read her mind.

"Yes sir," she murmured back. His hands were like heated promise on her skin, teasing and stroking as he stripped her dress away and then her panties. Her desire soared recklessly, immune to words or censure.

But his own libido repudiated delay, and he quickened with scorching haste, responding to her fiery ardor. His own pleasure was intensified by the opulent readiness under his fingertips, as though he only need touch her lightly here and softly there and kiss her thus and she was open and wet and ready for him. She was the most passionate woman he'd ever known, he thought with a flaring excitement. "You're way ahead of me, sweetheart," he murmured, sliding his finger over the dampness between her legs, stroking the slick entrance, slipping his fingers inside her heated wetness slowly at first, and then suddenly deeply so she cried out in pleasure.

"Good," she whispered when she'd caught her breath, and he smiled.

"Greedy."

"You betcha," she said, leaning back into the seat corner, her smile the equivalent of a feline purr. And her husky words were followed by her hands, sliding down his chest lazily to the buttons at his waistline. She unbuttoned and unzipped with seductive slowness. With her he was always in love for the first time, his mind clearly operating in a dimension over which he had no control. He waited for her small hands to touch his arousal, quivering with the rare magic of anticipation. Her fingers stroked the thrusting, pulsing tip, and his erection grew. When she clasped him in a slow rhythm, his eyes shut with the tide of pleasure flowing through his senses.

"Now, now . . . now," she breathily ordered moments

later, lifting her hips to reach him, her hands clasping his shoulders.

He took her the first time with his clothes still on because he couldn't wait any more than she. But later, when she was straddling him and moving gently above him in mellow contentment, he found time to pull his shirt off. "Nice muscles," she said, watching the ripple down his torso as he tugged the shirt over his head with both hands.

"I've been staying in shape for my Honeybear," he replied, his smile pure happiness.

"You don't feel weak, then?"

"I don't know," he said with a grin, "what do you think?" And he lifted her with his hips.

She didn't speak until the stabbing pleasure subsided. "Arrogant man," she said, though her sultry voice tempered her rebuke.

"Not me, ma'am," he drawled in western parody. "I follow your orders right ready. But, sweet missus, when you'all get tired of taking command, it's my turn." His grin was full of wickedness.

She lay in his arms the last half-hour, their clothes restored, the windows half-open to let the summer breezes alter the cool, air-conditioned scent of lovemaking and feverish bodies. His car was equipped with a small bar so they'd washed simply with lemon flavored Perrier—"like a camping trip"—Carey had said with a grin.

"I adore wealthy young men with soft leather backseats and discreet chauffeurs," Molly murmured, flushed with pink touches of color on her cheeks, her blue eyes luminous with impish cheer.

"I adore sexy young moms who adore wealthy young men." His golden hair blew a little in the window breeze, and his smile was lavish.

We agree on everything, then, she thought. *And when I join*

you on your mission to find Egon, one slight disagreement
shouldn't mar such unruffled compatibility.

Carey was humming a romantic fifties ballad from one of
those technicolor spectaculars MGM used to make. Feeling
very much in love, he realized he'd like to have Molly with
him on his search for Egon, if it were only a matter of
sleuthing down his hidey-hole. Unfortunately with Rifat in
hot pursuit, the risks were considerable. And when the shooting started, he wanted to be able to react without worrying
about Molly.

"Why does that sound familiar?"

"It was the theme from the late movie last night, and at
the moment I wholeheartedly agree with the cloudless lyrics."

"We have everything, don't we?"

"That's a fact." His grin was wide and sunny. "I think my
luck's changed."

"How much do you believe in luck?"

"Not exclusively, but I won't turn it down, either. And
your stopping at Ely Lake Park that Sunday was one hundred
percent bona fide luck, as far as I'm concerned. I didn't even
know where to begin looking for you."

She felt the solid warmth of his shoulder beneath her
head, the pleasant weight of his arm across her stomach, the
pleasure in his wanting her. "Happy?"

"Damn right." And he hugged her closer.

Bernadotte's home was large, built of pale local fieldstone
and reminiscent in both its size and sprawling central courtyard plan of a medieval monastery. How appropriate for a
hermit, Molly thought. And how inappropriate for his son,
profligate in all things. But, coming out into the drive to meet
them, Bernadotte was gracious and hospitable, not at all what
she had expected. He was in fact so far removed from his
normal composure that Carey was reminded of a remark his
mother had once made when he mentioned his father's

tranquillity. "You didn't know him when he was young, darling," she had said with a smile. "He was a very serious, pleasure-seeking man."

Carey saw the unutterable charm today, the attentive courtesy and captivating social loquacity he'd never before witnessed. The courtly gallantry Bernadotte showed Molly and the two young girls was unconstrained, as though he hosted parties of young ladies every day. They were instantly captivated. As Molly and Carey followed Bernadotte and the two skipping young girls into the house, Molly quietly said, "I thought you said your father was reclusive."

"He always has been," Carey slowly replied, astonished by the sight of the trio before him, his father bending toward the chattering girls, responding to them in ways that made them squeal with laughter.

"He seems wonderful," Molly said, watching her daughter's face glow with smiling delight, understanding where Carey had acquired his effortless charm.

"I told you he was anxious to meet you."

"You also told me he never had company, except your mother."

"Well, you're family now."

"Does he know that?"

"It sure looks like it to me," Carey replied with a grin. "I've never seen him so delighted in my life." Taking Molly's hand in his, he began walking again, his dark gaze on the extraordinary sight of his tall, white-haired father entertaining two nine-year-olds.

"In that case, I can relax. We passed muster."

"Darling, no one has to pass muster." But in a curious way, Carey, too, felt relieved. Knowing his father's eccentric attitude toward company, Carey hadn't been altogether certain of the degree of warmth his father would exhibit. Apparently Bernadotte was as enchanted as he with his daughter and future wife. Since he had been deliberately reticent over the phone, Carey used their first quiet moment together to explain the situation to his father.

The housekeeper, Mrs. Bailey, suggested she show Molly and the girls their rooms, and Carey took the opportunity to speak with his father. They all agreed to meet at the pool for lunch.

A few moments later, Carey and his father sat over iced tea in the library. Both men relaxed in the soft comfort of worn leather chairs. Carey had kicked off his sandals the minute he sat down; the glazed tile fronting the terrace door felt cool on his feet.

"She's a beautiful woman," Bernadotte said, thinking how perfect they looked together, golden beauty and youth. But more important he'd noticed how happy his son appeared, how he looked at Molly with a curious kinetic devotion, both volatile and ardent, like a fledgling young boy in love. This was dramatically different from the tolerant indulgence with which he'd viewed women over the years.

"The same one I spent my last summer with—before going out to U.S.C."

"I thought she bore a remarkable resemblance to the photo you kept on your desk that summer."

"And Carrie's my daughter." There was a world of pride in his voice.

Without a modicum of surprise, Bernadotte casually said, "I thought so. She's very much your daughter—her face, her movements, and horse-mad, like you were at nine."

"Perhaps it's genetic," Carey said with the doting smile of a father.

"Perhaps," Bernadotte replied softly, his smile nostalgic as he recalled his own youthful equestrian training under his father's tutelage. His father was patient and kindly to a young child, instilling in his son his own passion for riding. Something Bernadotte had, in turn, taught to Carey. And now his granddaughter had inherited their love of horses. "She has your hands. She'll be good." It was as if he read Carey's mind.

"I was about to ask if you would help Leon with her first lessons."

"Carrie and I have already agreed on five o'clock, after the heat of the day has passed." He lifted his brow in indulgent amusement. "She's insistent, just like you."

"Do you mind?"

"Of course not, can't abide tractable people. I would have known she was yours blindfolded. She has the same decisive way of making a question a foregone conclusion. And the inflections in her speech . . . I wouldn't have thought it possible to inherit those patterns, but—" He raised his tall crystal tea glass. "Thank you for a delightful granddaughter. I had, quite frankly, given up hope."

"You knew my feelings on Agent Orange."

"Yes . . . apparently you didn't know of her existence?"

"No." And then Carey filled his father in on the bizarre set of circumstances which had transpired, making Molly and Bart unaware of Carrie's paternity.

"You're a very lucky man," his father said at the conclusion of Carey's explanation.

"I know, and it makes this search for Egon doubly frustrating. Going off and leaving Molly and Carrie behind is difficult . . . unsettling." He looked across the small distance separating them, thinking how little his father had changed over the years, knowing he'd done the right thing bringing them here. "It's the hardest choice I've ever had to make, but I can't leave Egon out in the cold. You know what Rifat's like." In short, brusque sentences, Carey described his fear at seeing Ceci at the press conference, and his subsequent dash to the Merchandise Mart to find Carrie and Lucy safe only because of their own resourcefulness.

"They'll be safe here," Bernadotte assured him. "The surveillance cameras are quite effective, as is the monitoring equipment." Bernadotte preferred his privacy, and had developed a highly sophisticated electronic barrier around his estate as more of a hobby than a necessity.

"Do you have any idea where Egon might be?"

"My guess is he's making for his retreat in Jamaica. Since his villa is a mile up the mountain beyond the main road, Egon has this peculiar notion he's entirely hidden. Like a child covering his eyes who says, 'You can't see me.' I've never been able to convince him otherwise, and frankly never had the heart to disillusion him further. And perhaps the major attraction is the availability of drugs there. He'll be strung out—on fear and heroin. Not a difficult person to follow, I'm afraid. Rifat should be hot on his heels, but I may be able to beat him there by a few hours and meet Egon at the airport, a flight or so ahead of Rifat's men. I'm taking a chance by going directly to Jamaica, but Rifat will have to pick up his trail. I should be ahead of him, and if I'm lucky, Egon and I should be back here late tomorrow night, or early the following morning."

Bernadotte absorbed all the detail, offering no unwanted advice. "What explanation have you given Carrie?"

"None so far. We're here to see her new birthday horse."

"And Molly is amenable to your leaving and going after Egon? Surely Sylvie must have caused an irritable ripple or two." Bernadotte had never lacked for female company until he'd married Carey's mother, and he understood the subtleties of jealousy. And although he'd politely avoided Sylvie during her marriage to his son, he knew that Sylvie was difficult, thoroughly selfish, and rude.

"Between Sylvie and Molly's ex it was a toss-up on boorish behavior, but I think Molly's reconciled to my going. Reconciled—but reticent. I'm counting on you to take her mind off my absence. You'll enjoy her. She's outspoken, like Mother."

"Ah . . . so I have a reluctant—"

"Fiancée," Carey finished. "We're to be married as soon as she says the word."

"And when do you anticipate that?" Although Bernadotte's question was mildly put, the novelty of Carey pursuing rather than being pursued amused him. He decided Molly was very bright.

"She dislikes all the publicity surrounding my life."

"Truly?" His brows rose in skepticism. In his experience, women sought the spotlight.

Carey sighed. "Sincerely."

"An interesting conundrum for you, no doubt," Bernadotte replied softly and, in a thoughtful aside, asked, "How does your daughter feel about publicity?"

Carey grinned. "It's in the genes. She adores the photographers, wants a date with Chachi from *Happy Days,* and is wondering when she can have a role in my next movie."

"Ah, a sweet child," Bernadotte cheerfully observed. "And can *you* give it all up after all these years—the limelight and display?"

"*Because* of all the years, I can, without a backward glance. You, more than anyone, should understand my feelings. You'd led a life of some . . . irregularity before building this home."

"I envy you," his father said very quietly. His own dream had been the same—to live peacefully with Kirsti. But various egomaniacs had intervened, and their armies had crisscrossed his ancestral lands, taking away his patrimony and his darling wife. "My very best wishes for your happiness," he gruffly said, his sense of loss a dull ache of poignant regret. He'd never considered himself a romantic in his youth, but as he'd aged he'd begun to realize how fortunate one was to have experienced a deep, abiding love. So few in this world encountered their perfect lover or felt the startling intensity of passion so profound its memory never diminished. He and Kirsti had been fortunate.

There was a certain tranquillity to age, he reflected, that mellowed the inequities of life. With fondness, he looked at his son and wished him happiness.

"Thank you, Papa. And if all goes well, I'll be back with

Egon, Rifat will be checked, and hopefully, I can get on with my life."

"Surely," his father said, his finger tracing a path up the condensation on the tea glass, "you're not that naive."

Carey looked out through the open French windows under the low-pitched eaves to the sunwashed poolside, busy with servants preparing the luncheon table. He knew as well as his father did the brutal nature of the man he was opposing. "One step at a time," he said very slowly. "I have to get Egon out of danger. Rifat's been on several government hit lists for many years now—unsuccessfully. I don't know if I can do what they've failed to do."

"He won't leave you alone," his father quietly reminded him, "if you thwart him."

Carrie and Lucy had appeared in their bathing suits, watermelon pink and lime green accents against the lapis-tiled pool and were beginning to splash their feet in the sparkling water. An incongruous sense of unreality overcame Carey as he gazed at his daughter peacefully playing in the summer sun. He shouldn't be discussing Rifat's assassination with his father; he had no vested interest in Rifat's particular brand of banditry; all he wanted was a tranquil life with his wife and daughter.

"Wars are different now, but they're still wars, aren't they?" he said. "Only smaller and more frequent. I'm in this war purely by an accident of marriage." He leaned his head back against the worn leather and shut his eyes. "Shit."

"It might be possible to put together a team. I could check with Geoffrey or Rupert."

Carey's first response was to say, "Sure, check with your old network in MI6. Hire someone to knock Rifat off. Hire a dozen mercenaries and maybe one might manage what Rifat's numerous enemies to date have not managed." But he wasn't comfortable yet with coldly plotting an assassination. He still clung to a naive optimism that once Egon was safe,

Rifat would withdraw. Opening his eyes, he pulled himself upright and said, "I'd like to wait. Do you mind?"

"I prefer you not put yourself in undue danger."

"At this stage, if Jess and I take off say in an hour or two, we should be in Jamaica in good time—ahead of Rifat's men. Egon just left Nice yesterday, and if I know him he stayed in Madrid or Barcelona and caught a flight this afternoon. I might even beat him to Le Retour if he gets corrupted in Montego Bay." And he rose suddenly as he caught sight of Molly approaching the girls at poolside. "Molly's here. If I leave rather abruptly, make my excuses to her, will you, Papa? I'm counting on you to soothe any ruffled feathers."

Bernadotte set his glass aside and stood. The two tall men exchanged silent glances in the quiet room. "I'll do the best I can. But one last word of caution from an old man. I understand you must help Egon, but promise me no extraordinary heroics. He's not worth your life."

Carey smiled faintly, his dark eyes under his heavy brows intensified by the shadows in the room. He nodded his head. "Don't worry, I have too much to live for." He turned back toward the poolside scene and softly added, "I'm coming back to them."

Luncheon was cheerful, the adults all congenial, the children vivacious and full of questions. The menu was elaborate, both grown-up and childish fare offered in magnificent variety. Bernadotte insisted on champagne in honor of his future daughter-in-law and granddaughter. A buffet table was arranged at a poolside gazebo, complete with a lavish bouquet of roses and lilies. There was black and red caviar. Blinis were served hot in a napkin-lined basket with dill butter. Fresh figs filled with prosciutto and garnished with a caper dressing were beautifully cut in water lily shapes. Poached salmon, presented whole on an enormous silver fish plate, had been flown in fresh when Bernadotte heard Carey was bringing company home. A Greek lemon soup looked and tasted cool and delicious on the warm summer day, while tabbouli salad scented the air with mint. Chilled grape tarts looked like jewels on a silver tray. Molly thought the entire buffet table should have been photographed for a *House and Garden* cover. It was delightfully different from Chucky Cheese. But the girls' tastes had been catered to, as well, with peanut butter and jelly sandwiches cut into bunny shapes, small pizzas decorated with happy faces, hand-cut French fries, watermelon slices, and chocolate ice cream arranged in a large crystal bowl of crushed ice. They were enchanted.

An hour later, when Carey suggested everyone take a short nap before riding lessons, the children agreed. They were both so excited about riding—had already fed Carrie's new horse carrots and apples, and had checked out the riding ring with Leon—they were being on their best behavior so as not to jeopardize their lessons.

"I should have thought of a horse for a bribe before," Molly said, her grin teasing. "Usually when you say nap, you can count on a lengthy argument."

"Just watch me, babe," Carey teased back, "and I'll show you a thing or two about handling little girls . . . it's a lot like—"

"Don't you dare say it."

His look was innocent. "I was going to say it's a lot like being nice to their moms." But his grin was pure wolf.

"You're way too smooth, Carey Fersten."

"And you're so sweetly green, Ms. Darian, you could sell yourself for salad."

"A pleasant change for you, then," she replied.

"Amen," he said, and meant it with all his heart. Which made his next words doubly hard to say. They were almost to their room on the opposite side of the pool, and he touched her arm gently to stop her. "I have to check with Leon," he said. "I'd forgotten to see if we have boots for Lucy. I'll be right back." He felt a sinking sense of loss already, and he hadn't even left yet.

The face Molly turned up to him was smiling. "You won't be long?"

"A few minutes," he lied and, bending low, touched her lips in a light brushing kiss. He straightened and smiled. "Keep my spot warm." It was meant to be a casual remark, but he couldn't leave without touching her again. Taking her face gently in his hands, he bent and kissed her once more, a soft, lingering good-bye kiss. He had found her and lost her and found her again, and leaving her was the hardest choice he'd ever made. Damn. Why couldn't Egon be normal? Why did his drug habit fuck up everything he did? Why couldn't his family own a textile factory, so he could go to hell without bringing in the world's most dangerous terrorist as a partner on his ride to destruction? Yeah, sure. And as long as we're dreaming, let's end world poverty, too. In the meantime, Fersten, put on your spurs and *ride*, or Egon's going to disappear one bloody piece at a time. "I love you, Honeybear," he murmured as his mouth lifted from hers. "Always."

"Hurry back," Molly whispered.

And his startled expression was immediately masked with a smile. "I'll be back before you doze off."

But Molly had read his reaction properly; she knew he was leaving to go after Egon.

Immediately after Carey walked away, she entered their room, set her note to her daughter prominently in the center of the bed, and left to follow Carey. She knew her daughter well enough to know she would be the first to say, "Go, Mom."

Anticipating his swift departure, she'd changed before lunch into comfortable slacks and a cotton sweater. With a jacket clutched in one hand, she watched Carey stride toward the stables. He must have some last minute instructions for

Leon; she didn't believe the ruse of Lucy's boots for one minute.

Bernadotte's home was situated on a gentle rise overlooking a rolling panorama of hills and pastures and forest. The stables were closest to the house at the back, separated by a broad stretch of green lawn and a beautifully raked gravel turnaround for loading horse trailers. Directly east of the stables, beyond three fenced pastures, were the hangars for the planes. A hedged drive bordered the pastures, leading to the large airstrip cleared from the forest, and Molly made swiftly for the security of the hedge shadows. With Carey taking a detour to the stables, she'd have the advantage of arriving at the plane before him. And if by chance she'd misinterpreted and he did return to the house, she could simply say she'd gone out looking for him.

Would it be possible for her to board the plane undetected? How many people would be around the hangars and plane? Would she have to threaten Carey somehow to have him take her along? Was she overreacting? she wondered, struck by a niggling sensation suggesting she was overplaying the Nancy Drew clues. Then the jet engines roared into operation.

One gold star for Nancy Drew.

And one for a young woman who'd never done anything more exciting than fight her way through Frank Murphy's annual sale of designer dresses. She felt an exhilarating sense of adventure.

A new determination crept in past her initial fear for Carey that had impelled her to follow. Now the small impetus of reading the clues properly invigorated her, and she approached the entrance to the airstrip with a sleuth's caution *and* excitement.

There was no approach short of brazening it out that would get her across the broad expanse of lawn between the hedge and the hangar. She stepped out of the shadows onto the freshly mowed grass and walked briskly toward the strip where the large jet had taxied. Reaching the hangar, she stood still, gauging whether she'd been noticed. From where she stood with her back against the wall, she could see the ramp of steps had been wheeled up to the plane. Was Jess inside, or was he in the hangar? Were others accompanying Carey and Jess, or were they going alone? If she walked across the vast open tarmac to the plane, she'd be in perfect view . . . but her choices were limited. In broad daylight, any surreptitious approach was out of the question.

Just as she began stepping around the corner of the hangar, she caught sight of Carey coming across the pasture from the stables. Sliding around the corner out of sight, she held her breath and tried to concoct some plausible story should someone see her pressed against the wall. Damn! If she didn't manage to get on that plane, she was going to be left plastered to this wall when the plane took off. Taking a quick peek around the corner, she saw Carey no more than twenty yards from the hangar. Think, think! she commanded her flustered brain. Her options were rapidly dwindling to zero. Carey was between her and the plane without so much as a bush for concealment.

Wonder Woman or Superman would come in handy right now. Then she could dispense with the plane altogether. She could simply follow Carey through the sky like a human bird. Reluctantly discarding that plan, she was debating the possibility of dissolving into buckets of tears and pleading to be taken along when she heard Jess shout, "Come in here for a minute, Carey. I'm having some hassle with Duluth on filing the flight plan."

And Carey turned abruptly from his direct route to the plane.

"Thank you, God," Molly whispered into the blue sunny sky, "you're back from vacation. Just kidding," she quickly added, unwilling to tempt heavenly retribution.

As Carey entered the hangar, she didn't think. She didn't

weigh the odds. She didn't consider the chance that Carey or Jess might look out the window.

She sprinted.

Down the west side of the hangar, onto the warm tarmac.

The thirty yards between herself and the plane stretched like a shimmering mirage in the desert. It helped when you didn't have time to think. It helped when the blood was pumping so loudly in your ears, no other sounds intruded. But what helped most was the martinet on the phone giving Jess trouble over his flight plan.

"I'll talk to him," Carey snapped after the third explanation. And as Carey brusquely said, "Listen carefully. This is very simple . . ." Molly bolted up the steps into the dim interior of the jet.

She'd never been inside a private jet before. Scanning the arrangement of furniture to her left, the small lounge area closest to the door, and the hallway to her right, she cautiously turned right and took two tentative steps. Was anyone on the plane . . . perhaps in the galley? Was there a cargo area she could hide in? *Hurry, hurry*, an insistent voice reminded her. Another several steps and she saw the efficient chrome galley tucked away on her right. The door directly across the aisle was the bathroom, she discovered, after carefully easing the door open. One door remained. Taking a deep breath, praying no one was on the other side, she opened it. A compact bedroom with just enough space for a built-in bed and closet was decorated in black and poppy-red chintz.

A quick survey indicated one could not hide under the bed or in the closet, unless you were Houdini or an Indian mystic well versed in the more complex yoga positions. Her agitated mind was moving into overdrive in its insistent screaming, *hurry, hurry*, and a swift glance out the small curtained window froze her momentarily. Jess and Carey were walking toward the plane.

Pulling the bedroom door shut, she fled back down the

hall to the bathroom and slipped inside only moments before she heard Carey's voice.

"She wasn't very happy, but I didn't have any choice."

"It's for the best. Women always get in the way."

"Not always, Jess," Carey said, innuendo soft in his voice.

"Okay, but you know what I mean. Egon is going to be *trouble*. Hey . . . what the hell is the head light on for?" he asked, his voice suddenly changing.

Oh Christ, Molly forgot the damn light went on when the door locked. Her heart seemed to stop for endless moments as she heard Jess tugging at the door and muttering.

"Let it go, Jess," Carey said. "We can pry it open later. Let's take off. With Rifat after Egon, every damn minute counts. And pray for tail winds. I'm hoping like hell to beat Egon to Le Retour."

The sound of receding footsteps was Molly's cue to begin breathing again, and she inhaled carefully, making the least possible noise. She caught sight of herself in the mirror over the sink. She was ashen. So much for bravery and boldness; she'd probably drop dead at the sound of gunshots. But three normal breaths later, she realized she'd muddled through another crisis. What would Wonder Woman do next?

Almost an hour into the flight—definitely too late to turn back—someone approached her hiding place and began prying the door open. Rather than wreck the door, she unlatched the lock. The soft click of the lever brought instant silence.

Before she had time to decipher the sudden silence, the door shot open and she was facing the business end of a silencer affixed to a 9mm Beretta. Then she looked up into Carey's angry face.

"I should have known," he growled, "when you first raised your arms in the backseat of the limo."

"But your celebrated hormones," Molly purred, "were guiding your brains as usual, weren't they?"

"So far I've managed," he curtly retorted.

"One can only hope Rifat doesn't throw some nubile

young starlet into your path this side of Egon," she acidly replied.

"And all that smiling agreeableness," he said, furious his plans were jeopardized by her presence. "I should have known better. When you're that agreeable, I'd better watch my back."

"Don't fault me on hypocrisy, darling. 'I'm going to check on Lucy's boots,'" she mimicked.

"It was necessary." The anger in his voice was so controlled, it only carried the short distance between them.

Her face took on an expression of scorn. "*Your* deception is necessary, and mine is not? How convenient."

His hand dropped away from the door. Turning abruptly, he walked away and strode forward to the cockpit. At the moment he was too angry to trust his reactions. Molly's presence was going to bloody well fuck up everything . . . and he needed some time to unjam the overwrought circuits in his mind that were screaming abort! Abort!

It was too late to turn back if he hoped to beat Egon to Le Retour. Maybe Jess could stay with Molly on the plane, but Carey needed his help with Egon. Hell!

Molly watched him stalk away, enter the cockpit, and slam the door shut. Moving toward the couch and chairs arranged comfortably near some small tables, she sat down and waited to see if the plane would turn around. She'd only seen Carey that angry once before, and that was the night she left him in his apartment at Mrs. Larsen's to go off and marry Bart. His voice today had the same taut control, as though the softness of his tone could conceal his terrible rage.

But she wasn't eighteen any longer, nor daunted by his wrath. Why were his lies necessary, and hers merely disagreeable? Cautioning herself to remain calm and logical, she discarded her impulse to feel ill-treated. They both felt justified in their action. Now that she'd accomplished the first stage of this unusual expedition beyond the confines of her normal life, she intended to see she became an asset, not a hindrance. How best to deal with her angry lover?

She thought the old maxim "You get more flies with sugar than vinegar" held merit. Twenty minutes later when Carey emerged from the forward cabin, his scowl still in place, she said, "We're both adults, supposedly mature. I'm sorry. Could we talk about this?" And her smile was the very best soothing, dazzling look she could conjure.

"You're an impetuous bitch," Carey said in a deep growl, looking tall and menacing in the low-ceilinged cabin. "But I love you." And when he smiled, her face flushed warm from the glow.

CHAPTER 33

Egon was in a cold sweat in the bathroom of an Air France jet, and the stewardess was banging on the door. "Are you all right, sir?" she asked for the third time. Her voice was insistent now, but diplomatically muted to avoid disturbing the other first-class passengers. It was obvious Egon wasn't well; she'd seen enough druggies on this Marseilles–Jamaica run to recognize one when she saw him. As far as she was concerned, he could stay in there the entire flight, but a brassy redhead traveling with a man old enough to be her father was insisting the stewardess clear the bathroom for her.

Egon had taken one point with him—enough to last him to Jamaica—but the damn needle had jammed in the hem of his jacket, and he was having trouble getting it out without snapping it off. Jesus, if his hands would just stop shaking long enough to ease it free . . .

"I'll be out in a minute," he gruffly replied, his French touched with traces of his old nurse's Provence patois. When under pressure he lost the aristocratic polish his mother had insisted on. One's breeding was evident in one's speech, she'd always said, and on occasions when she was being particularly pedantic he would lapse into low German to annoy her.

Mama never forgot her family was landed in contrast to Papa's family's bourgeois roots. But 20,000 acres of marsh on the Baltic didn't buy that diamond tiara, now did it? Papa would retort when Mama put on airs. Papa was practical; while he didn't denigrate his title, he knew his power lay in wealth, not a coat of arms.

"Sorry, Papa," Egon said in a brief stab of remorse. It would have saddened his father to see him like this, and he often felt relieved that his father had died before the drugs. Wiping the sweat from his eyes, he spoke aloud in a low murmur, as if the sound of his voice would calm him. "Count to ten and breathe slowly." If he could relax, his hands would stop trembling. "Eight, breathe, nine, breathe, ten . . ." Now calmly slide the hypo out of the lining hem, he silently instructed, calmly, as if it didn't matter whether it came free or not. Ah . . . he had the plastic plunger now. Slowly . . . pull it out of the silk lining slowly . . . there. It's free!

And he wept with relief.

Five minutes later the first soothing traces were entering his bloodstream, and in two minutes more, steady again, the panic receding, his blissful sense of serenity returning, Egon told himself he'd stop the drugs first thing tomorrow. Once he was safe at Le Retour, he'd go clean again. First thing.

He looked at his watch. Four o'clock. He'd be at the villa by seven. Glancing in the mirror, he smoothed his hair, straightened his shirt collar, and eased back into his linen jacket. After disposing of the paraphernalia in the waste container, he emerged from the bathroom with a smile for the stewardess. "Forgive me, mademoiselle, I felt faint for a few moments."

"Are you better now?" she politely inquired, taking in the expensive clothes and Mediterranean tan.

"Quite fine, thank you."

It was a shame, she thought, watching him return to the row of seats he'd reserved to avoid having company. He was very handsome. And the nurturing impulse Egon so often triggered stirred in her. He was quite beautiful and obviously wealthy. What he needed was some woman to care for him and see that his melancholy disappeared from his eyes. For the remainder of the journey she was solicitous, enough so that the annoying redhead was heard to remark, "*Some* people in first class must be more important than *other* people."

She made the redhead's next drink so stiff, the bitch choked on it.

Shortly before they were to land, Mariel asked Egon if he cared to share the cab she had waiting at the airport. He'd mentioned he was going to his vacation home, and she had a three-day layover. Maybe he'd even ask her out to dinner. He had a charming smile, and his French reminded her of home, with its faint Provencal flavor. She couldn't actually say they'd had a chance to converse, but they'd exchanged the social pleasantries about vacations in Jamaica and the weather. If he accepted her offer to share a cab, perhaps she might discover the reason he attracted her so.

She had a smile like a young girl, Egon thought, tentative and even a bit shy, not at all the practiced expression one expected from someone in her work. She was small, shapely, he noticed, with a casual, brushed-back haircut and a minimum of makeup. "I'd appreciate that," Egon said, the decision simple. If he was going to retreat to Le Retour, it would be pleasant to have company. "Would you have time for dinner tonight?"

Her smile lit up the flashes of gold in her hazel eyes. When she quickly nodded in agreement, he liked the way her dark hair flared forward briefly to brush her cheek. With effort he restrained himself from touching the silken fall. Later, he thought. The heroin was making him whole again. All his receptors were pleasantly in tune, no agitation, no violence. He'd even forgotten momentarily that he was running for his life.

He had only a small leather carry-on bag with the barest essentials for traveling, and the cab Mariel had arranged for was waiting for them. Within minutes of landing they were on their way to Ocho Rios.

Two flights were scheduled to land yet from Europe, one from Rome, and one from Barcelona. Jess had been sent to check the arrival of any chartered planes, while Carey and Molly were waiting to see if Egon was on the Barcelona flight.

Jamaica was ungodly hot in June, and sweat was damp on her skin as Molly surveyed the passengers walking toward them. After their discussion on the plane—a mature discussion Molly was proud of—Molly stood beside Carey at the passenger gate hoping to see Egon and immediately whisk him away with them back to safety at Bernadotte's.

"If you want to help, okay," Carey had said seated opposite her across the small rosewood table in the lounge. "You and I will see if we can find Egon at the airport." How can she get hurt in an air terminal? he'd thought.

"Tell me what Egon looks like," Molly had said, pleased she'd presented her position so well. Carey understood how she felt and was willing to have her along. In the ensuing discussion, she forgot about Rifat. Carey was amiable, describing Egon so she felt she knew him even though she'd never met him.

But often in the course of their flight, Carey checked his watch. He was very much aware of Rifat, and time was about all he had on his side. Jess was great backup; he could fly or drive anything with a motor, but Molly was going to be a colossal hindrance. Goddamn . . . how can you love someone and be madder than hell at them at the same time? But in a mental exercise he'd developed in Vietnam, he forced himself to concentrate on the mission in hand.

1. Find Egon first. Maybe not too damn difficult; Ocho Rios was small.
2. If necessary, elude Rifat's men. Harder. Ocho Rios was small.
3. Get back to the plane.

So here he stood with sweat clinging to his skin at Montego Bay terminal, a building no larger than the gymnasium back home. He grew more nervous with each passing moment because the passengers were filing off now, and Egon wasn't one of them. He could have been wrong on his timing; it was possible Egon had caught a previous flight. It was also possible he was in the wrong place altogether, and Egon was huddled in some other part of the world. "Christ."

He didn't realize he'd spoken aloud until Molly took his hand in hers. "Maybe Jess found him."

He was having trouble being affable now, when it looked as though "Step 1" was fucking up in a major way. "Okay, let's go and see." But his tone was repressive, his scowl intense, and he swore under his breath all the way to the area where private planes landed. Jess was waiting for them, and Carey could see from a hundred yards away that he wasn't cheerful.

Now to sweet talk one of the reservation employees, and see if Egon had been on an earlier passenger manifest. Despite the realization Egon may have opted for another hiding place, Carey's gut feeling stuck with Le Retour. It had always been Egon's haven when his world was crashing around his ears. Carey had dragged him back to school a dozen times from Le Retour in the years he was married to Sylvie. He *knew* Egon would show up here sooner or later. He just hoped like hell Egon was sooner, and Rifat's thugs were later.

"No luck, boss."

"Ditto here. Do you want to see what you can get out of the cab drivers? I'll check the Barcelona flight passenger list. And I'll see what else is scheduled to come in this evening." Carey cocked one brow. "Use money."

The clerk politely explained to Carey that she wasn't allowed to show the manifest to anyone. It was distinctly against regulations.

"Perhaps you could just let me know if my brother-in-law was on the flight," Carey replied with a social ingenuity he was famous for, his voice as polite as hers. "He's been ill, and we're concerned since he didn't disembark. Perhaps I was mistaken on the flight number. I certainly would appreciate any help you could give me," and he placed four hundred-dollar bills directly in front of her. "His mother's worried. She sent me out to meet him," Carey added in a confidential tone, "and you know what mother-in-laws can be like." He smiled. "She'll have my head if I met the wrong flight."

The clerk smoothly picked up the bills without losing eye contact with Carey. "Of course, sir. In case of medical emergency, I could give you that information."

"I'd greatly appreciate it," Carey replied in the hushed tones a mortician would use with the family of the deceased.

No wonder the boy director was hailed as a genius. He was as good an actor as a director, Molly decided as she watched an expression of deep concern overshadow his features. The man was a natural actor.

The young woman looked up from the list almost immediately. "Mr. von Mansfeld booked two seats on flight 27, which just arrived."

"That's the flight we watched disembark. He wasn't on it."

"I'm sorry, sir. Perhaps he changed his mind."

"Would it be possible to talk to one of the flight crew?"

"I don't know if I can find them."

Another two hundred changed hands.

"I'll page the crew; someone may still be in the terminal."

"I'd be happy to pay for any information they might have." Carey's heart was thudding rapidly. There were endless possibilities why Egon booked two seats, then never showed up at the flight's destination. And most of the possibilities were unpleasant, with Rifat figuring very largely in them.

Egon and Mariel were seated in the backseat of a '66 Impala careening down the coastal highway to Ocho Rios. Egon was feeling fine, and the blue-green ocean on his left sparkled in the late afternoon sun. Mariel was cheerfully chatting beside him about the small children selling shells or the bucolic beauty of the occasional herd of cattle grazing on the coastal plain.

Their driver was keeping beat to the radio with one hand, steering with the other. Visibility around the curves on the coast road was limited, but he'd simply pull out, honk his horn, and accelerate around anything in his path. Even a large bus didn't slow him down. After that, Mariel clung to Egon.

"Want to stop for a beer or a Pepsi?" the driver asked in his British-accented Jamaican.

Egon knew that the residents in the shacks along the road lived off the tourists. "Sure, why not," Egon answered, content to be so near to home. When they stopped, Egon gave him a bill and said, "Why don't you get one, too."

Resuming their journey a few minutes later, they each had a cool Red-Stripe beer to sip on while the music played and the scenery unfolded for them like a travelogue for an ocean paradise. A few miles later on a portion of straight road, their driver turned round, took off his dark glasses, and inquired, "Looking for any ganja?"

"No, but I'm looking for something a bit stronger," Egon casually replied.

"My cousin can help you, mon."

"Good. No rush. Maybe tomorrow." Egon had his own supply at Le Retour, but he never passed up an opportunity to acquire more. He felt safe when his supply was comfortably large.

They passed Rose Hall. When Mariel mentioned that she'd never seen it, Egon promised to show it to her tomorrow.

"Is this your first time here?"

When she nodded yes, he said he'd have to show her the sights. They'd do the tour tomorrow. He pointed out Green Grotto Cave where pirates had hidden their contraband, and as they sped along the road he directed her attention to Runaway Bay where Columbus had landed.

They stopped for dinner at the Ruins just west of Ocho Rios. Seated at a secluded table with the view of the waterfall and tropical forest, they were served by two solicitous waiters. Egon dined regularly at the Ruins when he was at Le Retour, and he was known for his generosity. Feeling relaxed, Egon entertained Mariel with stories of his last trip to Paris when Sylvie had used him as buffer against Bernhardt. His descriptions of Bernhardt made her laugh, while his portrayal of the couturiers' inner sanctums, the models, and gowns were so perfect Mariel felt as though she'd been shopping with Sylvie herself.

"You'll have to join me sometime in Paris," Egon said. He looked lean and at ease sprawled in an empire armchair. "I'll show you my favorite playgrounds." He was dressed in buff and charcoal linen, his sport coat a small houndstooth check, his slacks a pale shade of charcoal, his natural colored shirt open at the neck. His long-fingered hands fascinated Mariel . . . elegant and aristocratic was her first thought. But he moved them with a restless mercurial energy that drew the eye, she was mesmerized by his compelling presence.

As their dessert soufflés were taken away, she reached out and lightly touched the pale golden hair growing in a thick pattern toward his wrist. She felt taut muscle beneath the silky golden hair and bronzed skin, and it surprised her momentarily. "Your hands are strong," she murmured without thinking.

"I ride," Egon said. "When the mood strikes me," he added with a grin. "Do you ride?" he asked.

"No, I'm afraid not."

"Would you like me to show you? I keep several horses at Le Retour?"

She smiled, liking his sincerity and his utter lack of arrogance. "I'd like that," she said.

"Good. Can you stay over a few days?" In the pleasure of Mariel's company, Egon had forgotten he was on the run. He was losing himself in the sense of security Le Retour always instilled in him.

"I've a three day layover."

"I'll have you riding out on the trail in two days. Wait and see . . . you'll love it."

She laughed at his enthusiasm. "Just a warning . . . I'm a lousy athlete. Don't be disappointed if I fall off."

"You can have Sylvie's Mannerheim. He's as gentle as a lamb. My sister doesn't like riding very much."

"Why does she ride, then?"

"Well, first Mama insisted she learn. Mama was from a Junker family which prided itself on its hunting lands. And secondly, Sylvie's ex-husband is a world-class rider; she pretended she adored horses for him. Carey realized how deep that affection went the first time he saw her ride. Anyway, Sylvie's old Mannerheim is like sitting in a padded rocking chair, I promise."

"In that case, I won't mind riding lessons. But don't feel you have to teach me to ride if it's an inconvenience." Mariel had never so instantly liked someone in her life, but she remembered her manners and also remembered Egon was from a very different world.

"No inconvenience," Egon assured her, reaching for his grappa. "I've all the time in the world."

CHAPTER 34

Rifat was infuriated by the wire his batman had brought him. Seated at his desk in the bedroom of his Rome villa, his bearing military even in a silk robe, he expressed his anger in a terse expletive. Rifat's man Yalcin, ignored his master's comment as any good servant would.

"Do you care to return an answer, master?" he inquired.

"No," Rifat retorted. "Wake me if there's any further message."

Yalcin knew enough to do that in any event, but the fact Rifat had mentioned it made this particular mission an important one. "Very well, sir." And he bowed deferentially before leaving.

"Jamaica," Rifat snorted in disgust, his hooded eyes dark with rage. Egon had eluded his men again. He crumpled the telex in an uncharacteristic show of anger. Flinging the ball of paper across the dimly lit room, he cursed Egon in several languages—and reached for the phone. Maybe it was time to consider the sister as a possible hostage. He wouldn't allow the prototype to slip through his hands, and if Egon proved evasive, the countess would be a bargaining chip of equal importance. Meanwhile the countess should be put under surveillance in the event she needed to be picked up. When the call went through, he spoke curtly into the phone, relaying his message in ciphered language. He was assured he would receive a report of her whereabouts by morning.

While Rifat was bristling in Rome and Ceci was drumming his fingers on the window of their chartered plane, waiting for it to touch down at Montego Bay, Carey was tracking down the third member of the crew and hoping she'd know more than the pilot and copilot. They had no idea of Egon's whereabouts, but they'd suggested Danielle, one of the stewardesses in first class. She and some friends were staying at a beach house in Ocho Rios.

Jess hadn't had any luck with the cab drivers. No one had seen a man of Egon's description. Now Egon was either ahead of him, not yet arrived, or in an entirely different part of the world. They would have to split up. Jess would cover arrivals, and Carey and Molly would proceed to Le Retour with a short detour to talk to Danielle. If it would have been possible to leave Molly with Jess, he would have, but short of tying her to a seat, he didn't see it as a feasible option. So while Jess stayed behind with orders to leave for Bernadotte's immediately if he found Egon, Carey and Molly took a cab to Ocho Rios.

"An extra fifty if we make it to Ocho Rios in record time," Carey told the cabbie.

"No problem, mon," the smiling man replied, turning up the volume on his radio.

"You might want to shut your eyes," Carey warned Molly.

And she did for the first two minutes, but curved roads and high speeds were stomach-churning with her eyes shut. Gritting her teeth, she braced her hands on the seat and watched the driver defy death a score of times in the next half-hour.

As they sped by the Ruins, Egon and Mariel were just

beginning their dessert. They jolted to a tire-squealing halt at the Hertz rental in Ocho Rios, an old red brick building with a large plate-glass window and worn wooden door.

Carey casually remarked, "Great driving, thanks," and paid the driver as though he were a passenger near death every day of his life. Pulling Molly from the car, he indicated the rental sign and asked, "Care to take over as driver?"

She felt like kissing the ground in thanksgiving, but in her best grown-up voice she said casually, "Sure."

"Good, cuz I've some chasing to do."

She lifted her brows in query.

"Looking for Egon."

"I knew that."

He grinned. "Women. You shouldn't even be here."

"No chauvinist remarks. I'm not sufficiently recovered from the jaws of death to be in fighting form."

He touched her cheek with a quick, brushing fingertip. "You're such a darling."

"No patronizing remarks, either. If I'm about to become your driver, I demand the respect due that position. We are not darlings. We are shooter associates."

For a moment he wondered if she was serious—but decided in the next moment she was not. "Where did you hear that?"

"On TV—where else?"

And for a second Carey wished he could turn off this program.

They drove out on the eastern tip of the bay to find Danielle. At least the beach cottage wasn't out of the way. Egon's villa was only another few miles down the road.

Over twenty-four hours had passed since Carey had decided to bring Egon in and fatigue was beginning to pervade his senses. Adrenaline could only sustain one so long. He'd hardly slept last night, his mind looping full speed on Egon's problem, and the hours today had been fraught with problems.

"I hope she saw him," Carey said as Molly pulled up to the hotel entrance.

"And if she didn't?"

"We'll go to Le Retour and hope he arrived before us. I'll be back in a few minutes. Why don't you wait in that parking lot across the way?"

"Yes, sir, captain, sir," Molly replied facetiously with a brisk salute.

"Now why didn't you do that back at Dad's when I wanted you to stay there?" he asked.

"Wanted to see the world, sir."

"Hope like hell you don't see more than you care to, soldier."

"Don't worry, sir."

"Shit," Carey muttered, but his smile was warm. How could she be so damn cheerful? And beautiful. Probably because she didn't have the slightest inkling of the danger involved. Which meant he'd better move his ass so Rifat didn't get too close to her. "Ciao," he said. "Don't move." And he was gone.

As he entered the main lobby, a small area the size of his bedroom with a ceiling soaring three-stories high, Carey passed a hundred-dollar bill to the manager, then asked for Danielle Garzin's cottage number.

The beach cottages faced the bay. He took the stairs down a floor to the open-air bar at poolside and, walking through, strode past the pool and out onto the sand. The temperature had diminished slightly with evening, and the breeze off the bay wasn't hot any longer. All the patios facing the beach were deserted, not only because of the off-season, but because late afternoon brought most guests inside to prepare for dinner.

At number 121, his knock on the glass door was loud and insistent but no one answered. He looked at his watch. Dammit, an hour and a half had passed since they'd landed, and time was a precious commodity. He peered through the glass doors for some sign of life, then checked out the two adjoining units in the hopes someone had seen her. They, too, were empty, but a radio was softly playing on a small table set between two cabana chairs on 121's patio, and a half-finished drink rested beside the radio.

Shielding his eyes against the setting sun, he glanced up and down the beach. With the exception of the young children who were beaching their jet-skis, he saw only two groups of people who could be tourists. And he hoped that the person who left the unfinished drink was one of the tourists on the beach.

He descended the steps to the beach, and strode swiftly toward the two women walking at the water's edge. "I'm looking for Danielle," he said as he approached them, but they shook their heads and answered in Spanish.

The second group consisted of two retired couples who looked like British tourists. They were collecting shells in a small, woven basket, and he turned back without speaking to them.

Standing on the nearly deserted beach, he gazed up and down its length once again while a wave of hopelessness overcame him. He'd been so sure when he'd left his father's, so sure he'd read Egon's mind correctly, so sure he understood Egon's feelings, certain he was on his way to Le Retour.

Now doubts were beginning to assail him, and if he were wrong, he'd be too late to help Egon. Rifat's men would get to him before he did. He shut his eyes briefly against the desolation sweeping him and took a deep sustaining breath.

He'd begun to turn away when out of the corner of his eye he caught a glimpse of shocking yellow between the spokes of the jet-skis chained to a palm. And as he focused on the tiny patch of brilliant color, a woman in a yellow bikini turned over so her oiled shoulder glistened in the setting sun. Walking closer, he noticed the Air France flight bag partially concealed by her beach wrap.

"Danielle?" he inquired.

Looking up at him over her left shoulder, the dark-haired woman said, "Yes?"

Bingo.

"Egon *was* on the flight," Carey announced, satisfaction evident in his voice as he entered the car and pointed eastward with a nod. "Danielle said her fellow stewardess Mariel took an interest in Egon and left the airport with him. So we're getting back on the coast highway," he explained as Molly backed up and turned out of the parking lot overlooking the tennis courts.

"So where's Egon? Does she know?"

"No, but my guess is he's playing kissy-face with his new friend up at Le Retour. I hate to break up a pleasant interlude, but Rifat's not likely to wait. Whoa! You need to drive on the left side of the road, darling, or we'll be a traffic statistic."

"Sorry."

"Want me to drive?"

"No, you give me directions. This I can do."

But when they'd covered the winding uphill miles to Egon's home high above the bay, the small staff he kept at the house hadn't heard from him.

Frustrated, Carey paced the large entrance hall on the main floor while Egon's steward looked on nervously. Awed, Molly eyed a statue reminiscent of a hellenistic sculpture she'd seen in a museum. The pale yellow and white color scheme complemented the cream exterior of the villa, one of the finest examples of colonial Palladian she'd ever seen.

Symmetrical stairways met on the main floor veranda and the entire facade faced the sea with enormous pilastered and pedimented windows exposed to the view and breeze.

"If we had time," Carey said, checking his watch, "we could afford to wait here for him."

"Could I have dinner served for you and the lady, Count

Fersten?" the steward courteously inquired, moving away from the doorway enough to enter Carey's line of vision.

"Thank you no, David," he said, shoving his hands in his shorts pockets and standing still for a contemplative moment. "Now where the hell would he go with a little French stewardess?" he muttered. Carey exhaled suddenly, his mind a muddle from trying to second-guess Egon, who at the best of times was erratic. On drugs, he was undirected impulse. In the meantime though, he'd better clear the house because sooner or later Rifat's men would show up and terrorize whomever was here.

"By the way, David, there's a bit of trouble following Count von Mansfeld. I'd suggest the staff sleep elsewhere tonight." He began pacing again, as if the physical activity promoted thought.

"But, sir, what if Master Egon arrives?"

"He'll understand, trust me. Now go pack what you need for a couple of nights and get everyone the hell out."

"But, sir, we're familiar with the master's scrapes. If the constable comes, we can deal with him."

Carey stopped midpace and swung around slowly until he faced Egon's steward who'd served Egon's father before him. Without terrifying David or being too explicit in front of Molly, he had to make David aware of the danger. "Egon's in more trouble than usual. Sylvie suggested you take a few days off and visit your family in the Blue Mountains like cook did once."

David and the servants had left once during the colonial upheavals of the fifties when some of the independence advocates had taken to the streets with machetes. Sylvie still talked about the stories old cook would relate of the bloody course of events.

"Truly, sir?" David carefully inquired, understanding the extent of the danger now.

"As soon as possible."

"And Master Egon?"

"I'm going back to find him and take him to my father's. He's somewhere between here and Montego Bay."

"Might I suggest—?"

"Rosie's?"

"Yes."

"He's with a woman already."

"Anyone from the island, sir?" David asked. Egon's companion might dictate the style of entertainment.

"No, an Air France stewardess."

"You might try the Ruins. Master Egon favors it."

"Good idea. Thanks, David." He smiled then, in both apology and understanding. Over the years he and David had seen to Egon's best interests on numerous occasions. "Remember," he softly said, his inflection suggesting the seriousness of the situation, "be out of here as soon as possible." And, striding toward Molly, he took her hand and pulled her out the door. "I'll drive." They were down the staircase and into the car with efficiency and dispatch.

"Why didn't I think of food?" he said, slamming the car into gear and accelerating out of the drive.

"Probably because if you were with an Air France stewardess you wouldn't be thinking of food," Molly sweetly replied.

"Great, I'm three thousand miles from home looking to stay one step ahead of the death squad and I've a comedian on my hands."

"It's the truth, admit it."

"Jesus, what a nag." But his voice was teasing and for a brief, insane moment he was glad she'd come along.

"I'm simply pointing out the reason for your oversight." Her voice was smug, but teasing too.

"I guess you're right," he replied. "They never did think about food."

She hit him then.

And he laughed. "You've led a sheltered life."

"Until now," she pointed out.

"You *should* be back on the plane with Jess."

"Don't want to."

"Impossible woman."

"But charming."

"Just *impossible* at the moment. You realize, of course, you're in the way." He kept his eyes on the road, both his hands on the wheel and was braking just before the curves, then accelerating into them with a speed much too fast for dusk on this narrow mountain road. "If he's at the Ruins, I'm going to bodily throw him over my shoulder and carry him out. You can make yourself useful by uttering polite noises to the stewardess and saying Egon's good-byes."

"Just like that. Won't she think it rude?"

"Not as rude as a 9mm round in her head. She'll thank you, believe me, for saving her family the expense of a funeral." Carey's voice was without a trace of amusement and Molly instantly recalled the attempt to kidnap Carrie. She still had trouble digesting the full impact of an act of violence like that directed at her family. Now that it was over, her first impulse was to dismiss it and forget it as some surreal infringement of her conventional life. And even here in Jamaica, racing down a mountain road as a magical lavender twilight settled into the anonymous gray of dusk, she seemed detached from the murderous danger of kidnappers and lethal bullets.

"Are you sure that Rifat is really after Egon?"

He *should* have locked her on the plane, he thought. It was a terrible mistake to have her along. "Can't be sure," he lied, thinking he'd drop her off at the Sheraton, book them a room, and tell her he'd be back to spend the night once he'd found Egon. *She'd* be safe then, and out of Rifat's way. He should have thought of it sooner.

"And Egon's fear might just be drug-induced."

"Could be."

"Maybe Carrie and Lucy *were* imagining things. You know how they go off on tangents when they're together."

Carey thought of the broken door jamb she'd obviously forgotten. "Maybe I *am* taking this all too seriously," he agreed in a voice he'd found particularly effective with nettled women and suspicious producers. "Probably read one script too many."

CHAPTER 35

Egon and Mariel were dancing on the small outside terrace. The last traces of sunset reflected off the water falling into the pool, sparkling saffron on mauve. They held each other close, moving slowly to the music, absorbing the pleasure inundating their senses.

"I'm glad I met you," she murmured, her face lifted to his.

"I should have met you years ago," Egon softly replied, feeling happiness for the first time in years.

"I would have been too young," she teased.

"I would have waited for you." His voice was low and hushed. Mariel was genuine and unaffected, with a warm vivacity that seemed to reach out and touch him. She'd talked of her home in Haut-Provence, of the countryside, and her family. Her conversation was eons away from the brittle banality passing for entertainment in his social milieu: seeing who'd outdressed whom; participating in silly games; overindulging to alleviate the lethargy, the excruciating sameness of the people and idle chatter. Mariel was like a fresh, cool sea breeze, and for the first time in many long years he thought beyond today.

"Do you have to go back?" Egon asked.

"No, not for three days," she answered, her cheek against the soft linen of his shirt, his scent fragrant in her nostrils.

That wasn't what he meant. "I mean can you stay with me."

She looked up, her expression bewildered. "I said I would."

He stopped dancing. "Forever," he said without emphasis.

She didn't realize this was the only commitment Egon had ever offered. She smiled at him. Misunderstanding both the meaning and significance of his words, she flirtatiously replied to what she interpreted as amorous banter. "Forever and ever."

"I'm quite serious," Egon said.

Her smile diminished as they stood in the center of the dance floor. "Please don't." She, too, had been touched by emotions so powerful she'd had to rationalize them away as the product of a tropical evening in the company of a wealthy young aristocrat with extraordinary charm. Egon von Mansfeld was beyond the pragmatic dreams of a young farm girl only two years out of Provence. *You don't have to say things like that. I'll stay with you for my three days without the facile words*, she thought. And in some ways his words tarnished her pleasure. A man so handsome and wealthy had surely used those phrases many times before.

Egon smiled then, a small, crooked grin. Hugging her, he said, "I'll tell you again in the morning when you know me better."

Responding to his smile, she brushed aside her misgivings and allowed herself to only feel the sheer joy of being with him. "I should like that immensely," she replied. "And if we're not dancing, could we go?"

Egon glanced around, startled to see the band was still playing while they'd become an obstacle in the center of the floor. "We can dance all night if you care to," he said graciously.

But she shook her head.

"In that case," he remarked, his lean face creased in a smile, "I'll show you Le Retour."

"And teach me to ride." Her voice was husky with double entendre.

His eyes held hers for a long moment. "With pleasure," he said.

Carey lost at least ten minutes arguing with Molly outside the Sheraton. The idea of her waiting while he searched for Egon seemed reasonable to him. Unfortunately, he was unable to convince Molly of his plan's merit.

"I'm not going in, and that's that."

"I'll carry you in."

"Try."

And her eyes were such narrow slits, he knew he'd be thrown into jail if he attempted that maneuver. "Look, I'll level with you. There's a certain amount of danger."

"I already know that."

"I won't be gone long," he countered.

"Then I won't be in the way for long."

He held his arm out the window to catch the last of the light and checked the time once again. He couldn't waste another minute. "Okay," he said, "you win."

"I don't want to win. I want us to cooperate."

"Cooperate, shit," he muttered, slamming the car into gear and taking the turnaround with a sharp jerk of the wheel and squealing tires. "Does this place look like fucking *Sesame Street*?"

"You needn't be grumpy," she said in the satisfied tone of a winner.

"Egon better be at the Ruins," Carey said in a very grumpy voice.

But he wasn't.

Carey was informed that Count von Mansfeld had left a half-hour ago.

"For?" Carey snapped.

"Le Retour, of course," the maître d' smoothly replied.

"You're driving like a madman," Molly remarked in as placid a tone as she could muster slung against the door as they rounded a curve at eighty.

"Keep it in mind," Carey growled, his frustration mounting. He couldn't shake the nagging fear that Ceci would appear before he could carry Egon off. Damn Egon's politesse. If he'd taken that sweet young thing straight to Le Retour instead of wining and dining her, they'd all be halfway back to the plane at Montego Bay by now.

"At least you know where he is."

Carey only grunted, his mind racing over possibilities for defense at Le Retour. What was the weapon situation? Egon's father used to keep some rifles in the study. They'd taken them out for target practice once, but how often were they oiled? It probably had been years since they were used, and this humidity was hell on metal.

"You can't always have your way, you know," Molly said in a small voice that brought his head around for a brief moment from the headlights' flaring gleam.

"I know," he replied with a sigh. Molly was unaware, he realized, that he had had his own way for a great many years now . . . almost without exception. And "cooperation" was almost as big an adjustment for him as it was for her to recognize there were paid killers in the world. Killers who were, at the moment, *probably extremely close* and checking their ammunition. "I don't want my way in an arbitrary sense, but will you promise me to listen if things start really heating up? You don't know—" He hesitated, and then simply finished, "just promise me."

"I can shoot, you know."

"I don't *want* you to shoot. Jesus, that's the last thing in the world I want you to do. Lie, humor me—just promise."

"Okay, okay. I promise."

"Thanks, Honeybear. I love you like crazy. Now if we can drag Egon out of his darling's arms in time, we might, we just *might* get the hell out of here healthy. It's only nine. Once we're back on the road past Ocho Rios, they can't tell one car from the other."

CHAPTER 36

*T*hey were just beginning to climb the upgrade into the hills above Ocho Rios after having stopped in town to get directions for Le Retour. Ceci rode shotgun, Deraille drove, and Reha assembled his assault rifle in the backseat. Their weapons had come over with their luggage in a crate with scuba gear. The rifle stocks were made of molded plastic to avoid detection on x-ray machines. But security wasn't a priority at Montego Bay, and they could have shipped them over assembled without problem.

"Remember," Ceci warned, "take von Mansfeld alive. If you have to shoot him, aim for an arm or leg. Watch it, with that rifle, Reha. It'll blow his leg off. I don't care about anyone else. They're expendable."

His companions were efficient and professional. His warning was only meant as a cautionary reminder for Reha, who took more pleasure in killing than was natural. Rifat needed Egon alive in order to have the prototypes delivered.

The fact that Le Retour was unstaffed struck Egon as unusual, but not unprecedented. From a quick survey of the kitchen and servants' rooms, he saw they hadn't been absent long, and on rare occasions they did go up mountain for overnight visits home. He hadn't been expected. Everyone would be back in the morning, he explained to Mariel. Taking a bottle of champagne from the refrigerator, he escorted her up the curved staircase to his suite of rooms facing the ocean.

The teakwood floors glistened warmly with the patina of time, and the simple four-poster bed crafted by the original plantation owner's slaves was an artisan's derivation of Queen Anne purity. Tall windows framed in sea island cotton opened onto a large balcony. White, hand-loomed cotton rugs were placed beside the bed, before two tall mahogany dressers and under the oversized cane armchairs situated so their occupants were afforded a view of the water.

"And flowers," Mariel exclaimed, as though her silent survey of the room's beauty had been audible to Egon. Dropping his hand, she moved toward an enormous earthenware bowl of white roses and buried her face in the delightful fragrance. Turning back to Egon with a smile, she said, "They *knew* you were coming."

"No, the flowers are changed daily. The freesia is my favorite," Egon replied, kicking off his shoes and strolling over to the bed. He set the champagne on the bedside table, adorned with a tall majolica jug of bright yellow freesia and baby's breath.

"Baby's breath too. Does everything grow in Jamaica?"

"Everything. Even an English garden was nurtured for centuries by the previous owners, although the climate is so tropical." He shrugged out of his sport coat and sprawled on the bed, his arms clasped comfortably behind his head. The crisp white linen bedcover felt cool against his body, and he peacefully watched Mariel walk from window to window exclaiming over the view of moonlight and sparkling sea.

"It's not hot up here."

"A fact the early settlers discovered immediately."

"How long have you owned Le Retour?" She turned from

he moonlit windows, her small form silhouetted against the
ilvery brilliance.

"My great-grandfather bought it in the eighties as a re-
reat. He was an amateur naturalist, and he enlarged the gardens, bringing in trees and plants from all over the world. Am
 boring you?" he asked politely. He wasn't generally a conver-
ationalist with a woman who aroused him.

"Will you show me the gardens in the morning?"

"I'll show you every last botanical eccentricity, if you
wish. Great-grandpapa brought over a gardener he'd stolen
rom the royal court and Herr Schramm oversaw an army of
native gardeners whose descendants still practice his style of
horticulture."

"My great-grandpapa raised cattle, and my grandpapa
and papa do the same."

Her words were like a soothing tonic, as though all the
tension in his body and mind, all the raw nerve endings he'd
been calming with heroin were tranquilized. He could imagine a quiet childhood on a farm generations old. Not that his
family's homes weren't venerable, but the frenzy of his
mother's social life was too prevalent, as was the unspoken
disapproval of their wealth. Their fortunes were fostered by
death. "My family made money on wars," he said. He'd had
no control over his feelings, no defense to bear the censure.
Unlike Sylvie, he was sensitive to the slurs. "Would you like
some champagne?" he asked, wanting to dismiss the plaguing
inequities. With Mariel near, he'd found a new ease in banish-
ing the past.

She came to him with a smile and sat beside him on the
large, linen-covered bed. Taking off her jacket, she watched as
he poured champagne into the two glass tumblers which had
been on the pottery tray beside the freesia. Everything was
anticipated and ready at hand, Mariel noted, down to the last
small detail. Danish biscuits, no doubt a favorite of Egon's,
were arranged on the tray, as well, only an arm's reach away.

New magazines lay on the tables beside the chairs. Even the cologne on the tallboy was unopened and new.

"Do you come here often? It's very beautiful."

"Not lately," he said, offering her a glass. "Although," he went on with a boyish smile, "if you like, we can come more often."

"Be careful what you say," she replied, her eyes serious. "I'm a simple farm girl and my head can be easily turned." Her smile was winsome. "And I don't care to be hurt," she added very softly.

"I'd never hurt you," Egon said, his eyes sober beneath the wave of blond hair falling across his forehead. "I'm an authority on the subject."

"Because of this?" Mariel said, reaching over to touch the needle marks on his bare arms. His short-sleeved linen shirt exposed the tracks of heroin use, and he didn't stop her from stroking the vestiges of bruises.

He gazed at his arms as though they were detached somehow, a landscape of misadventure he'd overlooked. "I forget how they appear to other people," he said, shrugging away the familiar sense of error. "It's not habitual. I go off and on."

"Could I help?"

He nodded, covering her small hand with his. "I'd like that."

"Tomorrow?"

"It's not very pleasant."

"Only if you want to," she quickly added, conscious of her overwhelming presumption. "I'm sorry, I didn't mean to be judgmental."

He smiled. "A crusading female."

"No!" Her small cry was instantly apologetic.

"Tomorrow's fine," he softly said, stroking the back of her hand, wondering for a brief moment why he was agreeing with such pleasure to undergo the excruciating ordeal. But his feelings were inexplicable—not muddled or distorted, merely inexplicable. And he savored the feeling of bliss.

Reaching over, he set his glass on the bedside table and said, "This may sound off-the-wall, but have you ever experienced bliss?"

"Do I have to answer that?" she replied, uncertainty in her voice. She knew him too little to admit to the sensation she was experiencing, and was afraid somehow he was toying with her.

"No—no," he quickly answered. "Are you through? Do you want more?" he asked. At her negative nod he set her glass next to his. "I'm sorry, I knew that was going to sound bizarre . . . and it's not the drugs talking. I've finally understood the sensation of bliss. That's all."

"What's it like?" Mariel asked with a childlike inquisitiveness he found endearing.

"It's warm," he said.

And she nodded in agreement, although he took it for understanding.

"Did you ever daydream as a child about something you wanted to happen and visualized how happy you'd be if everything worked out exactly like your dream?"

She nodded again, knowing how he felt, thinking he looked very strong, the muscles on his tanned arms powerful and taut.

"And it's like you've found the answer finally . . . and you wonder why you've never known it was there before."

"But it wasn't," she softly said.

"Exactly," he murmured. "Until now."

"Until now," she whispered.

Their hands met and twined, and they both smiled a secret, understanding smile that transcended all the unknowns in their lives.

And she bent to kiss him.

He stopped her short inches away, both his hands on her shoulders. "You don't have to worry about the needles."

"I'm not," she whispered and tried to kiss him.

He held her firmly, his tone level. "You should. It could be dangerous."

"You're not dangerous."

He sighed, wondering how much he should tell her, wondering if she'd accept all his other escapades as benignly. Should he say, "I have my own private physician who runs blood tests weekly, and I'm healthy." How would that play on the same stage with bliss?

"No, I'm not dangerous," he said, humbled by her utter faith in him. "And I'm going to kiss you. Don't move."

She held her breath until his mouth touched hers, and then exhaled a small sigh matched by his own gentle moan. Pulling her atop him, her slight weight effortless to lift, he held her tightly while they both felt the magic of warm daydreams come true.

After long minutes, he softly murmured against her mouth, "I'd like to—" he nibbled the sweetness of her upper lip, "take all night to please you." His mouth trailed over her cheek to her ear.

"But . . ." she teased, feeling him hard against her, hearing the husky rasp of his voice.

"But," he softly said, amusement in his eyes, "it's not going to work out . . . the pleasing."

"Until next time?" she finished with a seductive wiggle of her bottom.

"Which won't be all that long," he said with a sharp inhalation as she began to unzip his slacks. "Promise," he whispered, her hand stroking his rigid arousal.

He was proficient at undressing women, and her Air France uniform was discarded swiftly along with her lacy underclothes and nylons. She smiled when he brushed her hands away as she attempted to undress him. "You'll be way too slow." He grinned, kissed her straight small nose, and proceeded to shrug out of his clothes in record time.

She lay on his large soft bed, heated by his fierce desire, intoxicated by his impassioned need, feeling a sense of power and utter abandon. She would always remember the sweet tenderness in his beautiful eyes as he took her face in his hands and kissed her. "Hello," he breathed only inches from her mouth, and his smile held the promise of pleasure. "Welcome to Le Retour."

He was shaking when he entered her, touched by both passion and tenderness after a lifetime of pursuing only dalliance. But at least in his idle pursuit of pleasure he'd gained a flawless expertise, and he conscientiously set out to satisfy her. He moved with impeccable finesse.

As Mariel felt him glide inside her gently, she could almost anticipate each movement upward, and she trembled to feel him deeply and intensely.

He wanted more time, but knew that wish was useless in his present state. And rather than leave her unsated and possibly unhappy—something he rarely considered with the predatory glittering butterflies so often in his bed—he decided to discard thought of a leisurely lovemaking.

Egon concentrated on the readily roused portions of the female anatomy and proceeded to bring the lady to climax. It was a sensible action by a man known for his intemperance, for he wouldn't have been able to withhold his own intense orgasm much longer.

He felt as though he were drowning as he poured into her, his breath in sharp abeyance as acute pleasure washed over him.

And the small, soft woman in his arms wept with the intensity of her passion.

"Don't cry . . . I've hurt you. I'm sorry . . . don't cry," Egon murmured, bereft at his incompetence.

"No . . . no, it was beautiful. I've never—" She hesitated at the clinical word, translating it into the more lyrical French. "I've never experienced le petite morte . . ."

Oh Lord, he thought and damned his own selfishness. He could have made it so much better. Enfolding her in his arms, he held her close. "I think I love you," he gently said. He found the words infinitely easy to say, though he spoke them for the first time in his life.

"I think I like that," she whispered shyly in return.

And he knew he'd found his elusive paradise.

CHAPTER **37**

With every room at Le Retour lighted, Carey knew Egon had finally arrived. Without discretion he and Molly entered the house. Standing in the center of the entrance hall, he shouted, "Egon! Goddammit, get dressed!"

Then, grabbing Molly's hand, he swiftly moved toward the stairway leading to the third floor. "Pretty polite guy," Molly said, taking the stairs two at a time to keep up to him.

"No time for etiquette. Besides, Egon's used to me."

And that casual statement made Molly wonder how many times they'd shared the intimacy of amorous escapades. When Carey pushed open the door into Egon's room without so much as a knock, Molly hung back, uncomfortable with the idea of barging into someone's bedroom.

"Get your ass out of bed Egon, pronto. Sorry," he briefly apologized with a nod at Mariel who was clutching the bed-sheet to her chest. "But we've got to get out of here—*now!*"

"They might not come."

"And I'm the Virgin Mary. Get your clothes on."

Carey's sudden appearance brought thoughts of Rifat flooding back to Egon's mind. "Have you seen them?"

"No, not yet. We might make it out. Meet you downstairs

in three minutes. Here." He tossed Egon's slacks to him and walked out of the room.

"Let's see what we can find for weapons," Carey said, taking Molly's hand again and moving toward the stairway. "The study's downstairs."

"What was the girl like?" Molly asked as they descended the stairs. "Did she seem frightened at your appearance?"

Carey glanced at Molly, his expression bewildered. His thoughts were focused on the need to protect themselves. "I didn't look at her. She'll be down in a minute." He pointed toward a room at the base of the stairs.

"Can Egon handle a gun?" Molly asked.

"Yes," Carey said, "if the damn things aren't rusted shut." He was feeling extremely vulnerable at the moment with two women to protect and Egon's stability in question, though he'd seemed remarkably in control. One point for our side, Carey thought. When Egon was in command of his nerves, the man was prime. Like the time they were trap shooting in Austria, and he and Egon had both melted the bores on two shotguns, matching scores all afternoon. Egon had a good eye.

He glanced swiftly at Molly, as if to reassure himself. She smiled at him, and he squeezed her hand. She was so normal and rational, so fiercely lovable. Damn, she shouldn't be here. But then there shouldn't be brutality and injustice in the world, either . . . he couldn't control the universe.

After an inspection of the rifles and shotguns in the glass-doored cabinet, he found only two unusable. The others, while not modern assault weapons, were custom hunting rifles and shotguns capable of lethal damage. He was stacking ammunition on the large, polished desktop when Egon and Mariel appeared on the stairway. "In the study," he shouted.

Egon held Mariel's hand when he introduced her, and none of the blasé indifference was in his voice. Carey looked at her with interest; she was fresh-faced and unpretentious, with innocent eyes. A decided change from the European models Egon normally chose to amuse himself. The ones who pretended so much and so often, they were no longer sure exactly who they were. This young woman apparently knew who she was.

"So you're Molly," Egon remarked enigmatically when Carey introduced her.

"And you're Egon," she replied with a mischievous smile. "We've been tracking you for hours."

"I see why you married Sylvie," Egon quietly said. It wasn't the boredom of location in Yugoslavia, after all. Although dissimilar in physical details, there was a distinct *general* similarity between his sister and the woman Carey had called for so often when he was sleeping off some overindulgence during his enfant terrible stage. Egon had heard the name "Molly" quite regularly in those days.

"I'd love to sit and discuss my marriage to your sister," Carey said with a sardonic grin, "but with Rifat's gunmen close on our heels, I suggest we save our skins instead."

At Mariel's frightened expression, Molly soothingly said, "Carey's pessimistic by nature. I'm sure everything will be fine."

She should write messages for Hallmark cards, Carey thought, recalling Egon's sports car blown up on his doorstep. "Since there is a *possibility* of danger, the sooner we leave Le Retour, the better."

Mariel looked to Egon for explanation. "We'd better leave now to be safe," he said. "I'll explain on the way to the airport."

"Are you in trouble with the law?" she queried. There was no reproof in her voice, only concern.

"No."

"Which is why we have to hurry," Carey interjected. "The law at least might offer some security. You take this rifle, Egon. I'll take the other, and let's hit the road."

They were halfway down the outside staircase, the car no more than ten yards away when the AK-47 opened up and blasted the ornate balastrade a foot below them. Mariel screamed. Molly bit back her own cry as Carey whipped his rifle up and fired into the trees where the stream of red tracers originated. "Get back in the house," he barked, swinging around for a second to see if anyone was hit. "I'll keep them down. *Go!*" he ordered, and Egon herded them back up the steps while Carey emptied both five cartridge magazines into the trees. He heard the door open and thanked the darkness for saving them. Although the moon was out, sufficient shadow remained to make a moving target hard to hit at that range.

The familiar sound of gunfire had called all of Carey's old reflexes into action. He'd fired into the vortex of the red tracers—déjà vu, like a vivid movie in his mind. Even the warm, sultry night was the same, only the hordes of mosquitoes were missing. Where the hell were Ant and Luger when he needed them? he thought, crouching down behind the shattered stone railing to load the cartridges he'd stuffed into his pockets.

Reloaded, he scanned the tree line beyond the lawn, watching for movement in the suddenly quiet night. And he knew they were waiting to see what he'd do. For one thing, he'd better change out of this white T-shirt. He gauged the distance up the stairs to the door, slightly ajar now, with a portion of Egon's blond hair visible in the narrow aperture.

Sighting over the warm sandstone, he squeezed off five rapid shots, and then sprinted for the doorway. Egon fired across the lawn into the concealing shrubbery as Carey raced up the stairs in a crouching run, followed by a bursting explosion of flying sandstone as Rifat's men opened fire. Ricocheting bits of stone accompanied Carey's dash inside, and Egon slammed the door shut against the barrage.

"I hope she was worth it," Carey muttered, pulling Egon

away from the door. Even the six solid inches of teak wouldn't stop the AK rounds at close range.

"She was," Egon replied, his smile brilliant for a man under attack by bloodthirsty brutes who'd kill a man and eat a good breakfast five minutes later.

"It might be your fucking last fuck," Carey growled, frustrated by the damn timing. Another few minutes and they'd have been gone. "How the hell can you smile like that?"

"I have found bliss," Egon said. "I recommend it."

"Great. Glad to hear it. But I don't think the others in this crowd empathize with your current mood."

Mariel and Molly were huddled against the wall under the stairway, their faces ashen.

"But if some bloody miracle occurs, we might be able to blast our way out of here. How many did you see?"

Egon sobered immediately when he detected Mariel's fear. "I fucked up again, didn't I?" he said, the familiar pain back in his eyes.

Carey was immediately contrite. "Look," he said with a quick shrug, "maybe it's not so bad. I only saw three I think. How about you?"

Egon sighed. "Three. It's always the same . . . you have to come and save my ass. I'm sorry, Carey."

"Hey, hey," Carey said, taking his arm, "don't bum out on me now. We might manage if there's only three." *Only* three, he thought, am I the world's biggest optimist or what? They're fucking Rifat's front line. But he needed Egon functioning, not tripping out in his own little world. "Remember the shoot at Erhard's outside Linz? We paced each other all afternoon. Maybe we can keep them pinned down and pick them off. These custom rifles of your dad's are good for long distances with these full-size cartridges. Hell these are special competition rifles. Can you follow me?"

"Sure, Carey."

"With conviction now. I want to waste these suckers."

Egon's smile was faint, but hopeful. "I'll follow you, boss."

"Good, now let's get the women upstairs and we'll go stalking. Our great advantage is we know this place and they don't. I want to find their car."

After a swift detour into the study, the women were escorted upstairs past the bedroom floor into the attic. Handing Molly a shotgun and a rifle, Carey said, "These are for protection if you need them. But," he went on quickly, seeing the apprehension appear in her eyes, "you shouldn't. Just maybe."

"I can't stand waiting for a footstep on the stairs. Let me come with you."

Carey's first impulse was to brusquely refuse but that approach never worked with Molly. "Darling," he said, holding her lightly with one arm around her shoulder, "Mariel's about to lose it over there." And they both glanced at Mariel shivering in Egon's embrace. "I'm not saying you're not a great shot and we couldn't use you, but we need you here with her."

"I don't suppose she'll stay here alone."

"From the looks of it, she's going to fall apart pretty soon, and then Egon's going to get all emotional and I'd prefer that not happen. He can help me flush those guys out of cover; he knows this place inside out. Come *on*, Honeybear, be a dear and whip that female into shape . . . Please?"

"They're not going to just go away, are they?" Her words were mild despite their significant content, and she wondered for a moment if she was in shock. Is this normal when being stalked by killers, this unearthly calm?

She must be in shock, Carey decided, she was taking this much too serenely. He'd seen it before, when men started talking about their favorite songs or their girlfriend back home as shells started exploding. Shit. "Are you going to be all right? I've got to drag Egon out of here."

"I'm fine."

Oh Christ, he thought, looking at her standing there with a weapon in each hand, a pleasant smile on her face and that damn placid voice. He loved her more than anything, and he had to leave her here whether she could handle it or not; if he didn't move real fast, it was going to be over. "Thanks," he said in lieu of dragging her into his arms and never letting her go.

It took another few moments to persuade Egon to loosen his embrace. With an imploring glance over Egon's head, he silently asked Molly for help. Setting down the guns, she walked over and put a hand on Mariel's shoulder. "Egon, Mariel and I will be safe here."

"We'd better go," Carey declared, placing a heavy hand on Egon's arm. "We won't be long," he added with theatrical confidence. "Let's hit it." He felt like a goddamn coach at halftime, but the conclusion of this game was slightly more terminal, especially if he didn't pry Egon loose soon.

At last, Egon slowly relinquished his hold.

"Hurry back," Molly said with a bracing smile. Now she knew how the eternal female felt sending her man off to war.

"Take care," Carey murmured so only she could hear, "and don't let anyone in that door." The intensity of his tone was steel hard.

"Don't worry," Molly replied, warring impulses battling within her. "Good luck," she softly added as the door closed behind the men.

While she didn't consider herself some Amazon warrior, neither did she relish the idea of passively waiting to see whether Carey and Egon were killed. Certainly with three enemies outside they could use another weapon on their side. Although life and death situations were distinctly foreign to Molly's repertoire, she'd always prided herself on responding well to crises. She could help; she knew she could. And she was going to.

"Mariel, I'm going with them. They could use another

rifle. Can you shoot this if you have to?" Surprised at her solid conviction, Mariel's answer was unimportant. She was going.

When Mariel nodded, it was as though the movement confirmed Molly's resolution. "If it will help Egon, I'll do it," she said in a very small voice. "They're after him, aren't they?"

"Only because he owns a munitions factory," Molly clarified. "Otherwise he wouldn't be involved with men like those. Here, now look, this is all you have to do." And she placed the semi-automatic gun in her hands. "If a stranger comes through that door, pull the trigger."

Straightening her shoulders, she called on all her reserves of strength. "I'll manage. Now go, before you lose them." And, pulling up a dust-covered chair, she sat down and aimed the gun barrel at the door.

Molly glanced back once before she left and gave her an encouraging smile. Mariel was rigid as a mannequin, but the determination on her face was resolute.

With her adrenaline and heart pumping at maximum speed, Molly ran down the attic stairs, hoping Carey and Egon hadn't gotten too far ahead of her. But if they had, she'd already decided to exit the house through the study doors facing the veranda. Maybe she could serve as backup if Carey and Egon flushed the men out of hiding. The rifle felt solid in her hand as she paused on the second floor to listen for sounds. Nothing. The silence held an ominous quality; she knew that predators could be closing in, and were perhaps already in the house.

She was more careful descending the staircase to the main floor, keeping close to the wall. Her ears were alert to any noise. At the last step she paused before leaving the protection of the wall. Her approach to the study across the open area of the entrance hall was not conducive to stealth. With the shiny black-and-white marble of the floor, her footsteps would be audible. Certainly she'd be an easy target once she stepped out into the open foyer.

Apprehensively she took her first step away from the wall

and listened, her rifle held defensively, her finger on the trigger. Utter silence. Even the outdoor night sounds of frogs and crickets were muted by the thick stone walls. Just as she was about to make her dash across the large expanse of marble to the study, she heard a man's voice, and she moved back one step to the protection of the wall. She waited another slow count of twenty, but the sound was not repeated.

She couldn't stand pressed against the wall forever. Gathering her courage, she raced toward the study across the thirty feet of marble, through the partially open door into the sights of two rifles poised to fire.

Catching a glimpse of the rifle barrel and two shadowy forms, she dove for the floor just as she heard Carey mutter, "Oh, Christ . . ."

As she lay on the floor, he stalked over and stood silently over her, making no effort to help her up.

"You could have been killed," he growled.

"So could you," she replied. She knew damn well she'd come within a hair's breath of being shot; her pulse rate was still loud as a gang war in her ears, and she was bordering on hysteria.

He'd put a hunting jacket over his white T-shirt so he was dressed all in khaki. The only color catching the moonlight was his pale hair.

"You don't follow orders very well."

"I don't follow orders at all."

"I don't have time to watch you."

"You don't have to, and Mariel's in control."

He sighed and put out his hand to help her up. He didn't have any more time to argue. "Welcome aboard," he gruffly said. When she placed her hand in his, he pulled her up without effort.

"Thank you," Molly said. Standing before him, she was dwarfed by his size, but felt a new competence. "I'm a very good shot." She wanted to tell him she had a girl scout badge in marksmanship and was always a tomboy, but knew how ludicrous it would sound under the circumstances. So instead she said, "I can help."

He laughed, a dry humorless sound. "They don't say 'Take 2' if things don't go right, you know. You're risking your life."

"You are, too."

He shrugged. "You should think of Carrie."

"So should you."

"Okay, Honeybear. We'd better make sure we do this thing right, then. She needs us." And, putting his arm around Molly's shoulder, he gave her a hug. "Egon," Carey said, "we have backup now."

"Mariel's doing fine," Molly assured him. "She's determined to be brave and help you."

Even in the dim light Molly saw Egon's expression change to one of tenderness. "She's a remarkable woman," he said.

"Great," Carey said, wanting Egon to keep his mind on the problem at hand. "Now, if we're all ready." He looked at Molly. "You'd better take one of these jackets. You'll need it for your ammo." He passed it to her, and reached over for a handful of cartridges. Filling her pockets, he gave her a quick kiss and a shove in Egon's direction. "Follow Egon, he's going to lead the way around the house from the servants' entrance. I'll follow you. We're looking for their car first, in case they left a driver there we don't know about." With Molly between Egon and himself, he could protect her best. But her presence set his already taut nerves on edge.

They slipped out the back door without incident. Concealed by the shrubbery growing close to the stairway, they descended the steps. Every receptor on alert, they crept along the shadows of the kitchen garden wall, passed through the gateway separating it from the south lawn, and immediately stopped. The car was parked at the edge of the lawn where the rose garden boundary began, perhaps thirty yards away.

"I'm going to check the car out."

"There's no cover," Egon warned.

"They won't be watching the car. You two keep an eye on

that tree line." And he was gone before the arguments could start. Carey operated best on intuition and impulse—always had. Racing forward, he instinctively tumbled into a rolling dive milliseconds before the barrage of tracers reached him. He'd felt it like a sixth sense and dove for cover behind the car as if his guardian angels were still on full alert.

They wouldn't be firing like that at the car if they'd left a guard inside, so he could take a quick breath. They wouldn't attack in the open, either. Rifat's hired killers weren't looking for dead hero status. He wanted to look inside the car, though, hoping to get his hands on an assault rifle. It would even the odds considerably.

Egon and Molly watched with horror as the pattern of tracers sailed toward Carey, the flash and clamor erupting in the tranquil evening air. Then they fired into the trees in an attempt to protect Carey. The sharp retort of their rifles was distinct from the rapid barrage of terrorists' weapons.

But as suddenly as it began, the fusillade ended, as if in a freeze frame of time. All the participants waited and watched, poised to determine the next move. Normal night sounds and scents once again filled the moonlit scene of open lawn and car and bordering foliage: the low, muted whir of night birds and insects, the rustle of leaves stirred by the ocean breeze, the sweet fragrance of roses incongruous in this drama of death.

Ceci, Deraille, and Reha waited to see if others would join Count Fersten. He'd been recognizable by his size and gilded hair—and by his competence. Ceci was more cautious now. Count Fersten was an altogether different adversary than Egon. Had he brought reserves with him? With a brief movement of his hand Ceci indicated an extremely cautious advance toward the car, keeping well hidden in the shrubbery bordering the lawn.

During the pause Carey had crawled to the south side of the car and opened the back door. Raising himself a scant six inches, he glanced inside and was profoundly delighted. An assault weapon lay partially assembled on the floor. Risking another six inches of elevation, he reached for the pieces and carefully drew them forward. The process seemed endless in the intense silence of the night; in fact, eight seconds elapsed.

Then Carey scanned the area for movement. Assured they weren't within yards yet, he braced himself against the car and began working frantically assembling the weapon. As he snapped the pieces into place, repeating the never forgotten litany like a nursery rhyme from childhood, a flashback of horror materialized in his mind.

Charlie had overrun the perimeter wires in screaming waves at three A.M., and everyone was scrambling for their weapons, firing like maniacs, trying to stay alive when their minds were still sluggish from sleep. Carey had been firing at oncoming VC from a spider hole he'd found, but they just kept coming. The stack of belts at his feet was diminishing. He aimed a head shot at the enemy charging at him, and his M-16 jammed. Dropping down into the blackest corner of his hole, he'd feverishly broken his weapon down, trying to unjam the firing mechanism. He was halfway through, screaming in frustration and rage, when a VC came over the top firing. At the advice of a special forces cowboy he'd met one night in a hot tub in Saigon, Carey whipped a deadly knife out of his shoulder sling. He caught the attacking Charlie just under the rib cage with his blade and ripped him in half clear up to his head.

The assault had abruptly ceased moments later, as though Carey's victory had signaled retreat.

Shoving the magazine into place, he shook the disturbing images aside. Forcing away the bloody sights of death, he felt pleased Rifat's men had chosen a Kalashnikov. They never jammed.

Egon saw the small flurry of movement first. Molly nodded as he silently pointed out its location. "See them?" he whispered.

She nodded. "I'll take the last one, you take the other."

Their rifles poised and tracking, they followed the slight stirring as a branch shifted and a shrub quivered.

Carey was just rotating the selector to full automatic when Deraille and Reha opened fire on him. He rolled away from the rounds kicking up the lawn around him, scrambling backward and shoving the indicator onto automatic *hard*. Half-seated, he fired in a sweeping arc at the distant foliage just as Egon and Molly emptied their magazines into the trees. There were screams, but no one was able to determine their origin as everyone desperately reloaded. There was no time for conversation, no time to think; only speed and accuracy mattered now. Molly's hands trembled as she forced the new magazine into the breech. She was almost as fast as Egon, he noted as he whipped his rifle in position again and sighted in.

If he'd taken a second longer in his reloading, he would have been too late to see Ceci step out of the bushes behind Carey.

Egon's scream tore through the sultry night like a machete through gauze, a high-pitched, piercing wail of rage and appeal. "No-o-o-o!" And it echoed above the report of his rifle shots as he ran across the open lawn firing.

Ceci swung round at the cry and aimed automatically at the running figure, allowing Carey the split second he needed to redirect his weapon at Reha and Deraille as they came out of the woods at a run. It was his nightmare over again, and he held his finger solidly on the trigger as they came at him—a VC flashback of death and terror.

Egon staggered backward. Hit in the shoulder, the bullet had passed through his lung with the impact of a freight train. His arms flew outward as he slammed into the ground as if he'd been thrown by some giant hand.

Molly watched in horror as the man behind Carey who had just shot Egon, took careful aim—this time at Carey.

Focused on Deraille and Reha's assault, firing at the two killers who seemed to keep coming at him despite an onslaught of bullets, Carey was unaware of Ceci's objective.

There was no time for finesse or even thought; she barely had time to superficially sight in. Not realizing she was shrieking above the deafening roar of gunshots, Molly fired.

He fell, but like a marionette on strings, he pulled himself jerkily upright and stumbled back into the black shadows of the trees. She emptied her rifle into his back, but he wouldn't fall. Like a scene from a horror movie where ghoulish creatures survive every conceivable means of death.

When her ammunition ran out, she finally halted her own shrill cry. The silence was almost more ghastly than her wild howl.

Egon was spread like a crucified Christ on the manicured lawn, the bloody wound on his chest visible even from her position yards away.

There was no sign of Carey.

No sound.

And Rifat's men could be waiting in the trees.

Gulping back the suffocating sob caught in her throat, she forced herself to reload her rifle.

She counted her remaining magazines aloud in a low murmur to still her fear, as if the sound of her voice was protection from the danger surrounding her, as though the sound of her voice would guarantee Egon wasn't dead and Carey wasn't dead and nothing she saw would be real. She could create her own reality with her voice and ignore the one before her eyes.

As she counted the six remaining magazines, she looked up briefly to steady her nerves. Her fingers were shaking. She saw the pale glisten of Carey's head slowly appear above the automobile hood.

Dropping the rifle, she ran toward him without thought or consideration, without heed for his shouted cry, "Go back!" *He's alive!* The words clamored through her mind with such deafening fanfare, all else was obliterated. Perhaps she had a guardian angel, too, or perhaps her intuition was as splendid as Carey's. Without care for Rifat's men, she ran past Egon and past the spot where Ceci had stood only moments before. Falling to her knees beside Carey, she threw her arms around him and hugged him fiercely.

Carey hugged her back with one arm only, with the other he slowly swept the foliage with his assault rifle.

"You're alive," Molly whispered between sobs and tears and damp kisses. "You're alive!"

"You took a helluva chance," he murmured gruffly. "We don't know where they are." Carey was cold-eyed and tensely alert, though the feel of Molly next to him was sheer heaven.

"Egon's shot," Molly said, her voice suddenly unsteady. "He may be dead."

Carey didn't answer, his gaze still on the trees. Were Rifat's killers waiting for them to stand up and become better targets, or were they dead or wounded? His decision to stay quiet a few moments longer reminded him of all the rotten choices he'd been obliged to make day after day in Vietnam. They were wretched choices like this, selfish and cruel and pragmatic. The kind that kept you alive.

"In another minute I'm going to stand up very slowly and we'll see if they're dead or gone or still around."

"Don't," Molly pleaded.

"I'll take it real slow. We've got to help Egon . . . he saved my life." Carey hadn't seen Ceci until Egon's scream warned him, and without that alarm he'd have been cut in two with rounds. Taking a deep breath, he slid his arm from around Molly's shoulder. "Don't move," he cautioned. And very slowly, inch by inch, he raised himself from the ground until he was standing. "Stay here," he ordered, "while I check for bodies." And in the shuddering aftermath of the nightmare she'd just lived through, Molly didn't raise her voice in dissent.

Carey had to be sure. Even though Egon may be bleeding

to death, he couldn't take a chance they were using Egon for bait. He stepped into the shadows of the trees and disappeared.

The minutes Carey was gone seemed like a thousand terrifying lifetimes as Molly sat huddled by the car, alone in the silent, moonwashed night. She strained her ears to catch some sound of Carey's direction, but it was as if he'd left her alone in an alien world, and she felt fear creeping closer like an unseen enemy.

It seemed like terrifying hours, though it was only minutes later when Carey reappeared, carrying two extra weapons. "Two dead," he said, "and a trail of blood down the mountain. The third man."

Egon felt like he was suspended in air, his whole body floating somewhere above his head. His collapsed lung only allowed slow little sucks of breath, and he waited for the blackness to descend—the kind he'd always heard described before death. The low murmur of Carey's voice drifted across the lawn. He tried to shout to him, but he couldn't draw enough air into his lungs. Then, as he lay there waiting to die, and no blackness or dazzling light appeared, it occurred to him that perhaps he wouldn't die. And a spirit of hope possessed him. He moved his hand slightly, feeling the damp grass. But when he tried to move his legs, they wouldn't move, and the effort brought choking blood into this throat and mouth. He thought with despair: *I'm going to bleed to death.* The silence became alarming instead of comforting. Was Carey dying, too? And Molly? Would Rifat's men find Mariel and kill her also? In agony he lay bleeding into the grass, unable to move, suffocating from lack of air in his lungs.

He closed his eyes. When he looked up again, Carey was kneeling over him, his face a mirror of despair.

"I can't feel my legs," Egon said, but his voice was so weak Carey had to put his head next to his lips to hear him.

"It's all right, Egon," Carey said. "You're going to be all right." And he looked away so the lie wouldn't show in his eyes. Egon's right shoulder was torn apart, and the sound of his lungs was like so many he'd heard in Vietnam before the blood choked off all the air.

"I did fine this time, didn't I?" Egon whispered. "I stood up to Rifat."

"You were great," Carey said, tears welling in his eyes. "You saved my life."

Molly knelt near Carey, tears streaming down her face. Wanting some miracle to make Egon whole again, she watched him struggle for air.

"You . . . owe me . . . now." Egon's words were the merest whisper of sound, and the smile he attempted the most stirring act of courage Molly had ever seen.

Carey nodded, not capable of speaking.

"Mariel—" Agitated, Egon tried to say more but, gasping for air, he fell silent.

"I'll take care of her," Carey promised. "My word on it."

And the panic on Egon's face subsided. "Love you," Egon whispered.

"I love you, too," Carey murmured, his voice husky with emotion. As Egon's eyes closed, a strange anger overcame Carey . . . as though he could fight death or stay its hand. He wasn't going to let Egon die. He'd breathe air into his lungs if need be, and replace his blood with his own. But he needed a doctor most. Galvanized into action, he stood in an abrupt movement. "Stay with him," was all he said as he ran toward the house.

He got a call through to Jess, and said, "Get a helicopter. Egon's wounded. Bring a doctor. He'll know where Le Retour is. Hurry." And he hung up, slamming the receiver down and reaching for a drapery at the same time. Pulling the curtain down with a rough jerk, he tossed it over his arm. Grabbing a tablecloth off the dining room table, he ran back to Molly.

Outside, Carey tore the cloth into strips and began bandaging Egon's bleeding shoulder. Molly watched him gently pack the wound and bind it tightly until the worst of the bleeding was under control. Then he covered Egon with the heavy velvet drapery to prevent shock. While he dressed Egon's wound, he kept looking up, listening for the chopper, pausing for a second in the hope they'd hear the sound of its approach. "You'd better get Mariel. They could be here soon," he told Molly.

When Molly brought Mariel down, she knelt beside Egon, took his hand in hers, and prayed. He was no longer conscious. His breathing was shallow and labored, his skin completely drained of color.

No one spoke.

In the aftermath of the horror she'd witnessed, Molly felt drained and lifeless. Carey held her in the security of his arms. She leaned back against his chest, letting the emptiness in her mind calm the memories of the awful destruction. When she began to shake, Carey's arm tightened around her, his voice soothing. "It's over. Hush, hush, it's over." Carey placed his other hand over Egon's, as if he could pass his own energy into his friend, as if he could protect both people he loved with his own powerful strength.

He looked like some great white hunter in khaki jacket and shorts, both stained with Egon's blood. His feet were bare, his tanned body sweat-sheened from his exertions, his gilded hair in spiked disarray under the tranquil tropical moon. He was disheveled and bloody, but steady, and cool, alert for the sound of Jess's approach.

For a disquieting moment she thought: *I don't know this man, this unflagging, proficient killer who can go through all this untouched.* She sensed the inherent power he possessed, like some inhuman machine without feeling or sentiment.

But it wasn't true. His face ached from the powder burns, and he was exhausted now that his adrenaline had stopped pumping. And bloody images haunted his mind—all the killing ones from Vietnam.

He heard the faint rhythm first. "Jess is here," Carey said. Releasing Molly, he bent low over Egon. "The doctor's here, Egon, You hear, brat? The doctor's come." He thought there was a glimmer of movement beneath his eyelids, but when he looked again there was only quiet and the face of death.

Sylvie was the first one off the chopper. When she came within range, Carey shouted, "If you're not going to help, get the hell away." He didn't want any scenes or screaming tears or questions. He didn't care why she was here or how she'd arrived. All that mattered was grabbing at the slim chance Egon had at life. "And if you know how to pray," he added, as she halted in midstride, shocked at his brutal tone, "you'd better start."

Continuing past her, he helped unload the oxygen and stretcher. He answered the doctor's questions in succinct phrases, and wordlessly aided the doctor when he eased Egon onto the stretcher.

Subdued by Carey's warning and the sight of Egon's grave wounds, Sylvie was remarkably quiet. She only said, "We'll follow you," when Carey informed her he was bringing Egon to Miami. Her private jet which had landed in Montego Bay, was parked near Carey's.

The flight to Miami was funereal. Carey wouldn't talk, but sat with his elbows propped on his knees and his head in his hands. Mariel had found a rosary somewhere, and the doctor and two nurses who'd joined them at the airport spoke in the hushed tones of a death watch.

Carey seemed remote from the man Molly had loved long years ago in their heated summer of passion. Even the sweet, caring man she'd rediscovered short weeks ago had disappeared. She found herself with a silent, merciless gunslinger, a competent killer who had taken control with quiet efficiency as though he stalked hired assassins every day of his life.

The flying bullets had been *too* real, as were the deadly tone of Carey's voice and the ice in his eyes. She felt a small shiver of fear travel down her spine. Did she really know him at all?

Their arrival at Jackson Memorial Trauma Center didn't alleviate her feelings of uncertainty and doubt. Carey Fersten, a VIP of the first magnitude, was treated with deference by everyone from the admitting clerk to the head surgeon.

Although Carey was concerned for her comfort, Molly found him curiously detached, as if he found it odd to see her still beside him as they entered the trauma center. And much later, when the team of doctors had stabilized Egon's shocked and damaged body, he'd said in a cool voice, "Would you excuse me for a moment, darling? The doctors want to brief Sylvie and me on Egon's condition." And he walked away with his beautiful ex-wife. His head was tipped low in conversation, giving every appearance of being deeply attached.

Mariel, who had scarcely said a word or looked up from her rosary, patted Molly's hand in comfort.

Molly silently cautioned herself against reading erroneous interpretations into Carey's tenderness toward Sylvie. Good Lord, she chastised herself, he loved Egon, and the next hours could see his young friend gone forever, could see Sylvie's only family disappear forever. They needed each other now, and she'd be the most unfeeling monster to deny them the solace they found in each other.

At last everyone re-assembled in the waiting room. While Molly, Sylvie, and Mariel sat and listened, Carey asked questions about Egon's condition.

The doctors didn't have much hope. Egon had been given last rites. Even if he survived, there was a possibility his paralysis would be permanent. A bullet had lodged near his spine, and was in too precarious a position to attempt removal. Continued pressure was aggravating the paralysis, but surgery now could be lethal.

"I'm so sorry," Molly said softly.

Mariel cried without uttering a sound.

And Sylvie threw her arms around Carey's neck and wept.

They stayed at the hospital through the night. Carey arranged rooms for them, but no one could sleep with Egon near death. Carey, Sylvie, and Mariel took turns at his bedside.

When he wasn't with Egon, Carey prowled like a caged tiger. *I'll kill him for you, Egon*, he silently vowed, his need for revenge terrifying in its violence. And later, when he sat by Egon's bed again, watching him struggle to breathe, all his anger and frustration was directed toward Rifat. "Live, Egon, just live," he whispered to the still, quiet form attached to all the machines and tubes and tanks. "I'll kill him, I promise."

Rifat's greed had to be stopped, his senseless brutality brought to an end. Carey had never considered himself a crusader; he avoided politics and causes, always contributed anonymously to charities, not wanting the publicity. Even his impulse for soldiering in Vietnam had been inspired by family tradition, rather than patriotic zeal.

But now a black and savage vengeance overcame Carey, a murderous rage that demanded retribution for what Rifat had done to Egon. People like Rifat preyed on weakness and fear. They didn't take the chances themselves. They only gave the orders, detached from the human suffering, the unmitigated terror their greed imposed on other human beings.

For the first time in his life, Carey was a zealot. All he could think of as he sat at Egon's bedside was the retribution he would exact. Nothing else distracted his thoughts, no room existed in his mind for other emotions. His urge to kill was the only positive energy he felt.

The doctors held no hope for Egon.

As he waited, Carey planned every move: what he'd need, how he'd enter Rifat's house, the equipment necessary to avoid detection. "Come on, Egon," he softly pleaded, bending near so Egon might hear him, "keep breathing." Like an older brother promising to fight the playground bully, Carey said, "I'll kill Rifat for you."

And he smiled when he saw a tiny flicker of Egon's eyelid. "Hold on, brat. I need you to make my life interesting."

That afternoon the doctors made a cautious prognosis. Egon's kidneys had begun functioning, an improvement that moved him into the everyday miracle stage.

It was near midnight when he opened his eyes—only once, but he focused on Carey.

"Welcome back," Carey said softly.

A dozen times Molly had begun to say, "I'm going back home." But her declaration would seem tactless and disrespectful when Egon lay dying, so she stayed and watched Carey withdraw into himself.

Molly had had her taste of adventure. Now, in the shrouded gloom of Egon's death vigil, her swift journey into near extinction was enough to last her ten lifetimes. No longer exhilarated or impelled by a need for self-reliance, she only experienced an enormous despair. Disillusion had set in, and all she wanted to do was crawl into her sheltered cocoon and pretend men didn't kill other men over drugs and guns and money. She wanted to go back to Carrie and bring her home. Just before dinner, she told Carey her wishes.

"You can't," he said bluntly. "Not until Rifat's terminated."

"Terminated?" A sharp criticism was delivered with the single word. "Why don't you say what you mean?" They were standing in the hall near the windows overlooking the parking lot, where waves of heat rose from the asphalt in transparent vapor.

"Okay, killed. Better? I'm going to kill the mother-fucker," he said with ruthlessness, his eyes black with hate.

She took a reflexive step backward. "I don't know you like this," she whispered.

"The war was over when I met you," he curtly replied.

"Have you . . ." she hesitated, not knowing why she felt impelled to ask, thinking maybe there was a simple answer to understanding this stranger standing before her. "Have you killed many people?"

"Lots," he said in a voice devoid of warmth.

That wasn't the simple answer she wanted to hear. It was exactly opposite of the answer she wished for. She felt the hair rise on the back of her neck. "I want to go back home," she said. This time, he didn't argue.

"Fine," he said, his voice level and empty. "I'll take you to my father's."

"When can I go *home?*" Her words were determined.

"Afterward."

"After what?"

"After Rifat's dead."

CHAPTER **38**

They left late that night, after Sylvie had been sufficiently placated and Mariel settled into the room next to Egon. They drove to the airport like two silent strangers, and once they boarded the plane Carey excused himself to join Jess in the cockpit. Egon was alive; at least their mission had been partially successful, though the extent of his injuries was grievous. Molly wasn't so sure her relationship with Carey hadn't suffered an equally unfortunate mutilation; he was not the man she thought she knew. He was disturbing and unfamiliar, and she was forced to face the very real possibility she had fallen in love with a memory, not the existing Carey Fersten.

Although Carey knew better, he couldn't make himself give Molly all the necessary explanations and assurances. He wasn't up to the argument of whom or what was more important. He was going to kill Rifat or die trying. That was just the way he felt, and he didn't want to have it analyzed or examined or negated.

————

Their arrival at Bernadotte's was subdued. Molly didn't argue when Carey suggested she go to sleep while he filled his dad in on the events in Jamaica.

Bernadotte was concerned for Egon's life, but more apprehensive about his son's intractable obsession with Rifat's death. Once he realized Carey wouldn't be deterred, sensible man that he was, Bernadotte took it upon himself to offer whatever help he could. The two men sat up that night planning the operation.

"He must be cordoned off from the world," Bernadotte said. "He hasn't survived this long without the most sensitive security system, and he may be expecting you if one of his men got away."

"I can't be certain if the man survived. There wasn't time to follow him. It's possible the third man is dead."

"Nevertheless, Rifat will be alerted as well if his men don't return."

"Fucker's always alert. You know what my first instinct was when Egon got mixed-up with the bastard? I thought: maybe a small missile through his bedroom window or a bomb under his chair in his favorite restaurant. But no, I'm too damned civilized now. A dozen years away from Vietnam and you begin acting normal. Your first impulse is no longer shoot first and check out the corpse's identity later."

Bernadotte heard the anger in his son's voice, and was reminded of the glimpses he'd seen of that same white-hot rage when Carey had first come home. He'd been mostly silent and uncommunicative, but on rare occasions a television newscast or a newspaper article would set him off, and an explosion of words would come tumbling out, words of tragedy and loss, of the horror that passed for war. "A car bomb might be effective. And safe."

"His vehicles are checked before he steps foot in them."

"Maybe a woman could carry something into his bedroom, or say, at a restaurant and leave it."

"That's been tried. The woman's body or what was left of

it turned up in the Tiber two days later. Besides . . . I want to see the fear in his eyes before I kill him."

"I felt that way about the Russian artillery crew that bombarded us and killed Kirsti. I understand how you feel."

"I don't know if I can do it—manage to get to him," Carey said, "but I have to try. Do I sound deranged?" He smiled then, in a rueful grimace, and drained the glass of tea his father had brewed for him.

"You can't be perfectly normal with your mother and me for parents," Bernadotte replied with his own smile, aware of the idiosyncracies in their personalities. "All I ask is that you take all the possible precautions. The image of the lone, heroic gunslinger is a literary device. In the real world, a well-devised plan with a team to implement it is more effective."

"I'm going to ask Ant and Luger for help with the logistics. If they can supply me with some interesting weapons, I'll be in good shape."

"Are they coming here?"

"No, not with Molly and Carrie . . . and Lucy. I'm flying out west tomorrow morning." He sighed then, and recrossed his legs. "Molly doesn't understand," he said.

"Why should she?" Bernadotte quietly replied.

"I know." Carey slid lower on his spine, his expression disgruntled. "She wants to go home."

"And what did you say?"

"*No*, of course. She'd be completely vulnerable to Rifat."

"Does she understand?"

"Not emotionally."

"But logically she does."

He shrugged. "Perhaps."

"So there's trouble in paradise."

"You bet." He raked his hands through his hair in exasperation. "Would you make it as pleasant for her as possible? Try to explain—oh hell, I should do that, but dammit, I'm not up to it right now." He sighed again. "After Rifat, I'll explain."

"I'll do what I can," Bernadotte promised, "and if it's any

consolation, Carrie and Lucy are happy as clams here. It won't be difficult to convince them to enjoy a few more days of vacation on the farm."

"Great." And Carey's eyes glimmered with hope. "Tell me what they've been doing. I'll bet Leon is pleased to have another Fersten under his tutelage. Isn't she wonderful?"

The night passed swiftly as Bernadotte filled Carey in on the activities at the farm. Then the two men began to plan the mission against Rifat.

They were having breakfast when Molly joined them.

"You didn't come to bed," she said, surveying the weariness on Carey's face and the golden stubble beginning to show along his jaw.

"Papa and I couldn't sleep. Did you rest well?"

"Yes, thank you," Molly replied. In fact, she had hardly slept, waiting for Carey to come, wanting to talk to him, wanting assurance against the doubts assailing her. When he didn't appear, the old uncertainties held sway.

"I'm flying out this morning but Papa will keep you company," Carey told her at the breakfast table. She couldn't scream or make a scene or even ask for an explanation with Bernadotte there. Now she knew why he hadn't come to bed.

Carey Fersten didn't want to argue or offer any more explanations. He also didn't love her enough, she thought, to care how she felt. She replied in as pleasant a tone as his, "Have a good trip. Will you be long?"

There was an infinitesimal pause before he answered, "I don't think so."

"I was hoping to go home soon," she said.

"Could I call and let you know on that?"

"I'd appreciate it."

They could have been debating the condition of the lawns at Wimbledon, Molly thought with resentment, they were all so damned civilized.

Carrie and Lucy came bounding into the breakfast room a moment later, easing the tension. The girls were dressed for their riding lessons, and so absorbed in their excitement over learning to jump that the topic took precedence over eating.

"Do we have to?" Carrie complained when Molly said, "Now sit down and eat," and she looked to her father for support.

"Do what your mom says," Carey directed, "and I'll go with you."

"Will you? Wow! Grandpa said you and Tarrytown can do five feet. Will you take me over?"

"Let's start a little lower," her father cautioned. "I didn't jump five feet my first week."

"You will though, won't you? I mean later—maybe when I'm lots better—take me over that high?"

"Sure, Pooh, I promise."

After the girls had bolted their breakfast, Molly was invited to accompany them, but declined, saying she'd follow along later. Her mood was still acrimonious enough to make polite conversation a trial, and she didn't care to risk even a mild scene in front of the girls. After some calming moments in her bedroom in which she counseled herself into a functional courtesy if not a sincere one, she walked down to the small jumps Bernadotte had set up near the stable.

But as she approached the jump area, it was empty. Leaning on the white, painted fence that wound for miles over Bernadotte's land, she searched the rolling hills. Several of the green pastures were occupied by grazing horses, but no riders were in evidence.

Just as she was moving away to return to the house, a wild, exhilarated cry carried faintly to her ears, the sound vaguely reminiscent of her daughter's voice. And when she turned back to investigate the direction of the high-pitched scream, she saw the horses in the distant pasture lift their heads in curiosity. A moment later, two horsemen jumped the farthest fence into their pasture, and shot toward them.

The horsemen broke through the maddened scuttle of the herd, making for the opposite fence. They cleared the three-rail fence as though it didn't exist, and galloped toward the stableyard. As they drew closer, Molly saw the two girls seated in front of the men, their hair streaming behind them, their little legs bouncing wildly, their hands clutching the saddle pommels. Carey was holding Pooh with one hand, his reins with the other, and she could see their smiles even from her distance. Lucy was equally cheerful in Bernadotte's care, and she saw the youngsters wave to each other in joyful excitement.

The horses came up the rise at enormous speed, digging in with long racing strides. When Molly realized the men were going to attempt the high fence into the riding ring, her hands went unconsciously to her mouth in horror. *They're fools*, she thought, petrified and appalled. Mad, mad fools . . . and they were jeopardizing the lives of two young girls. No wonder Carey was so impossibly heedless and wild—his father was exactly the same.

As they careened toward the high fence, she shut her eyes, unable to watch the bloody carnage.

"We won! We won!" she heard her daughter crow a moment later in lieu of the crashing noise she'd expected. Her eyes snapped open to observe her daughter twist around in the saddle and throw her arms around her father in jubilant victory.

"Tarrytown's fresher," Carey modestly said, "or Lucy and Grandpa might have beat us. But you were great. I hardly had to hold on to you at all."

"Nice riding," Bernadotte said to his son, pride in his voice. Carey had managed to get two strides ahead at the last fence and held it up the hill.

"Thanks, Dad." And he remembered all the times his father had taken him over the jumps as a young boy to teach him the joy, the inexpressible sensation of soaring through the air.

"But *we're* going to beat. *them* next time, aren't we, Bernie?" Lucy emphatically declared, patting Bernadotte's favorite mount Daxon on the neck.

Bernie? Carey speculated in astonishment. His father had never allowed that diminutive.

"We have to," Bernadotte casually replied, as though little girls had called him Bernie all his life. "How else can we keep the racing interesting?"

"Mom, Mom, did you see us?" Carrie shouted, loosening her grip on her father and searching out her mother.

Molly's heart was still caught in her throat. She was having trouble finding her voice, but she nodded at her daughter's bright-eyed face and tried a shaky smile of her own. Despite her own terrifying fright, her daughter was perfectly comfortable on that huge beast, leaning back against her father who was equally relaxed and at ease. Carrie would ride like that someday, she thought, under the Fersten tutelage. She was both fascinated and petrified by the awesome size of their mounts; they were so powerful she couldn't imagine her small daughter controlling them, not to mention jumping them over fences higher than her head.

"You've got to try it, Mom!"

Right after brain surgery, she thought, but she said instead, "It looks like fun."

Carey had walked Tarrytown closer to the fence. "I hope you don't mind," he said, his exhilaration restrained now under his cool courtesy. "She wanted to try the fences."

"I don't mind," Molly replied. "What a beautiful horse." And she gingerly patted Tarrytown's nose.

The big bay twitched his head away as if he recognized hypocrisy, but Carey gently forced him back and made him stand politely under Molly's stroking palm.

She envied Carey his confident skill and effortless rapport with horse and child alike. But most of all, she appreciated his loving attachment to Carrie. Even if she couldn't always understand the complexity of their relationship, he was sincerely devoted to his daughter. And she was grateful. "Carrie's really enjoying herself," she said.

His eyes held hers for a moment over the head of their daughter. He wanted to kiss Molly and tell her how much he loved her, but then the old arguments would begin again about how much love was love. "So am I," he replied, silently promising himself to heal the hurt in her eyes once he came back. And he hoped with all his heart he'd be coming back.

CHAPTER 39

S o the modern-day gunslinger rode off in his silver plane to make the world safe for young drug addicts, vulnerable females, and small children, Molly indignantly mused several hours later. She was lying by the pool in the warm afternoon sunshine, listening with half an ear to the girls splashing in the water. It wasn't that she didn't understand Carey's mission. She even admired the bravery and courage required to take on the Rifats of the world who barricaded themselves behind bastions of killers.

But her understanding didn't mitigate her resentment; nor did her admiration detract from her sense of affront at being captive at Bernadotte's until such a time as Carey determined the danger past. Perhaps what rankled most was that he didn't ask her permission.

Carey Fersten was too selfish, spoiled, a wealthy young man who did as he pleased. Had always done as he pleased. She knew that ten years ago, and she knew it now. He would expect her to make all the concessions, like his asking her to leave for Australia for a year. Gloomy shades of her marriage to Bart began darkening her already ferocious mood. And then, of course, she sullenly thought: Don't forget all the women.

Even Bernadotte's charm reinforced her assessment of Carey. He was utterly charming just like his father, and that only increased her testiness.

Carey had made arrangements to meet Ant and Luger in San Francisco, a midway point. Ant drove up from the sparsely populated forest south of Carmel where he lived in his cabin at the end of a dirt road. Luger gave his secretary the day off, put a closed sign in the window of his modest insurance agency an hour north of the Bay, and, entering the south-bound freeway, set the cruise control on his Buick at seventy.

In a basement restaurant in Chinatown the three men exchanged pleasantries while the waiter filled their table with all the specialties of the house.

"How's the third wife?" Luger asked Ant, good-natured teasing in his voice. "Last time I saw you *this* was going to be the one."

Ant was a handsome Hispanic with an eye for the ladies and the looks to attract them. "I think it's the backwoods," he replied with a grin. "Once they're around for a few months, they complain about no shopping and TV. I dropped the last one off at her mother's and said, 'It was nice.' So how's *your* old lady? Still singing in the church choir?"

"She plays the piano for the choir," Luger seriously replied as though the distinction mattered. Methodical and pragmatic, Luger was a detail man.

"That's great. Ain't that great, Carey?" Ant teased. "The world needs more of that kind of stability."

"We can't all help the divorce lawyers pay for their BMWs," Luger retorted.

"Hey . . . we all do our bit for the economy. Besides, I don't have a high overhead like you do. An office *and* a secretary . . . pretty damned IRS productive, I'd say."

"Carol sends her love," Luger said, as though suddenly recalling the message he'd been entrusted with. His austere face had earned him the nickname Luger because he looked like every typecast SS colonel in the movies. "She said to say hello to whichever number wife is currently residing in your redwood forest."

Luger was the type of guy who genuinely enjoyed visiting at the coffeeshop in town, who discussed the last city council meeting with the postmaster, who found great satisfaction sweeping the sidewalk in front of his office in the morning and exchanging opinions on the weather with whomever passed by. He'd seen Ant's multilevel home built on a rocky mountainside years ago. As he gazed at the stone, stained glass, and redwood building resembling a sculpture more than a home, he'd remarked, "Wouldn't want to insure that with the mudslides and fires. 'Specially with the state of your road." It had taken them forty-five minutes to navigate the switchbacks up the mountain. While he understood Ant's need for isolation, Luger had always figured there was plenty of time for solitude in the grave.

"There might not be a number four. I'm getting used to no bitching. It grows on you—you know—the peace and tranquillity . . . no yak-yak about the hours in the lab and I've been busy."

Antonio Ramos made a very profitable living as an explosives expert for both sides in the bomb business. Legitimate work paid Uncle Sam his portion and his extra projects kept Ant's Swiss bank account healthy.

"Was that Monte Carlo bank bomb yours?" Luger asked.

"A beauty."

"I thought it sounded like yours. No one heard it, even though the restaurant next door was open on Sunday."

"I'm getting good." Ant winked and touched his thumb and middle finger to his lips. "Refined. Like good sex."

"Speaking of which," Carey interrupted.

Ant grinned. "The world-class stud speaks."

Carey shook his head. "I swore off. I mean the bomb. I need one."

"Carey Fersten swore off women?" Ant said, checking his watch. "It must be here—the end of the world. Bend over and grab your ankles, Luger." His smile was accompanied by a disbelieving look.

"I'm in love," Carey said.

"Jesus, it really is the end of the world. Is that why you need a bomb?"

"Can it, Ant, he's serious," Luger admonished.

"About what?"

"About both."

"So what do you need?" Ant asked, all the teasing gone.

"I need some C-4 devices, and some suggestions. I may have to get into a villa that's tighter than Spandau Prison. The man's had so many assassination attempts on his life, his place is damn near impregnable."

"Never," Ant said softly.

"I was hoping you'd say that."

"When do you need this stuff?"

"As soon as possible . . . with some weapons for long-range attack and contact weapons, Luger. Whatever you think I can use."

Behind Luger's office was a small room concealed by his bookcase of insurance yearbooks. Inside he had what he called his "hobby equipment"—a collection of state-of-the-art weapons he'd assembled with a passion he reserved exclusively for them. He had contact with the weapons specialists of the world and prided himself on knowing the market.

"I have a couple TOW missiles you can practically carry in a suitcase, and a new Beretta with a state-of-the-art silencer. How much can you carry?"

"Probably only a backpack. I may have to go in over the roof. Just what I can carry comfortably and move fast."

"Who's the unfriendly?"

"Shakin Rifat."

"Oooeee," Ant softly exclaimed. "The killer king of the banditos. What's he done to you?"

"He's been shaking down my ex-brother-in-law, and the kid can't take it. Right now Egon's about dead in a Miami hospital. One of Rifat's shooters used him for a target." Carey put down his chopsticks and pushed his plate away. "I had a lot of time to think, sitting at the hospital, and I thought maybe someone should send Rifat on that last fine mile."

"It's been tried before," Luger said.

"I know."

"So how you getting in when others haven't?"

Carey lifted one shoulder slightly in a faint shrug. "I'll take a look when I get there."

Ant glanced at Luger and grinned. "Sounds like this guy needs some professional help along."

"No . . . no way. It's my vendetta. I just came here for the equipment."

"As it happens, I've a delivery to make in Liverpool for the Provo boys," Ant went on, as though Carey hadn't spoken. "Then on to Switzerland to brown bag the cash. I'll be pretty damn close to Rome by that time. Maybe I'll take a run down to check out the women, now that I'm available again."

"You're always available," Luger said between chews of pork lo mein.

Ant picked up a spun-sugar apple slice. "Someone's got to pick up the slack for you faithful guys who stay off the market. I look at it," he said, the glittering confection lifted to his mouth, "as equalizing the universal equation."

"Fucking is what it is," Luger said matter-of-factly, shoveling a shrimp into his mouth.

Ant assumed an expression of mock pain. "The man has no poetry in his soul."

"Cut the crap, Ant," Luger remarked, his tone good-natured and mild. "You don't have a soul."

"Nor do any of us," Carey said with a smile. "As I recall, we all sold ours to the devil if he'd produce a woman out in the bush after two weeks on patrol."

"And then those nurses on a fact-finding tour for the

dickheads at the command center showed up in three Hueys. You're right. We lost our souls, fair and square."

"But with a smile on our faces."

"Every part of me smiled for the next week. Even my toes. As I recall even Luger cracked a grin once or twice that week."

"Shit," Luger disclaimed, but his harsh features were transformed by the faintest of smiles.

"So when do we leave?" Ant inquired.

"You don't."

"It almost sounds as though he doesn't want us along, Luger."

"And I've never been to Rome. Selfish, if you ask me."

"Wants all the fun for himself."

"He always was selfish. If I remember he kept two of those nurses for himself and the rest of us had to make do with one apiece."

"You're right. And now that Shakin Rifat's the target, he wants all the glory."

Carey leaned back in his chair and looked at his friends who were grinning like they'd drunk too much rice wine. "Rifat's about ten-to-one odds—against."

"Then you need us *bad*."

"This is the least rational thing I've ever done."

"No—flying that Phantom you stole out from under Colonel Drake's nose was. He'd have shot you on the spot *if* he'd found you."

"Okay," Carey said, "*one* of the least rational."

"So we'll come along to stabilize your gyro." Ant's voice softened, and his eyes lost their amusement. "We're going, right, Luger?"

Luger continued pouring his cup of tea, as though a mission against the bloodiest terrorist in the world was like answering his secretary's request for a new stamp meter. "Right," he said.

Ant spread his hands wide and looked at Carey, "There you go, John Wayne . . . you got yourself a posse."

Carey gazed at the men he'd lived through the hell of Vietnam with, whose friendship hadn't faltered or lapsed like so many once they'd landed back in San Diego. They were no longer young boys with a reckless courage; they were older now, more pragmatic. And more skilled. "Thanks," he said, his deep voice hushed. "Thanks a lot."

CHAPTER 40

With his Brazilian buyer anxiously awaiting delivery of the prototypes, Rifat was setting his alternate plan in action. He'd recently received verification that Sylvie remained at her brother's bedside in Miami. If he died, she would no doubt return with the body to Germany. But while Egon lived, Sylvie was fixed in Miami, He would need a few days to put together another team.

Timur had flown Ceci home. He was recuperating now in his suite on the second floor of Rifat's villa, feeling remorseful and depressed.

Shakin Rifat, much older than Ceci, was less daunted by failure. Had he been, he never would have survived the coup which ousted him from power and made him an exile from his country.

"Regroup, my boy," Rifat had explained to Ceci, his fondness for the young officer genuine. "If every general gave up after being outflanked, the map of the world would be considerably altered. Simply attack again, immediately, while the jubilant cheering is still echoing in the enemy camp. We'll merely take the Countess von Mansfeld in Egon's stead. And you may entertain her in her detention." Rifat's background relegated women to a limited number of functions, the majority of which pertained to service to men. He would offer Sylvie to Ceci as a present. "How is your arm healing?"

The bulletproof vest had saved his life, but Ceci looked very unhappy, his pride buffeted by his failure. Dressed in a silk robe of deep forest green, he lounged on an oversized Renaissance sofa, his left arm bandaged and in a sling. "Well enough, sir," he replied, unable in the depths of his depression to appreciate the surgeon's skill which had repaired damage so severe, a lesser expertise would have meant the loss of his arm.

"Good. Now, enough self-reproach. I expect you to be fit enough by the end of the week to welcome the countess."

They landed in Rome near midnight, a day later. Jess had piloted and they unloaded the boxes of tack and saddles themselves. Customs officials barely glanced at the equipment, since Carey was known by reputation and had been coming over for competitions since he was a boy.

He was playing in a polo match, too, he told them, which accounted for his extra gear. His jumpers and polo ponies would be flown over in a few days.

Ant remarked to Luger as they entered the limousine waiting for them: "Don't get too used to this preferential treatment they give counts, Luger. When you get back to Taylorsville, you're going to have to take out the garbage, same as ever."

"They like horses," Carey noted. "Every time I come over to compete, they remember my last win."

"What happens when the horses don't come over?"

"Plans change. A horse isn't sound enough for a race. You cancel out. They understand. Hell, with this ungodly hot weather, I'd decide not to bring my horses over, anyway." A sultry blanket of heat lay over Rome, even at two in the morning.

When they arrived at the apartment Carey had rented, they quietly unloaded the heavy boxes and carried them up to the second-floor sitting room. After parking the car in the courtyard, Jess joined them at the table where they all sat studying a map of the city.

Ant was to reconnoiter the area immediately adjacent to Rifat's villa, while Luger explored the environs of Rifat's office building. Neither man was familiar to Rifat, and with tourists at their peak, two more men with guidebooks and cameras shouldn't attract notice. Jess and Carey worked on a time-table of escape routes back to the airport, in the event heavy weapons were required. Explosions of that magnitude would attract attention . . . and the carabinieri. They would have to exit the area swiftly.

When Ant and Luger returned with the details of the buildings, grounds, access points, and security system, they drew up floor plans and argued about methods of attack.

Luger favored his TOW missile fired from the back of a truck parked a block away from Rifat's office. "There's enough heavy traffic near the square so a truck wouldn't be conspicuous. If I can get the angle right, I can blow Rifat and his car to hell."

"What about the risks to innocent pedestrians?" Carey remarked. "His office is on a busy square, and I'm not out to get anyone but Rifat."

They discussed the possibility of planting a C-4 bomb in the office, but decided there was no guarantee it would kill only Rifat. Again, innocent people would be endangered.

Everyone knew almost at the onset what would be required, but first they methodically eliminated the less risky procedures. Even if they could plant a bomb on his car, they'd have to wait for a day he was alone to detonate it, increasing the risk of its discovery. In any event, Carey didn't want to wait.

Carey subscribed to Rifat's methodology of attack. He believed in a rapid offensive, for personal as well as logistical reasons. He wanted Rifat dead, and he didn't want time to dwell on the danger to himself and his friends. He particularly didn't want to have time to think about all he had to lose; he couldn't afford to hesitate. He needed his mind unobstructed for action.

They finally decided to go into Rifat's villa the following night from the rooftop across the street, and Ant volunteered to see if he could get inside for a glimpse of Rifat's protection.

Posing as a Mexican reporter, Ant appeared at the villa and tried to get an interview with Rifat. He was ultimately refused as he'd anticipated, but returned with a pleased smile on his face.

"When they heard I was a Mexican reporter, the butler wasn't sure what to do. While I was standing in the entrance hall waiting for Rifat's secretary to be wakened, I had a look at the cameras and surveillance. A guard was monitoring a bank of TV screens in a room off the hall, and since he'd just been delivered his breakfast, the door was open. I gave him a cheerful, 'good morning, nice weather' kind of greeting. It's about all I know in Italian. He shook his head and slammed the door in my face. But I caught a glimpse of the screens before the door shut, and evidently Rifat doesn't allow cameras in his private rooms.

"And as far as the detection devices at the front door and hall windows, I just happen to have a laser which keeps the beam intact even when it's broken. That alarm won't be set off when we enter the house."

"Something new?" Carey looked at him intently across the remains of breakfast al fresco. Being able to enter the villa undetected was worth a great number of points for their side.

"Yeah." Ant smiled. "My retirement fund. Evidently Rifat might have something going in our hemisphere to the south because his secretary was actually polite when he told me, 'No interview.' "

"We're set, then." There was a new energy in Carey's voice.

"Everything on track, except . . ."

"Except?" Carey probed.

"If Rifat doesn't feel the need for camera surveillance in his private apartments, he may have some other defense."

"We'll find out."

They napped that afternoon, ate lightly, then geared up while Jess packed the car with all the necessary equipment. The saddles and tack were carefully resettled atop the mortars and assault weapons, the detonators and missile sights hidden beneath one level of the carefully constructed wooden crates.

Jess was to wait for them at a prearranged site, down the hill from Rifat's villa. He would be inconspicuous even if the house exploded in a ball of fire.

"Heaven forbid," Ant said with a wide smile.

"I haven't fired a baby TOW in a long time," Luger commented, longing evident in his voice. But at the warning light in Carey's eyes, he quickly added, "Relax . . . I'm under control."

Carey didn't relax completely, however. Handing Luger a firing mechanism was a bit like putting a woman in a jewelry shop and saying, "Don't touch."

Shortly after ten they walked into the area in timed intervals. Dressed in dark cotton shirts and slacks, wearing sneakers and carrying canvas bags, the men resembled tourists out for an evening stroll. Slipping into the building across the street from Rifat's through the back door of an antique shop, they carefully moved up the stairs past two levels of apartments and climbed up onto the roof through a wooden trapdoor at the back of the third-floor hall.

Since there were still sounds of activity in the apartments below they maintained complete silence when they assembled on the roof and waited for darkness to descend. They spent their time preparing their weapons and rappelling equipment. Their rappelling gear was a lightweight aluminum rope with a grappling hook on the end to which special harnesses were attached both for men and weapons.

Shortly after eleven, when a cloud temporarily covered the small quarter moon, Ant threw the grappling hook and caught the roof parapet the first time. Carey led the team across in a smooth routine, without noise or problems.

The roof was a shallow pitch tile. After silently pointing out the beam of light protecting the perimeter, Ant adjusted his laser device to jam the beam to a continuous on position, and they dropped over it onto the tile. They unstrapped their MP5s from their backslings, clipped the explosive packs to their belts, and crept slowly toward the peak.

Typical of many Renaissance villas, Rifat's was built around a central courtyard, quiet and shadowed now under the thin moon, but patrolled by two armed guards. Lying flat on their bellies, Carey's crew peered over the peak searching for Rifat's suite, the private rooms facing on the courtyard.

The second- and third-floor balconies rimming the courtyard shadowed the windows of the villa, partially obscuring the numerous windows. Silently the three men perused the portion of the villa opposite them, searching for some clue to Rifat's rooms. Figures passed by windows occasionally but they were armed guards dressed in fatigues. The guards at least explained the reason Rifat's rooms weren't surveyed by monitor screens. Apparently, he preferred the privacy accorded by hall guards.

They all counted as they lay on the rooftop. The sultry summer night was more appropriate for lovers than assassination, the perfumed scent of the courtyard flowers heightened the incongruity of their mission. Luger indicated by sign the number of guards, pointed out their positions, and without speaking asked verification of his total. Ant and Carey both agreed, and all three realized they were moving into an armed camp. Although no direct sign of Rifat had been seen, the concentration of guards on the east wing of the second floor strongly suggested the location of his suite of rooms.

They entered the villa through a narrow attic dormer. The process of slowly easing it open in full sight of the courtyard below was a slow, nerve-racking procedure. Especially when a nest of sparrows disturbed by their manipulation erupted into a brief agitated squawking. For the next few minutes the men lay flattened against the roof tiles, still warm from the sun.

Instantly the guards looked up, contemplating the half-dozen circling sparrows silhouetted against the nebulous gleam of the moon. After what seemed endless minutes, they went back to their gossip and cigarettes.

I'm getting too old for this, Carey thought, sweat beading on his brow. His cheek was jammed tightly to the smooth clay tile, his heart pounded. But when he glanced over and caught Ant's wink and smile, he remembered his heart had pounded as violently at eighteen. And the sight of Luger's cheerful face, slightly blackened, convinced him some things never change. Luger was enjoying himself. Luger had always been the nerveless one, while Carey and Ant and Mac had sky-rocketed through a mission high on adrenaline.

Right now Carey had enough adrenaline pumping into his body to keep him awake for a month. He signaled he'd go through the dormer window first. Servants had slept under the dusty eaves in past decades, but the attic was empty now, except for the distinctive pink beam of light crossing the large space six inches above the floor. Ant's smile was smug as they stepped over the colored line of protection without marring its perfect symmetry.

The floor immediately below the attic contained small rooms. They paused, listening carefully, and realized from the unmistakable sounds of snoring that the rooms contained sleeping men. Rifat had at least two platoons of guards in residence. They moved on with great care, each covering a door with his weapon as they went down the carpeted hall to the stairway.

They paused at the top of the stairwell, weapons poised up and down the staircase, knowing when they descended to the second floor they would be on the level of active guard operation. They also had to pass the living area before reaching Rifat. If that wasn't daunting enough, even if their mission was successful, they would have to return the entire distance they'd traveled in order to escape back across on their wire. Rifat had chosen his villa well. Solid walls buttressed him on two sides, while the third side overlooked a steep drop into a Roman temple complex: The only point of access was the street side, which they'd used for entry.

Carey led the way down the stairs, one cautious step at a time. At the bottom, he eased his head around the corner of the wall just enough to survey the second floor hall. The lengthy corridor was elegantly appointed with Kazak carpets loomed to order, their distinctive red-dye weft enhanced by the bold dragon pattern popular in that region. The original beechwood paneling had darkened over the last four hundred years to a sepia shade brightened by the addition of several large, gilded mirrors.

Although the hall was luxuriously appointed, the interior space was spare and uncluttered. By design, Carey presumed. Rifat chose not to impair his line of fire with large potted plants or console tables that would divert his guards from their target.

As if on cue, a guard walked into the apex of the juncture where the north-south corridor met the east-west length. Carey watched the man turn in a loose military rotation, then disappear out of sight.

Okay. They had to get by him and whomever else was patrolling that wing. And there was nothing to do but move forward and see what they found when they got there. Silently, Carey signaled the position of the guard, took a deep breath, then stepped out onto the carpet. There was no point in moving slowly in the wide open spaces of the corridor; there was more safety in speed. Carey sprinted down the muted softness of the dragon-patterned rug. Ant and Luger were right behind him, their weapons poised to fire.

The view of the next corridor reminded Carey of a military base. A guard station was situated halfway down the hall, two armed guards were seated at a table adjacent to a solid steel door, no doubt the entrance to Rifat's private quarters. It explained the relative laxness of security in other portions of the mansion. The outer perimeter was protected by an electronic surveillance beam, and guards patrolled the street entrance and courtyard. Rifat lived behind a coded entry door defended by two armed men. Four, Carey corrected himself, as two more appeared from what must have been a guard room to the left. Shit. Maybe there were ten more in there.

Measuring the distance to the door with his eyes, he turned back to Ant and Luger. Speaking for the first time since they'd reached their rendezvous, he murmured, "There's four I can see. I'm going to try and draw some of them down this way. You two target the ones at the desk. Wish me luck. I know about twenty words in Turkish." And unfortunately, he thought, most of them were only appropriate in the boudoir.

Raising his voice sufficiently to reach the guards but not carry to the floor above, Carey delivered rapid fire guttural phrases having to do with one's heritage.

Without hesitation two guards ran toward him, their weapons raised. Stepping out into the corridor, Carey fired at them with two well-placed controlled bursts. Even before they began falling, Ant and Luger had squeezed off their own rounds. The two men at the desk lifted slightly from their chairs before their bodies were thrown into the wall. Even though the men were shot with silenced weapons, it didn't mean noise was eliminated. The impact sent the guards flying backwards as if they were rag dolls.

The distinctive muffled sound of the rounds hitting home was followed by a noisy disturbance as the two guards in the corridor fell heavily to the floor, and the men at the desk collapsed with a tumbling clatter of chairs. They knew the sounds would be heard by whomever was behind the steel door, so they raced forward to drag the bodies out of sight. In seconds the four guards had been unceremoniously dumped in the small alcove that had apparently served as a locker room. Then they waited.

The wait wasn't long.

The steel door opened, and two men stepped through it, their weapons drawn. One man turned to glance into the alcove only inches from Carey, who was crouched behind the door. The other guard stood in the open doorway, holding the heavy plated steel with one hand and his weapon with the other.

As the first man walked into Carey's range, he seized the man's collar and twisting hard, pulled him down. The swift hauling motion dragged his throat onto Carey's knife. The second man never had time to digest what was happening, because Ant came up off the floor under the table and finished him just as neatly.

Carey was on the wrong side of the door to see what was happening but he observed Luger's signal, "One coming." He'd take him. And although the man came out in crisp military style with his weapon aimed and someone behind him for backup, Luger shot them both before they were over the threshold.

Now was the time to attack.

Ant went in first because he was closest, followed swiftly by Carey and Luger, and the thirty-round magazines of their guns rippled across the chests of the two guards reaching for the phone on the table in front of them. Out of the corner of his eye, Carey caught a glimpse of movement and, swiveling, shot the last guard with a burst between the eyes.

It took only an exchange of glances for each man to know what to do. They cleared away the bodies, stacking them in the alcove and closing the steel door in the event it was timed to an alarm, they reloaded and proceeded to their next barrier.

They knew they had only minutes at their disposal. Ant began setting his plastique on the lock of the second steel door to Rifat's inner sanctum. The explosion was a muffled sound, the lock disintegrated. They rushed through the door into a plush foyer carpeted in an unusual yellow ground kilim and walled in a glittering succession of mirrors.

Absolute silence greeted them.

They fanned out in a choreography from the past, rehearsed to perfection in another killing field long years ago. Each moved forward carefully, every reflex on alert, nerves taut.

They found him two rooms away, seated behind his desk. When Carey suddenly stepped into the room, his assault weapon trained on Rifat's chest, he greeted them without surprise, with unusual calm. Unknown to them, the explosive charge had set off his warning system, and the villa was on full alert.

"Count Fersten, I thought you and I might meet again." And he crossed his hands on the leather-covered desktop as though a submachine gun wasn't pointed at him. As though he wasn't responsible for half the terrorist attacks last year. As though all the people dead because of him were numbers in a ledger of profit and not human beings with families who perhaps couldn't even begin to understand the reason for their deaths.

"You were harder to find this time," Carey said, remembering the last time they'd met in Cannes with sycophants and starlets surrounding him, not steel security doors and armed guards.

At Rifat's casual words, Ant had moved over to the windows facing the courtyard. Easing the drapery aside a scant inch, he surveyed the scene below. It was full-scale mobilization with armed men racing toward Rifat's wing, and every light in the villa illuminated. "The troops are out, Carey. Time to go."

"In a minute." He wanted that minute. He wanted Rifat to

suffer a brief moment for what he'd done to Egon. For what he'd done to countless, nameless people in his rise to power. There was a rumor he collected ears and brought them out at dinner parties for effect. It almost made one consider torture in return as biblical justice.

"You'll never get out alive," Rifat said, his voice moderate, the burgundy silk of his dressing gown, a vivid splash of crimson in the glow of the desk lamp. "I've sixty men garrisoned here." His smile held no geniality.

"A few less," Ant said, his gaze still fixed on the courtyard below, "on the other side of those steel doors."

"My commendations on your skill." Rifat's smile thinned. "No one's ever gotten this far."

Luger was guarding the doorway. "Let's go," he muttered.

And when Carey rotated the half-turn to interpret the intensity of his voice, Rifat's hand moved a scant few inches toward the silver inkwell in the shape of a small cannon lying directly in front of his clasped hands. The flash of red caught as a periphery image warned him, and Carey fired without aiming. The impact blew Rifat back, but he recovered a moment later to his smiling, upright self.

A bulletproof vest, Carey thought just as Ant said, "We're outta here."

"One second."

"A half a second, that's it."

"My dear count," Rifat said, his voice grating with animosity at the first serious threat to his life in years, "you don't have a half-second." He drew from his pocket a small automatic handgun, firing it before his hand had lifted. And if Carey hadn't automatically moved in practiced reaction to a pointed gun, he would have been gut shot . . . or lower. Instinctively he aimed for Rifat's head and fired—one close-patterned burst that no one could survive.

Luger slammed the bedroom door shut behind him just as the sound of shattering glass echoed through the shadowy room.

"That's for Egon," Carey said as Rifat's body fell heavily to the floor, his head splashed in bloody pieces across the torn drapery and broken glass of the window behind him.

"No way we're going back the way we came," Luger said, shoving a large dresser in front of the door. "They're halfway down the hall already."

"They haven't climbed the balcony yet," Ant declared with a tight smile. "Let's try a little Tarzan shit." He was already uncoiling the nylon rope hooked to his belt harness. "Hey, Carey, are you fucking back in this world yet?"

But Carey didn't hear him, transfixed, not by the sight of Rifat's remains, but by a memo sheet on Rifat's desk with Sylvie's name, the name of the Miami hospital, and Egon's room number scratched across it in bold script.

"We've got to get out of here," Carey said aware of Rifat's auxiliary plan now that Egon was beyond kidnapping.

"No shit," Ant muttered, exchanging an ironic lift of his brows with Luger.

The sound of running feet was audible now, much too close for comfort. The next sound they'd hear would be splintering wood as the door was shot open.

"I'm going up and out of here," Ant said. "You two cover my ass while I find something to anchor this rope to." And following Ant, they stepped out onto the balcony through the smashed window. After looking in both directions they opted for the more dimly lit area to the left. Undetected, they raced down the length of the veranda, away from the commotion concentrated in the area around Rifat's suite.

At the corner they stopped, assessing where best to gain access to the roof. The balcony supports were smooth marble columns unsuitable for climbing, and the balcony eaves were without decorative detail. "Christ," Ant swore. There was nowhere to secure a rope, and even a grappling hook would never catch on the polished handrails. "I'm going to see if I can slip this rope through the third floor balcony railing. Hang on to me, 'cuz I'm going to have to *lean* out." It went without saying the third man would cover them against attack. Down below them the courtyard was a hive of activity with soldiers running, orders being shouted, and sounds of frantic movement, but no one had seen them yet, concentrating as they were on racing to Rifat's quarters. "Shit," Ant swore, the eave on the balcony obstructing his view, "we could use Mac's long arms right now."

"Here," Carey said, "let me try. I'm taller." Jumping onto the railing, he grasped the marble column with one hand and leaned out past the roofline. Extending his hand, he felt the coiled rope being slapped into his palm. With a swinging toss he threw it toward the third-floor railing. It slid off and tumbled back down. The noise levels below were escalating. He heard bursts of fire power and wondered if they were through Rifat's bedroom door yet: Lights were coming on even in the formerly dark rooms of the mansion.

Gauging his distance carefully, Carey swung the weighted rope upward again in a slow, looping arc. Though it flipped over the marble railing, it didn't have enough trajectory to continue downward so a knot could be secured. Carey swore.

Ant swore.

Luger checked his clip.

Violently jerking the rope down, Carey meticulously coiled it so it wouldn't tangle. Leaning out so far the muscles in his arm strained with the effort, he tossed the coil of rope up a third time.

It ascended into the silvery moonlit sky in a lazy, curving sweep as though time didn't matter. Carey watched the rope sail skyward. His mouth was dry, the tension in his body acute. How long would it be before they were observed, like sitting ducks in a target gallery? And still the rope rose in its indolent course.

A silent prayer was forming in his mind when the soft nylon drifted over the railing. His prayer was changing to a pleading appeal as the free weighted end snapped through the balustrade uprights with a small purring whoosh.

So far so good, he was thinking, as though the rope were listening to his encouraging words. It was descending downward now.

Hurry, he silently admonished, fucking hurry! Time was precious. He tried to mentally speed up the formulaic equation for gravity as the rope seemed to sink downward in excruciating slow motion. He heard the machine gun blast tearing up the barricaded door. If this bloody rope didn't touch his fingers soon, they were all in deep shit.

Every muscle in his body strained toward the rope, his arm extended to its absolute limit. And then the slippery nylon touched his fingertips. He grabbed it and hauled it down. Thank you, God.

They were up the rope and onto the third floor balcony with a buoyant agility that overlooked the fact they had a long way to go yet.

"The rest is a piece of cake," Ant jubilantly declared. "Look at all the damn chimneys. Now watch this cowboy technique." As good as his word, he lassoed a chimney easily, and they pulled themselves onto the roof without mishap. They were all silently congratulating themselves when the first shots rang out, narrowly missing Luger, who was closest to the edge of the roof.

They scrambled up the roof and over the ridge peak, followed by a barrage of bullets and flying pieces of tile. Out of sight of the courtyard now, they ran, dashing over the rough roof surface as though it were a flat track.

Their rappelling line was two hundred yards away when the first guard came out of the dormer window they'd used for entrance into the villa. He reached the roof peak just as Luger began hooking his harness to the wire. The burst of bullets raked the parapet above their heads, and they dove out of sight behind a chimney.

"Ant and I'll keep them down on the other side of that ridge. You go over first, Luger."

Discussion was unnecessary; they'd performed this

procedure so many times as a team, their roles had become automatic. Luger moved out first because he was a flawless shot at long-range.

Ant went next because he couldn't sprint as fast as Carey. And when Ant and Luger were both away, Carey would race for cover. It had developed into such a routine maneuver, they'd begun calling it their football play, as if the game of battle were stylized and amusing.

But the roof ridge presented a formidable bunker for Rifat's guards, and no jungle or underbrush existed to conceal one's retreat. There was no cover at all until they dropped below the parapet and hung from the rappelling wire.

Carey and Ant tore up the roof ridge while Luger made a dash for the wire, and both breathed a small sigh of relief when they heard the added sound of his fire power behind them. He was over and in position.

Once Luger was adding to their defense, Ant ran for the wire. Reinforcements were continually coming up—Carey could tell from the additional rounds bombarding them and the increasing number of shouting voices. He hoped there weren't any zealots in Rifat's troops; they'd be hard to keep down. Mercenaries were a different matter. Trained and skilled and deadly, they still preferred collecting next week's paycheck. Zealots alarmed him, their mad eyes reflecting the chaos in their minds.

A man screamed and then another. He knew that sound. Good. Two less—whatever their persuasion. And he glanced toward the parapet, gauging the time it would take Ant to cross. He wasn't staying on this side a second longer than necessary. Emptying his magazine in a spraying sweep across the roof peak, he was crouched behind the chimney in the process of reloading when his instinct for self-preservation screamed, *Go!* Without hesitation he dropped his rifle and ran. He never, *never* ignored that voice.

They hadn't expected him to break cover without firing, and he had a few scant seconds of reprieve before they began sighting in on him. He was up on the parapet and then on the wire before the first guards rose in pursuit. He heard Luger's shouted warning, but didn't slow down as the first rush was almost immediately followed by a full-scale charge. Ant and Luger were doing their best to stop them, but it was possible several might make it to the parapet. Carey was halfway across the thirty feet in a light run when a stream of bullets flashed by him so closely he felt the heat on his face. "Cut the wire," he shouted, "cut it." His additional directive erased the first shocked look from Ant's face, and he was reaching for the wire with his cutters when Carey leaped the last eight feet for the roof. In midair he heard the snap as the taut wire split apart and saw the welcoming grin on Ant's face.

An enormous explosion erupted behind him. He rolled to his feet and he saw Luger with a missile launcher balanced on his shoulder, a look of infinite satisfaction on his face.

"Where the hell did that come from?" Carey inquired, breathless and astonished.

"Brooks Air Force Base."

"I didn't mean that."

"Helluva nice hole over there," Luger remarked, and Carey turned to see the entire roof, half Rifat's villa, and the pursuing guards disappear in a blaze of fire.

On the ride back to the airport, Luger explained: He'd brought the TOW missile to the antique shop earlier in the day and had hidden it in the stack of empty boxes outside the back door. Making sure he was the first one to arrive at their rendezvous that night, he'd carried it up to the roof before Carey and Ant arrived.

"Fucking pyromaniac," Carey grumbled, though his grin belied his words. "You should be committed."

"Stopped 'em, didn't it?"

"Stopped the entire operation of the villa, not to mention calling out half the fire trucks in the city."

"Any problem there?" Luger replied angelically.

Carey's grin widened. "Hell no. That was one big mother of a blast, though."

"Yeah . . . it was a beauty," Luger replied with the fondness parents reserved for compliments on their children. "Although it's small in relation to other missiles."

"How do you get your hands on those?"

Luger smiled. "Privileged information."

"That means he stole it," Ant interjected, sprawled in one corner of the backseat, a Mexican beer in his hand.

"*I* didn't steal it. I purchased it," Luger explained as if the distinction were important.

"I think we're all aware of the occasional lapses in integrity in the Defense Department and its agencies," Carey noted, wiping the camouflage black off his face. "So what do you have from your supermarket for Miami?" Carey had briefed them on the memo on Rifat's desk and their need for haste, since they had no way of knowing if Rifat had set the operation in motion yet or not. But they were safest assuming the mission to kidnap Sylvie had been initiated. They had to proceed as though the danger to Sylvie existed. If it did not, they would all breathe a collective sigh of relief.

In the meantime, Carey called Sylvie and, without alarming her into panic, explained she should hire extra guards and stay in the hospital until he arrived.

CHAPTER 41

The wing was bristling with off-duty police officers when they returned to Miami. Sylvie had taken Carey's order to heart. But essentially she was calm. Everything was fine, she told him. She had hired a great number of security and there was nothing more to worry about. Although Carey was slightly more cautious than she, he did have to agree they seemed protected behind the barricades of police officers. No one was allowed in or out of the wing unless they were personally approved by Sylvie or himself.

Egon was still on the critical list, but not worse, the doctors' prognosis one of guarded optimism. "He may live," they said.

"Great," Carey replied. "What about the paralysis?"

Their faces became more somber at that point and none dared offer hope.

"Surely someone can try operating. What the hell does he have to lose?"

His condition was too critical, they replied. He would never survive the surgery.

Carey dropped the discussion. Clearly some research was necessary, other specialists had to be called in. All avenues would be pursued later when the threat to Sylvie was resolved.

After stopping by to visit Egon and Mariel, Carey called Molly.

Rifat was dead, he said.

And she asked quickly if he was all right, her voice concerned and warm.

He was fine, he replied.

Could she go home then? she asked, her tone more controlled and less vital.

He wanted her to wait a few more days, he politely mentioned, until he reconciled the threat to Sylvie.

"Are you with Sylvie?" she inquired, and the brittleness in her voice was unmistakably cool.

He wished he didn't have to say yes. "Just for a few more days," he said.

"Your father's waiting to speak to you," she declared. "Thank you very much for calling."

He swore under his breath, but when his father came on the phone he merely related the pertinent events, explained the necessity for a delay in Miami to stave off a possible threat to Sylvie, and ended by telling his father he would be home as soon as possible.

"I'm very glad you're safe," Bernadotte replied, "now let the security earn their keep and stay out of the way."

"No one can get through this phalanx of guards, Papa. Rest easy."

He'd stopped by Sylvie's sitting room to discuss the new doctors they should call in for Egon. When the cleaning woman walked in, the hairs on the back of his neck stood up. Looking over at her, he told himself he'd been without sleep too long and was overreacting to every stimuli. She was just a plain young woman with black hair pulled back carelessly in a net cap, a dark complexion, and a strange way of holding a mop.

He'd spoken perhaps a half-dozen more sentences to Sylvie when her odd grasp on the mop handle registered in his mind. Continuing to speak to Sylvie, he turned his head a minute degree and glanced once again at her hands.

She had long red nails and a fifty dollar manicure, and if he didn't miss his guess, she'd probably never held a mop in her life.

"So if you agree," he went on, his heart rate accelerating, "I'll have Allen get a team to research the best specialists in spinal surgery, and we'll have someone out here in a couple of days." It wouldn't do any good to take this woman and leave the rest of her colleagues untouched.

"I'm fully in agreement," Sylvie said, waving the woman away from her side of the room. "And Egon is, as well. The young girl he finds so entrancing is afraid of everything, but she hardly matters. I say get the best and tell them we want the bullet out."

The woman had mopped the same area of floor for quite some time. The sooner Carey alerted Ant and Luger the better. He moved toward the door, watching her out of the corner of his eyes. She was intent on his progress.

At the doorway, he paused. "Do you have that phone number of the clinic in Denver?"

Sylvie nodded, sorting through several sheets of paper on the table near her chair.

"Do you mind giving it to me?" He held out his hand. "And I'll call after I talk to Egon."

She thought it odd he didn't move, only stood with his hand out waiting for her to bring it to him.

Walking over to him, Sylvie handed the paper to him.

And when he said, "Thank you, darling," and pulled her into his arms for a kiss, she knew something was wrong. She'd been trying to get Carey to kiss her for three years, and he'd avoided her every advance. "Do whatever she says," he murmured into her ear. "The cleaning woman . . . I'll be right behind you." Relinquishing his grip, Carey patted her on the shoulder and, in a bolstering voice, said, "Keep up your spirits now, sweet. Egon needs you cheerful."

Shutting the door behind him, Carey signaled Ant and Luger, who joined him as he walked away down the hall. "The cleaning woman is one of them," he said. "We'll follow her out when she takes Sylvie and get the rest of them. Or as many as we can."

He preferred not involving the hired security guards. They'd been only told the Countess von Mansfeld was being protected from unwanted publicity. In addition to not completely trusting outsiders, some of them could be in Rifat's hire. Ant and Luger were the best. He felt secure.

"Are we taking prisoners?" Luger asked.

"No," Carey briefly replied, and turned into a small shower room three doors down from Sylvie's suite. "We'll wait here."

In only a few minutes, Sylvie and the cleaning woman walked out of Sylvie's room, apparently in friendly conversation, although Carey knew the woman was holding a gun under the stack of towels in her arms. As they reached the doors exiting the wing, Sylvie asked the guard on duty if he would go to her room to get her purse she'd forgotten. "And if you don't mind, you could escort me to dinner. I can't tolerate another meal of hospital food." Her smile was relaxed and flirtatious.

Thrilled by the prospect of accompanying Sylvie von Mansfeld to dinner, he readily responded and swiftly left to do her bidding, leaving Sylvie and the cleaning woman alone at the exit to the west wing.

They were out the door and halfway down the hall when Carey, Ant, and Luger slipped through the doors behind them, staying far enough back to remain out of sight. The woman took Sylvie down the service stairs. After a judicious interval, the men followed, Luger carrying his small canvas bag of weapons. She took Sylvie all the way down to the basement and, without a glance backward, proceeded briskly out into the underground lot.

The men had armed themselves on the descent. Sylvie's blond hair was easily visible above the parked cars even in the dimly lit garage. Splitting up, each man trailed the two women, flanking their progress.

Carey heard the car ignition before he saw it, realized the woman had stopped with Sylvie as though she were waiting for the car turning the corner of the aisle ahead. Knowing that Ant and Luger would cover him, he stepped out into the aisle and shouted, "Sylvie!" He waved as though he were trying to catch up to her.

As the dark-haired woman spun around, he was already running toward them. He saw the surprise in her expression, saw her toss the towels aside. While her arm was swinging up to aim her pistol at him, he pumped three rounds into her head from hip level. Still rushing forward, he grabbed Sylvie around her waist and they both tumbled behind a parked car just as the black Mercedes applied its brakes.

"Stay down," he ordered, aiming for the tires and firing the rest of his magazine into the two front tires. Even if the car was bulletproofed with specially equipped tires, you could usually slow it down with a few well-placed rounds in the tires. And Luger was carrying some weapons effective against bulletproof glass. As Carey reloaded, the car moved forward again, its damaged tires diminishing its speed. "Have you got them?" he shouted out, neither Ant or Luger visible.

"I got them," Luger replied, his voice cool and without emotion.

And as he watched, a barrage of gunfire tracked symmetrical paths down the windows on both sides of the car, shattering the glass. Careening out of control, the car slammed into several parked automobiles before it came to a shuddering stop fifty yards down the aisle.

The men arrived at the Mercedes with poised weapons, but no one moved inside. Both men were slumped in the front seat. Ant opened the doors with gloved hands and double-checked.

"And now we disappear," Ant said, turning back from his task.

"Right," Carey agreed. "I'll get Sylvie and call you at home in a day or so. No sense in overloading the police with a lot of paper work."

Ant grinned. "A true model citizen."

Luger was repacking his canvas bag, more intent than Carey on avoiding the police since his weapons were all illegal.

"And thanks," Carey said, his voice subdued. "I owe you."

"Forget it," Ant said.

"My pleasure," Luger quietly retorted, his bag slung over his shoulder. "That TOW was a beaut . . . lit up half of Rome."

For a moment it seemed nothing had changed, and Carey was years younger seeing Luger and Ant coming back from a mission with that same elation. Although their worlds had turned full circle countless times, the sense of accomplishment was the same.

"Come to my wedding," Carey said, putting his hand out.

"Wouldn't miss it," Ant replied, grasping Carey's hand in a street-smart high sign.

"Carol likes weddings," Luger said, "so we'll come." And his hand gripped Carey's in a firm, hard clasp.

They turned then, and melted into the shadows.

CHAPTER 42

He returned to Sylvie and helped her to her feet. She looked pale and disheveled, but wasn't hysterical.

"Did you get them all?" she asked, glancing at the dead woman lying on the cement. Her voice was more shaken than he'd ever heard.

"I think so . . . and with Rifat dead—" He shrugged, not able to give her an iron-clad guarantee. "This should be the last attempt." He looked at the pistol he still held in his hand, then slipped it into his sports jacket pocket.

"You saved my life." Sylvie's eyes misted with tears, and her pouty mouth quivered.

With Sylvie, one never knew if she was playing a role or was sincere, but neither possibility interested him, so Carey smiled and said, "With a great deal of help from Ant and Luger. About which—" He glanced around, concerned with discovery before he had time to rehearse Sylvie's story. "Listen, darling," he coaxed, "we've got to get out of here. Ant and Luger don't want to be involved." Taking her hand, he began pulling her toward the service stairs, hoping no one would drive in or step out of the elevators in the next thirty seconds.

"Why ever not?" she asked, trying to keep up with his rapid stride.

"Mostly because all their weapons are illegal, and the police would take issue with their possession of them. Both Ant and Luger occasionally tread the perimeters of the law." Opening the stairwell door, he ushered her in.

"But they helped save my life. I'm sure the police would understand."

"Uh, darling . . ." He indicated they were going up. "Some police might understand, and then some may not. Neither Ant nor Luger care to take that gamble. Understand?"

Sylvie glanced over at Carey as they ascended the stairs side-by-side. "Well, certainly I do. Why didn't you say your friends were criminals? Sweetheart, my lips are sealed, absolutely."

Rather than argue with Sylvie's interpretation, Carey quickly agreed. Subtlety escaped Sylvie's comprehension.

"How will you explain the bullet holes in the car, though?"

"I'd just as soon not explain anything." And he'd prefer to plead ignorance to the entire episode in the parking garage. But he knew Sylvie was seen leaving with the cleaning woman who now lay dead with a bullet between her eyes, and he wasn't going to be able to carry off the denial.

"Carey, dear, I absolutely insist you get the credit for saving my life. You were terribly heroic, and you deserve the kudos."

"No publicity . . . I don't want it."

"Nonsense." The old Sylvie was back now that she was removed from the scene of bloodshed. "You shot that awful woman and saved me from kidnapping. I owe you my life." Her voice trembled in a dramatic inflection sure to carry to the last balcony.

"Cut it out, Sylvie. This whole thing has to be played way the hell down."

"Fine. Protect your friends, if you wish. Say whatever you

want about the car. I'll cooperate with your story, but I *will* not be silent on your extraordinary act of bravery."

Sylvie and publicity were a natural combination like heart and lung function; one didn't exist long without the other. The question was how to keep her under some semblance of control so Ant and Luger would be protected and his part in the episode limited.

He talked very rapidly on the last flight of stairs. They would deny all knowledge of the men in the car. Carey would admit to shooting the cleaning woman when she threatened Sylvie's life. Perhaps the two dead men in the car were part of some drug dealing vendetta. With the current daily total of murders in Miami, that suggestion wouldn't be unreasonable. He had fired at the car he would admit, only if ballistics tests implicated him, and in the panic of the moment missed, hitting the tires.

So when the police officer hired to guard the door into the west wing questioned Sylvie about her disappearance, her story was intact.

A tear even slid down her cheek when she breathlessly began: "I was almost kidnapped! If not for my dear ex-husband Count Fersten who fearlessly placed his own life in jeopardy to save mine," she paused for dramatic effect, "I should be *this very moment* a captive."

Within twenty minutes the hospital was aswarm with police, reporters, photographers, and television crews. The police were insistent for details, the reporters clamoring for interviews and a press conference.

"No press conference," Carey snapped.

"Darling," Sylvie cooed, playing for the audience, "don't be so modest!" And she launched again into her now thoroughly rehearsed version of her heroic salvation from kidnapping.

Carey kept his distance from the press and tried unsuccessfully to pry Sylvie loose, once the police were nominally satisfied with the fabricated story. "Sylvie, that's enough," he muttered, his jaw clenched tight in restrained anger.

"Just one more question, darling," she replied with a smile, blowing him a kiss. "Isn't he a darling?" she purred to the crowd of reporters in the hallway. "A modest hero."

Those words segued into the TV evening news. *"Isn't he a darling?"*

Then Sylvie came on the screen looking flushed and beautiful, only recently saved from abduction by her ex-husband. She blew him a sultry kiss as only Sylvie von Mansfeld could. Every man in America watching the six o'clock news wished he were the recipient of that kiss from the most sensual, pouty lips in the world.

Molly was grateful Bernadotte and the girls were still out riding; she was saved from having to hide her humiliation from all of them. She had been sitting in the cool, dim study, sunk in one of the soft leather armchairs, feeling sorry for herself even before the news item flashed across the screen.

With Carey gone, so many of the differences in their lives had taken on more forbidding proportions, starting with Sylvie. With time on her hands, Molly had escalated them into *enormous* differences. The past still haunted her, with all the old residual insecurities intact. She hardly knew Carey. Just how much of a life together could be based on an overwhelming passion, she wondered, when both of them were strangers to each other beneath the all-consuming desire?

Then she would remind herself, her feelings alone weren't at stake. Carrie mattered tremendously, too, and she adored her father. She mustn't be hasty or rash, Molly cautioned herself, swept away by some terrible jealousy over an ex-wife and in so doing harm her daughter. But in the next heartbeat, Sylvie's picture reappeared in her mind, Sylvie with invitation blatant, Sylvie who was more important at the moment than she.

Immature, immature, she chastised herself. Good God, he had to stay . . . the woman's *life* was in danger. But the admonition didn't stand up for a minute against her demon of jealousy. Dammit, he was every woman's goddamned hero. He was her *daughter's* hero. Age was not a consideration in female adoration. Every female who came within ten feet of Carey Fersten adored him. Without exception.

When Carey called, although she tried to behave in a civilized way, Molly's resentment was obvious.

"You made the six o'clock news," she said. "Congratulations." But her voice wasn't congratulatory, and she wanted to blurt out more. Is she still hot for you? How does it feel to hold the world's sexiest woman? Do you think of me when she's purring in your ear?

Instead, she said, "Carrie's missing her two weeks of camp we'd scheduled last winter," she said. "If the danger is over, I'd like to go back home."

"Leon can drive you. I'll fly into the Cities tomorrow. The police are being," he paused, not wishing to go into any detail of the abduction attempt, "well . . . police."

"I might still be at Kichigoomi tomorrow, dropping off Carrie," Molly rebuffed.

"I'll wait at your place," Carey replied.

"I may be *very* late."

"I'll keep the light burning in the window."

She needed some time to herself, Molly decided, to sort out all the Fersten charm against Darian reality, to deal with Carey's terrorist connections impinging on her daughter's normal childhood, to come to terms with the glitz and glamour surrounding an international film director in contrast to her perhaps idealized notions of a peaceful life in an old factory turned home and business.

Seeing Carey's childhood home had reinforced her impressions of aristocratic wealth and privilege. Although Bernadotte was a natural, unaffected man, he accepted all the prerogatives of affluence casually as though living in a mansion surrounded by servants, having one's own stable and airstrip were normal. While she admired his lack of pretention, she perceived a patrician noblesse he didn't even realize he exuded.

How many differences of attitude would surface day after day, month after month, between herself and Carey? Would he think her bourgeois—a Cinderella with cinders on her feet. Would she find him condescending? She embraced the melting pot ethic enough to question why a duke or duchess, a prince or princess was fawned on by society, splashed across the pages of *W* or *Town and Country* or *People*, when in fact, many were, at base, ignorant and boorish. With a reverse snobbery of her own, it annoyed her when wealthy ladies proudly said the millions they spent on couturier clothes were helping the economy and all the charity functions they attended were a noblesse oblige impulse to aid the needy. She found such hypocrisy offensive when children were living through blizzards with their parents in cars, cold and hungry and bewildered. And she was afraid her anger would appear incomprehensible to someone who didn't know the price of anything.

She *liked* to bargain shop. It was one of her favorite rushes . . . to buy something for fifty percent off.

The prosaic daily cycle of living might prove disastrous; she thought of the daily aggrievements that had slowly decimated the fabric of her marriage to Bart. A marriage she'd entered into with positive hopes for success. Maybe the strongest love diminished to dust in the battlefield of misunderstandings. And if there were easy answers to the question of love, all marriages would be eternal smiles of bliss. Since so many weren't . . . it further shook her already shaky convictions.

She wanted some time, she decided, alone at home to ponder the riddles of the universe and the lesser earthly dilemmas relating to herself and Carey Fersten. And relating to Sylvie. And Egon. And to enormous wealth which shouldn't be a problem but was. And to every other topsyturvy emotion concerning cabbages and kings. Damn. Where was her Cinderella happy ending?

CHAPTER **43**

Carey spent the evening with Egon, talking about Rifat, the abduction, and all that had transpired to disrupt their lives. As he rose to leave, he said, "Eat and do your exercises. I'll be back in a few days with some doctors who'll take out that bullet in your spine. Allen's checking the current research for me. You'll be walking again in no time."

Egon smiled, strangely content even with his paralysis. Mariel was seated beside his bed, her hand clasped in his, her smile and presence the cause of his content. "The world sure looks good," he teased, "when you consider the alternative. And even if"—he put up a hand to stop Carey's protest— "even if things don't work out," he quietly said, a new maturity in his tone, "I'll consider myself extremely fortunate. Now stop worrying about me and go back home to Molly."

"And the film," Carey said. "Allen says Tangen is raising the roof about production delays. So I'll see you in a few days, probably over the weekend," he added, moving toward the door. "Keep an eye on Sylvie." She was like a loose cannon, totally unpredictable.

"And then?" Egon retorted with a grin, knowing as well as Carey she was ungovernable.

"At least warn me if she's heading my way," Carey replied, grinning back, "and I can plan a defense."

"I'll keep her here as my ministering angel, unless of course, she becomes bored with the role."

"A good possibility with Sylvie. She has the attention span of a puppy." Carey was standing by the door, pleased at the sight of Egon and Mariel so obviously happy despite the daunting circumstances of Egon's injury. "Well . . . take care," he said, and with a casual wave he was gone.

Carey slept on the flight home. Assuming Molly wouldn't be back from her trip to camp till midmorning at the earliest, he made arrangements to meet Allen at the airport so they could discuss both Egon and the state of their film.

Sitting across from him in the comfortable lounge of Carey's plane, Allen told him a team of doctors had been assembled and would depart for Miami in two days.

"Thanks," Carey said, stirring two extra spoonfuls of sugar into his coffee to help keep him awake. "I appreciate all your work."

"No problem. With all the new data bases available, we came up with a list of names immediately. Checking them out took a little longer. No bullet holes in you?" Allen was drinking Red Zinger tea from a Styrofoam cup he'd brought on board. His baseball cap sat backward on his head, a sign he was tired.

"Nope. I can run faster. Egon played the hero."

"The papers say you did, too."

"That's all Sylvie's hype. Ant and Luger were with me—and that's security, let me tell you. Look," he said, uncomfortable with Sylvie's publicity, turning the discussion from heroics, "my apologies for bringing you down here this early, but I'm going to spend a couple of days with Molly, and I wanted to get the business taken care of first."

"Speaking of business," Allen cautiously advanced, "what

do you want me to do about Tangen? He's screaming cost overruns like it was his own money." Allen's eyebrows rose resignedly. "All those days you were gone . . ."

"Stall him another few days. I'll talk to you tomorrow or the next day. Right now, I'm going to see Molly, and I don't give a damn about Tangen."

Allen swallowed and said, "Okay, Carey, whatever you say." But he had visions of money being blown away in the wind, and his practical soul was gulping hard.

CHAPTER 44

When Carey stopped by Molly's shortly before noon, his daughter answered the door. "Dad," she squealed and launched herself at him like a catapult.

Scooping her up in his arms, he hugged her close, and thought: Now I know I'm truly home and safe. But she squirmed a moment later, and he realized he was holding her too tightly. Setting her back on her feet with a brushing kiss on her cheek, he said, "I thought you were going to camp."

"Not me, Dad. I can get eaten alive by mosquitoes in the park across the street."

"Your Mom *said* you were going to camp."

"Not me," she cheerfully repeated. "I hate camp. You have to see me ride, Dad. Grandpa said I'll be as good as you someday—maybe as good as him," she added with a grin.

And Carey's uncharitable thoughts about the deception of camp were distracted at the word, Grandpa—a pleasant, warm-sounding word, redolent with granddaughterly affection. "You must be hot," Carey said, ruffling her pale, silky hair, " 'cuz Papa still holds some racing records from the thirties."

"Good gene pool, hey?"

His daughter's maturity always surprised him. "Must be,

Pooh," he agreed with a grin, "because after only a week on a horse, it sure isn't the training."

"I have to meet Lucy halfway; she's coming over, so I'll see you later," she declared with childlike obliviousness to the fact he'd risked his life twice in the last few days for her sake. "Mom's downstairs talking to Theresa about everything she missed. She'll be thrrrrrilled to see you," Carrie teased.

His welcome was considerably less than thrilling, however, when he walked into Molly's office. It was, in fact, cooler than he'd anticipated. He sat for twenty minutes waiting while Molly and Theresa went over the outgoing invoices. And if they hadn't been interrupted by the lunch hour, his wait would have been longer.

"I'd like some time to myself," Molly blurted out the second the door closed on Theresa. She had to express herself before Carey's charm and beguiling tongue could change her mind. And she stayed at her desk as if she could barricade herself from his persuasive allure.

"No," he said, expecting dissent, but not like this. His dark eyes glittered dangerously beneath his black, scowling brows. He was too tired to deal dispassionately with their differences, but he had to take it slow or risk worse disagreements. So he steeled himself to calmness.

"I'm afraid it's not open to discussion." Molly kept her voice as moderate as possible. She was trying to be sensible about her feelings, not adversarial. She understood that Carey didn't have misgivings—he never did it seemed—and she wondered whether she'd not traveled as far as she thought from the young girl she'd once been. But maybe that was the essential difference underneath all the superficiality of Carey's wealth and glamour. Maybe they had fundamental differences in personality. She was never adamantly certain like Carey. Molly had always been prone to intellectualize and rationalize every emotional crisis. She was probably doing that again, but she'd feel more secure in her final decision if she gave herself time to examine her feelings beyond the overpowering passion she felt for Carey. Was passion enough? Would it sustain the good times and the bad times? Would it even endure? Or was passion, desire, lust, and love all one? Was she killing their relationship by dissecting it to death?

"Everything is open to discussion," Carey emphatically replied, his scowl unaltered, his voice a low rumble.

"Everything?" Molly retorted, taking issue with the unspoken demand in his tone. "Like Sylvie's clinging presence in Miami? I don't recall discussing the situation."

"It was an emergency." His voice was strained.

"So is this—so I don't make another mistake."

"Don't compare me to Bart," he snapped. Then his voice changed, and he quietly said, "Let's talk about this."

"I don't want to now."

"I'm sorry about Sylvie."

How many others would he be sorry about—later—someday—two years from now? Although he said he loved her, it seemed from her vantage point, his love was flexible. "I am, too," she quietly said. "Sorry about the killings and about Egon. How often do you think we're going to be sorry about things if we get married?"

"We can *work* it out."

"I have to work it out for myself *first* before I can begin the cooperative working out."

"Jesus, Molly, I'm sorry as hell Egon got mixed up with Rifat, but I couldn't leave him out there."

"I know. I *know*." She wasn't unfeeling. "That's not the point."

"So hit me with the point," he said, unmoving in his chair, his face expressionless.

"The point is," she slowly replied, "whether *I* want, whether I want my *daughter*—"

"*Our* daughter," he tersely interjected.

"—to enter a lifestyle," she went on, ignoring his challenging interjection, "so far removed from what we're familiar with."

His eyes closed and he suddenly felt his aching weariness. "Dear Christ," he said softly, and when he opened his eyes his gaze was moody. "We've been over this a dozen times." He sighed. "I'm truly apologetic for all my goddamn money, and I suppose the title, too—although you know as well as I do that I don't even use the damn thing. I'm penitent as hell I ever slept with a female other than you in my entire life. What else?" he said sarcastically. "Oh shit—the guns, of course. I can't help it. I can't walk away from my past, although I would if I could for you." He ran his fingers through his hair and sighed again. "Do you know how unimportant all this is?"

"In your opinion," Molly said in a prim voice he'd never heard before, and he scrutinized her quickly at the unfamiliar sound. "I'd like a week or so to myself."

"Don't say you need breathing space or I'll puke."

"No, I won't."

"What if I say make up your mind right now or fuck it?"

She only gazed at him without answering, and if she'd been less involved in her own disordered emotions, she would have noticed how tired he looked.

He hadn't slept well in days, and wasn't currently equipped to deal with Molly's uncertainties. "Just remember," he said, rising in a swift movement as his temper surged. "Pooh's my daughter, too and if your *decision* should be negative to my interests, I'll fight you for custody." He was near the door when he finished and, despite his anger, an overwhelming sadness struck him suddenly like a blow. "I don't want to fight," he said quietly.

"I'm sorry," Molly whispered.

His expression was searching and critical for a moment, then calm. "So am I," he said crisply, and left.

CHAPTER 45

S he hadn't expected him to agree, but Carey's chill anger, his threat about child custody, and the absolute grim blackness of his scowl had shocked Molly. Was her request so devastating?

Maybe she was too removed from adolescence to still be indulging in her search for identity. Maybe she was selfishly egotistic to be making decisions for two other lives beside her own. *Maybe* Carey was right and they could work out their differences later.

Leaving the office, she decided to go upstairs to the apartment and rest over the lunch hour; she was feeling a curious light-headed sensation, brought on no doubt by her emotional turmoil. But when she reached the apartment, Carrie and Lucy were watching TV at blast-off volume, each word blaringly clear as she lay in her bed next to her daughter's room. Unable to relax, she rose from the bed. Straightening the pleated skirt of her white linen suit which wrinkled if you even looked at it and slowly walking to her daughter's room, she opened the door and said, "Why don't you play outside? It's such a nice day."

No one responded, since they couldn't hear her with the

TV broadcasting for the entertainment of the entire city block. Molly moved closer. "Don't you think it would be a nice day to play outside?"

Carrie looked up, said, "Okay, Mom," and with a smiling wave went back to her Batman and Robin program.

Molly turned the volume down herself and said, "You girls should go outside on a beautiful summer day like this."

"Sure, Mom. Turn the sound up a little, will you? I can't hear."

"I'm trying to rest."

"Sorry, Mom, we'll move closer. Lucy did you see that Batmobile burn out of the cave? I want one of those, Mom." Both girls' eyes were glued to the TV screen.

"I'll get you one this afternoon," Molly replied, mildly sardonic, "right after I fuel up the Rolls."

"Great, they have them at Children's Palace, on sale this week. Six ninety-five."

She was absolutely adorable, Molly thought with unconditional motherly pride, gazing at her daughter sprawled out on the bed, her chin resting on her crossed arms, her pale hair pulled in a spiky ponytail. Just like her father. And in so many ways she was oblivious like him to the angst of daily living. She should try and develop a similar competence at avoiding anxiety.

"I'm going to try and sleep for a while."

"We'll be quiet, Mom," her daughter said to Batman and Robin.

But she couldn't sleep and only managed to wrinkle her suit past wearing. As she was changing, she caught sight of herself in the mirror and noticed her unusual pallor. She rationalized it away as the result of all the tumultuous activity of the past weeks and her erratic eating schedule. She'd eat a good lunch for a change, and restore some color to her cheeks; she'd make something nutritious and nourishing. But when she opened the refrigerator door, a peculiar smell assailed her nostrils, triggering an instant wave of nausea. She hastily pushed the door shut. She'd have soup instead, she decided, driven to a seated position at the kitchen table by the passing queasy sensation. Her mother had always made her chicken noodle soup when she wasn't feeling well. Wouldn't it be just her luck, she reflected, working up her energy to prepare her lunch, to have picked up some damn exotic virus in Jamaica? But when the bowl of soup wafted its warm aroma through the kitchen, she wondered whether Campbell's had changed their recipe; the odor was distinctly different. After two spoonfuls she felt worse instead of better. She called the office then, said she'd be an hour late, and went back to lie down.

Who wouldn't feel less than in peak condition after the unsettling events of the last weeks? She'd dealt with kidnapping, murder, and terror. She couldn't expect to experience a shocking journey into a hellish world without suffering some physical reaction to the horror of it all. Now that her life was restored to her normal activities, in a matter of time, this nausea and dizziness would disappear. A few more days, and she'd be perfectly fine.

At least the paparazzi had departed from her doorstep, intent, no doubt, on their next morsel of gossip, and her sidewalk was restored to its familiar quiet. She was relieved of that additional tension. And there was comfort in knowing overnight wonders in the scandal sheets were simply that—a sudden flash of interest—eyed, speculated, probed, and then as rapidly forgotten. Would it be possible, she wondered, her reflections more placid now as she began dozing, to become inured to their dogged curiosity as Carey was? Would she no longer notice them after a time? Would she become as sensational as the sensational Carey Fersten? Or as worldly? Could she marry a man she loved beyond reason but didn't really know? And on that unanswered question, she fell asleep.

———

The next morning an extravagant basket of exotic lilies was delivered. The scrawled note was brief: "Day one and counting. Six to go. I love you." Carey's sentiments were like him: direct, without apology, and imbued with a provocative vitality.

She set the flowers on the foyer console. She found herself more vulnerable than she expected to Carey's thoughtfulness. But she remained painfully aware of his engaging charm. He was familiar with the game of love, an expert at the chase. He had, after all, set records for acquisition.

If she married him, would she begin hearing whispers of his affairs once the passionate glow of their love softened? Or more aptly, with his track record, how long would it be before she heard the whispers. And would she ever be able to come to terms with Sylvie's possessiveness? Knowing Carey's affection for Egon, surely Sylvie would enter their lives on occasion. She had to weigh his charm against her vulnerability, his past against her hopes for the future. She had to find some reasonable answers to the confusion that preyed on her heart.

In the meantime, she received a daily floral offering and love note. But as the third day passed, and then the fourth, she found herself no nearer a resolution; the same combination of anxieties relooped through her brain without even a basic sorting process to eliminate her minor concerns.

Her dilemma was like the bad ending in a movie she'd recently seen in which the protagonists walked away from each other because neither had sense enough to go for the brass ring. She hated the movie after she saw the ending; she hated the characters for their small, bleak view of happiness. But this wasn't a movie, it was her one and only life, and she was afraid the pain would come too soon to compensate for her brief moment of happiness.

She was well and truly bewildered.

And then, he didn't call; even though she hadn't wanted him to call, he actually *hadn't* called, which put an entirely new complexion on her anarchistic thinking. It was easy to

send flowers and clever notes; he didn't even have to lift a finger to do that, someone else could take care of it, like Allen,
who practically ran his entire life, anyway. And maybe it
meant he was too busy with Egon or *her* to even think of the
woman he claimed he loved more than anything. Anything,
sure, after the film and Egon and Sylvie with the name that
sounded like her parents knew she was going to be a damn
two syllable movie star from the cradle. Damn, damn, damn.
She missed him. She missed him terribly.

As if life wasn't miserable enough, the phone rang on the
morning of the fifth day and Jason Evans's lubricated voice
greeted her hello. What now? she thought. Does he want a
pound of my flesh before the renewal is up?

He was sending over the papers on her repaid note, he
said.

"Repaid?" Molly had to stifle the squeal coming up from
her lungs.

"Yeah, last month by Phoenix Ltd. I thought you knew."

She'd die before giving Jason the satisfaction of knowing
she was completely ignorant of the repayment. She dissembled shamelessly. "In the excitement of my vacation in
Jamaica—I just returned a few days ago—the note completely slipped my mind. You know how it goes, Jason, it's
fun, fun, fun." She tried one of those trilling laughs, but
winced at the brittleness. Jason didn't seem to notice; brittleness, no doubt, was a way of life for him.

"How's your love life?" he said with his usual subtlety.

"Probably better than yours, Jason, although possibly not
as quiet. You don't like them to talk, do you? Until they say,
'Drive me home, Ken.' "

"Cute."

"When I want to discuss my love life with you, Jason, I'll
give you a call." And she hung up on him with a satisfaction
so profound, she felt giddy.

How had Carey accomplished the payment? she wondered. The answers to her naive questions were obvious.

Carey Fersten had a reputation for doing pretty much what he pleased, she reflected, an uneasy resentment simmering beneath her gratitude. However benevolent his action, his presumptuous meddling in her financial affairs reinforced all her nagging insecurities. She refused to concede her hard-won independence to a man who ordered the world to his perfection.

She didn't want, didn't need, wouldn't tolerate an authoritarian husband.

She had lived through too many unhappy years with Bart, who viewed a woman's role as somewhere between household furniture and a mannequin. She had survived too many desperate months after the divorce wondering if her business would succeed another day or through another payroll or past another quarterly tax payment. She and Carrie had struggled through those bad times when each new account was cause for celebration, when she and Theresa would re-work the numbers, shuffling and cutting until all the monthly bills were covered—just barely. And now, at last, when she was seeing daylight for the first time, she *would not* give up all her triumphs and achievements for love.

Her sudden emphatic decision after days of bewildering confusion was startling at first and coldly unromantic. For a brief transient moment she felt as though she had forsaken dreams of a lifetime and a thunderbolt would strike her dead for her unorthodoxy. But she was still sitting at her desk, intact and whole a few minutes later, feeling a flush of pleasure at the prospect of emancipation. Emancipation not only from her past, from the divorce and unhappiness of those years, but an emancipation from so many of the stifling rules she'd always considered requisite to a woman's fulfillment.

She was free from the limiting strictures she carried from childhood. She was also assured now she could succeed in her business. And yes, she had to admit, she was cheerfully self-indulgent at times. Without guilt.

And if she smoked, she could have dressed in a three-thousand dollar dress to lounge in one of those ads declaring: You've come a long way, baby.

Still seated at her desk with the sound of Jason's unctuous voice grating on her memory, she decided she was ready. She was ready to negotiate her love and future happiness from a position of strength, an autonomous, self-reliant sense of self and purpose.

She would not give up her business nor her independence, and if Carey Fersten needed capitulation on either count, he wasn't the man she wanted to marry. That was the bottom line on her personal integrity. After that point was established, she'd enter the discussion about other issues like Australia, pursuing women, Sylvie and Egon's likely presence in their lives, submachine guns and counter-culture types, paparazzi, and sundry facets of the glittering film world.

CHAPTER 46

Carey hadn't called because he was trying to play by her rules. It was hard; he'd picked up the phone a hundred times that week, only to slam it down in frustration a moment later. He was short-tempered—rare for him, a man who prided himself on self-control—and everyone on the cast and crew had begun glancing at him out of the corner of their eyes as he passed, in the event they had to jump fast. And he'd apologized for his curtness more in the past few days than he had in a lifetime.

He'd promised everyone a bonus if they finished by Friday, driving them unmercifully, single-minded in his goal. Perhaps as stubborn as Molly and as self-indulgent, he admitted freely his wishes were purely selfish: He wanted her and he intended to get her. By her rules this time, but by any rules or no rules if necessary.

When the week was over, Molly's apartment resembled a hothouse for orchids and rare lilies, and the florists in Minneapolis were richer for her impetuous stand on integrity.

Carey had called the evening of the seventh day and, like a

polite suitor, circumspect and well-mannered, his voice smooth as velvet, had asked her out for dinner the following night.

His knock on the door came precisely at eight.

His knock came so perfectly as the second-hand swept toward the twelve, Molly wondered if he'd stood outside her door waiting with his fist raised until the exact moment.

He was bronzed and beautiful, each silky hair on his gilded head in place, his gray double-breasted suit impeccably tailored, his white-on-white patterned shirt crisp, his Lyon silk tie soft as Southern speech, a startling magenta alstroemeria blossom in his lapel buttonhole. Perfection stood before her, and for a brief moment before he smiled he looked like a scrubbed and combed young boy ready for his first date. His smile however, conjured the familiar Fersten sensuality, and his lazy drawl further blurred the young schoolboy image. "Good evening, Ms. Darian, you're looking . . . splendid." His eyes traveled in slow assessment from the top of her shiny blond head down to her green and white silk print dress to the tips of her toes and eventually back to her face. His teeth flashed white, and he winked. "As usual."

And against all prudent admonitions to remain judicious in her response to the Fersten charm until their discussion was concluded, she couldn't help but return his grin. "Thank you, Mr. Fersten. May I return the compliment. I've never seen your hair so perfectly combed."

"I bought a comb today as an indication of the full extent of my commitment."

"I'm flattered."

"Good. In that case," he said with a smile, "my ten dollars wasn't wasted. I hope you're ready now, because I can't guarntee this veneer of perfection very long. Once I move, it may shatter." And he shook his head suddenly, as if breaking free of the stifling ideal, his burnished gold hair rearranging itself to its familiar disorder.

He was cheerful on their way downstairs as if the past week hadn't intervened in their relationship. He filled her in on the progress of the film, as well as on Egon's current state of health. "I flew down overnight to see him day before yesterday. The doctors are running additional tests, trying to decide how to operate."

"I'm happy he's feeling better," Molly replied in a polite tone, but her stomach did a brief flip-flop as she visualized Sylvie greeting Carey. Even with Molly in the same room, she'd had no compunction about falling into his arms. How close had she been two days ago, with Molly a thousand miles away?

"I talked to Papa this morning," Carey said, opening the outside door for her, "and he misses Carrie. By the way, where is she?" He had expected his daughter to greet him, since eight o'clock was well before her bedtime.

"She's sleeping over with Lucy. Lucy has a new video game they've been trying to master the last few days."

"Does Pooh need one?"

"No," she said too quickly, her tone as abrupt as a treaty negotiator determined not to relinquish another foot of motherland soil. Immediately embarrassed at her rudeness she added in a more moderate voice, "Actually, she's waiting for some new model due out next fall. Maybe then."

"I miss her," Carey said quietly, haunted the past few day not only by his differences with Molly but by unwelcome thoughts of possibly losing his daughter.

She had no response. Carrie had been asking for her father all week.

"Where's Carey?" her daughter had asked.

"Gone."

"Are you two fighting again?"

Molly hadn't answered for a moment, trying to formulate an acceptable reply. Although she had expected Carrie to begin one of her curious Freudian interpretations, she had merely said, "I miss him, Mom." And she didn't sound adu

t all, she sounded like a little nine-year-old girl who missed
her dad.

"It was only a week," Molly replied to Carey, a touch of de-
fensiveness in her voice.

"You're right," he lied. "The week flew by."

Paradoxically, his casual reply was as irritating as a complaint would have been, and Molly took brief mental pause to
consider her irrationality. Everything had been irritating her
lately, she reflected, as though her world had tipped askew.

As Carey opened the garden gate, she stepped through
and saw the parked car. It was small and sleek and expensive.

"No limo?" she remarked, immediately wanting to bite
her tongue at the pettish insult.

"I wanted to be alone with my girl," Carey replied, his
smile ignoring the peevishness of her tone, and she was
handed into the low vehicle with faultless courtesy.

Short moments later, Carey slid into the driver's seat,
brought the powerful engine to life, and deftly wheeled the
car out into traffic.

Molly glanced around the beautiful hand-crafted interior,
its walnut dash panels waxed to a soft luster, the smell of
leather mingling with Carey's faintly woodsy cologne. "This
must be yours. They don't rent these in town do they?"

Carey shrugged, intent on the driver ahead of him, whose
left signal was flashing while he exited right onto the freeway
entrance. Downshifting around the slow-moving car, he
replied with his familiar reticence, "It's mine I think . . . You'd
have to ask Allen."

"You don't know if it's your car?" She was vaguely offended by his casual admission.

"Look, Honeybear," Carey replied, glancing over at her
briefly, his dark eyes reflective, "I hear the warning whistles of
temper. I wish I could give you the right answer, but I own
several production companies and corporations. I can't personally keep track of everything and still devote the time I

want to making movies. Allen directs all those things for m
so I can concentrate on the films."

"Will he be taking care of me, as well?" She shouldn't hav
said that; she should have waited for a calm period after din
ner when they were sipping liqueurs. But then, she'd neve
had much restraint.

"Of course not," he said cordially.

"And I'd appreciate someone telling me when Phoeni
Limited decides to pay my bills." She sounded like a petulan
child, but his extreme tranquillity was provoking her. I'n
paying you back every penny."

"Suit yourself, Honeybear."

There. That same placid tone as though he *were* dealin;
with a child. And no acknowledgment of the two hundred
thousand dollars he'd paid on her note. Although, she
thought, nettled by his calm, two hundred thou was probabl
pocket change for him. "I mean it, Carey." She didn't want t
hear another word in that condescending tone of his; she
didn't want someone taking care of her. "I want to run m
own life!"

He pulled the car over to the curb and stopped in a fev
short seconds. Gently taking her hands in his, Carey said, "N
one wants to run your life, Honeybear. I only want to shar
it with you. Stay with me. Love me. Be the mother of m
child. Let me make you happy. And we'll work it out any wa
you say."

Molly could feel the tears filling the back of her throat
"I'm sorry," she whispered, feeling her face flush hotly. Hi
wealth, heritage, and profession couldn't simply be nullifie
because the distinction between her life and his was an issue
"It's been only Carrie and me the last few years and that ol
factory building that's home and work and recreation . .
and maybe my own pilgrimage toward freedom. Now sud
denly I'm up against a conglomerate with production com
panies and film corporations and—" She took a gulpin;
breath to still the turmoil in her mind and stomach. "You se(

not just Carey Fersten the boy I fell in love with, but . . .
erything else that goes with him. I'm not good," she said, a
all winsome smile curving the beauty of her mouth, "with
blicity people."

"You don't have to be."

"I don't want photographers hounding me."

"I'll see that they don't."

"Carrie needs a normal life—*without* terrorists."

"I'll *make* it normal. I'll do anything I have to. I mean to
ep you this time, Honeybear. I won't lose you again."

"Just tell me," she softly pleaded, "I won't be overwhelmed
your business and entourage and threats to our lives. And
vie," she murmured in a whisper, wanting to add "and all
e other women."

"Everything will be reconciled, I promise. I love you and
u love me. Nothing else matters. Now tell me you love me.
eed to know every five minutes for the rest of my life."

"I love you," she whispered, fighting back the tumult of
r emotions.

"I love you, Honeybear, more than anything."

And then she threw up all over the burled walnut dash-
ard.

rey held her head as she bent over to empty the rest of her
mach on the plush wool carpeting. When it was over, he
lped her sit upright again, silently wiping her face dry with
linen handkerchief. Reaching into the back storage area,
pulled out a bottle of spring water, opened it, and handed
o her.

She smiled her appreciation, took a sip, and rinsed her
uth.

Taking the bottle from her hand, he recapped it, then set it
the floor behind his seat. He slipped a gentle finger under
r chin and asked, "Do you have something to tell me?"

Molly looked into his earnest dark eyes, her own expression both bewildered and alarmed. "No," she whispered, horrified. "You're wrong."

His dark brows, so dramatic in contrast to his hair, rose mild incredulity. "Wrong?" he returned very gently. "Again?

"Absolutely," she whispered. "Positively." But there w more than a hint of tentativeness in the last word.

He didn't reply, but his eyes were alight with pleasure. A ter a moment of silence, he patted her hand, a tend smoothing caress, and said, "I'll be right back."

She watched him dodge two cars as he ran across t street, then push through the heavy bronze doors of an el gant hotel. Returning in less than five minutes, he pull Molly from the car, escorted her into the hotel through t magnificent lobby, and took her in the elevator to the t floor. Still without a word, he unlocked the hotel room do walked her through a sitting room decorated with hunti prints, through a brocade and gilded bedroom, into a bat room that would have done justice to Nero. Opening t glass shower door, he pushed her in, followed her and shov the gold embellished door shut. Taking her by the shoulder he pressed her gently against the tiled wall. He moved h hands upwards until they rested on the emerald tile, palr down and braced on either side of her head. "You're not ge ting out of here until you tell me what that little episode the car was all about," he said.

"You mean about me running my own life?" she said in very small voice.

He shook his head.

"You mean about the publicity people?" Sublimation its finest.

"Hey, I've got all night."

"I'm going to faint," Molly whispered.

"I'll hold you up. Now, sweetheart, the question that tak home the grand prize," he gently posed, his powerful body close she could feel his warmth. "Are you pregnant?"

"I can't be."

"Any good reason why not?"

Her eyes were wide. "It hasn't been very long."

He could barely hear her voice. "It only takes once," he gently said. Lifting his hands away from the wall, he brushed the silky weight of her hair behind her ears and held her face tenderly cupped in his hand. "And I stopped counting a long time ago."

"I don't think so." She felt sick again, as if her body disputed her statement.

"Lord, you're naive, Honeybear. Why the hell can't you be?" he murmured. "It's pretty natural, after all, unless they've changed the rules without telling me."

Looking up into his gorgeous eyes lit with an inner glow of happiness, she asked in a hushed voice, "Do you think I am?"

"I sure as hell hope you are," Carey replied, his own brand of raw vitality burning through his deep voice. His pulse raced with an excitement he'd never felt before. "It's time Pooh had a brother or sister, and if I'd known of her existence, I'd have barged into your life long ago and insisted on —husbands be damned. You've always been mine, Honeybear. We both should have admitted it years ago."

She touched him then, as if touching him made it all real, her hands reaching up, cool and slender, to rest on his temples and shiny hair. She could feel a warm pulse beneath her palms.

"You're cold," he said with concern, covering her hands with his.

"I'm happy."

"I'll keep you warm." And then his brows drew together in alarm. "Do you feel all right?"

She nodded. "I should have known," she said quietly, as if thinking aloud, "but I thought my nausea was because of all the . . . well, frenzy and commotion lately."

"Instead, it was me and my wanting you so badly that first night at Ely Lake."

"I wanted you more."

"We both wanted what we'd missed all those years."

"And after you—we—found out Carrie was yours . . ."

He grinned. "Yeah . . . so what did you expect, Ms. Darian?"

"You don't mind then? I mean, I never even thought . . ." She blushed. "Although I suppose I should have. But—if I am, do you mind?"

"Mind?" He took a deep breath, then released it slowly, his eyes filling with tears. He'd be here this time for the first smile and the baby's first unsteady steps, for the first soft cooing word and the first day of school—all the precious milestones he'd missed with Carrie. "I thought I'd never have children of my own," he said in a whisper, "and now, Honeybear, you're going to give me two. Mind?" He swallowed hard and wondered how to fully express the sweeping scope of his joy. "Let me give you the universe wrapped in a silver bow," he said, jubilation in the rich timbre of his voice.

"I don't want the universe, I only want you."

"Ask for something." He was elated, dizzy with rarefied happiness. "Everyone always asks for something." That he fully accepted. "Diamonds at least or a villa."

"I don't want to hear about everyone, Carey Fersten." Molly's lush lapis eyes began smoldering with flashes of heat.

How disarming, he thought, and sweetly cruel to be reminded a portion of the world practiced sincerity. "Retracted love," he replied, intent on accord, his sensibilities attuned to every nuance, every desire, every whim she might fancy. "The world of sycophants and glitter have jaded my more wholesome instincts. It's been too many years. I forget there are people who aren't always expecting something."

The incipient anger faded in Molly's eyes, and she saw Carey in a different light. Although he'd meant it as a simple declaration of fact, she hated the thought that people had always demanded something of him. "Let me," Molly mur-

ured, brushing the strong line of his jaw with one finger,
give *you* something instead."

"You have already," he replied with a quiet intensity. "I
eed you passionately, desperately." He inhaled deeply.
Without reason or pride."

"You have me," she whispered, touched by his admission.
veil of restless moodiness seemed to descend immediately
ter his disclosure. He was a man of both reason and pride,
rmerly untouched by love, and disquieted by this new vul-
erability. "And you have Pooh, too."

He smiled then, the hint of melancholy erased by the
und of his daughter's name.

"And maybe a son next time, so think of it as not only
aving me to drive you mad on a daily basis, but two more
ungry mouths to feed."

He grinned. "In that case, I'll buy another cow and plow
p the north forty."

"Somehow I can't picture you milking a cow."

"Perhaps I should do what I do best then. Have my stew-
d hire a couple of nannies, a decorator for the children's
ooms, one governess for Pooh," he looked at her quizzically,
ad her expression correctly and said, "no governess, right.
'e'll hire a trainer for Pooh's riding, instead. What have I for-
otten?"

"Don't ask me, I've never seen a nanny in my life. I was
inking more along the lines of leaving our schedules open
nough to take care of the children ourselves."

"Children." He said the simple word with reverence, and
is hands were trembling when he pulled her close. "Do you
now how far away that word makes the jungles of Vietnam?"
e looked down at her but really didn't see her for a moment,
ansfixed by memories. She could see him returning to the
resent, and his hands closed more tightly on her shoulders.
And whether the baby's a boy or girl, Honeybear, it doesn't
atter. So you have to marry me now. I knew I'd get you one
ay or another." He grinned.

"Scheming villain."

"Right." He lifted one dark brow in a leer. "And you'r‹
the pure and innocent young milkmaid. A very hot one,
might add."

"We try to please the villains of our choice."

"How nice. I look forward to act two. Is that the wed‹
ding?" He smiled then, a faint, teasing curve of his mouth‹
"You say the word, darling, large, small, extravagant, sim‹
ple—whatever kind milkmaids prefer—it's yours."

"And what about the milkmaid's business," Molly aske‹
quietly. It was her second thought after realizing she'd marr‹
Carey anywhere, anytime.

"Let's not talk about it now," he replied, bending dow‹
to kiss the tip of her nose, "and spoil all this grand, undi‹
luted joy."

CHAPTER 47

They should have food sent up, he said, scrambled eggs and cinnamon toast maybe, something light for her stomach, and champagne to celebrate. He added with a grin, "I'll drink yours."

And he ordered flowers, baskets of white roses.

Too many flowers, she anxiously said, watching a parade of young men carry in the white wicker baskets. But Carey only shrugged, took off his jacket, pulled off his tie, and asked, "Would you like mousse for dessert? I'm trying to think of digestible foods. Or a sorbet or maybe a fruit . . . strawberries?"

"Okay," she said, and he knew she was feeling better.

"All three," he told the waiter, who stood at attention, his pen poised. "And maybe some ribs, for me," he ordered, with a smile at Molly. "And steamed fish for you?" He looked at her for confirmation and nodded. Dropping into the chair beside her, he leaned over to kiss her lightly on her cheek. "I'm going to adore watching you get fat," he murmured. "We need a vegetable," he asserted, as if remembering the additional food group like a dutiful father, "for junior or juniorette," he whispered in Molly's ear.

"Do you have asparagus?" he asked the waiter.

"Green or white, sir?"

"Green, we're trying to be healthy."

"That's enough," Molly cautioned. "You're beginning to sound like a nutritionist. I can't eat all that."

"Humor me," he said, his voice low, cheer radiating like sunbeams from his eyes. "This is my first baby." And he kissed her again.

"The waiter," Molly murmured, not accustomed to living her life as Carey did, with servants continually around.

"He doesn't mind."

"Please?"

"That'll be it," Carey said to the waiter. He smiled then, to mitigate his crisp dismissal and said, "Thanks a lot . . . appreciate your patience." Rising from his chair, he followed the man out into the small hallway. "She's having my baby," he quietly told the waiter, holding the door open, "so she's a little touchy."

"Congratulations, sir," the young man said. "I understand."

"Oh, and bring up some rice pudding. She likes it."

"Yes, sir, right away, sir."

"No rush . . . really."

"Yes, sir, I understand, sir," the waiter immediately interpreted. "We won't hurry."

"Thanks. It's a great day, isn't it?"

"Yes, sir, I know what you mean, sir. It certainly is."

"Now let's get your dress off," Carey said as he reentered the sitting room. "Hey, altruistic motives only," he went on, his arms out, his smile wide. "I just thought you might like to— ah, send that to the cleaners."

They showered. Wrapped in the hotel robes, they lay on the satin-covered bed and smiled and talked and lightly kissed. Carey apologized for the decor; Molly said it didn't matter a bit. He promised her the real thing—rococo palaces in France and Bavaria—as soon as they left on their honeymoon. She said a tent in the backyard would be palatial, if he were beside her.

He said he'd be happy to arrange it. Her backyard or his? He didn't mention, cautious to keep the dialogue discreetly removed from controversial facts, that his backyards were in California, Tahiti, London, and Greece.

She only wrapped her arms around his neck and languorously murmured, "Mmmm." The literal translation was hazy, but her meaning was clear. He smiled into her warm blue eyes and whispered his undying love for her.

When the food came, the very first thing Molly said was, "Rice pudding? How did you know?" Her eyes were wide in wonder.

"My gypsy blood," he teased, but in truth he'd remembered she'd mentioned it once years ago and it had come to him like some flashback as he was standing in the hall talking to the waiter. She'd always eaten it at her grandmother's, she'd told him then.

"I love you," she said, her heart filled with inexpressible affection.

Carey arranged the food on the bed, and they tasted everything, kissing between bites, feeding each other a spoonful or forkful if a flavor particularly appealed to them.

Carey stopped eating first and lounged on one elbow, watching her. The whiteness of her robe heightened the fairness of her hair, its simplicity enhanced the clarity of her beauty— her small, straight nose, the pink opulence of her well-formed mouth, the Scandinavian classic purity of her cheekbones and her eyes, heavily lashed and blue as a summer sky. If he wasn't so selfish, he'd put her in one of his movies; but he was, and he had no intention of sharing her with the world.

She reached over for a strawberry, and her robe fell open

slightly, the fullness of her breasts briefly revealed; the creamy texture of her skin a subtle contrast to the immaculate whiteness of her robe. White but not white, warm and soft and touched with rosy iridescence. He felt his erection rise. When she put the strawberry in her mouth whole, he experienced a rush of heat racing through his veins.

"Are they good?" he asked, content and happy, knowing he would touch her lush creamy skin, feel its smooth warmth, and feel himself inside her.

Molly turned to him and nodded, her mouth still filled with strawberry. Her smile was an upcurving of red lips damp with strawberry juice.

He couldn't resist. Stretching up, he tasted the sweetness of her mouth. "They are good," he agreed a moment later. He returned to his lazy sprawl, the pulsing of his arousal keeping time with his heartbeat.

"Aren't you hungry anymore?" Molly asked, tiny flutters of desire distracting her own appetite.

"Depends." His entire body, lean and tanned and minimally covered by a robe made for a much smaller man, was invitation.

"On?" She knew the game, and relished the soft promise of the sound on her lips.

"What you have to eat."

His dark eyes were half-closed, and she wondered if that seductive glance was intrinsic or learned in bedrooms all over the world.

She moved her hand in the minutest gesture, indicating the trays of food spread on the bed. Her own seductive smile was indeed inherent and natural. Without the virtuoso practice of his.

"We always did get along," he murmured. He could feel the heat rising through his body.

"At least in bed," she replied in a husky contralto.

He glanced at the food, then at her. "Was the sorbet good?"

"It was cold," she softly said.

"Did you like the chocolate mousse?" The rich resonance of his voice stirred all her nerve endings to life.

"It was too dark."

They weren't talking about food; they were talking about unhurried intoxication ... heedless of the world around them. Their world had narrowed dramatically to two people, very close, on a small portion of a large bed.

"I've never eaten rice pudding." He hadn't moved, not a muscle, not an eyelash, and then one dark brow lifted in query.

"You'll like it," she said.

He moved then with a swift, fluid grace, and cleared off the bed of trays and dishes. Almost cleared off the bed ... except for the pudding.

His bronzed skin seemed darker against the white terry-cloth robe, his hair more golden in the half-light of evening. His eyes were the midnight black of velvet dreams. They were her tiger eyes, their tempestuous beauty mixed with a moody restlessness mirroring his mercurial nature. And they were smiling for her.

When he untied his robe, shrugged it off, and dropped it to the floor, her pulse responded with its own internal storm. His wide muscular shoulders exaggerated his height, and he was solid strength and lithe elegance in such perfect balance, the symmetry of nature deserved blushing honors. He was much too beautiful.

And when he moved toward her and lowered himself to the bed, a rush of flickering shocks trembled through her body. She felt defenseless in a splendid, flaunting way, waiting for him to touch her.

He picked up the silver bowl of pudding and handed it to her. "Hold this," he said, placing the small ornate dish in her hands and closing her fingers around it with a gentle pressure of his large hands. "And then I don't have to reach for it."

Her body reacted instantly to the scented tenor of his

voice and the intimate suggestion of his words, and her hands trembled slightly holding the bowl.

"Don't drop it," he murmured, steadying her arms with his palms. "I need that."

The rice pudding was prepared more elaborately than her grandmother's, folded into rich whipped cream and then frothed into a smooth, fluffy cloud. A faint fragrance of cinnamon drifted up from the bowl.

"Am I going to like it?" Carey asked, observing the direction of her gaze.

Her thick lashes lifted, and the intensity of her blue eyes held his for a moment before she said, "I'm sure you will."

"You have some first," he said softly, scooping his index finger into the fluff and bringing it to her mouth.

He waited the merest fraction of a second until she opened her lips as though yielding to his silent directive, and then he slid his finger into her mouth. She felt the small invasion with a responding heated flame deep in her stomach, and he shut his eyes for a brief moment of pleasure when her lips closed over his finger. "You're warm and wet," he murmured, sliding his finger out again and dipping it once more into the pudding. And he rubbed the sweet whiteness over her lips this time, then bent to lick it off. He sucked on her bottom lip first, and then her top while she sat very still and let the throbbing between her legs inundate her mind.

"You taste good," he whispered, his tongue drifting over the curve of her upper lip. "Do you taste good everywhere?"

"I hope so," she breathed, her eyes audacious with lust. "I truly do . . ."

"Would you like your robe off?" It was a gentle query with a faint dulcet undercurrent of command.

"Yes," she answered. "And hurry," she added with an imperiousness of her own.

He laughed. "And if I don't?" he inquired.

"I'll kill you."

His eyelids drooped in insolent reply. "Your loss," he said softly.

"I'm still holding this bowl of pudding," she threatened.

"Which I'm sure you'll enjoy later, if you see things my way."

"How much will I enjoy it?" she inquired.

"A lot," he promised, unabashed at his proficiency.

"You're pushing it, Count Fersten."

"I know. You're extremely hard to push ... it makes the game so much more fun."

"I'll get you for this."

He smiled. "Maybe." He touched her cheek with the lightest fingertips. "You look hot."

And she was. She was so damned hot it brought back memories of high school when you'd pet and play and never consummate the ardor because everyone was too young to know what to do. But your body would throb for hours afterward, on fire for an elusive release. But it was no longer elusive, and she wanted to feel the fevered, hot-blooded liberation, and she wanted right this very moment to *feel* him.

As his fingers touched the ties of her robe, she moaned, a low, whimpering sound of wanting. She felt the searing path of his hands over her breasts a moment later, as he eased the garment off, taking the bowl from her briefly so she could free her arms.

He painted the crests of her breasts then, quickly and delicately, with the creamy froth as though he had a job to accomplish. She was both unnerved and tantalized by his detachment, as though she were a human sculpture he was decorating with skill and finesse. His touch was sensitive as he smoothed the creamy confection over her nipples, and he smiled as they hardened and distended beneath the cool dessert like crowning ornaments swelling for him.

But when he bent his head a short time later to taste his handiwork, he was no longer concerned with haste. He leisurely sucked and licked and nibbled until Molly would have collapsed had he not held her upright. He had to take the bowl from her hands and lay her back against the pillows a few moments later, because her eyes had closed and she was too absorbed in the waves of pleasure flooding through her body to be aware of the outside world.

How long could she sustain such intensity, she wondered, before she died or fainted or disappeared into another dimension? If she weren't so selfish, she'd hate him for being so expert. His mouth was like heaven, consigning her into blissful Elysium until suddenly the pressure of his lips intensified, sending a river of sensation flooding down through her body. Her pulsing hunger approached uncontrollable limits. He bit her then, tiny, lush, perfectly restrained bites, and she screamed as a rushing conflagration ignited every feverish nerve.

He waited for her heated cry to dissipate in the mauve twilight of the room before he gently spread her legs and settled between them, stretching out his long body without urgency, as though he had a horizonless span of mauve twilights at his disposal.

"I want you," Molly whispered, her eyes shut tight against her headlong plunge into ecstasy.

"I can tell," Carey softly replied, stroking the satiny flesh inside her thighs.

"Hurry."

"No."

"Please . . ." Her breathing was accelerated, her cheeks flushed.

"I don't like to hurry." And he smoothed his pudding-dipped fingers over her hot, throbbing dampness. As the striking coolness covered her heated flesh, as his fingers stroked and gently stretched to fill her sweetness with *his* dessert, nothing mattered but feeling. The entire focus of the world was beneath his hands, and she rose into his manipulating fingers, greedy and burning. When he replaced his fingers a moment later with his tongue, she trembled violently, as though she were a celibate nun who'd never been touched.

He reached up to soothe her tremors, his warm palms gliding over her arms first, then tenderly over the fullness of her swollen breasts. They drifted downward long moments later, across the smoothness of her stomach, to reach finally the torrid center of her longing. And he used his long fingers gently, massaging, guiding the direction of his mouth and tongue until he'd appeased his appetite for creamy pudding and deprived Molly completely of reason. She was floating in a nirvana of the senses, her entire body attuned to the progress of Carey's lips and tongue, her only conception, a flooding, intense pleasure beyond conceivable words. She had forgotten in her eagerness how he could maintain the intensity just short of the extreme limit that would take you over the edge. She'd forgotten, but he never did.

And moments later, when he moved from his languorous ease, adjusted himself above her, and entered her with a gliding force that drove in to touch the very center of her being, she dissolved around him in blissful release.

He smiled. In so many ways she was practical or contemplative, but never in bed. Making love, she exposed herself spontaneously to feeling as though it was pointless to settle for less. He'd always adored her hedonistic, unreserved intemperance.

And she his. "Thank you," she whispered, brushing her hands through his scented hair and sighing a small blissful rush of air. "I owe you."

"I'll be collecting in the next few minutes," he replied with a smile, his rigid arousal buried deep inside her. "Rest for a second or so."

"That long?" Her half-lidded gaze was amused.

She stretched luxuriously then, a sensual, sybaritic movement he felt tighten around his erection. When he groaned in pleasure, she murmured, "Ready?"

Once, late that night, she sensed his shock, although his expression was hidden in the shadowed room.

"Where did you learn that?" he growled, territorial prerogatives obvious in the bite of his voice.

"I read," Molly sweetly replied. "Everyone can't visit the plush red-light districts."

"And if I don't believe you?"

"Can I help it if I'm a liberated woman?" she teased, savoring both his shock and possessiveness. It would never do to let a man like Carey Fersten take her for granted. She rather preferred keeping him on his toes.

"Not anymore," he snapped.

"We'll see now, won't we?" she replied, moving beneath him in a unique and tantalizing way.

Absorbing the shimmering, exquisite sensations for long, distracted moments, Carey swallowed hard before he muttered, "Damn you."

"And I love you, too," Molly purred.

He demonstrated then, moody and fevered, who exactly could do what to whom, but the delirium encompassed them both and through the night they pledged themselves to each other in a flaming passion that had survived separation and loss, intact and whole and glorious.

CHAPTER 48

L ater, twined in each other's arms amidst the shambles of the satin and velvet bedclothes, Molly smiled up at Carey. "You're marvelous at suppressing evening sickness," he said.

"I'd be happy," he murmured, a lazy smile on his face, "to serve all your medicinal needs. Consider me on twenty-four-hour call. And since I caused this nausea in the first place, it's only fair I do my duty to alleviate it."

"I've never considered you as particularly dutiful," Molly replied, her grin mischievous.

"Fatherhood has startled me into a reappraisal of priorities. Duty first from now on. I'm yours to command," he finished facetiously.

"Don't go to Australia."

His smile flickered for a moment, and then was placidly restored. "Let's talk about it later. I'm still basking in the pleasure of this prenuptial evening romp. The loss of several million dollars requires a discussion of some length, and I'm not up to the task at the moment. Hit me with something easier."

"How much are you up to?" Molly queried, only half-teasing.

Moving away, she sat up cross-legged, her back straight and her eyes intent.

Carey's hands went out to stop her. Then, changing his mind, he let his hands drop back onto the sheet. Reclining against the lace-trimmed pillows like a golden surfer, he said, "Anything under ten mil, I'm braced and ready." His smile was the enchanting one he saved only for her.

"I don't want you to see Sylvie again."

"I don't intend to."

"You sound sure."

"Sure as the sun comes up over the Leonidas mine and sets over the ballpark. For you, Honeybear."

"That's pretty sure. How do you know she won't appear on our doorstep again? And she's still with Egon."

"Wrong."

"Oh?" It was a soft inquiry potent with ruffled feelings.

"I talked to Egon this afternoon. His surgery is scheduled for Monday, if all goes well . . . and the doctors are extremely optimistic. One hot-shot young turk is betting him he'll be skiing by Christmas. On that happy news, Sylvie excused herself from his bedside and flew back to Nice. It seems some gala in Monaco was determined to go on without her. I expect she's dancing under an enormous chandelier at this very moment, exchanging banalities with some man who's suggesting they share breakfast together."

"How can you be so flip about her?" Molly still retained a modicum of suspicion after watching them at the Trauma Center. They'd been more than casual friends, and it showed.

"I'm not. It's the simple truth. La Dolce Vita, Monaco style. Sylvie thrives on it."

"As you once did."

"*Did* is the operative word, I believe," Carey replied, his dark eyes grave.

"Did you ever love her?" Molly asked the old question answered so many times before, but never with the finality that would shut the door on that period in his life.

Carey gazed at her for a long moment, wishing he could find the words that would make her understand how little Sylvie meant to him. He shook his head, no, finally, and shrugged, remembering those years. "Sylvie felt it was time I got married," he said, as if trying to find the answer himself. "I wasn't conscious of much of anything in those days, so I said, why not? A combination of circumstances which proved disastrous. It was a stupid mistake."

When he saw the alarm on Molly's face, a terrible dawning of uncertainty and fear, he added in an even tone, "Don't be afraid. It's different with us. *We're* different. I didn't love Sylvie. You didn't love Bart."

Molly's expression registered shock.

"You didn't love him," Carey repeated. "You loved me."

And she knew it had always been true, though she'd locked away the truth all those years ago. Locked it away behind the wedding arrangements and the impossibility of leaving Bart and their families and friends in limbo at the church. And then she'd thrown away the key when she discovered she was pregnant. One loved one's husband, that's the way things were. You especially loved your husband when you carried his child.

"I know," she quietly said, pained and honest. "I always loved you, I never stopped loving you. I'm sorry."

He understood her apology and all the sadness behind it. "Just never leave me again."

He opened his arms, and she went to him.

CHAPTER 49

After Pooh's return from Lucy's the next morning, when they told her they'd decided to get married soon, she scarcely changed expression. She was sitting on her old wooden rocking horse that still held its place of honor in the living room. Kicking it in a leisurely movement, she said, "I knew it. Mom's been moping all week. She runs for the phone every time it rings. We can't walk through the apartment without knocking over a basket of flowers—I see there's more." She cast a random glance at the new baskets of white roses. "And Mom hasn't hollered at me once this week. I thought she was sick. Are we going to move?" she finished, as though her abrupt question was a perfectly logical conclusion to her statements.

"Ah . . ." Carey awkwardly began.

"Er . . ." Molly exhaled painfully.

"I want to be a flower girl," Pooh declared, "with a long dreamy dress, flowers in my hair, and silver shoes."

"Of course," Carey quickly replied, relieved at the new direction of the conversation. "You and your Mom decide what color dress. *Silver* shoes?"

"Jennifer Porter thinks she's hot 'cuz she's got silver shoes."

"Good enough reason for me," Carey said with a grin.

And the difficult topic of moving was brushed aside in favor of a discussion of flower girl dresses.

Carey took them out for dinner that evening, and they celebrated their coming marriage in ten-course magnificent style. And much later Pooh was tucked into bed after an extemporaneous story of rabbits and enchanted forests.

Carey and Molly spent a blissful night in their own enchanted land, and when morning came their wedding date on the following weekend had been decided. The decision to tell Pooh about the coming baby had been made. The wrap-up schedule for the picture five days hence was decided. Even the honeymoon had been decided.

Southern France for all three-and-a-half of them.

Only the decision about their working lives hadn't been decided.

Cowardly, they'd avoided the subject.

CHAPTER 50

When Carey arrived on location in the late morning, he immediately went to the trailer and rummaged through the file drawers. Five minutes later, he called in Allen from the final scenes being set up in the meadow near the lake.

After a brief exchange of amenities, Carey said, "I'm tossing another mess into your lap, Allen. Call and tell our lawyers they're going to be busy in the next few weeks. I just tore up my contract with Allied International to direct that film in Australia."

Allen sat down hard, taking off his baseball cap in an unconscious gesture of shock. His horrified glance was no surprise to Carey. "You can't," he exclaimed as vehemently as his breathless lungs would allow.

"I already did," Carey replied with a much-too-cheerful demeanor for a man who may have committed financial suicide.

"You're ruining yourself," Allen pronounced, his mind racing through the possible loss of income totaling millions on top of Carey's determination to make this immigrant movie that may or may not make money, not to mention the losses suffered during the weeks he was gone on his murderous mission.

"Christ, Allen," Carey responded, "I don't *need* all this. I lead a simple life. I know how to run my own camera."

"Jesus, you're not some long-haired juvenile director with a creative dream, Carey, You're incorporated ten times over now." And you don't lead a simple life, he thought, unless royal prerogatives had reached the masses when he wasn't looking. "You've a wife and daughter to think about, or soon will have," he added in an attempt to reach the starry-eyed man he'd known as a hard-headed pragmatist for eight long years.

"And another child on the way."

Allen's eyes bulged out. "That kid really is yours."

It stopped Carey for a moment—Allen's inherent disbelief—even after all the weeks of legal maneuvering to put Pooh in his will. "*Both* kids are really mine," he said very simply.

"Good God, then, Carey, think of them. If you renege on that contract—" Allen exhaled violently at the thought of all the dire consequences.

"I'm not exactly penniless, Allen. I think I'll survive. You're better off not going in for these big productions, anyway."

He was sounding more and more like the barefoot man Allen had first met at Cannes long ago. "Shit, Carey, don't go native on me. This is more millions than—"

"I'm not impressed, Allen," Carey interrupted. "If you recall," he went on very quietly, "those millions and some of the people behind those millions were the reason I left Hollywood in the first place."

Now *that* sounded *exactly* like the barefoot man at Cannes. And that integrity was what had always appealed to Allen. You could count on the man. Always. Ever loyal, Allen sighed deeply and gave up. "You're sure?"

"Sure as hell. If I don't have Molly, there aren't enough millions in the world to make me happy. Clear?"

"As crystal." Allen smiled then. "Who the hell would ever think you'd find the end of the rainbow way the hell up here."

"It's where I lost it in the first place. Why shouldn't I find it here?"

"And all those women around the world waiting their turn?"

Carey laughed, a pleasant sound full of pleasure, without regret. "They're all yours, Allen. Be my guest. My Honeybear is all I need."

On the term of endearment, Allen's glance swiveled to the small honey-colored teddy bear mounted in a delicate bell jar which had always held a place of honor on Carey's desk. "For her?" he asked. "That was hers?"

Carey nodded.

"And Golden Bear Productions?"

Carey shrugged. "What else?"

"Holy Christ, would the gossip columnists have a field day with that," Allen teased. "You, the guy who didn't believe in romance. Only amour."

Carey smiled. "If you dare, Allen," he said, humor weaving like children's laughter through his voice, "I'll find you, no matter where you hide."

"Bloody hell," Allen exclaimed, "under that man-of-iron will beats the mushy heart of a romantic."

"More to the point, a mushy heart that just had me tear up my contract. So call the lawyers."

"Okay, Carey. What the hell? My broker can learn to live a little cheaper."

Picking up the torn scraps of contract, Carey said, "Put these in a box, will you, Allen. And have it gift-wrapped. Wedding paper, I think."

"That's a thirty-million-dollar gift, you damned fool."

"She's worth every penny of it."

CHAPTER 51

The film was finished. Carrie was in bed. It was the evening before their wedding. Contrary to custom, Carey refused to stay away from his bride-to-be, and they lay together in bed, the TV on but unwatched, the lights of the city spread out below them in a colorful array, framed in the floor-to-ceiling wall of windows.

"You're subdued tonight, Honeybear. Having cold feet?"

With her cheek resting on his chest, her hand trailing slowly over the hard muscles of his stomach, Molly murmured, "Not a chance. You're trapped this time, and no mistake."

"Ah . . . a predatory woman. After my own heart."

"You never did like the passive, gentle type, did you?"

"Nope—not my style. Too damn boring. Now a woman like you—temperamental, opinionated, dare I say, aggressive? Love every tiny little inch of your opinionated body."

"Speaking of opinionated, I've made a decision." Sitting up suddenly, Molly rose from the bed.

"Hey," he protested, "if you're leaving me, you know the old saying—over my dead body. I'm not about to let that happen a second time."

"Only getting you a present," Molly shouted from the

dressing room where she was digging through her purse. A moment later, walking back to the bed lush in a rose silk robe Carey had had flown in from Paris, she held out a heavy envelope. "My gift to you," she quietly said.

Taking it, he patted a spot on the flowered sheets. "Sit down, Honeybear. I've something for you, too. I was going to wait until tomorrow, but why not now?" Graceful and lean, he twisted around to reach his leather travel bag on the floor near the bed. She watched the play of muscle down his body from shoulder to thigh. Tossing aside clothing, he found what he was looking for—a small flat package exquisitely wrapped in silver foil paper and white lace ribbon. Rolling back onto the bed, he offered the package to Molly. "Happy marriage, Honeybear." And he lounged back against the pillows to rip the envelope flap open. His eyes shone with both tenderness and amusement when he extracted the colorful brochure of homes for lease in Melbourne, and the catalogs of private schools in that city.

Molly had carefully untied the expensive ribbon and folded away the paper the way her mother always did. She was piecing together the ragged edges of several sheets of legal-sized paper she'd taken from the small box. Perusing the first paragraph of a partially assembled page, her gaze lifted to Carey's.

"This is the nicest gift I've ever received," he said, holding the brochures and catalogs aloft, his dark eyes full of love.

"You gave this up for me?" Molly whispered.

"For us," he quietly replied. "For all of us."

"It's too much."

"No more than you gave up for me."

"You really don't mind about Australia?" She was almost afraid to mention it. Life was too perfect, and her gypsy soul was screaming, "Don't be stupid."

"Plenty of time for that when the kids are older," Carey said. "I'm going to be a father, you know."

"Yeah," she said with a grin. "Someone told me about

that." And then her voice became very small. "Are you really pleased?"

His lazy, seductive smile appeared like sunshine after the rain, and he whispered, "Come here, Honeybear, and I'll show you how pleased."

ABOUT THE AUTHOR

Susan Johnson, award-winning author of nationally bestselling novels, lives in the country near North Branch, Minnesota. A former art historian, she considers the life of a writer the best of all possible worlds.

Researching her novels takes her to past and distant places, and bringing characters to life allows her imagination full rein, while the creative process offers occasional fascinating glimpses into the complicated machinery of the mind.

But perhaps most important . . . writing stories is fun.

Don't miss any of the sensuous historical romances of

Susan Johnson